Maureen's eyes burned with righteous fury

"Maybe you think I'm a fool," she said, struggling to wrest herself from his powerful grip. "I don't have your money—or the proper equipment. But I want this ranch to *be* something someday. I'm going to make everyone who ever doubted me eat their words!" Tears stung her eyes. Try as she might, she couldn't fight them.

Then Brandon kissed her softly. He pulled back and let his eyes delve into hers. It was not the kiss but his eyes that rendered her motionless. She stared at him, shocked and speechless.

"Maureen," he whispered quietly in a way she'd never heard her name uttered before.

This time when he kissed her he pulled her body next to his. He clasped his hands around her waist and pressed her closer. Maureen could feel every inch of him, from his knees to his shoulders.

And this time she did not resist.

Other Avon Books by
Catherine Lanigan

ADMIT DESIRE
BOUND BY LOVE
SINS OF OMISSION

and writing as Joan Wilder

THE JEWEL OF THE NILE
ROMANCING THE STONE

ALL OR NOTHING

Catherine Lanigan

AVON BOOKS ◆ NEW YORK

ALL OR NOTHING is an original publication of Avon Books. This work has never before appeared in book form. This is a work of fiction, and while some portions of this novel deal with historic occurrences and actual events, it should in no way be construed as being factual.

AVON BOOKS
A division of
The Hearst Corporation
105 Madison Avenue
New York, New York 10016

Copyright © 1989 by Catherine Lanigan
Front cover photograph by Walter Wick
Published by arrangement with the author
Library of Congress Catalog Card Number: 88-91376
ISBN: 0-380-75459-2

First Avon Books Printing: December 1989

AVON TRADEMARK REG. U.S. PAT. OFF. AND IN OTHER COUNTRIES, MARCA REGISTRADA, HECHO EN U.S.A.

Printed in the U.S.A.

RA   10 9 8 7 6 5 4 3 2 1

*This book is dedicated to Texans,
both the native born and the transplants
who have adopted her and carry her spirit
in their hearts*

Acknowledgments

This book came to pass because I was gifted with many wonderful friends, some very old and very dear, and some new, who are equally treasured.

My thanks and gratitude for their help, guidance, and wealth of information about themselves, their lives, and their Texas; and to the non-Texans who saw my vision and cheered me on.

Nancy Ames; Terry Anzur of KPRC News in Houston; Jean Hale Coleman in Los Angeles; Gwen Davis; Charlotte Dial in Los Angeles; Frank Dobbs; Susanne Jaffe, my editor; Carole Keeney of the *Houston Chronicle;* Jo An Kent; Dorothy Lanigan, my mother, who spent weeks in libraries from Florida to Indiana researching for me; Harold Lipton in Los Angeles; Barbara Mantooth; Maureen Miles; Norma Myers; Marvin Myers; Lynn Nesbit, my agent; J.R. Richard, my husband; Ryan, my son; Tena Glenn Rogers; Harriet Rosmarin; Suzanne Saperstein; David Saperstein; Judy Schaefer; Beverly Bennett Wilson; Chet Warner; Steve Zimmermann; and Sherri Zucker.

1

♦

Zimbabwe, southern Africa
September 1985

A ZEBRA MOVED into frame. The slender blonde lifted her right arm and delicately laid the back of her hand against her forehead. She remained motionless as the clicking sound of a camera broke the silence. A hot breeze blew sand in her eyes, but she didn't flinch. Instinctively, she lowered her arm and lifted the sequined black lace skirt of the Giorgio Armani gown she wore. She adjusted the sleeve of the black-and-white batik jacket.

"Shit!" she muttered under her breath. Her arms were an inch and a half longer than average and she always had trouble with sleeves. She tilted her head and looked at the camera dead-on. She flashed her million-dollar smile.

"Fantastic!" Maureen said, and squatted close to the ground for a different angle. "Now move back one pace. That's it. I want to get all of the zebra in this one . . ."

"What zebra?" Bitzy asked, but did not lose her poise. She was being paid over a hundred thousand for this assignment, and Bitzy believed that kind of money bought professionalism.

"The one that's gonna get you another cover."

Bitzy beamed. "You think?"

"I know," Maureen said firmly. She stood and let her camera dangle from the leather strap she wore around her neck. Everyone from the wardrobe coordinator to the guide knew the gesture. The day's shoot was over.

Instantly, there was the sound of many voices. The other two models, Verona and Sally Martin, were on their first assignment for *Ultra Woman*. Both were young, hopeful, and yet to make their mark as top models. They did as they were told and only complained between themselves about the inconveniences, the hot African days and the cold nights. They were awestruck at their good fortune. Being assigned to a Maureen McDonald shoot was unheard of for girls with their lack of experience. They also knew Maureen had chosen them herself. An added bonus.

Verona had a haughty, eastern Old Guard look, with chestnut hair pulled back in a chignon and aristocratically fine bones. Sally looked as if she'd just been plucked from the wheat fields of Kansas. She had long, honey-blonde hair and freckles. Though she hailed from Lake Forest, Illinois, hers was a look that made one believe in the kind of youthful innocence that had gone out of fashion with Janet Gaynor.

Maureen packed her camera and lenses herself. No one in the company dared touch her equipment, for they knew she was almost superstitious about it. She had one Minolta, two Nikons and her favorite, a Hasselblad complete with Carl Zeiss lenses from Sweden. It had been a gift from her Uncle Mac when she was first hired at *Ultra Woman*. She had just closed her case when Sally and Verona walked up.

"Miss McDonald . . ."

Maureen looked up and was hit by an orange shaft of setting sunlight. Sally shifted her weight and cast a shadow over Maureen's face so she could see. "Yes?"

"Do you think . . . well, that it was good today?"

Maureen smiled. "Anxious to get back to New York?"

"Oh, no! It's not that . . . not at all. I just . . ." Verona stuttered.

Maureen thought she'd never get used to seeing these fabulously beautiful girls become tongue-tied around her. "I guess I'm the only one who ever sees the beauty in this place."

She looked around her at the scrub grasses, the sparse but monstrous trees, the rolling ground and, far in the distance, the Inyanga Mountains. It was a land filled with challenge, wild beauty and grace. This was her fifth trip here in two years. She'd have to come up with yet another scheme to cajole Michael into an African shoot next year. This year, with the release of *Out of Africa*, he had been almost forced to send her. It was *her* idea to shoot not only the Safari collections, but the Armani evening clothes as well, against African sunsets. The pictures were the best she'd ever done. More important, she'd been able to stretch a one-week shoot to twelve days. There were still a half dozen gowns to be photographed. Maureen wouldn't have to leave yet.

"We'll be wrapping up in a couple days." She looked at the forlorn faces. "Cheer up. I have a surprise waiting for us when we get back to camp. I'm having ice cream flown in from Victoria Falls."

Verona forced a smile. "Great." She looked at Sally and then they both turned and walked away.

Verona waited until they were out of earshot. "Ice cream? What about boyfriends?"

Sally harrumphed at her cabinmate, picked up the skirt of her black-and-white silk chiffon and climbed into the Jeep. "I'd rather have the ice cream."

Maureen checked to be sure everything was packed. They wouldn't be coming back to this particular site again. She put her case in the back of the lead Jeep and climbed into the passenger's seat, next to Ualla, her driver and guide. "It was a great day," she said to him.

Ualla nodded. "All days are good in Africa, Missy."

"So true," she said, smiling, and they sped away.

Camp was situated only fifty miles into the bush from Victoria Falls. Its thatched-roof houses made of mud and grasses were surprisingly cool during the day and warm at night. Grouped in a circle were eight houses, a main "dining hall," a "kitchen" and three bath huts. There was running water, telephones, television, radios and a stereo, all powered by a generator. *Ultra Woman* provided the best for its employees. There was a maid for each house so that no model or crew member was bothered by domestic duties. All meals were prepared by an excellent chef who hailed from Philadelphia.

Maureen wore a light cotton batiste robe as she towel-dried her hair. It was an hour till dinner. This was her favorite part of the day. She could see the last shafts of sunlight as they spewed from the sinking orange sun. She sipped a tall glass of iced fruit juice, then sprawled across her bed, thinking that she could stay here forever.

Africa reminded her of the Texas ranch her Uncle Mac owned, where she'd spent every summer of her childhood. Though she and her parents had lived in Manhattan, Maureen had always liked Texas better. She liked the feeling of openness where animals and man were free to run, free to be themselves. She had felt safe on the ranch and much loved by her uncle.

Maureen sighed. Suddenly, the phone rang. She knew who it would be.

"Michael," she said.

"Hey, babe. How's it goin'?"

"Great. Just fantastic. I'll make history with the shots I got today."

"Good. 'Cause I need you back here tomorrow. I've made all the arrangements. You catch the ten o'clock out of Victoria Falls . . ."

"Wait a minute, Michael! We're not finished here. . . ."

"You're finished when I say you're finished."

"Michael . . ."

"Didn't you hear me? I need you."

"I heard you," she sighed. "What do you need me *for?*"

"I've got advertisers chewing my ass out because you're a week overdue here."

Maureen frowned. It was just as she'd thought. "I guess I misunderstood you, Michael. You mean *the magazine* needs me."

"That's what I said, 'I need you.' It's all the same."

"Not to me it isn't."

"Don't start this crap again. . . . You're in Africa, for Christ's sake! We'll talk when you get back. Dinner tomorrow night. How about the Water Club?"

"Just one more day, Michael. That's all I need." She paused. *"Please?"* God, she hated begging.

"No! You get your ass back here. . . . ASAP!" he yelled angrily.

"Okay! Okay . . ."

"That's a good girl."

"Michael, do me a favor?"

"What's that?"

"Don't be condescending. You got what you wanted. Leave

it at that.'' She hung up without saying good-bye. She looked at the black telephone and wondered if he'd gotten the point.

"Probably not,'' she said as she stood and began to dress.

Maureen walked into the dining hall, where everyone was already seated. All heads turned, for she looked fabulous in a khaki dress with lace underskirt. Her black hair fell straight down her back. She tried to smile, but she could tell she was fooling no one. She sat next to Bitzy, and as she did the waiters took their cue and began the hustle of serving the crew of *Ultra Woman.*

"What's wrong?'' Bitzy asked her best friend.

Maureen looked down at the artistically arranged food on her plate and sighed. "Nothing like being in love with the boss to kill an appetite.''

"Oh, *him,*'' Bitzy pouted with the most photographed pout in the business.

"We're going back.''

"We all knew we would,'' Bitzy teased.

"No, I mean in the morning.''

"But I haven't even worn the white sequined chiffon! What about the pictures we were gonna do at the falls?'' she asked, truly disappointed, for she knew what Maureen could have done with her, the sequins and the rainbow over Victoria Falls. Bitzy had *dreamed* about that one shot. She had *plans* for it. Her publicist was already spending the commission he was going to make off the stories for *People* and *Us* he was going to book for her.

Bitzy shook her head firmly. "He can't do this to me! Tell him I refuse to go back till we finish.''

"You tell him,'' Maureen said. "I pushed hard to get what I did from him. I know what he's like when he starts screaming 'advertisers.' After two years, you learn the signals.''

Bitzy bit into a vegetable that looked like zucchini but that she knew was not. "And you know them all?''

"All.''

"Oh, too bad.''

"Huh? What are you talking about?''

"Come on, Mo. You know. No more mystery left . . . deadsville.''

"Mystery? There's never been any mystery to Michael. That's what I like . . . love, I mean, about him. I want some-one who is dependable, predictable.''

"All these years I've known you, Maureen, and I've never heard you say this. Your whole life is creativity, a quest for the new, the different, the innovative. You're constantly changing your mind about what you want. One minute you want me at the top of the mountain and the next you want me at the bottom."

"That stuff is different. That's my work. Besides, I do know some things I want. I want a family. A real home. I'm ready for commitment. Can you imagine what kind of a relationship Michael and I would have if I didn't use my *head* about things?"

"Yeah! Dy-no-mite!"

Maureen scowled. "Chaos is more like it. Michael is my rock. I need some order, logic in my life. Michael is everything I want in a man. He's respected, successful, kind, generous . . . and he loves me."

"I haven't seen any engagement announcements in the paper." Bitzy knew she was striking a nerve, but she wanted to help.

Maureen was instantly on the defensive. "And so how is John, the journalist?" she asked, referring to Bitzy's boyfriend.

"In Ottawa on assignment, missing me. You know our *plan* even better than I do, Mo. We're going to be married next fall. Two more years of modeling for me, then we pack up and head for the mountains so John can write his novel and I can have babies. We *are* committed, Mo. We're both headed in the same direction. You deserve better than Michael . . . someone who wants to go there with you."

"I can't plan fantasies like you. *My* priorities are straight."

"Yes, but are Michael's?"

The waiters cleared the dinner plates and brought the ice cream Maureen had ordered for her hardworking crew. Maureen's head was pounding the more she thought about Michael. She didn't want to admit that Bitzy was right. Their relationship was becoming even more strained as of late.

For over two years, Michael had been her lover and employer. Michael Grayson was thirteen years older than Maureen, and at forty-one he ran the largest and most lucrative women's magazine in the country. (*Ultra Woman* had topped *Cosmopolitan*'s circulation in 1983.) He was also the sole owner. Michael had been on the cover of *Time* and had been written about in nearly every business magazine in the country. Men emulated him. He was handsome, divorced and sought after by half the single women in New York. Maureen was envied by many people simply because of her association with Michael. "Michael Grayson's girlfriend" was a moniker Maureen despised. Its whole connotation clouded the lustre of her own fame as a photographer. It had always been important to Maureen that she have something of her own. She wanted to "be somebody" in her own right. Her accomplishments could never come through a man. Not Michael, and certainly not anyone else.

They did not live together because Maureen had told herself that she wanted her *independence*. Michael, too, had agreed it was better. To her knowledge, he'd been faithful to her, and she had no reason to doubt him. The truth be known, she thought it a human incapability to fit another woman into Michael's work schedule.

This year Maureen had turned twenty-eight, and as the end of her twenties closed in on her, she, like most people, was reassessing her life. Introspection told Maureen that she was not happy. She wanted more from Michael. She wanted a real home and children. She wanted to be *married*. Typically, the more she pushed Michael, the more he pulled away. She became depressed, and they argued constantly whether she was in Africa, Australia or New York.

Maureen felt that much of life was going to pass her by if she didn't make a change. Family had always been important to her, even though she was an only child. Her parents had died in a sailing accident when she was twenty-five. Her only relative was her father's brother, Mac, who lived thousands of miles away in Texas. They'd been close, and she'd spent her childhood summers at his ranch. But once she'd graduated from Skidmore, she only saw him once a year when he came to New York to spend Christmas holidays.

Those days after her parents died, she'd been alone, afraid and vulnerable. She had been looking for changes then, too. After a great deal of thought, she left her job as a photojournalist with the New York *Daily News* and took a more lucrative job at *Ultra Woman*. For a time, the security of the high salary calmed her fears, and then Michael had filled that awful void.

Now she needed to learn what she truly wanted. She was no longer in mourning and she was not afraid of the future. With glaringly honest eyes, she looked at her life and knew that only *she* was responsible for the predicament she was in. For too long she'd placed too much importance on financial security—at the sacrifice of her needs. She had revered her independence, and now she saw that it was only an illusion.

Michael had told her over two years ago that they would get married someday. She had believed him then. But for Maureen, someday was here.

She looked around at her crew as they finished their meal. It was time to get on with her life. She rose to tell them the news.

"Listen up, everyone. There's been a change in plans."

A hush fell over the room.

"We need to get an early start in the morning. Five o'clock. We're flying back to New York on the ten o'clock plane."

Verona let out a whoop. "Did you hear that, Sally? We're going home! I never thought I could miss Randy so much."

Sally nodded and looked at Maureen. "She doesn't look too happy about it, does she?"

"No, she doesn't," Verona observed as Maureen left the hall and walked outside.

Sally's cornflower blue eyes narrowed slightly as she considered Maureen's behavior. "You'd think she'd be itching to see her man, too. Wouldn't ya?"

"I suppose so."

"I find that very interesting."

2

◆

THE JET LANDED at Kennedy. As was his custom, Michael sent three limousines for Maureen and the crew. Bitzy rode with Maureen because they were not going home as were the others. They were going directly to the *Ultra Woman* offices on Fifty-seventh Street.

Bitzy wanted to see the pictures as they came out of the lab for herself. It was part of her contract and, tired as she was, she wasn't about to give up her long-fought-for privileges. Bitzy was twenty-four years old. At a time when many models found their careers over, Bitzy's was just beginning. Taking her cue from supermodels such as Cheryl Tiegs and Christie Brinkley, she hired the best managers and attorneys to handle her. Bitzy wanted to be more than just a cover girl. She wanted it all: marriage to John; two, maybe three children; and she wanted to help him achieve his goal of writing his novel. To ensure her future, she had to make the best of today. Bitzy left nothing to chance.

Maureen was silent, thinking about what she would say to Michael. She'd almost felt tears in her eyes as they flew over Victoria Falls. She'd had the sinking feeling she would never be coming back. She was proud of the work they'd accomplished, but she could have done more. Perhaps that was one of her problems. She was always demanding the best out of herself—and everyone else around her. It was obvious that Verona and Sally were more than glad to be back home. Even Bitzy had been ready to come back. *She* had been the only one who could have stayed, and stayed. . . .

Maybe she had been too rough on Michael. Maybe he was right to make her come back. He'd been pretty good about her extensions when she asked for them. Everyone had a breaking point, and perhaps Michael had met his. Michael worked under constant stress, and she'd only added to it with her demands.

Bitzy looked at Maureen. "Uh-oh."

"What?"

"I can tell by that look in your baby blues that you're feeling guilty."

"I am not," Maureen said, thinking that Bitzy was positively scary sometimes the way she could read her.

"Well, you better not. I'm still pissed 'cuz we didn't get that picture. I'll back you up, if you need it."

"Thanks." Maureen smiled. "But I think I'll be okay."

The limousine pulled to a stop. Maureen didn't wait for the driver to open her door, but bounded out and across the sidewalk to the glass doors of the *Ultra Woman* building.

Bitzy watched, stunned, as Maureen vanished inside. "Shit!" She shook her head and followed.

Maureen went straight to Michael's office. She didn't knock, but went right in. He was on the phone. He glanced up, nodded at her. She flashed a smile. He didn't react, but kept on with his conversation.

"I told you a million times, Stan. Now just do it the way *I* want it done and there'll be no more arguments."

"Michael . . ." Maureen went to him and put her arm around his shoulder. He leaned up and kissed her cheek. He put his arm around her waist.

"Knock it off, Stan. I mean it this time." He slammed the receiver down.

"I missed you," he said, grabbing her and pulling her onto his lap. He kissed her deeply.

"I missed you, too," she said.

He looked at her and laughed. "Your nose is sunburned."

"Huh? Oh, yeah. It's the hot, dry season there."

He pushed her out of his lap. "Yeah? Well, it's hot here, too. Where's the film?"

"I'll take it downstairs now."

"You didn't drop it off on your way up?"

"No, Michael. I wanted to see you. I didn't want you to be mad . . ."

He sighed, exasperated. "If I don't have those pictures by six tonight, I will be mad."

"Jesus! I've only been back five minutes and you're starting already. I'll take them to the lab." She spun on her heel and stormed out.

"Maureen. . . . Mo!" he shouted. But then the phone rang. He picked it up, knowing it would be an emergency. It was *always* an emergency.

Maureen waited with Bitzy to see the proofs. As she had expected, the pictures were her best. She pored over them, scrutinizing every detail. They were artistry, the best the fashion industry had to offer the public. It made her both humble and proud to know that God had given her the talent to create this kind of beauty on film. She was lucky, she knew, and she never took her talent lightly.

"These are wonderful, Mo. Every time I see your work I think, How can she ever top this? And then you do. You're amazing."

Maureen smiled, looked at her watch. It was 5:45. "Well, I'll be truly amazing if I can keep a lid on Michael." She scooped up the proofs and raced to the elevator. In minutes she was in his office.

"Incredible . . . Fabulous. Jesus! Look at this one!"

"I could've done great things with the falls, Michael."

He scowled at her. "I don't need anything more than this." He kissed her. "Why don't you go home and get changed? I made reservations for nine o'clock at the Water Club."

"Sounds lovely."

She kissed him quickly and left.

Maureen met Bitzy in the hall.

"Mo! I was trying to find you." She leaned closer. "John just called and said he was picking me up and taking me to Windows on the World for dinner."

"That's big time for him. What do you think it means?"

"I don't know. Maybe he sold a publisher on his idea. This has all the earmarks of a celebration."

"I agree. Now you'll have to think of something romantic for afterward."

"Mo, dear, as an artist being original won't be a problem. As I've always said, my creativity begins in bed."

Maureen laughed and shook her head. "Bitzy, don't ever change."

"Nevah, my dear!" Bitzy walked away waving her arm flamboyantly over her head.

The driver was waiting for her when she emerged from the building. He opened the door for her, this time being quick enough to beat her to it. She nestled back against the grey leather seat, feeling secure once again.

She had a good life, she thought, and she wondered what there was inside her that was constantly wanting to jumble everything up. Millions of people would kill to have her life. No other photographers were chauffeured around town in a limousine. But thanks to Michael, that and the best tables in the best restaurants were always at her disposal. She *always* got the best seats at the Shubert and Winter Garden. But then the line that divided his influence and her fame became fuzzy. It was *her* money that had bought her condo on Eighty-first Street. She was responsible for the small but excellent collection of lithographs she'd started three years ago. Trips were usually working vacations through the magazine. She paid for her own clothes, food, insurance.

"God! What's the matter with me?" she mumbled as she leaned over and took a Perrier from the bar. "I'm acting as if we're dividing up property after the divorce!"

She looked out the window as the car sped past couture dress boutiques, jewelry stores and furriers. She had always lived in this part of Manhattan, but today, more than ever, she realized what a tiny part of the world she'd experienced.

Her father had been a successful stockbroker. Her mother had always stressed a good education, but had prepared her to be the wife of a successful man, just as she was. As the storefronts fused into a collage of neon and bright colors, she remembered back to the spring of 1983. She had been with the *Daily News* four years when she met Michael Grayson at a press interview. She remembered shooting an entire roll of film that day. Michael had been the "man of the hour," with his publication soaring to the top that March. Michael had been impressed with her, too, because he'd made her a job offer the same day her photos came out in the *Daily News*. She accepted.

He set her up in a studio to do fashion layouts. But rather than being fun, the work was unchallenging and boring. Four months later, she walked into his office with her resignation papers. It was a day she would never forget.

"I quit," Maureen said firmly.

Michael was stunned. He'd only talked to her a few times when they'd consulted about a specific layout. He'd assumed she was happy. Her work was beyond reproach. *He* couldn't have been happier.

"So, what do you want? More money?"

"I want out. Plain and simple."

"You can't just walk out."

"Who said so?"

"Well, I did. I'll raise your salary."

"That's not enough."

"Double it, then."

"You don't understand. I'm stifled here. I want to go back to news work. I'm a photojournalist. I don't want to take pictures of pretty girls."

"No? You wanna go to the Middle East, I suppose. Get your head blown off. Or worse, get thrown in some rat-infested jail."

"That wouldn't happen to me."

"Grow up. Of course it would."

"I don't care," she said, standing on principle now. "I have to have more than this."

Michael pounded on the desk. "God damn it! Nobody walks in here and just quits for the hell of it!" he yelled. He continued yelling, and the glass walls began to rattle. Michael was oblivious to the stares he was getting from the staff outside his office. Writers and secretaries raised their eyes from their word processors, peering over each other's heads, trying to see who was causing all the commotion.

Maureen yelled right back at him. "You're not God, you know! You can't tell me what I want and don't want! I quit!"

She started to walk out. Michael hustled around from behind his desk and grabbed her arm.

"No!" he said as she spun around. They were face-to-face, angry sparks igniting their tempers. "What kind of fool are you? Don't you know that *Ultra Woman* is at the top? I can make you famous. I can put your name on the lips of every advertiser, every publisher in the business."

Her blue eyes bore into his. She did not relent. "Well, I can't get there from the inside of a studio."

"And just where would you like to work?"

Maureen had to think fast. She needed an outrageous comeback to keep his attention. "Africa! I want to go to Africa."

"Jesus! You're gonna cost me a fortune . . . ."

She noticed that he pulled her a bit closer. His voice was softening, but the look in his eyes was becoming more intense. She found herself responding to him. "I know. But you said that I would be famous. Show me how badly you want to keep me."

"I'll show you all right," he said. He then notified his secretary that he was leaving for the rest of the day.

Michael took Maureen to a tiny, romantic restaurant in the Village. He bought champagne and agreed to all her requests. He would give her all the location shots she wanted, and at double her salary. They rode in his limousine with soft music playing. And when he leaned over and kissed her, Maureen felt all the excitement of their earlier encounter all over again. She felt alive; she felt she was in love.

Instead of taking her home, he took her to his penthouse, where they made love all night. They had been lovers ever since.

"Miss McDonald?" the chauffeur said.

"Yes?" Maureen snapped out of her reverie to find herself at home. She stepped out of the car and waited while the driver took her bags out of the trunk. The doorman rushed to help.

"Welcome back, Miss McDonald."

"Thanks, Eddie." She patted his arm. She'd known Eddie since her parents moved to this building when she was ten years old. When her parents died, she found that her father had never believed in insurance. He had put all his money into stocks, which did well until the downturn a year after his death. Maureen took what profits were left and put the money in the bank. There wasn't much, but it was enough to give her a feeling of security.

Eddie and the driver helped her with her bags. She tipped them both and let herself into her apartment.

She threw her coat over the sofa and quickly went through her bills. She never received "mail," she thought. Not even junk mail.

She flipped on the radio to her favorite soft rock station, went to the kitchen and got a Coke. As she passed by the answering machine she absentmindedly turned it on and then went to her bedroom to unpack.

She sorted the dirty clothes . . . nearly everything . . . from the clean and put her makeup away. The messages were the usual. The framers calling to say her newest lithograph was finished. Her dentist's office reminding her of an appointment on Tuesday for a filling. After ten such messages, she heard an unfamiliar voice. One with a Texas accent.

"Miss McDonald," the voice said. "This is Sylvester Craddock in Kerrville. I'm calling to inform you that your uncle, Mac McDonald, passed away yesterday evening late. As attorney to his estate, I felt you should be informed immediately. I can handle the funeral arrangements if you're unable to come to Kerrville. Call me at area code 512-444-8890."

The machine clicked off and rewound itself automatically.

Shock held Maureen rigid. Her mouth went instantly dry as her eyes filled with tears. "It can't be . . ." She raced to the machine and fast-forwarded the tape. She replayed the attorney's message. "No!" she cried, and covered her face with her hands. "Uncle Mac . . . you're all I've got . . ."

She looked up at the enormous Remington oil hanging over the fireplace. Uncle Mac had given the painting to her mother, his sister-in-law, nearly twenty years before, hoping to convert Jillian to the country. But Jillian had been born and reared in New York City. A model for four years before marrying Hal McDonald, Jillian had been as much a city girl as her daughter. She'd taught Maureen how to fast-walk from their apartment straight to the dress department in Bloomingdale's in fourteen minutes. Jillian had hated Texas—or *any* outdoor area that didn't have sidewalk cafes and a telephone on every corner. Jillian had been hard-pressed to develop a taste for the Remington, but it was Western art at its zenith, and because it would please her husband, she displayed it proudly.

"Uncle Mac . . ." Maureen looked at the overstuffed flowered chintz chair her uncle always occupied whenever he came to visit. Most times he spent the entire night in that chair, not wanting to sleep in the cramped confines of the "study," which was really a converted pantry.

She remembered the summers she'd stayed with him. He'd taught her to ride, even rope. He'd never married, but he was happy. He wasn't a hermit, and he'd told her he must be a throwback to the old cowboys who never needed anyone, just the freedom only the land could give. Truly, Mac had never seemed to fit into the modern world. He had been happy out there in West Texas. She knew he would want her to make certain his funeral was in keeping with the way he had lived his life.

Maureen's hand was still shaking when she picked up the receiver and punched out the numbers that would connect her with Kerrville. The phone on the other end rang four times. She looked at her watch. It was only six o'clock in West Texas; perhaps he might still be there.

Her call was picked up on the fifth ring by a woman.

"Mr. Craddock's office," she said breathlessly.

"Oh, thank goodness. I was afraid you'd be gone."

"I was just on my way out."

"I won't keep you long. Is Mr. Craddock in? This is Maureen McDonald."

"Oh! Miss McDonald, he left about an hour ago." There was sympathy in the secretary's voice. "May I leave him a message? I know he is anxious to speak with you."

"Yes. Tell him I most definitely will fly to Kerrville to make the arrangements . . . for my uncle. I'll call tomorrow and tell you what time I'm arriving."

"Very well. And . . . my condolences, Miss McDonald."

"Thank you," Maureen said, and gently laid the receiver down.

Maureen nearly let herself give in to her grief, but instead she called the travel agent the magazine used. The offices were closed. She telephoned the airlines directly and booked her flights, first to Houston, then on to Kerrville. She would be in Texas by late afternoon.

Maureen went back to her bedroom and started going through her closet trying to find things to pack. She wanted to keep busy so she couldn't think. But as she tossed dress after dress onto the bed, suddenly she sank down into the little antique chair.

"Uncle Mac . . . I never bought a dress to wear to your funeral! I never thought you'd die. . . ."

Maureen could do nothing to stop the flood of tears. She cried for nearly two hours as she walked from room to room remembering every word she'd ever spoken to her uncle, enjoying and hating the flood of memories that were meant to comfort but only brought pain.

She was in the bathroom washing her face when the telephone rang.

"Are you standing me up or did you just forget?" Michael asked half teasingly.

"Michael . . ." She checked her watch. It was a quarter after nine. "I really don't feel like . . ."

"Hey! I cut my meeting short just so I could be with you."

He said the fatal words at a time when she was in much need of comforting. She felt like a child who needed desperately to be held, to be reassured that she was loved. She needed to know that somehow, someone would make the world right again. "I'm on my way."

She was numb during the cab ride to the restaurant. As the maître d' escorted her to Michael's table, she wondered if she was being fair to Michael by expecting him, a mortal, to nullify the pain that death had caused.

He stood and kissed her. As she sat across from him in the booth, she noticed he'd ordered champagne. The bottle was half empty.

"You look like shit. What happened?" he said.

"My uncle died." Her eyes filled with tears, but she squeezed them back. She gulped a glass of champagne and wished it were straight scotch.

"The one in Texas?"

"Yes."

"How?"

"I . . . don't know," she answered, wondering how she could not have asked Mr. Craddock's secretary such an important question. "I called the attorney who left a message on my recorder. He wants me to make the funeral arrangements."

"I see . . ." Michael held her hand. "You'll need to leave tomorrow, right?"

"Yes. I know you have work you wanted me . . ."

He clutched her hand. "Fuck work. I'm not a tyrant, you know. You couldn't help this. It would be wonderful if you could stay here, be with me . . . the magazine. But you can't."

She smiled. It felt good. "Michael, you're so good to me."

"I know. And don't you forget it. Listen, are you really hungry?"

She shook her head. "Not really."

"Me either. Not now, anyway. Whaddya say we go back to my place? I haven't seen you for almost two weeks and . . ."

"It's a wonderful idea," she said.

Michael paid his bill and then kept his arm around Maureen as they waited for the valet to hail them a cab. As they rode to Michael's penthouse on Fifth Avenue, he held her close, rubbed her shoulder and arm and recited the ages-old, soothing, nonsensical things one says to a loved one during times of grief.

When they made love that night, Michael restrained himself and was more tender than usual. He held Maureen close until he fell asleep. Maureen rolled to her side, still trying to find comfort in his tenderness. But she felt empty. She felt no joy in their lovemaking. She guessed everyone felt like that when death hovered over their lives.

Again, Maureen could not stop her tears. She thought she'd stifled her sobs, but she woke Michael. He pulled her close to him again.

"Don't cry, please. I know this is a difficult time. But it's not the end of the world."

"You don't understand, Michael. Uncle Mac is all I have . . . had . . ."

"But . . . you still have me," he said.

She snuggled down into his shoulder so he couldn't see her eyes in the moonlight that flooded the room.

"Yes, Michael. I still have you." Oddly, she was not reassured.

3

♦

Maureen landed at Kerrville Municipal Airport at four o'clock the following day. Since there was no commercial air service to Kerrville, Maureen had had to book a chartered flight out of Houston. Fortunately, there had been only a one-hour layover between her flights. Over the years, Maureen had flown in an odd assortment of "aviation equipment," as she called these refurbished relic planes. She was not frightened of them, and as a general rule they were just as dependable as the newest commercial jets. But this trip was not a location shoot; there would be no happy times on this trip. When she walked down the roll-up steel steps of the small aircraft, she felt completely drained.

Sylvester Craddock had rearranged his schedule so that he could meet Maureen's plane. Since she was the only female passenger, he walked straight up to her. "Miss McDonald. I trust your flight was not difficult."

Maureen shook the tall, slender man's hand. "It was fine, thank you," she said. She noticed that he wore a tailor-made Western suit in a dark camel color. He placed his cowboy hat upon his head as he took her hanging bag from her.

"That's too heavy for a lady. . . . Let me get that bag, too," he said, referring to her suitcase.

"I can manage," she replied. She looked down and saw that his boots were expensive, cream-colored eelskin. She smiled when she noticed that he was wearing a string tie with a silver, turquoise-studded "slide." It looked like the one her uncle had always worn.

He ushered her to his sparkling clean navy Cadillac. She noticed as he placed her things in the trunk that the car still bore dealer plates.

"I like your car," she said, trying to make small talk.

"Why, thank you. I just landed a big case. I thought I'd celebrate." He held the door for her and even picked up her full skirt for her, so not to catch the hem when he closed the door.

As soon as he started the car, Maureen asked, "How did my uncle die?"

"Heart attack. He went quick and fast, Miss McDonald."

"You can call me Maureen," she said, not used to this profusion of Southern gallantry. "To my knowledge, he'd never had any trouble with his heart."

"I know what you're thinking. And fifty-six is young. Hell, that's only a few years away for me," he said reflectively. "But Mac, he worked hard, maybe too hard, on that ranch. It's not an easy job. And he didn't have much help."

"He did when I used to visit. But that was seven years ago."

"A foreman, one maid and two drifters does not run a place that size. He had nearly four hundred thousand acres."

"Four hundred thousand? I thought it was one hundred thousand!"

"That's what he bought initially. But over the last decade he'd been buying up small parcels here and there. Not many people around here knew about it until a few years ago. He was always pretty quiet about his business. Kept to himself mostly."

"And you've been his lawyer all this time?"

"Not really. Mac didn't believe much in lawyers. But I did handle his will for him. I suppose that's what you're most interested in."

"What?"

"The will, the ranch." He smiled with a smug, condescending grin that made her nerves jump.

"I came here to give my uncle the kind of funeral he would have wanted," she said firmly and with a bit too much strain in her voice.

"Sorry," he said. "I know how you New Yorkers are. Always wanting to get straight to business. I thought—"

"You thought wrong," Maureen interrupted. She suddenly realized that what she had thought was gallantry was condescension. She wondered which he thought less of . . . women or New Yorkers.

They rode on Highway 27 past Schreiner College, through the middle of town and out to the west toward the ranch.

Maureen could feel the tension between them growing. Out of the corner of her eye she caught the looks he gave her. But it was he who broke the silence.

"He left everything to you. The ranch, the cattle, the mineral rights, the cash."

"Everything?" she asked, and then realized he'd had no other heirs. "What will I do with it all?"

"My advice is to sell it. *You* certainly couldn't run it. There are several ranchers in the area who already expressed interest in the land. I don't think you'd have a difficult time finding someone to take it off your hands."

"Take it off . . . Why? What's the matter with it?"

He gave her that same patronizing look. She ground her teeth, but kept silent.

"It's a bit run-down. Everyone knows that. Old Mac always had more important things to do than run his ranch."

"What on earth are you talking about?"

He chuckled. "Gold, little lady. Old Mac was convinced he was going to find gold on his land. He said the conquistadors left wagonloads of the stuff in the hills he owned. He put every nickel and dime of profit from the ranch into his prospecting. When he wasn't working with the cattle, he was digging for gold. I'm not sure if it was the hard work that killed him or the realization that he was never gonna find that gold."

"Oh, Uncle Mac . . ." she whispered to herself.

"Yeah, Mac's brain got more half-baked as the years caught up with him."

She looked at him. "You don't have much respect for him do you?"

He kept his eyes on the road. "I never speak ill of the dead."

"Just of the living?" she said sarcastically.

They continued the drive in silence. Maureen couldn't wait to be rid of this egotistical man, who obviously had little love for his client. It was her guess that his fee from her Uncle Mac's estate was paying for his shiny Cadillac.

North of the Guadalupe River in the heart of the hill country, Maureen finally rode through the gates of McDonald Ranch.

Suddenly, it all came back to her: the craggy hills, the yupon and oak trees, the terrain that was more rock than land. There was the sparkling creek that ran in back of the house. And the house itself.

It was fashioned of stone and had been built in the late 1890s by a cattle baron. It rose two stories high, with a red clay roof and two round towers at each end. It was an odd blend of arched Spanish windows and colonnades and English doors and rooflines.

There was a two-story-high porch that wrapped around the entire house with stone balustrades and huge arches and that kept the beating sun from baking the interior and allowed breezes to flow through the house. The outside walls were fourteen inches thick, insulating the interior against the harsh seasonal weather.

Since she had not seen the house for over seven years, she had expected it to be smaller than she remembered. But she found the opposite to be true. It loomed over the land, the fenced-in horse corrals, the rock-strewn and stubbly grassed "yard" and the neglected vegetable garden on the east side near the drive.

Reverently, Maureen mounted the steps to the house. The house seemed more frightened and alone than she did. She turned to Sylvester.

"I'll be staying here."

"What?"

"I can make the arrangements from here. What funeral home did you say he was at?"

"Earlman's."

"I'll take care of it. And I'll call the pastor at Trinity Baptist Church myself."

"I must advise against this, Miss McDonald. You'll be much more comfortable in town. I've made reservations at the YO Ranch Hilton for you. Why, I'm not sure there's even food in the house."

"Juanita is still here, isn't she?"

"Yes. She's at her mother's today. But she'll be back tonight."

"Then I'll be fine."

"Have it your way," he said, and took her bags from the trunk. He followed her directly into the foyer.

Maureen laughed. "Only in Texas would anyone *not* lock the doors."

He handed her the keys to the house. "In case you can't break your habit. I'll formally read the will after the funeral. You know my number in case you change your mind and decide to move back to town."

"I won't," she said, and ushered him to the door. She watched as he drove away.

She was glad to have this time alone to explore the house. At first glance it looked fine. It was clean. Juanita had seen to that. But as she entered the old panelled living room with its soaring ceilings, oak columns and parquet floors, she realized that it was in need of much work.

The plaster was cracked and peeling in many places. The wallpapers in the dining room, study, library and foyer were peeling right off the walls. The floors were warped, uneven and needed refinishing. The draperies needed to be replaced, as did some of the window frames, which were also warped.

When she walked into the kitchen she realized she'd forgotten that Mac had modernized nothing. As a child she'd paid no attention, but today it all registered. The stove was a gas-burning monstrosity from before World War II. The refrigerator was small and just as old. She found that the freezer section was totally inoperable. There was no dishwasher, no garbage disposal and barely any counter space. The linoleum floor pulled up at the edges and was black with grime that had been ground into the surface. No amount of scrubbing would ever make it clean. Again, the plaster was cracked and everything was in need of a new coat of paint. When she turned on the faucet, it sputtered and spewed and pipes throughout the house rattled loudly.

She flipped round switches; they were the original switches, from when the house was wired before World War I.

Maureen went upstairs. There were six bedrooms and three baths and a sitting alcove at the end of the hall. There was furniture in only two rooms: Mac's and Juanita's. Two of the baths were usable, but needed all new fixtures and lighting. The third bath was a disaster and had probably not been used since Mac bought the house in 1948.

Maureen hauled her bags upstairs and instantly began clearing out Mac's closet and drawers. There weren't many clothes. Mostly Levi's, plaid shirts, two suits, both of which were kept neat inside cleaner's bags. He had four pairs of boots; all were worn and scuffed. His drawers revealed little about the man, except that his maid kept his things clean and neat. In the bottom drawer, however, she found a scrapbook.

She sat on the floor and opened it carefully.

"Why, that's me!" she said, flipping the pages, watching herself grow in the carefully arranged succession of photographs. There were valentines she'd made for her uncle, and homemade Christmas cards. There was a picture of herself sitting atop the horse she'd ridden when she and her parents visited the ranch when she was five. There were ten pictures of her sitting in the lap of the Macy's department store Santa from the time she was one until she was eleven. She remembered that the year she was twelve she had refused to go again. Instead, she sent a picture of herself in front of St. Patrick's Cathedral. Next to the picture he'd written: "My baby grows up."

Maureen hugged the album to her chest, then rose. She would give all his clothing to the Trinity Baptist Church for the pastor to dispose of properly. The album she would keep.

As she came down the stairs, she saw a shadow at the front door.

"Juanita? Is that you?"

There was no answer. She continued down the stairs, and when she got to the door she saw there was no one.

Maureen felt an eerie sensation course her back. Just to be on the safe side, she bolted the front door.

As she walked toward the kitchen, she heard the back door slam. "This time, I know I'm not crazy," she said, and rushed into the kitchen.

"Juanita!"

The old Mexican woman spun around, her black eyes wide in her round brown face. "Miss Maureen!"

"I knew I heard someone! I'm so glad you're here!"

"Si! Me, too!" Juanita hugged her. "Let me see you. Too skinny. Your uncle Mac, he no like."

Maureen smiled. "Perhaps I am. I'm sure you can change that for me."

"Si. You sit. We talk." Juanita pulled Maureen over to the ranch oak table and chairs. She nearly pushed her down into the seat. Juanita began hustling around, chopping vegetables, then making flour tortillas. "How you get here?"

"Mr. Craddock brought me."

Juanita shook her head. "Mac no like him. Bad man."

"Well . . . he's a bit prejudiced, but I don't know if he's bad. Anyway, I don't want to talk about him. Tell me, Juanita, is it true that Uncle Mac did not suffer?"

Juanita stopped rolling flour. "With his heart he always suffered. But not like you think. Mac, he never found what he wanted. But he was never in pain. He did not linger."

"Mr. Craddock told me about the gold. How Uncle Mac was always looking."

Juanita shook her head, and when she did her long, grey ponytail flopped against her back. "Mac, he a lonely man. I tell him find a woman. But he never listen. He should have children, I say. But he say he got Maureen. I say that not enough for anyone. Gold *never* make anyone happy."

Maureen sighed. "How right you are, Juanita."

"He give you ranch, no?"

"Yes, he did." Her eyes surveyed the disastrous interior around her. "But I'm afraid it's going to take a lot to make this place livable again. I doubt anyone would want to buy it in its present state."

"You sell the ranch?" Juanita asked incredulously.

"Of course. What else can I do with it?"

"I . . . never thought . . . Mac, he give the ranch for *you*. You must stay here!"

"I can't stay here, Juanita. I have a life in New York. I have a career, a very good career. A man who loves me."

Juanita's eyes darted quickly to Maureen's left hand. "If he love you so much, why you not his?"

Maureen's back stiffened at the mention of the sensitive subject. "People don't just jump into marriage these days. . . ."

Juanita looked back down at her tortillas. Maureen could tell she wasn't buying any of this. "Anyway, I'm a photographer, not a rancher. I came here to take care of Mac's funeral and make certain he had a proper burial."

"Then you do as he wished."

"What's that?"

"Bury him under the big oak close to the road. He loved that tree. He say he want to rest there. Then, you stay here, where you belong."

"Yes, I could do that. But I won't put any marker up since I still have to sell the ranch and I certainly wouldn't want to lose a buyer who might have superstitions about gravesites within view of their front window. It would make Mac happy to be buried there. Still, I know that *I* belong in Manhattan and not in Texas.''

"Humph!" Juanita growled.

Maureen could tell the subject was not completely closed. "Are there any boxes around?"

"Yes. In the bunkhouse. I'll get them."

"I'll do it."

Maureen left through the back door. She noticed that this part of the house, which faced northwest, needed repairs. The gutters and downspouts were rusted and practically falling off. The stone here was worn by the elements more than on the south side. She walked along the rock-edged path to the bunkhouse.

She knocked on the screen door. It, too, needed replacing.

"Yo!" a scratchy male voice answered.

Before she could respond, a man in his mid forties, with black hair and brown eyes, came to the door. He was a bit taller than Maureen, with narrow hips and a huge belly. He smiled, but his heavily hooded eyes were wary. She disliked him on the spot.

"I'm Maureen McDonald. Mac's niece. I was told there were some boxes in here I could use."

"Wahl, howdy. I'm Wes Reynolds . . . the foreman. My condolences on your loss, Miz McDonald. I've worked for your uncle for five years, and I was mighty sad over his partin'.''

"Thank you, Wes," she said uneasily. She didn't know what there was about him, but he made her nervous. She guessed it was the tension of the trip.

"I'll get them boxes for you," he said, and quickly scrambled to the storage room. "I'll carry them up to the main house for you, ma'am. I know how tired you must be after your trip . . . and all . . .''

Maureen walked alongside him, noting that he stepped back a bit to allow her more room. He couldn't be more courteous and here she was thinking ill of him. She must be more tired than she thought.

"Tell me, Wes, where are the other workmen?"

"Just Rusty and Grady left. They went on into town until the funeral. I guess they'll be movin' on."

"Why's that?"

"Well, everybody around here sorta figured you'd be sellin' the place. No need for hands if there's no work."

"But couldn't they work for the new owner?"

"Could. But these things take time. A man's gotta go where there's steady work."

"What about you?"

"I figured you might need my help for a few weeks, till you get things set up for the sale. There's still cattle to tend."

Maureen stopped and looked at him when they reached the back door. "That was very generous of you, Wes. Thank you."

"No problem," he said as he placed the boxes in the kitchen. "I want to do all I can to help. City girl like you is gonna have a tough enough time . . . and then there's the funeral and all . . ."

Maureen couldn't believe her ears. Did she look as inadequate as everyone here believed her to be? True, she didn't know anything about ranching, but she'd always considered herself a self-sufficient person. She wasn't helpless.

Maureen tried to ignore Juanita's looks as she took the boxes up to Mac's room. She thought it odd that Juanita should want her to stay on the ranch and yet that Wes knew she should go. Juanita, obviously, was speaking from the heart. Wes, from his head.

When they entered the bedroom, Maureen instantly fell to the task of packing Mac's clothing.

Suddenly, Juanita screamed. "Santa Maria!"

"What is it?" Maureen cried, seeing Juanita's terrified face.

The old woman was literally shaking. She pointed to the bed. Maureen looked down. There, atop the bed, was a small, antique Indian doll whose head was unattached.

Maureen bent over. "A broken doll . . ."

"Don't touch it!" Juanita screamed.

"I don't remember seeing it in the drawers. It must have rolled out of his clothes. Maybe we can glue it."

"It's a bad sign!" Juanita warned. "They want you to leave this house. Leave this place."

"Who does?"

"The ghosts!"

Maureen laughed and patted Juanita's arm. She was not about to get into a discussion about the metaphysical with an obviously superstitious woman. "That suits me just fine. You're the only one who wants me to stay. As soon as I finish my business, I *will* leave."

Maureen tried not to let Juanita see her tears as she placed bundles of clothes into the boxes. With each opened drawer, Maureen was flooded with a new set of memories, familiar smells; at times, she almost felt as if she could hear his voice.

She turned to Juanita. "I miss him," she whispered, then put her head on Juanita's shoulder and let her grief escape.

4

♦

MAUREEN WATCHED as the casket was automatically lowered into the ground. She looked up through the widespread branches of the century-old oak tree. A hot, late-summer breeze rustled the leaves, but the branches, so old and firm, did not move. She felt a tremendous sense of peace at that moment. She knew that this was what Mac had wanted.

The past two days of arrangements had drained her. She had expected all Mac's friends to be at the funeral service. But besides herself, Juanita, Wes, Rusty and Grady from the ranch, only the pastor of Trinity Baptist Church was in attendance. She didn't understand it. Mac had been a lovable and generous man, he'd liked people and liked having a good time. It didn't make sense that his neighbors would do no more than to send the ostentatious flowers that filled the house. But then, perhaps none of them had allowed themselves the luxury of knowing her uncle the way she did.

Sylvester Craddock arrived late, but did follow the entourage back to the ranch. She could tell he was anxious to read the will.

The Earlman brothers gathered up their equipment and began loading the hearse while their Mexican gravedigger filled the grave.

"Sylvester," she said, turning to the attorney, and then suddenly stopped. Her eyes focused on the road leading to the ranch. A spiral of dust rose into the air. It moved toward them at a dizzying speed, and as it did she was able to see a chocolate brown Jaguar convertible. It was driven by a blonde-haired man wearing Ray Bans. The car braked to a dramatic halt. The driver got out of the car and walked toward her. Suddenly, he smiled. It was a smile she would have known anywhere.

"Alexander!" she cried, and rushed toward him.

He whipped off his sunglasses and opened his arms. He held her close and then kissed her cheek. "I would have come sooner, but I was in Mexico. I just heard . . ."

Maureen stood back. "I'm so very glad you're here." She smiled as she looked at him. "You've grown up."

"So have you," he said, eyeing the way her silk dress clung to her curves.

She laughed. "I never thought you'd be quite so . . . handsome." And he was. Excruciatingly so. He was a bit over six feet tall, with strong, wide shoulders and a lean torso. He was not at all the scrawny boy, with hair so white it blended into his even whiter skin, she remembered. His hair had turned to gold, and his tan made his green eyes flash in his face. They were the same eyes that had charmed her years ago. Alexander Cottrell lived on the ranch to the north. His mother had been very strict with him as a child and did not allow him to "consort" with anyone on the McDonald ranch. But to Maureen's delight he disobeyed his mother and sneaked over to ride and play with her week after week, year after year. They'd exchanged a letter or two over the years, but when she quit coming to Mac's ranch, they'd lost touch.

He held her hand. His was warm and firm, just as she remembered. "I'm glad you're here," he said, "but I wish the circumstances had been different."

"Me, too," she said, feeling his sympathy. "I can't get over how you've changed. I'll bet all the girls in the county are after you."

"Not the right one."

"You're not married?"

"No. Are you?"

"No," she said.

Just then Sylvester Craddock coughed. Maureen reluctantly looked over at him. "I'm sorry. I suppose we ought to tend to business so Mr. Craddock can leave."

Alexander shook Sylvester's hand. "Didn't mean to hold you up. It's just that I haven't seen little Mo for a long time."

Sylvester sniffed. "I wasn't aware you were acquainted."

Alexander smiled with that elfin half smile that Maureen

was certain had broken a thousand hearts. "Neither was my mother . . . until I told her where I was going today." He looked at Maureen. "Guess it's too late to whip my backside now."

Maureen laughed. "Let's get this over with so we can talk." Maureen took Alexander's hand and led him into the house.

Alexander took her aside. "I'll get myself a drink and wait in the library until you finish. I don't want to intrude."

She appreciated his gesture. "It won't take long," she said.

In the huge wood-panelled salon, Maureen listened as the attorney earned his fee.

"As I said when you first arrived, Mac left everything to you. Lock, stock and barrel. There is a provision for Juanita. He left her five thousand dollars and all the furniture in her room."

"That's not very much," Maureen said, thinking that Mac normally would have been very generous with a devoted employee of over twenty years.

Sylvester took off his glasses. "Perhaps I'd better state the facts. This ranch isn't worth much."

"But you told me there were over four hundred thousand acres."

"True. But he's got a lot of outstanding debts."

"Why?"

"I tried to break it to you the other day. Mac put everything into his ridiculous gold hunts. I know you haven't had time to go into the horse barns, where he kept equipment. The storage shed is jam-packed, and I'd think even the closets and attic in this house, going by what he's told me. Just the week before he died, he spent over seven thousand dollars on a computerized gimmick that is nothing more than a metal detector."

"Oh, God."

"For years he's raised his cattle only to support his efforts in his treasure hunt. He has not modernized a thing. The pickup truck is four years old, but paid off. He's got some farm equipment left, but it's all in need of repair. He sold his plane four years ago. When the rest of Texas was gearing up, Mac was gearing down."

Sylvester went on to tell her how Mac had sold bits and pieces of the ranch to make ends meet. The antiques were gone, the paintings sold at auction. She could see for herself how little Mac had put into maintenance and renovation. The lawyer painted a bleak picture for Maureen. Mac had been very foolish when it came to his money.

Sylvester shook his head. "He was a crazy old Yankee coot, all right."

"My uncle was a wonderful man, Mr. Craddock, and his money—or what there is of it—is helping to pay your bills. Leave your papers with me. I'll take care of everything."

Sylvester gladly did as she requested. "You Yankees are all alike. You think you know everything and you know nothin'. This is a hard land, Miss McDonald—and my professional recommendation is that you'll need all the friends you can get."

"Thank you," she said, stepping aside so he could pass to the hall. "I'll consider what you said. Good day." Maureen ground her jaw as she watched him leave. No one had ever told her she couldn't do something. She had spent her life being told she could do anything if she wanted it badly enough. Her father, uncle, mother, even Michael, had all believed in her, or at the very least, her talent. Of course, she had no intention of staying in Texas, but all the same, she'd still like to make Sylvester Craddock eat his words.

Maureen slid the carved pocket doors open and smiled. Alexander was leaning against the heavy oak mantel looking up at the Remington above him. He smiled when Maureen entered.

"I didn't know he had this piece."

"It's a copy."

"What?" Alexander looked at it more closely. "It's a damn good one."

"He sold the original years ago, according to his attorney. Mac gave my family a Remington . . . now I'm not sure if it's real or not."

Alexander walked over, took her hand and together they sat on the worn Victorian settee. "I know there's nothing I can say to make your pain any less, but I want to help, Maureen." He moved a bit closer. "I know you'll think this strange . . . but I always knew you'd come back."

"Why?"

He chuckled, but his expression was serious. "I never forgot you, not really. I knew you had an exciting life in New York, your career . . . men, probably lots of men, huh? Well, anyway, I remember how close we were when we were young.

Remember the time I came and got you at midnight and we
went riding in the hills till dawn and Mac never found out?''

"He knew. He never said anything, but I think he
knew. . . .''

"My mother would have beaten me to death if she'd known.
Yeah, Mac probably did know. . . . That's what made him
special. I think he . . . liked me . . .''

"Of course he did, Alex. Everybody here did.''

"Yeah.'' His eyes flashed with pleasure. "Even Juanita.
She liked me cuz I liked her cookin'.''

They were both smiling now, remembering the past.

Maureen caught his enthusiasm. "Remember the time we
were supposed to be feeding the horses and kept jumping
into the hayloft? We laughed so hard . . .''

". . . I remember the dreams we had then. The plans we
made that day . . .''

Maureen looked at him. "You said you wanted to own the
biggest ranch in Texas.''

"Still do,'' he said, laughing. "You said you wanted to be
a grand lady, live in a big house and have three children.''

"Still do,'' she said, peering into his eyes. "Funny how
life doesn't work out the way we planned.'' She sighed. "But,
I was only eight years old then.''

He was holding both her hands now. His face was very
close to hers, but he kept himself in check. He seemed to be
exploring her soul. She wondered what he saw. "Don't you
still dream, little Mo? Don't you have plans for your life?''

Uncomfortable with his probing, she eased back in the settee. "You sound like Bitzy.''

"Who's Bitzy?''

"My girlfriend in New York. She has her entire life planned
out. I even think she knows where she wants to be buried. . . .''

"Plans are all right,'' Alexander said, "as long as you
allow for flexibility.''

Maureen watched as Alexander sped away in his Jaguar.
She walked down the hall and into the kitchen. Juanita, Wes,
Grady and Randy were seated around the kitchen table, the
remnants of Juanita's enchiladas on their plates. They looked
up at her expectantly, waiting to hear what she would tell
them.

"Wes, do you know anything about accounting?''

"Enough."

"Tomorrow, you and I are going over all Mr. Craddock's papers to find out exactly where we stand."

Rusty's brown eyes darted over to Grady. "How . . . how much longer will you be needin' us, ma'am?" he asked. They were cowboys in the true sense of the word. They were loners, never needing anything but a ranch to work and pack-able possessions. They never stayed in one place very long, kept mostly to themselves and never, never formed relation-ships. However, jobs were important to them. They went where there was work.

"I would appreciate it if you wouldn't move on quite yet. Wes told me yesterday the cattle are ready to go to market. I'll need you for that. Can you stay on and help?"

Rusty gave Grady the high sign. "That'll be fine. But we'd like to get settled in some place before winter hits."

"I have no problem with that. I'm not sure how long it takes to sell property around here, but if you'd like, I could arrange with the new owners to keep you on as hands . . . as part of the sale."

As she expected, Juanita was the first to speak. "You makin' big mistake." She lowered her voice to a hush. "Even the ghosts say you stay."

"What?" Grady and Rusty said at once.

Wes cocked his head to the side. "What're you sayin', Juanita?"

"She found a broken Indian doll in Mac's bedroom."

Wes roared with laughter. "Juanita, those Indian ghosts are gonna be the death of you. Nobody believes that stuff."

Juanita lifted her fat chin defiantly. "Mac, he always be-lieved me!"

Maureen felt the tension in the room at the mention of Mac's name. Maureen's eyes darted from Wes to Grady and then Rusty. They all looked away from her, like children in a classroom who didn't want to be called upon. Was it really true? Had Mac been as daffy as everyone seemed to think? Maureen needed answers.

"I'll be in Mac's study if anyone needs me. I want to review the books."

Maureen spent the rest of the day going through Mac's drawers in his mammoth rolltop desk. In the study closet were three sets of file cabinets. Instead of receipts, bills, and projections for the ranch's yearly profits, she found stacks of research on Indian folklore, gold mining by the Spanish conquistadors in the sixteenth century, and extensive histories of Texas, German settlers and Spanish noble settlers. She found everything except what she needed to determine the real worth of the ranch.

She pored over the attorney's papers, the mortgage and loan papers she'd found. She used her pocket calculator to make some rough figures. She found a recent agreement signed by Mac to sell 150 head of cattle to the government of Venezuela. They were expecting shipment by the end of October, only thirty days away. She wondered if she could find a buyer that quickly who would handle the sale for her.

Maureen made a quick list of the top cattle-producing states; Florida, Illinois, Indiana, Kansas and Texas led the list. But these cattle were not for slaughter. These were breeding cattle. And Texas led the list in cattle breeding for the world. She would have to depend on local interest to produce a buyer.

She shuffled through the built-in drawers on the far wall. Many were warped and obviously had not been opened in years. She found accounting books, but nothing was accurate. There were papers dating back to 1948, when Mac originally purchased the ranch. She even found the original house plans. Mac had been a pack rat and terribly disorganized. She wondered how he paid his taxes every year.

Uppermost in her mind, however, was the nagging thought that above all, Mac had wanted her to stay in Texas. He'd left everything to her safekeeping, but she lacked the knowledge and . . . the determination to keep the McDonald ranch in McDonald hands. She felt incredibly guilty.

"I know you can hear me, Uncle Mac. I promise I'll find someone who loves the ranch as much as you did."

By seven-thirty her back ached and her head throbbed with the jumble of information she'd been exposed to that day. Just as she was rising and about to go to the kitchen, the phone rang.

"Michael." She said his name with a smile.

"How are you, babe?"

"Okay. Not wonderful, not bad." She paused. "It's . . . tough, you know."

"Yeah. So, are you coming home tomorrow?"

"Tomorrow?" She looked around her at the forty years' accumulation of papers that was all of Mac she had. "No."

"Why not? The funeral is over."

"Michael, there's the ranch to consider. It has to be sold"— she looked at the crumbling plaster—" and repaired."

"You've never heard of real estate agents? They are marvelous, enterprising people. You pay them money and they take care of things like ranches."

Maureen stiffened at his patronizing attitude. Had he always been like this and she'd never paid attention, or was this some new tack? "Michael. This ranch is more than bricks and boards and nails. There are the animals to consider and people whose lives depend on it."

"They'll survive. In the meantime, I need you back here."

Maureen stood her ground. "I'll come back in ten days."

"Ten days? Jesus! Between this and Africa you'll have been gone almost a month!"

"I can't help it. This is a working ranch, Michael. I have obligations. It's like a corporation. You wouldn't just dump your magazine overnight without trying to make an intelligent decision about it."

"What decision are you talking about? You only have one option, Mo. Sell the damn place."

"Michael, try to understand. My uncle spent his life building this ranch. His heart and soul are connected to this land."

"Yeah? Well, your heart and soul are in Manhattan."

"I'm not so sure . . ." she mumbled under her breath.

"What did you say?"

"Nothing."

Just then there was a pounding at the front door. Maureen heard Juanita's familiar shuffling feet as she answered the door. Juanita, her smile wide, came to the study's doorway with an enormous bouquet of three dozen yellow roses. She handed them to Maureen.

"How beautiful!" Maureen exclaimed as she pulled out the card.

"What's beautiful?" Michael asked on the other end.

"I just received three dozen roses." They were from Alexander. The card read: "These are not for Mac, but for you, for coming home."

Michael paused on the other end. Something was not right. "Another funeral arrangement?" he asked pointedly.

"No. They're from an old friend. Alexander Cottrell. He was the only neighbor who attended the burial ceremony."

"Yeah? How 'old' is this friend?" Michael asked.

"My age. We were playmates when we were young. He lives on the ranch to the north of here. It's the largest breeding ranch in Texas. So he says."

"Rich, huh?"

"I suppose."

"Mo . . . I was thinking that since you can't come to New York, maybe I should fly out and see you this weekend. I could use some time away. I know I can't go another ten days without seeing you."

"You'd do that?"

"I just said I would."

"Oh, Michael, you don't know how happy you've made me."

"I love you, babe."

"I love you, Michael," she said as she bent over and sniffed the roses. "You'll love it here. It's so beautiful. God's country."

"I can't wait to see it . . . and you. Good night, Mo."

" 'Bye, Michael." She hung up the phone, feeling wonderfully elated. It was the first show of commitment she'd seen from Michael in months. Perhaps her absence had made him realize how much he needed her. She hoped they would progress to the next phase of their relationship. She hoped he might even propose. She hoped for a lot of things.

Juanita took the flowers from her. "I put these in water." She started toward the doorway. "We have visitor for weekend, yes?"

"Oh, yes. A very special visitor. Everything is going to be . . . great."

5

♦

"THIS IS GOD'S COUNTRY?" Michael Grayson mumbled to himself as he emerged from the charter plane and was hit with a blast of hot, dusty wind. His tie blew up into his face, and he nearly lost his balance on the metal roll-up steps. He heard Maureen's voice before he saw her.

"Michael!" she cried, and raced toward him. She nearly knocked him over in her exuberance. "I'm so glad to see you."

He held her momentarily. "What a trip! I can't believe people still fly on crates like that."

Maureen chuckled, thinking of the different contraptions she'd flown in all over the world for the good of *Ultra Woman*.

Michael looked askance at the beaten-up relic Maureen referred to as a "truck." He gingerly placed his chic, new, MCM luggage in the rusty back bed. As they drove to the ranch, Michael filled Maureen in on all the latest news from New York. He handed her a letter from Bitzy, which she stuck into her purse. He told her about his problems with the advertisers, the editors, the free-lance writers and the distribution. It was the same old song. Finally, he quieted down and looked out the window.

"Hell, this looks like your photographs of Zimbabwe," he said, stunned at the realization.

"I know. I've always loved it here."

"I could have saved a bundle by doing the shoots in Texas. Shit."

Maureen sighed, exasperated. "I do believe our readers could tell the difference."

"Possibly," he said, vowing at that moment to schedule more domestic shoots. With the dollar falling on foreign markets it was the economically prudent thing to do. He looked over at Maureen. "I'm already glad I came."

Maureen's eyes narrowed beneath her sunglasses. "Really? Why's that?"

Michael didn't like the edge of her voice. "I missed you more than I thought." He leaned over, kissed her cheek and then slid his arm around her shoulder. He felt her relax. He'd said the right thing.

"So, did you get an agent yet?"

"I'm interviewing two today after we get back."

"Great," he said and kissed her again.

They drove through the gates to the ranch and up to the house. Michael got out of the pickup and slammed the creaky door.

"You weren't kidding. This place is a disaster." He saw her frown. "But quaint, Mo. Very quaint."

They went inside.

"Juanita!" Maureen called.

Juanita shuffled in from the kitchen, dusting flour off her hands. "Si?"

"This is Michael Grayson. Michael, this is Juanita."

"Hi," he said, noticing that Juanita was giving him the once-over.

"Would you show Michael to his room?" Then she turned to him. "I'll fix us a drink."

Juanita pulled Maureen aside and whispered conspiratorially, "Señorita, you have a visitor."

"Oh? One of the real estate agents?"

"No." A deep voice came from the salon. "Just me."

Maureen and Michael turned around to see Alexander. Maureen smiled, went to him and kissed him on the cheek. "Alex. I'd like you to meet Michael Grayson."

Alexander shook Michael's hand exuberantly. "Welcome to Texas, Michael."

Michael did not smile. He *knew* he'd been right to make this trip. "Thanks," he said curtly.

Silence filled the air like loud tambourines as the two men assessed each other. It was Alexander who kept the mood light.

"You two attend to your business. I'll make the drinks."
Alexander winked at Maureen and flashed her his boyish
smile. He retreated to the kitchen for ice.

Michael followed Maureen and Juanita up the stairs. Maureen showed him the guest room.

"What the hell is this? We aren't sleeping together?"

"I . . . uh . . . I'm staying in Uncle Mac's room."

"So?"

"It's just that . . . I'd feel awkward . . ."

"Shit, Mo. The man is dead. Give me a goddamn break."
He picked up his monogrammed hanging bag and flung it
over his shoulder. "Or is it pretty boy downstairs?" Michael's dark eyes lit with anger.

Maureen suddenly realized why Michael had made this trip.
He was jealous. It was a good sign.

"Alexander is just a friend," she said firmly. "We were
kids together."

"Well, you're not kids anymore. And I'm the one who's
sleeping with you. Don't forget that."

"I won't." She smiled as he walked out of the guest room
and down the hall to her room.

He left his things for Juanita to hang up. He opened his
briefcase, and he looked around the room.

"There's no phone in here?"

"You can use the one in the study. It's private there."

He pulled out his black telephone book. Maureen stiffened.

"Michael, you just got here. Couldn't this wait? Alexander's here and . . ."

"Just one call. It won't take long, I promise."

"Okay," she said, and they went downstairs.

Maureen went into the salon. Alexander, as usual, was all
smiles. He held out a glass to her. "You like margaritas? I
make the best."

"Sounds great."

"Where's Michael?"

"Business calls. You know."

Alexander didn't miss the disgruntled look on Maureen's
face nor the way her eyes lost their earlier gleam. "Hey! How
about all of us going for a ride later on?"

"I'd love it! I haven't had time to do more than visit Esprit."

"Mac held on to that mare?"

"Alexander . . . this is Esprit's daughter. She's beautiful. Dark chestnut like her mother."

"You and Esprit had a real rapport, didn't you?"

She laughed. "I used to think she could talk to me. She always knew how to cheer me up."

He put his drink down and took her hand. "I wish I could do that for you."

"Why on earth would you say that? Everything's fine now that Michael's here."

"Alexander peered at her. "Is that so?"

"Yes," she said, knowing she wasn't convincing anyone.

Alexander saw the downturn in her mood. Quickly, he started into a light banter about their childhood days. Maureen laughed often at his jokes and at the way he was able to bring the past back to her as if everything was happening to her right now. She liked how he made her feel that she was special. The time passed. Alexander refilled their drinks. They continued talking. It wasn't until Juanita announced the arrival of one of the real estate agents, Kristin Jenkins, that Maureen realized nearly two hours had passed.

"Where is Mr. Grayson, Juanita?"

"Still on the telephone."

Alexander rose. "I'd better go. I'll call you later about that ride. Hire yourself somebody good, darlin'," he said. This time as he left he kissed her quickly on the mouth.

Maureen was a bit stunned. She lifted her finger to her lips and touched the place where she still felt the pressure of his mouth. She watched as he slid into his shiny Jaguar.

Alexander put on his Ray Bans, started the car, opened the sunroof and turned his cassette player on full blast. He sang along with the old Ronettes tune, "Be My Baby."

Alexander continued singing along with the music and re-played the song four times before he arrived home. Everything was working out just as he'd wanted. He would have good news to report to his mother. . . . Maureen was going to sell the ranch. He would place his bets on Kristin Jenkins's getting the listing. Kristin was good. He could easily cut a deal with her; she might even reduce her commission if she thought he'd sleep with her.

Alexander was glad Maureen's boyfriend had showed up. The guy was such an asshole it didn't take much for Alexander to look good in Maureen's eyes. He couldn't believe this jerk was letting Maureen run around the country without his name on her.

Texans knew a good thing when they saw it, and they put their brand on it. A man would have to be blind and a eunuch not to be attracted to Maureen. On that score, Alexander did not fault Michael. Alexander found it nearly impossible to keep his own hands off her. But he had to be careful. He wanted more from Maureen than just sex. He would wait till the time was right to make his move. Alexander guessed that he had already won her trust. She'd really climbed into all that stuff about their childhood.

"Poor kid," he said to himself. She was all alone now, and that was the way he wanted it. Alexander could see that the end of Maureen's affair with Michael was just a matter of time. He believed that if he pushed her—just a little, and in the right direction—he might be instrumental in eliminating Michael Grayson as a factor in Maureen's life.

It had been a long time since he'd felt this good about life . . . about himself. He hoped the feeling would last a long, long time. He rewound the Ronettes tape and played it one more time.

6

♦

"I HATE HORSES!"

"Come on, Michael. It'll be fun. I want to show you the ranch. We can go up into the hills and have a picnic."

"I already have indigestion from Juanita's cooking. Does she put jalapeños in everything?"

Maureen was losing her patience. "Everything except fried eggs!" she quipped angrily. "Is there nothing you like here? So far you've complained about the weather, the house, the bed, the food, the people. I'm surprised you haven't packed up and left. Maybe you shouldn't have come here after all."

"You don't mean that. You've been under a tremendous strain the past few days, and I understand that." He put his hands on her shoulders. "You're the one who needs this ride, not me. It's gonna get better. You hired this Jenkins woman to handle the property for you. You can go back with me to New York on Monday. Everything will be back to normal."

Maureen still felt as if she were being squeezed in a vise. She should be more relaxed, and she wasn't. She'd taken care of all the business she could; someone else would carry the ball from here on out. Michael was right. She should feel better. Instead, she felt worse.

Michael sensed her tension. "Look, I've got some calls to make. You go for your ride. I'll be just fine."

"I'm sure you will!" she hissed and slammed the front door on her way out. It was exactly as it had always been. Michael needed nothing but his business. There was no room for her. She strode angrily to the horse barn.

45

Wes saw her coming and waved. "Mornin', Miz McDonald. You wanna see Esprit?"

"Yes. Would you please saddle her up?" She glanced toward the house. "I need a breath of fresh air."

Wes wisely turned around and went straight to the barn. He thought surely by now the arguments in the ranch house would have abated. But obviously tempers were just as hot now as they had been last night.

Wes led the chestnut mare into the sunlight. He gave Maureen a boost into the saddle and handed her the reins. "Have a nice ride."

She was still incensed over Michael, and her cheeks were blazing red as she galloped through the scrub grass and scraggly trees toward the hills. The morning sun rose in the sky and warmed her back. As she rode harder, the wind rippled through her long hair. She spurred Esprit on to the top of the highest hill, where she could view the entire valley.

When she could go no higher, she paused for a moment before dismounting. She stroked Esprit's nose, and when she did the mare bowed her head, as if craving more attention.

"I guess we all want the same thing, don't we, girl?"

Maureen felt her anger abate; in its place remained a thin gauze of despair. She crouched to the ground, then sat Indian style and plucked long pieces of grass one by one out of the hard earth.

"This weekend has been a disaster," she moaned. Nothing had turned out the way she'd thought it would. Obviously, she'd read Michael wrong. She had thought he would propose. She'd thought things would be different because they had been apart for so long. She'd been wrong about everything. Michael's trip here had only shown her that a future with him was impossible.

She lowered her face, cradled it with her hands. "How could I have not seen it before? Two years . . ." But, she *had* seen it. They were lovers and that was all they would ever be. It had been Maureen who'd done all the work in their relationship. It was clear to her that they could go on forever as they were, never committed, never truly being intimate. Truth be told, they weren't even good friends. They had few friends in common . . . a point Bitzy always made. Perhaps this *was* the normal course relationships took. They had finally come to the river, and if they couldn't cross it together then it wasn't meant to be.

She realized she wasn't angry with Michael. She was angry with herself. She'd been less than honest with him for a long time. She'd pretended she was content with the status quo. Michael could only take his cue from her. Bitzy was right. She *did* need a man who would go there *with* her. She wanted more for herself. It wasn't fair to Michael to expect him to change.

Michael did not need her. He needed only his work to make him happy and a woman who wanted no strings. Perhaps other women could be satisfied with that, but she couldn't. Not ever. Michael's compulsion with work was *not* a slam against her personally. She could see that now. They were just two different kinds of people.

Maureen also knew that she would have to be the one to make the changes. Michael never would. For him, everything was perfect.

She looked up into the clear blue sky. Pink-and-white clouds swept across the vast canvas like long, thin fingers. Maureen knew now that her future was not with Michael. But her career was.

"Damn!" She thought of the life-style she had in New York, her fame, the respect she had among those in the industry. She was proud of all she'd accomplished. And yet, she wanted to climb higher. She knew she was capable of more than fashion photography.

Knowing Michael, there was a good chance he wouldn't fire her after she broke off with him. After all, Michael always had the best interests of *Ultra Woman* at heart. He would never do anything to jeopardize his circulation or the support of his advertisers.

Maureen was confident that she could keep her job for a while until she figured out what she really wanted to do with her career. And, she thought as she rose and mounted Esprit again, there would be more time to think about careers once the business of the ranch was settled.

"First things first," she said aloud.

Maureen rode slowly back to the house. When she entered the house, she heard Michael from the hallway. He was shouting again . . . long distance.

Michael slammed down his coffee mug on the desk. "Christ, Murray! Do I have to stand over your shoulder all the damn time? Why is it that if I'm not there everything goes to hell in a handbasket?" He paused and then ran his hand through his hair. "Okay. I'll take care of it first thing Monday morning . . . I can't do anything about it now! I'm thousands of miles away!"

He slammed down the receiver. Maureen walked over to him. She took a deep breath. Making the words travel from her head to her lips was not as easy as she'd thought.

"Pretty tough day, huh?" she asked.

"The worst. Murray has managed to piss off two major accounts. He told the Revlon people about the concessions I gave to the Estée Lauder execs. The last thing either one of them would call me is Mr. Wonderful, which I *used* to be."

"I'm sorry, Michael."

"It's not your fault."

"I think it is."

"What?" he asked, finally looked at her . . . really looking at her.

"If it weren't for me, you'd be in New York and would have handled this problem hours ago. Even yesterday."

"But I wanted to be with you."

"No you didn't, Michael. Not really. I see that now."

"What's going on here, Mo? Did you really meet Sir Lancelot in the hills?"

"This has nothing to do with anyone except you and me. Certainly nothing to do with Alex. You didn't come here for me, Michael. You came here for your—your ego. You thought your territory was being threatened. Alex is not a threat."

"This is ridiculous," he said, rising. "I love you, Mo."

"I think you *think* you do. But whatever love that is, it's not enough. I'm going to say this plain and simple, Michael. I want more than just weekends with you and a quick ham sandwich at noon in your office twice a week. Your career is enough for you, Michael. But your career isn't enough for me."

"Why do I get the feeling I've heard this before?"

"Maybe you have—when your wife left."

"That's a low blow."

"It's the truth, Michael. For some reason, you keep picking women who want marriage and families, and yet that's not what you want at all."

"I'll decide what I want."

"You have decided. You decide every day when you refuse to get any closer to me. We have never been really intimate—"

He interrupted her. "No? I thought we had a great sex life. Or maybe you're some new kind of actress I don't know about."

"That's not it at all. Intimacy is something entirely different. And I'm not saying there's anything wrong with the way you live your life. It just isn't for *me*, that's all."

"What the hell is this, Mo? I come all the way here . . ."

"And you've spent the entire time on the phone to New York. Don't you think I know you were up two hours before me to start your calls? You are miserable here, Michael. Admit it. And I'm miserable living a lie. There's nothing in this for either of us. Can't you see that?"

"I can't see. I won't see. What is there about you women that you *have* to be married? Why can't things go on the way they were? We were happy."

"Yes, we were—for a while. But I went beyond that. I passed you."

"Not the way I see it. You haven't grown up at all. The world is a cold, rotten place, Maureen. There are no ivy-covered cottages. There are no little cherub babies that come down from the heavens just to make you happy. Things aren't that simple. Life's a bitch and then you die."

"I don't think so, Michael."

"Maureen, listen to me. You've never known anything in your life except the pretty things. You've never had to scrape in the gutters, with the rats, just to survive. You've never had to cheat or steal to get what you want. You probably can't imagine what kind of person would stoop that low. Let me tell you, circumstances can make almost anyone do anything to survive. Survival is all there is. You've been sheltered all your life. Hell, I've even helped out on that! I didn't want you to know how bad it can be, looking over your shoulder, constantly watching to see who's gonna bite your ass next. Wise up, little girl. You've got a good thing with me. Don't blow it."

"Michael, if this means you intend to fire me, then so be it. I can find another job. I'm good and we both know it. But it's not fair to either one of us to keep up a relationship that is based on job security. We both deserve better than that."

He looked at her. He'd never seen her this resolute, except for the day she'd come into his office to quit nearly two years ago. This time, however, if he took her in his arms, it would be disastrous. He knew Maureen well enough to know that she didn't arrive at decisions easily or lightly. She'd been thinking this one through for a long time. He also knew that once she made up her mind she wouldn't change it. He'd known for months that things weren't right between them. Perhaps that was why he'd come here—to force her hand, force her to make his decisions for him. If he were honest with himself, he was just as tired of the situation as she was.

"Maybe this *is* the best thing, Mo. I don't have the time or the energy to spend on you . . . trying to help you find your happiness. I already was happy. I can be that happy again."

"I have no doubt you can, Michael," she said, thinking that he asked so little for himself that it was an easy bill to fill.

He picked up the telephone. "Information, please. I need the Kerrville Municipal Airport."

Maureen watched numbly as a cloud of dust rooster-tailed behind Michael's taxi. She'd wanted to drive him to the airport, a last gesture of sorts, but Michael had declined.

She had her ten days to get things in order at the ranch and get back to New York. Michael would hold her job that long before he started interviews, he'd told her. He wouldn't wait forever.

She knew she'd done the right thing, but still she felt scared and very much alone. She'd felt this way—actually, a hundred times worse—when her parents died. She would never get used to this insecurity, this feeling that the earth would open up at any minute and swallow her up. She knew she was a strong person, but sometimes strength hid itself quite conveniently.

"Señorita." Juanita approached her cautiously. "I . . . I must go into town."

"What for?" Maureen asked, still staring at the empty road.

"Groceries . . . then the butcher's."

"I'll do it," she offered. She wanted to get her mind off Michael. "Do you have a list?"

"Si. I get it."

Maureen went to the study and took the truck keys off the desk. She also grabbed the tally of figures she and Wes had come up with. Now was as good a time as any to visit the real estate agent, Kristin Jenkins. She needed to arrive at a reasonable asking price for the ranch, so that Kristin could plug the information into her multilisting computer.

Maureen frowned as she scanned the list of debts outstanding against the ranch. It was a bleak picture. Sylvester Craddock had been right. There wasn't much left. The night before Michael had arrived, she, Wes and Juanita had gone through the storage sheds, the closets, every place on the ranch where Mac had stowed his gold-mining gear. She'd made a list, and it was extensive. Mac had spent a small fortune on equipment that did little else but sustain his dream.

Maureen planned to sell every piece. Tomorrow she would place ads in two mining-and-geology magazines. She needed to purchase a telephone recorder to take the messages that came in from the ad. She hoped there would be many callers.

She walked out the back door and found Wes walking toward the old pickup.

"Do you need the truck?" he asked.

"Yes. I'm going into town."

"I need some supplies for the cattle. Can I hitch a ride?"

"Sure," she said, and they both climbed in.

They rode in silence for quite a while. Maureen was aware of Wes's gallantry in not saying anything about Michael's departure.

Wes fidgeted in his seat, lit a cigarette with a Zippo and then shoved the lighter back into his jeans pocket. He flicked the ashes out the open window. "I know you got a lot on your mind, Miz McDonald . . ."

"It's okay, Wes. Out with it."

"It's about the cattle, ma'am. I need to make arrangements to get them to Venezuela. I know you're pushin' to sell the ranch and all, but I don't think them cattle can wait that long."

"I know, Wes."

"Mac worked real hard to get that contract with the Venezuelans. Miz Cottrell wanted that deal for herself *real* bad."

"Alexander's mother?"

"Yes ma'am. Mac worked on that deal for months. Miz Cottrell's got the finest breeding cattle in these parts. But the Venezuelans couldn't meet her price. That's how Mac swung them to his favor. He sure was excited when he closed it all up. It was the first time he got the best of that old bitch . . . uh . . . Miz Cottrell, I mean.''

"Is she as bad as Alexander makes her out to be?"

"I don't know about that . . ."

"He's always talked about her with half reverence and half anger . . . ever since we were kids. I never paid much attention. I was never around long enough for it to make any difference to me. She can't be all that bad."

"Oh yes she can! I worked at Devil's Backbone for three years before signing on with Mac. That woman rules that place with an iron fist."

"I'd think with a ranch that big she'd have to be that way."

Wes shook his head. "That woman is pure rawhide. She don't have no feelin's at all. She thinks of nothin' but that ranch—of makin' it a success. She's gonna die makin' it the biggest and best in Texas."

"I know the type," Maureen said, thinking of Michael. "People like her are survivors."

"Is that what you call it in New York?" Wes laughed and flicked his cigarette butt out the window.

Maureen pulled the truck to a halt in front of Kristin Jenkins's office. "I should only be about an hour. You take the truck and meet me back here. Then we'll get Juanita's supplies and head back to the ranch." She started to walk away. "Oh, Wes! I didn't give you any money. Do you charge it or what?"

He reached into his back pocket and pulled out a checkbook. "I've got the ranch checkbook. I'll just pay for it."

Maureen raised an eyebrow. "Where did you get that?"

"I've always done it this way. I've had check-signing privileges since I signed on at the ranch."

"Oh, well, I guess if that's what you and Mac decided . . ."

"It saves a lot of time and hassles. It shouldn't be more than a couple hundred dollars for everything."

"Okay. Well, keep the receipts for me, too."

"Yes, ma'am." He smiled brightly and then pulled away from the curb.

Maureen walked into the real estate office. The secretary announced her to Kristin.

Kristin came into the reception area and greeted Maureen

with a friendly smile. "Good morning. Isn't this a lovely day?"

Maureen had been so depressed over Michael's departure she wasn't aware if it was sunny or raining. "Yes. Lovely."

Kristin was dressed in a pretty blue silk dress that dramatically enhanced her auburn hair and blue eyes. Kristin was thirty-five years old, slender and average height. She was single, supporting two young daughters. She must be doing fairly well, Maureen thought, for she wore real diamonds on her ears, hands and around her neck. All were mounted in expensive settings. Kristin obviously was used to the finer things in life. Her skin was still tan from the summer, and Maureen surmised that Kristin did not spend all her time working.

Maureen followed the agent into her office and sat on a hunter green, upholstered chair. "How close are we to arriving at a price?"

"Very," Kristin said, pulling out a thick file. Maureen saw, in this light, that Kristin's face was more deeply lined than she'd noticed before. Sunbathing was taking its toll. It gave Kristin a harsh look. "I'd like to ask two-point-two million."

"Whew! That seems like a lot. Is it?"

"It's a fair price. Depending upon how fast you'd like to get rid of the property . . ."

"As fast as possible."

"Well, that may not be easy to do. If we must rely on local interest, it will have to sell to someone who is only interested in adding the acreage to their existing ranch. For new blood to come in, we'd have to make some costly repairs to the house, the barn, the bunkhouse . . ."

"How costly?"

"Several hundred thousand . . . just to make things livable."

"I can believe that!"

"You might be wise to sell parcels of the land. You could keep some for yourself if you want."

Maureen had not considered this. She felt uneasy sitting here in this office discussing the sale of Mac's dream. Again, she felt guilt creep around her and envelop her in its web. "I hadn't thought of that alternative."

"I suggest we try to sell the ranch as a whole right now. If we don't get any interest in a month or two—"

"A month or two? How long will this take?"

Kristin looked puzzled. "Miss McDonald, have you ever sold any real estate before?"

"No."

"Ah." The agent nodded her head. "Well, a piece this size should take nearly a year."

"A year? I haven't got a year to fool with this! I have to get back to New York. I have a life there." Though not as much of a life as I used to have, she thought.

"I'm sure you do."

Maureen was suddenly confused. She didn't know what was the right thing to do. How naive she'd been to think someone would simply waltz in and take over the ranch. Settling matters between herself and Michael was enough decision making for the time being.

"Kristin, I'd like to think about this for a day or two. I'm not sure how I'd like to go about it."

"That's fine. Call me and let me know. It's your decision."

"I know," Maureen said glumly. She rose, shook Kristin's hand and left.

She walked out into the sunshine and saw Wes leaning on a parking meter and talking to Alexander. They were both laughing.

"Alex . . . I didn't expect to see you today."

He took his hands out of his pockets and smiled at her. "Why not?" He kissed her on the cheek. His eyes flashed impishly when he looked at her. The breeze lifted his gold hair. He pushed it back with his hand.

She felt reassured whenever she saw Alex. He wanted to help her, she could see that. He seemed to go out of his way to make her feel a part of things. He'd been like that as a child. She gestured with her hand toward the real estate office. "I had some errands to do . . ."

"I know. I asked Juanita where you were."

"You followed me?"

He smiled. "Sure did. I wanted to see you."

Wes coughed, shuffled his feet, then lit a cigarette. He was clearly embarrassed by Alexander's pointed comment.

Alexander glanced at Wes. "I'll help you with your errands. Wes doesn't need to hang around anymore."

"Okay," Maureen said. "I'll meet you at the ranch," she

said to Wes, who then climbed into the truck with a silent nod and drove away.

They took two carts at the supermarket and filled them. As they travelled down each aisle, Alexander spoke about some of the escapades they'd had as children. He could feel Maureen moving closer to him with each story. They paid for the groceries and then loaded them into Alexander's Jaguar.

"It's been a busy weekend for you, hasn't it?" Alexander said, opening the sunroof.

Maureen took a silk, leopard-print scarf out of her purse and tied it around her long black hair.

She looked at him and wondered how much Juanita had told him. Everything, she guessed. "Very."

"If you ever need anyone to talk to . . . I mean . . . just friend to friend . . . I want you to know . . . I'm here."

"Thanks," she said, and patted his hand.

He grabbed her hand and held it. "I wish there was something I could say that would help."

Maureen wished Bitzy were here so she could bare her soul. She felt uneasy showing her vulnerability to Alexander. It was silly, she knew, for it had nothing to do with her trusting him, but more to do with his maleness. It was just that she'd always shared such things with girl friends. She was being unfair to Alex, who obviously only wanted to help. Maureen had to talk to somebody.

"It has been hard," she said with a sigh. "I keep going through Mac's things over and over. I guess I keep thinking that I'll find him there underneath all those old papers. That's pretty dumb, isn't it?"

"No." He kept his eyes on the road. "I don't have anybody in my life I'd ever feel that way about. In a way, you're very lucky."

She looked at him, wondering what it was that he was trying to tell her. She pitied him, not being close to anyone in his family. She wondered if his devil-may-care attitude was a cover-up for unhappiness.

"Michael left today, didn't he?" Alexander said.

"Yes, he did. We had a terrible weekend. We fought constantly."

"I know."

"How? Did Juanita tell you?"

He laughed. "She didn't have to. Half this county knows

about the rows between you and Michael. How he wouldn't even finish a meal without a phone stuck to his shoulder. Gossip travels fast in these parts. Ranch hands have quicker communications than AT&T.''

"I can see that.''

"Don't get huffy now. We're all used to it and you're not, that's all. If you'd ever ask your help, you could find out all about my fights with my sister . . . and my mother.''

"Really?''

"Yep. Really. For instance, the first day you got here, my housekeeper had already heard the story about the broken Indian doll and your ghosts.''

"Oh, for Pete's sake. Juanita can get carried away.''

"True. But everyone around here knows about her superstitions. And anything like that coming from the McDonald ranch is . . . well, expected.''

Maureen's lips pursed tightly together. "Didn't anyone like Mac?''

"I did. But no, not many did.'' He glanced at her as he rounded the turn under the iron arch of her ranch. "But it's not their fault. Mac *was* a bit strange these last few years. He was filled with gold fever, Maureen. He was obsessed with finding the stuff. And he cut off everyone and everything else to pursue it. Don't form judgments about the people here without all the facts.''

"But you liked him.''

"Yeah, I did.''

"God,'' she sighed as he braked the car. She looked up at the house. It seemed to be begging her to repair it. "What am I going to do with all this?''

"You could sell it to me.''

She spun around in the leather seat and looked at him wide-eyed. "You'd be interested in buying the ranch?''

"I might. If the price was right.''

"What for?''

"What it was meant for. Cattle grazing.''

She paused for a long moment. "You're serious.''

"Absolutely.''

"Okay. Put together an offer and I'll consider it.''

"That's fair enough,'' he said, and quickly pecked her on the cheek. When he pulled back he gazed into her blue eyes. "You sure turned out beautiful.''

"Likewise,'' she said smiling.

He placed his hand on the back of her neck. He pulled the scarf off her head and let her hair fall around her shoulders. This time when he kissed her, he took his time. It was a gentle kiss, a friendly kiss. It tasted of times past. It helped shore up the shaking timbers beneath her.

7

◆

ALEXANDER WAS WHISTLING as he pulled the Jaguar to a stop beneath the portico to his mother's house. He picked up Maureen's scarf and held it to his nose. It smelled of Opium perfume, just like Maureen. He smiled and got out of the car.

He went into the mansion, crossed the expansive foyer and went to his office just under the circular stucco-and-black-ironwork staircase. He closed the door.

He placed the scarf in the top left-hand drawer and locked the drawer. He placed the tiny gold key on his key ring. He didn't want anyone to invade his privacy. Alexander was a stickler about privacy.

Just then he heard a knock at the door. He opened it.

"Mother, come in," he said courteously.

Barbara Cottrell, dressed in a stunning St. John knit suit, crossed the room, her straight back keeping her magnificent shoulders level and her head high. She was an incredibly beautiful woman. At fifty-five, she looked younger than women fifteen years her junior. But then, Alexander thought, she took better care of herself than most women did. She had exercised all her life and rode on horseback, but only near dawn or at nightfall, when the sun could not damage her skin. She had a weight trainer who came to the ranch three times a week. Her diet was vegetarian, even though she raised prime cattle. She had a facial, a manicure and a pedicure weekly by a woman she visited in Dallas when she flew there in her private plane every Wednesday morning on business. She was always immaculately dressed, though she preferred gaucho pants and loose blouses. She had always been more at home in boots and trousers than in ball gowns.

Barbara's snow-white hair was perfectly coiffed, as always. She sat on the leather sofa opposite Alexander and lifted her green eyes to him. He smiled, for today he had good news for her. News that would please her. And more than anything in the world, Alexander lived to please his mother—then he would win her respect.

"Where've you been so early, Alex?"

"I saw Maureen today."

"Oh," she said, starting to rise. "I thought it was something important."

"It is—for us."

Barbara lifted a dark eyebrow. "Oh?"

"She is going to sell the ranch. I told her I wanted to make a formal offer."

Barbara kept her cool demeanor. She never allowed herself to show excitement. It was a ploy she'd learned from her father when he was dealing with business associates. She never wanted anyone to know what she was thinking, not even her son. "She'll sell all of it?"

"I think so. She doesn't want to stay here. She's anxious to get back to New York and her job."

"How much does she want?"

"I don't know. But Kristin is handling the property for her. It won't be hard for me to find out."

"Do that. Then let's make our offer as quickly as possible. I don't want anyone else to beat us out of that land."

"Anyone else?" He was momentarily puzzled. "You mean Brandon Williams might be interested, too?"

"Brandon always wants what I want. People of his sort are constantly struggling to better themselves. You remember that, Alexander. I don't ever underestimate him, either. He's risen very quickly."

"Twenty years is hardly a skyrocketing pace, Mother."

"Don't contradict. Since the day he discovered oil on his land, he's been after me—after Devil's Backbone."

"No one's ever seen evidence of that, Mother." Alexander had heard this scenario a thousand times over the years. Barbara had some kind of vendetta against Brandon, simply because his family did not possess the ancestry that Barbara's family did. Barbara could tolerate "poor white trash" only as long as they kept their place. She believed that success was the God-given right only of those who could trace their lineage back five hundred years. Brandon, however, had become a super-success. He'd crossed over the line that separates the old Southern gentry and the new rich. He was accepted in the best social circles, and it was Alexander's observation that this was the sin for which Barbara could never forgive him . . . her jealousy and pride forbade it.

Alexander didn't care what Brandon did or didn't do. He didn't care where Brandon's ancestors came from, nor what they had done in the past. All he wanted was to make Devil's Backbone the biggest ranch in Texas. He wanted it to be bigger than the King Ranch, even bigger than XIT had been in the thirties before it broke up. On that score, he and his mother concurred.

Barbara kept her hands calmly folded in front of her. "I don't want Brandon to get a chance at that land, Alexander. Is that clear?"

"Perfectly. And don't worry. Maureen will do anything I tell her."

"Anything?" Her eyes registered surprise.

"She trusts me. In a way, she's a lot like you, Mother. She trusts the past."

"Then she's a wise person." She rose and walked to the door. "Hopefully, she will be wise enough to see that her grazing lands could not be in better hands than mine. I'm depending on you, Alexander, to get those lands for me. It would please me enormously."

He beamed. "I would think so. We stand to double the size of Devil's Backbone."

Barbara smiled, too. "Think of it. No one could touch me then, not even Brandon Williams." She opened the door, paused and turned back to him. "You feel strongly about your influence on her, Alexander?"

"Yes, I do."

"Then I think it's time I met Miss McDonald. Invite her to a barbecue next Saturday night. We'll invite all the neighbors. Then we will announce to everyone that we are buying the McDonald ranch."

Alexander hesitated. "But what if she doesn't accept our offer?"

"Give her whatever she wants. It's my guess she's more worried about finding a buyer at all than about the price. Call

Kristin. Get the facts. Honestly, Alexander," Barbara said with an exasperated tone, "must I tell you how to do everything?"

Barbara left the office. Alexander was thrilled with the day's development. He didn't even pay attention to his mother's last dig.

"Maureen, I love you!" he shouted to the walls. "You don't know it, but you're going to make me a very happy man."

He picked up the telephone and dialed Maureen's ranch. Her phone rang three times before she answered.

"Hi," he said. "You left your scarf in my car."

"So I did." She paused. "Thanks for helping me today."

"Anytime. Listen, I called to invite you to a barbecue on Saturday night. Can you make it?"

"I'll check my incredibly filled social calendar," she said, laughing. "What time?"

"Seven. I'll pick you up."

"That's okay. I can drive."

"I'll pick you up. I wouldn't want anyone to think a beautiful woman like you was unescorted."

"Flattery—"

"Always works," he interrupted. "But I'll see you before then. Okay?"

"Okay. 'Bye."

Alexander hung up the phone. Everything was working out just the way he'd planned.

Maureen opened her left eye and squinted at the wind-up alarm clock. It was twenty past midnight. Silver moonlight streamed into the room through gossamer thin curtains. She opened both eyes, sat up, rammed her fist into the down pillow and rolled onto her back. This time, she *would* sleep. She closed her eyes. Five minutes later, they popped open again.

"This is useless," she mumbled, and sat up. She pulled on her satin Christian Dior robe and slid her feet into a pair of white satin slippers. They looked incredibly out of sync with the Navajo rugs, battered wooden floors and forty-year-old furniture.

She went downstairs, got herself a huge glass of milk and went into Mac's study. She sat in the wooden swivel chair and snapped on the desk lamp.

Absentmindedly, she shuffled through papers she'd looked at a dozen times already. If Alexander would buy the ranch from her, all her worries would be over. She could go back to New York knowing that the land was being put to good use. Maybe she could push him to employ Juanita at the Cottrell ranch house. She knew she could get Alex to keep Wes and the other hands on. Then she could go back to her life with a clear conscience.

She leaned back in the chair, thinking about the world she'd left behind in New York. She missed Bitzy already. She thought about the apartment, her other friends, her work—and Michael.

She looked around the room at the old, leather-bound books, the disarray that was half her efforts at sorting through Mac's life and half Mac's efforts at keeping his life in chaos. She'd never felt about any place the way she did about this old house. She liked the old relics that were here, the chandelier made of longhorns, the leather furniture, the wood walls and floors.

There was something here that pulled on her the way no other place did.

She opened drawer after drawer looking for things she didn't know she wanted to see. She opened the bottom drawer and lifted out a stack of papers. Then she saw that there was a false bottom to the drawer. She slid the piece of wood out. She found a leather-bound diary.

Slowly, she opened it. She felt chills course her spine. Mac's familiar scrawl covered the pages. The entries were months, sometimes years, apart, but lengthy in content. They were introspections, dreams and hopes. As she read her uncle's innermost thoughts, she was struck by the realization that at no time was there any doubt to the man. Negativism was not in Mac's vocabulary. In 1971, when he was severely ill with pneumonia, he expressed his desire that everything on the ranch be put in order—he intended to leave everything to his brother, Hal, to be kept in trust for Maureen.

Maureen was surprised. She had only been fourteen at the time.

She read further. Again in 1979 he spoke of willing the ranch and the gold he knew he would find to Maureen. Mac's last entries looked as if he'd known she would be reading this diary.

This land has been my life. It has given me a sense of history, of myself, I could never have found anywhere else. I have found a freedom to be myself, explore myself and the world in an environment that is unfettered by the world. Sometimes, I feel as if I'm living in another time. Maybe I should have been born a hundred years ago, and just missed the boat. I want Maureen to live here, away from New York and the frivolities I see there. I hope I'm not pushing too much Thoreau on her, but even if she were to live here only a year, I think she would discover more about herself than her life anywhere else could teach her.

I want her to have dreams, which I see she has none of. I have mine of finding my gold, which my heart tells me is here. My heart tells me that Maureen belongs here.

The entry was dated September 23, 1985, the night before Mac died.

Maureen burst into tears. Her head dropped to the desk, and she folded her arms over it as if she were sheltering herself from the pain.

"No, Mac," she growled as she raised her head to look down at the words again. "Dreams? What did dreams ever get you? Debt, the loss of your friends and now . . . nothing."

She slammed the book shut. "Why couldn't you leave it alone? Why couldn't you have lived!"

Anger filled her head and dried her tears. She shot out of the chair and raced out of the study, then down the hall and out the front door. It was as if she were running away from him. She went to the horse barn and saddled Esprit. She pulled the cinch too tight, and the horse whinnied.

"There, there, girl. I'm sorry." She swung up into the saddle.

She galloped past the corrals, the horse barn and the fields of tough grasses behind the ranch house and headed for the hills. Moonlight rode her back like a silvery cloak. The slopes became steeper, but she did not slow down. Yupons and cedar trees sprinkled the hills. Scraggly oaks spread their wide branches and cast rickety, dark shadows on the hard limestone-and-clay earth. Esprit's hooves clanked against the jagged rocks as she rode higher. She galloped through a shallow crystalline creek whose source was to be found higher up in the hills.

She rode to the highest slope and pulled the horse to a stop. Green-silver moonlight bathed the valley in an eerie glow that allowed her to see for miles. It was a clear night; the stars overhead were huge and close. She felt as if she could reach out and touch them. She could make out the house and the white fence that surrounded it. Everything below her was still and peaceful. But as she sat, she knew the hills were alive with activity. She saw a white-tailed deer dart among the junipers. The deer was more curious about her than she was about it. Mockingbirds flitted overhead, and a wild turkey ran across the base of the hill. She knew there were cougars, bears, wolves and jaguars in the hills to the west, because Mac had warned her about them when she was a child.

For days Maureen had been pitched back and forth between her desire to return to New York and her responsibility to Mac's dying wish. It seemed that every time she even thought about her job, her friends . . . Michael, she felt pulled back to this place.

She should have already placed everything in the hands of an accountant and Kristin and let it go at that. She should have helped Juanita find other employment. She should have already booked a flight back to New York. But she hadn't.

If she were truthful with herself, she'd purposefully decided to stay a few days longer just to go to the barbecue with Alexander. Searching further, Maureen also knew that it wasn't that she wanted to be with Alexander so much as it was that the barbecue gave her another excuse to stay.

"It is the land that draws me," she said aloud. "I've always loved it. Michael was right. I went to Africa because it reminded me of here. Perhaps it's more a part of me than I know."

Unused to making decisions with her heart, Maureen sifted through all this information and came to the conclusion that it was her responsibility to Mac that was making her think these things, feel this way. Her decisions had always been based on logic, she told herself. This time was no different from the rest.

Logically, she had little to return to in New York. She and Michael were past history. Her job would be difficult under the circumstances. She knew she would have to leave *Ultra Woman*. She would miss Bitzy, but that was all.

Maureen drank in the scent below her. Never before had she felt so at home as she did here. She tried to visualize

Manhattan—the skyscrapers, the noise, the bustle. But it had become a distant bell.

As she rode down from the hills that night, she had quieted the turmoil within herself. She would stay in Texas.

8

BARBARA COTTRELL STOOD at the top of the circular stucco staircase with its inlaid Spanish tile steps and lacy black iron railing. Half a dozen Mexican women scurried across the enormous foyer carrying food and flowers to the terrace outside. Barbara smiled to herself, thinking of the hundreds of times she'd witnessed the same scene in this old house.

She looked around her at the white stucco walls; the dark, heavy-beamed ceilings; the chandeliers made of longhorns; the leaded-glass windows and doors. She loved this house even more than had her father, Alexander Kern, for whom she had named her son. It was he who built the house in 1920. Though the Kerns were originally from England, they came to Texas in 1812 from Boston, where they had been engaged in shipbuilding.

The ranch house was architecturally Spanish in flavor, but most of the furnishings were family heirlooms. The foyer was filled with Chippendale chairs, Hepplewhite tables and Mexican clay pots filled with colorful begonias and impatiens. Barbara loved the enormous salon the best, for it had six sets of leaded French doors that opened onto the terrace and pool area. Barbara loved gardening and so, with much care and the constant surveillance of three gardeners, she was able to create lush greenery in a land that was mostly rock.

When she'd embarked on her plan twenty years ago to build a formal garden, she'd hired bulldozers to clear out the land, scoop out the earth three feet down and replace the rock and clay with rich, black soil she'd had brought in by truck from

Nebraska. The result was a dramatic display of year-round color that was admired by all who saw it. So fabulous was it, that Barbara's garden had been photographed by *Better Homes and Gardens* and *Architectural Digest*.

Over the years she'd increased the half dozen oak trees that guarded the front of the house to over forty-eight trees that surrounded not only the house but the acre and a half of garden, pool and tennis court area in the back as well.

Barbara believed that everything could be manipulated, even nature. It was this credo that had made her one of the wealthiest women in Texas. Barbara owned the largest cattle-breeding ranch in the state. It was not the largest ranch, for none of her cattle were for slaughter. Barbara's business involved the freezing of cattle sperm and embryo implantation. Barbara's cattle were the best and always brought the highest prices at auction.

Barbara could not tolerate anything that was not the best. She knew *she* was the best. Her mother had told her so. She came from family she could trace back to the Crusades. She had the royal blood of King Richard the Lionhearted in her veins. Barbara's mother, Anne, had drilled her often and extensively on her family lineage. She taught Barbara about family pride. She explained to her daughter how important it was that she live up to her lineage. Barbara must always be the best at whatever she did. Anne taught her daughter that, along with her birthright, she also carried the responsibility to give back to the world more than what she took from it.

Therefore, Barbara had always been politically active, even as a teenager. She was allowed by both her parents to form her own opinions and then to fight for those causes. Much to her father's dismay, Barbara was not a Republican, as he was, but a Democrat like her grandfather Kern. It had often been said in Kerr County that Alexander Kern taught Southern Democrats *how* to be Southern Democrats.

But in those days, just after World War II, when the world was settling down to peace again, Barbara had been seventeen and the motivations behind her political enthusiasm had more to do with her heart than with causes and party platforms.

It was a time when Barbara learned a great deal about pride, the restrictions of her lineage, and about heartbreak.

It was a beautiful autumn day, and her parents had agreed to allow the Young Democrats to hold a rally at their ranch.

None of the youngsters was of voting age, but they were the volunteers the politicians needed to stuff mailings, make telephone calls and do all the legwork that keeps a political organization alive.

Barbara had worked with a few of the group in town on Saturday mornings. It was there she'd met John Williams, a new boy in town, who had moved to Kerrville from Odessa. She knew little about him, other than his devotion to Lyndon Johnson, the strongest advocate for better education Texas had ever seen, and that he had incredibly blue eyes. Barbara couldn't wait for her parents to meet him.

Barbara watched as he piled out of a wood-panelled station wagon with four of her classmates. He wore blue jeans, boots and a plaid shirt.

Barbara waved to John, then rushed up to meet him.

"Hi," he said, looking down at her. "You look . . . you're beautiful."

Barbara's long, naturally platinum blonde hair was in a ponytail. She tugged on the pearls she wore, hoping she wasn't blushing too much. "Thank you." She looked at him again, thinking she'd never seen anyone so handsome. "I'm glad you came. I want you to meet my parents."

He took her hand and held it gently. And as they walked through the huge ranch house and out to the terrace, where the cooks were grilling hot dogs and music was playing from a jukebox, Barbara did not notice how John's eyes took in every little detail.

"You have your own jukebox?"

"Yes. I love giving parties. Daddy put the brick terrace in so we could jitterbug out here. He thinks we get too wild sometimes."

John's smile was wan, but Barbara was aware only that he was still holding her hand.

She led him over to her parents. "Mother, Daddy, I want you to meet John Williams."

"How do you do, sir?" John said politely, and shook Alexander Kern's hand.

Anne looked at her husband, then back at Barbara.

"Barbara tells us you're new in town."

"We just moved here from Odessa. My pa used to work the rigs. He was let go about three months ago. So we sold everything and moved here."

Anne's eyes narrowed as she continued her scrutiny. "And what does he do here?"

"Oh, we bought the Banning ranch on the east side of Devil's Backbone."

"You what?" Alexander Kern boomed in shock.

"We bought—"

"I heard you," Alexander said, trying to contain himself. "I wasn't aware that it was for sale."

"My pa says it was pure luck. It was just meant to be. He went down to the real estate office the day we hit town. Mr. Banning was in there talkin' to the agent. Said he'd decided to cash in . . . now that there was no reason for him to stay."

Anne's eyes saddened. "Both his sons died in the war. I can understand . . ."

"Well, Pa walked over and asked how much he wanted. They wrote up the deal right then and there."

"How long ago was this?"

"Three weeks."

"Three weeks," Alexander said to himself. "I never heard a word about it. No one in town said anything about Banning's leaving."

John was confused. "Is there some reason they should have?"

Alexander lifted his chin imperiously. "I would have given him twice what your father paid for it."

"Why?"

"Because I wanted it. I could use more grazing land."

And then Barbara watched as her father's countenance altered. She saw him as she'd never seen him before. His back straightened and his eyes blazed.

"I should have had that land," Alexander growled. "I have a right to that land. You and your family have no business even being here. I've seen your kind before—trash, that's what you are, poor white trash. I've seen what you do to good land. You abuse it, work the life out of it because you don't know enough. Then, when it's nothing but waste, you'll leave it . . . and go on to the next place. Your kind never settles down . . . always drifting . . . always taking . . . never giving."

"Daddy!" Barbara screamed in shock. "John's not like that!"

"The hell he isn't."

John Williams stood riveted to the spot. His face was red

with anger, his eyes blazing as hotly as Alexander Kern's. Barbara saw John's fists clench and then tremble as he struggled to control his temper. "You're wrong, Mr. Kern. Dead wrong. We may not be rich like you, but we know there's more to a man than where he came from and how much money he has. Someday, Mr. Kern, I'll make you eat those words. We're not leavin' this place. Not my pa, or me. Never! You hear me? Someday, I'll be calling the shots. And if I don't, then my children will . . . cuz we ain't leavin'!''

John spun around, took one look at the young faces staring at him and raced through the house and out the front door.

Barbara turned a tear-streaked face to her father. "How could you do that to him, Daddy?" She started to run after John, but Alexander grabbed her.

"Don't," he said.

Barbara twisted out of his grasp and fled into the house. Her mother followed her, holding Barbara close as she burst into tears.

"Your father is right, Barbara. John isn't the boy for you. He's not our kind. You could never be happy with anyone like that. His world is so different from ours.''

"That's not true, Mother," Barbara sobbed.

"Think about it. Could he ever give you pearls like the ones you're wearing? Or the clothes we bought in Dallas? What about these parties? He'd spend all his life trying to please you. And then he would come to resent you. He would be miserable. And so would you.''

Barbara listened to the Frank Sinatra song playing on the jukebox. She could hear more of her friends arriving out front, their horns honking. John didn't own a car . . . not even a truck. She wondered if his father did. Her mother was right. She hated her mother then, for knowing so much, for being so right.

Barbara walked to the window. John was nearly out of sight. She felt her heart sinking. She wondered if she would ever feel that special way again.

"Señora? Mees Cottrell?" Maria, the housekeeper, said. "You want Jose to set the bar in the garden or the house?''

Barbara shook the memories out of her head. "The garden, of course. Did the extra ice arrive?''

"Si.''

"Good. I'll come to the kitchen in a minute.''

"Si." Maria hastened back to her duties.

Barbara was aware that John's son, Brandon, would be at the party tonight. Her father had been right. John Williams, his father and John's wife, Alice, had all worked themselves to death on that ranch. But it was Brandon who had made his father's prediction become a reality.

John had died in 1966, when Brandon was eighteen. Six months later Brandon had run a geological survey on the eastern portion of the ranch and found oil. He became a millionaire at nineteen. For the past twenty years Brandon had parlayed his money into one business after another. He was one of the richest men in Texas.

Barbara thought about that day back in 1947 when her destiny turned a corner. She never did feel that way about a man again. She married Tom Cottrell two years later. Her mother approved. He was *her kind*. They had two children. He had two mistresses. Barbara's parents died and she took over the ranch. A year later, when she was thirty-two, Tom died when his horse came upon a rattlesnake and bucked him off. He hit his head on a rock and died instantly. Barbara did not cry at the funeral, and neither did Alexander, but her daughter, Shane, did.

Barbara had not seen Brandon since the Governor's Ball in Austin when Mark Dixon was inducted over three years ago. She was always busy with her work; he was forever flying here and there. She did not make a practice of inviting him to her parties, but when it was inevitable, he graciously sent his regrets. Brandon was aware of the animosity she felt for him, but she was certain he didn't know why. How could she tell him that, because he looked *exactly* like his father, he reminded her too painfully of a time long ago . . . of dreams that did not come true.

9

◆

MAUREEN THREW a silk Ungaro on the bed. A tailored Bill Blass suit followed. Then came the black linen Anne Klein she'd worn to Mac's funeral.

"None of this is right!" she complained. In all these years, she'd never met Alex's family. She wanted to make a good impression. Even if she'd brought her whole closet from New York she wouldn't have anything to wear to this party.

Juanita came into the room carrying a stack of towels. "What the matter?"

"Just what does one wear to a barbecue in Texas, Juanita?"

The Mexican woman shrugged her shoulders. "Jeans. Pretty dresses."

Maureen frowned. "You're a lot of help."

Juanita went to the closet and went though the clothes. Then she picked up the silk Ungaro from the bed. "Wear this."

"You think so? It's rather plain."

"But very sexy . . ." Juanita's eyes twinkled as she felt the clingy fabric and pointed to the low-cut V neckline.

"Well . . . I guess it's all right."

"You hurry. Señor Alexander will be here soon."

Maureen checked her watch and saw that Juanita was right. She bathed quickly and was spritzing herself with Opium perfume when Alexander arrived.

"Incredible," he said breathlessly as she descended the stairs.

73

"Are you sure this is all right? I didn't think I'd be going to a party."

"It's perfect."

She smiled and took his arm. "I'm so glad you asked me."

"Me, too," he said, and kissed her cheek.

When Maureen and Alexander arrived, there were already over a hundred people in attendance. The enormous ranch house was decorated with pots of blooming geraniums and greenery. There was a mariachi band that walked around the terrace and gardens playing, and on the far side of the pool, beneath a canvas tent, a country-and-western band was setting up to play after dinner.

Under another red-and-white striped tent were rows of picnic tables covered in red bandana print cloths and centered with red, white and blue flowers. On the west side of the pool were long buffet tables laden with food. There were a half dozen trays filled with sliced brisket of beef, huge glass bowls filled with coleslaw, potato salad and pasta salad. There were baskets mounded with corn bread and crocks of ranch beans.

Alexander spied a waiter carrying a tray filled with glasses of white wine. He signalled to him and handed a glass to Maureen.

She sipped her wine and looked around. "I was right. This dress is wrong."

Everyone was wearing Texas Chic—suede, rhinestones, denim, lace underskirts and diamonds. Even in Tiffany's Maureen had never seen so many jewels. And she'd never seen so many worn with blue jeans before. Texans, she found, obviously had a penchant for large diamonds. From what she could see, anything under five carats was used as a baguette.

But none of the guests was dressed as impeccably as the hostess.

Barbara was speaking with the state's attorney general as Alexander and Maureen approached. *Magnificent* was the word to describe Barbara, Maureen thought. Alexander had told her his mother was fifty-five years old, but she didn't look a day over forty. Her hair was thick, wavy, long and snow-white. She had fabulous bone structure; a narrow, perfect nose; huge, sparkling green eyes and flawless skin. She was wearing a black suede skirt with a black leather cummerbund. The jacket was collarless, with enormous bouffant sleeves, and sprinkled with silver studs across the back yoke and down the sleeves. In her ears were diamond stud earrings. She wore a silver-and-diamond collar around her neck and a cuff of diamonds on each wrist. There were four diamond rings on her fingers. Her boots were black suede and snakeskin.

Barbara was intimidating without even opening her mouth. And she knew it.

"Mother," Alexander said, taking Maureen's arm possessively as they stood next to Barbara. Barbara's eyes quickly glanced down at Alexander's hand. Alexander dropped his hold. "I'd like you to meet Maureen McDonald."

"I'm pleased to meet you," Maureen said.

"Yes. And after so many years." Barbara carefully surveyed Maureen, and Maureen detected a note of disdain in Barbara's voice. Barbara turned to the friends standing next to her. "I have only recently learned that when Alex was a child he used to visit Miss McDonald every summer." She turned back to Maureen. "Tell me, are you still a corrupting influence on my son?"

Maureen gasped. But Alexander laughed.

"I hope so!" he said, nodding to the others, who then exhaled their tension and laughed with him.

Barbara was smiling. Maureen was not.

Maureen knew Barbara had meant the dig as some kind of warning. But for what? Not to take her son from her? Yes, that had to be it.

"No more than he corrupts me," Maureen retorted, and she noted that Alexander was pleased with her barb.

"You misunderstood, Maureen. I've heard only the loveliest things about you."

Maureen was still wary of her. "From whom?"

"Why, Alexander, of course."

Everyone chuckled. Though Barbara began a light banter of social conversation, Maureen caught the almost imperceptible hardness in her eyes whenever she would look at Maureen. She noticed how Alexander had taken a slight step away from Maureen. Barbara's influence on her son was formidable. He seemed unaware of his telling gestures. Maureen wondered how far Alexander allowed his mother's influence to rule his life. Did he do it out of respect or resentment? As a child he'd tried to rebel against her to get her attention. Maureen thought he'd found a new tack.

Finally, Barbara put her hand on Maureen's shoulder and took her aside. "I know this evening could be difficult for you, after your uncle's passing. If you need to leave early, I'll arrange for the chauffeur to take you home."

"I'm sure I'll be fine."

"I just want to help," Barbara said.

Maureen turned to Alexander. "How about that dance you promised me?" As they walked away, she noticed the surprised looks on the faces of Barbara's friends. "Did I do something wrong?"

"Not many people walk away from Barbara Cottrell unless she has dismissed them."

"I'm not 'many people.' "

"I know," he said with a grin, putting his hand around her waist as he began Maureen's first lesson in the Western two-step.

The music ended, and Maureen and Alexander went through the buffet line, then sat at a long table. Alexander had just introduced her to some friends from Dallas when two stretch limousines pulled up on the left side of the gardens. They parked in a small paved area that was surrounded by huge oaks lit with security lights.

Maureen had worked with beautiful women and fabulous clothes for years. It took a lot to impress her. On this night, Maureen was impressed.

All the doors on both limousines opened as if by synchronization. Slowly, one gorgeous woman after another emerged. Some were escorted, some were not.

As they piled out, Maureen realized that she could not tell the age of a single woman. They were all somewhere between twenty-five and fifty-five. They all had the kind of skin that only the best cosmeticians and plastic surgery can offer. They had perfect, nearly adolescent bodies; the kind of bodies that, if not granted by nature, could only be maintained by rigorous dieting, exhausting exercise, massage and luxurious pampering. Their coiffures were precisely cut, colored and curled to enhance each face. Maureen wondered if Mr. Kenneth would be the last person out of the limousine.

Each was more expensively dressed than the last. The first woman to catch Maureen's eye was a tall, slender, auburn-haired beauty wearing a blue denim Western dress with a double white-eyelet petticoat that skimmed the top of her black-and-white "pony" boots. She carried a pony purse to match. She wore silver crescent earrings paved in diamonds and a five-inch-long crescent of diamonds around her throat. She had high cheekbones, even, dark olive skin and deep emerald eyes that gleamed happily in the light. But of all the things about her, Maureen was most struck by the woman's carriage. She didn't walk so much as glide; and as she drew closer and spoke quietly to friends, Maureen had the impression of a Persian queen greeting her loyal subjects. There was nothing haughty about her manner, but rather an innate sense of her position, her responsibility to give of herself. Maureen could tell that she was not only admired but loved.

The bevy of beauties descended upon the crowd, greeting everyone with smiles and laughter. It was as if someone had sounded a gong; it was now official, the party had begun.

"They're like dolls," Maureen said to Alexander.

"What do you mean?"

"They're so perfectly beautiful . . . like they were molded of wax. They have everything. Money, beauty, and friends. Look at how everyone is itching to talk to them, to be around them."

"True. These are among the richest women, richest couples in the state. They have power."

Maureen gazed at him, then she quickly looked around to find Barbara. She was standing at the far side of the pool observing the "show." Her cool, formidable smile was in place. Barbara was indulging the "dolls," letting them have their entrance, as one would humor children. Barbara waited patiently, and then, one by one, the women approached her, paying their respects as worshipers would at the sanctuary of a god.

"But none of them have the power of a Cottrell."

Alexander's thin smile was perfunctory. "None."

Maureen glanced up to see a petite blonde woman leaning over her shoulder, her eyes on Alexander.

"Alex, darling. How *are* you?"

"Wonderful, Charleen. You're looking fabulous, as always."

And indeed she was. Her brown eyes danced with merriment in a heart-shaped face. Her skin was as flawless as that of any fifteen-year-old model Maureen had worked with. She wore a peach-colored suede jumpsuit drizzled with rhinestones. Her boots, purse and belt were all custom-made of matching peach-colored eelskin. Where other Texans wore silver-and-turquoise jewelry, Charleen's was gold and aqua-marine. Maureen guessed there wasn't a stone on her throat, ears or wrists under ten carats.

"Charleen," Alexander said, "I'd like you to meet Maureen McDonald."

"McDonald?" Charleen's round doe eyes widened in surprise. "Why, you're the girl with the ghosts."

"Ghosts?"

Charleen caught herself. "My sympathies about your uncle," she added almost as an afterthought. "Tell me about your ghosts."

"I don't know what you're talking about."

"Your maid told my maid all about it. How you found the broken Indian doll."

"It was just one of my uncle's mementos."

"I wouldn't be so sure about that. I know all about these old tales. A broken doll is a bad sign."

Maureen shook her head. "This isn't voodoo, you know. Juanita gets carried away about such things."

Charleen was disappointed. "Have there been any other occurrences?"

"No."

"Not at all?" she nearly whined.

Maureen smiled. "Sorry. None."

"Well, if it was only one time, maybe there isn't much to it after all. But if there is . . ." Charleen's eyes were expectant again. "Let me know. Okay?"

"I think you'll find out about it as quickly as I will."

Charleen laughed. "You're right about that!"

"Do you live near here?" Maureen asked.

"I have a small place to the southeast of your ranch. It's not a working ranch like these others."

"No," Alexander grinned mischievously. "She only works her rigs."

"Ghastly-looking things on the north side of my land, near the Williams property. But I don't complain about them. They do pay the bills." She laughed again. "I heard you're from New York. A photographer . . . you know a lot about fashion working for *Ultra Woman*, I suppose. My favorite magazine, by the way. I just love New York. I go as often as time permits. I love the shopping, though of course it's not as good as Paris, but then Paris is the best. Paris is all there is . . . really. Don't you think?"

Maureen liked Charleen instantly. She seemed not to have a care in the world other than having a good time. Maureen wondered what that would be like—to be a doll.

Charleen turned around, searched the crowd a bit and then motioned to a friend. "Lynn. Lynn! Come here. I want you to meet Maureen."

A curvaceous blonde wearing a hot pink suede Western dress with black leather epaulets and a black belt, hat and boots emerged from the group of dolls. Her even smile was wide in her square face. But as she took Maureen's hand to shake it, Maureen thought she'd never seen such sad blue eyes.

"Glad to meet you."

"My pleasure."

"Maureen's the girl who inherited old Mac's ranch," Charleen explained.

Lynn nodded her head.

"I always liked Mac," Charleen said. "We used to exchange ghost stories . . . not very often, though. He liked being by himself."

"I liked him, too," Lynn said.

Maureen remembered the day of the funeral, and her resentment over the poor showing that day surfaced. "If you liked him so much, why didn't you come to his funeral? Why weren't any of these people there?"

Charleen's perfectly arched eyebrow shot up. "No one told you?"

"Told me what?"

"There wasn't a soul in the county here that whole week. All the men were on the Tejas Vacqueros Ride and all the women were in New York. I think Barbara was the only woman who stayed home."

"Hell, Charleen, why should she go? She isn't married," Lynn said with a clear note of derision in her voice.

Maureen was confused. "A ride?"

Lynn was the first to speak. "All the men in the county—well, those that aren't worried about a paycheck every Friday afternoon—leave home for a full week the last of September every year to 'play cowboy.' They rope calves, have rodeos, drink and carouse. Men stuff." Bitterness sat on the edge of Lynn's mouth as she spoke. "While the men are away, all the wives go to New York to buy their fall wardrobes. We do it every year."

"Yes," Charleen said with a secretive warning signal in her eyes, "every year."

There was some kind of code between the two women that Maureen didn't understand, and something told her she didn't *want* to know, either.

"But you said you were in Mexico . . ." Maureen said to Alexander.

"I was. First time I've missed the ride in years."

When Maureen turned back to Lynn she felt as if she were looking at a mask, not a person. Lynn's voice was bubbly, her mannerisms and smile a trifle forced. "Alex isn't married, so the last week of September isn't as expensive for him. I put Burt back a bundle this year." She leaned forward conspiratorily. "I bought a Fendi fur. It's drop-dead stunnin'!"

"So is the price tag!" Charleen quipped.

"Is your husband here tonight?" Maureen asked Charleen.

"No. I've been widowed for ten years. My date's over there," she said, pointing to a middle-aged man wearing a charcoal grey Western suit. "He's fun but not important. Since I have no one to care what I do, I always go to New York with the girls. We have such a good time."

They talked about the plays they'd all seen both off and on Broadway, the restaurants they liked in common and the newest, most fashionable boutiques in Manhattan. Maureen was surprised. These women knew more about New York and Paris than she did.

Alexander had just come back with drinks for the three women when suddenly he stiffened.

"Oh, my God. Not tonight . . ."

Maureen followed his gaze, as did Lynn and Charleen.

Standing at the microphone in front of the band was an outrageously dressed young girl. She wore her white hair "punked" on top and cellophane-colored in deep, vibrant purple. She wore a tie-dyed, shocking pink headband, a dangling cross of diamonds in one ear and a chartreuse feather in the other. Her eyes were ringed in black kohl so that she looked like a raccoon. Her lips were outlined in black and filled in with lipstick. She wore an outfit of old long johns and sweatshirts that even the costume designer of *Flashdance* would have pronounced too provocative. On her feet were scuffed, old, brown English riding boots. Amazingly, no matter what the girl did to camouflage herself, she remained incredibly beautiful. Maureen was fascinated.

"Okay, everybody! Gather 'round. We're gonna play some *real* music for you now!" The girl zipped over to the corner and pulled out an electric guitar. She gave quick instructions to the band, who nodded and then joined in. She smiled at the crowd and jumped into a rendition of electric vibrations and sounds only Van Halen could love. She screamed and sang obscene lyrics, jumped up and down and gyrated across the small stage. The band members followed along, but their faces were filled with confusion. The mixture of their country twangs and the punk girl's electric gymnastics on her guitar assaulted Maureen's ears. Maureen could tell that everyone else agreed with her. Blessedly, the rendition came to a blaring halt. The applause was meek.

"Jesus! Who was that?"

Alexander scowled. "My sister."

As he walked over to the girl, Maureen's eyes instantly found Barbara.

Barbara spoke to her friends in the buffet line as if nothing had happened. She laughed; she greeted a tall, dark, ruggedly handsome man. Maureen was baffled.

Lynn leaned over. "Everyone indulges Shane, even Barbara." She followed Maureen's gaze. "That's my husband, Burt, talking to Barbara now. He's probably offering his services. Sir Galahad—coming to the rescue."

"Cut it out, Lynn," Charleen warned.

Maureen still did not understand the private banter between Lynn and Charleen, but right now she was more fascinated with Shane.

Alexander had taken his sister firmly by the arm, but the girl wrenched free. They stopped, exchanged some obviously heated words, and then she followed him over to the table.

"Shane," he said sweetly, "I'd like you to meet Maureen McDonald."

"How do you do?" Maureen said.

"Not too fucking well tonight," Shane said, grinning mischievously. "These assholes don't appreciate good music."

Charleen got up to leave. "Come on, Lynn."

"What's the matter? You don't like my music either?"

Charleen looked Shane in the eye. "I don't like what you're doing to yourself, Shane. You used to be such a sweet girl till you went to Hollywood."

"Shut up, Charleen. You don't know anything about it," Shane retorted.

Charleen pushed past her and Lynn followed.

Alexander was steaming. "Why do you do that? She's one of Mother's best friends."

Shane stuck her chin out at him, her eyes glistening with anger. "That's why . . . you asshole. So now that I met your newest lay, can I go?"

"Christ! Yes! Leave."

Shane spun around on her heel, grabbed a tall drink from a waiter's tray and walked up to a man nearly twice her age and pinched him soundly on the buttocks. He jumped, then laughed when he saw her. He put his arm around her shoulder and kissed her deeply. Maureen thought Shane was going to swallow his tongue. She also noticed that the man wore a wide, gold wedding band.

"I apologize," Alexander said.

"Is she .. always like that?"

"Usually."

Maureen watched as Shane went from man to man, greeting them all in much the same vulgar manner. The more Barbara ignored her daughter, the more outrageous Shane's behavior. Finally, she walked off with a man who looked to be about twenty-five years old, much closer to Shane's age than any of the other men.

"Is that her boyfriend?"

"Shane doesn't believe in exclusivity. She won't be happy until she has the undying devotion of every man in the county."

"You don't seem very sympathetic toward her."

"I'm tired of being her champion. Charleen was right. Ever since she went to Hollywood to be an actress, she's gone off the deep end. Nobody can control her."

"Is she any good? As an actress, I mean."

"A couple of episodes on 'Falcon Crest,' a 'Fall Guy,' a month and a half on some soap opera and a movie of the week. Mostly she took acting lessons, singing lessons and guitar lessons."

"Sounds expensive."

"All Shane's endeavors are expensive . . . in one way or another." He sighed, then walked her to the dance floor. "Forget about her. I have. It's the only way."

They danced, and as they did Alexander introduced Maureen to others on the dance floor. Maureen was still trying to decipher Lynn's strange code with Charleen and Shane's unusual behavior. No wonder Mac had kept to himself so much. Never before had she met people like this. One thing she had to say for Texans, they were certainly individualistic and unafraid of showing it.

When the music stopped, Lynn and Burt Bean were standing next to Alexander and Maureen. Lynn introduced her husband to Maureen.

"I'm delighted to meet you, Maureen," he said charmingly.

Lynn was just about to say something when she stopped. "Alexander, you didn't tell us *he* was going to be here."

Alexander turned toward the house. "I didn't think he would."

"Well, I'll be damned," Burt said, smiling. "Wonder of wonders."

"What?" Maureen glanced from one to the other.

Lynn whispered in Maureen's ear. "Over there, standing by the patio doors. That's Brandon Williams. To my knowledge, this is the first time he's ever shown his face at one of Barbara's parties."

"Why?"

Lynn chuckled. "Probably because Barbara doesn't invite him. I wonder why she did tonight?"

Alexander knew. If he worked everything precisely the way he'd planned, he would give his mother the crowning achievement he'd always dreamed of: doubling the size of Devil's Backbone. Barbara had invited Brandon so that he could witness her coup in the company of all their friends.

Barbara left the small circle of guests she was speaking to and went to Brandon. Maureen watched as the very tall, wide-shouldered man greeted his hostess. She noted that they were courteous to each other, but that was all. She couldn't see the man's face or his expression. There was only the outline of his body with the light behind him. Unlike the other guests, he wore no hat and an ordinary business suit. His only distinctive Western gear was his boots.

Alexander grasped Maureen's arm. "I haven't had a chance to show you the garden. There's a Japanese pond with goldfish the size of trout. What do you say?"

"Sounds lovely."

They walked into the subtly lit garden. Maureen marvelled at the flowers and English hedges. Reflexively, she thought it a great place to do a shoot. She could see Bitzy in an Oscar de la Renta ruffled gown sitting in the white painted Victorian gazebo.

They sat on a wicker love seat.

"Kind of a lot to take all at once, isn't it?" he asked.

"I'm not overwhelmed, if that's what you mean."

"You should be."

"Why?"

"Everything that's happened to you the past week. Plus trying to get everything in order on the ranch. That's what I wanted to talk to you about. Remember I told you I'd make you an offer on the land?"

"Yes, but I . . ."

"Kristin will bring the papers by on Monday, but I couldn't wait till then. I'm prepared to offer two-point-two million for the place. Your asking price."

"My God!"

"I want you to know that someone who loves the ranch like Mac did will be looking after it. You know he was always special to me."

"And you to him."

"I think he'd approve. And I didn't want you to have to go through a long, drawn-out bargaining war with some outsider. We'll use the land strictly for grazing so we wouldn't abuse anything."

"Alexander, I—"

He wouldn't let her finish. His excitement had overtaken him. "I'd hope that you'd want to come back and see me sometime. See the ranch, I mean. I was thinking, too, that when I come to New York, we could spend some time together. I don't want this to be the end, Mo, but the beginning for us. I think it's a generous offer and . . ." He looked into her eyes.

"Yes, it's a very generous offer. I don't know what I'd do with that much money."

"You could probably start your own magazine!" he said, laughing.

He moved closer. His arm slid around her shoulders. She saw moonlight sparkle in his eyes. She could hear the music playing softly in the distance. When he kissed her, she gave in to the kiss. She put her arm around his neck and kissed him back.

"You don't know how happy you've made me. I can't wait to tell Mother!"

He jumped up so quickly, pulling her along with him, that she didn't have a chance to tell him that she had no intention of selling the ranch. If he was this happy about her, then he would be even happier when she told him she would be staying in Texas.

"Alexander . . ." She tried to stop him as he pulled her behind him.

He rushed up to the bandstand and stopped the music. Everyone turned expectant faces to them. Maureen was embarrassed standing there with him. She saw that Barbara had an oddly triumphant look on her face.

"May I have your attention, please? I have an announcement to make. As you all know, this is Mac McDonald's niece, Maureen. She and I have known each other since we were children. I wanted all our friends here tonight to be the first to know that Maureen has just now agreed . . . tonight . . ." He looked at her.

"Alexander . . ." Maureen said in an urgent whisper, "please stop."

"Maureen has agreed to sell the McDonald ranch to me . . . to Devil's Backbone. I want to propose a toast . . . to Devil's Backbone. Soon to be the largest ranch in the great state of Texas!"

Alexander watched as a genuine smile of pleasure etched itself across his mother's face. Her green eyes shone with pride. It was a moment he'd lived for all his life. He'd tried in a thousand ways to make his mother look at him like that, and never succeeded before. The riding trophies he'd won, the good grades in school, the adoration of young girls, the long hours he toiled for the ranch, the business meetings he conducted in Dallas and Houston—none of those things had brought the slightest word of praise from her. He'd always felt like a failure in her eyes, or at best, simply insignificant in her opinion. Today, he felt like a man . . . a king. He would relish this feeling for a long time to come.

The whooping, hollering and commotion that began was enough to break Maureen's eardrums. She blushed dark red from both embarrassment and anger at Alexander for jumping to conclusions. She had no choice but to rectify the mistake before any more damage was done.

"Alexander! Why did you do that? I never said I would sell to you!"

"What? You most certainly did. Just now . . . in the gazebo."

Maureen stepped up to the microphone. "Everyone . . .
please. There's been a terrible misunderstanding here." She
tried to speak over the ruckus. "Listen to me, please!" Finally, there was quiet. "I'm sorry, Alexander. I know you
meant well, but the truth is . . . I'm *not* selling the ranch.
Not to Devil's Backbone. Not to anyone."

Gasps of shock, rumbles of confusion and incredulous
glares met Maureen as she looked at the crowd. She saw
Barbara's smile vanish. Oddly, her face was now expression-
less. She didn't seem surprised at all.

"Please understand. Alexander made me a very, very generous offer. It's just that . . . I can't sell the land. My uncle
wanted me to stay here, to live here. He felt that I belonged
here. And I think I do, too."

Everyone was stunned. Silence reigned until a singular loud
clapping broke through the air.

Shane moved through the crowd toward Maureen, still ap-
plauding. She stood at the base of the bandstand. "Good for
you, honey. Let 'em know you won't take their shit."

"Shane!" Alexander growled. He was crushed. His moment of victory had not lasted ten seconds. But in that space
of time he'd found the one way to his mother's heart. He knew
his destiny now more than ever before. He must convince
Maureen to sell her ranch to him . . . at any cost.

Shane raised her half-empty tumbler of Tanqueray. "You
blew it, Alex." She guffawed.

Enraged, Alexander jumped down from the bandstand and
grabbed his sister. She tried to squirm away from him, but
he was much stronger. He led her away from the crowd and
into the house.

Barbara gave the signal to the bandleader to start the music
again. He edged Maureen off the stage.

As if they were day players in a movie company, everyone
began dancing again. Maureen watched dumbfounded as Barbara peeled her cold green eyes off her and went back to
being hostess. She neither followed Alex into the house nor
sent a servant or friend to assist him. Barbara seemed totally
unaffected by her daughter's behavior. She cared nothing
about Alexander's blunder nor his humiliation.

Maureen felt terrible. She'd never intended to hurt Alexander. He was her friend.

"Miss McDonald?" A deep, velvety male voice came from behind her.

"Yes?" She kept her eyes on the house where Alex had gone.

"May I shake your hand?"

"Sure. What for?" she asked, pivoting.

Standing in front of her was the man whose silhouette she'd seen earlier. He was incredibly handsome, even more so than Alexander. He must have been six-foot-six, she thought. His wide shoulders tapered to a very slender waist, and though he wore a business suit, she could see the outline of well-developed thigh muscles through the material. He had thick, wavy hair that he wore parted on the right side. He had a high forehead, a straight, prominent nose and even, full lips. When he smiled at her, he had dimples in his cheeks that gave him an angelic look that was at odds with the seductive gleam in his clear blue eyes.

His hand was twice the size of hers, and when she held it she felt as if a wave of electricity had shot through her. Her mind went blank and her heart raced.

"I never thought I'd see the day when someone bested the Cottrells."

"I didn't mean to."

"Too bad. It would have been more exciting if you had."

He was still holding her hand. Or she was holding his. She didn't know which. She didn't really care. She couldn't remember what he said two seconds after he said it. And she didn't know what she said. She only knew that for some reason she couldn't take her eyes off him and she couldn't move from the spot. She noticed that *he* had no trouble speaking. He stepped closer. As he spoke she had the craziest impulse to simply close her eyes and immerse herself in the sound of his voice.

Snap out of this, she told herself.

"You are?"

"Brandon Williams. My land connects with yours."

"Yes. So I understand."

"I was sorry to hear about your uncle. I was in Saudi last week. I just got back tonight."

"Seems everybody was somewhere . . ."

He placed his left hand over both their hands. His voice was very low when he spoke. "I won't kid you. I didn't know your uncle very well. He didn't go out of his way to be neighborly, but then, not many people around here have ever been overly friendly to me. I guess I just lumped him in the same bag with everyone else. I think I might have missed something by doing that.''

She peered into his eyes. There was no malice there, no manipulation. But then, she thought, perhaps she was only seeing what she wanted to see. He was charming, handsome and very sensual. She didn't know what he really wanted, except that he must want something, otherwise he wouldn't be talking to her.

The whole night had been confusing to her. She didn't understand Alexander's sudden offer to buy the ranch any more than she understood his sister's bizarre behavior or Barbara's coldness. This man was a total stranger and she was reacting to him like a starstruck teenager. She had to clear her mind. He was handsome, but, after all, she'd worked with the best-looking male models in the business. Maybe she'd had too much to drink.

''Tell me, Mr. Williams, why do you think people aren't friendly to you?''

Just then someone bumped into Brandon and his face came very near Maureen's. She could almost hear her heart slamming against her ribs. She held her breath. She had the most incredible impulse to kiss him. She wondered what it would feel like to have his lips touch hers. But before she could indulge further in the fantasy, he was speaking.

''Folks around here have always been prejudiced against the Williams family.''

''Why is that?''

''We aren't *real* Texans.''

''What does that mean?''

''My family only goes back three generations. And we were poor.''

''Does that matter?''

''To them it does.''

''Does it matter to you?''

''No.''

''Maybe, Mr. Williams, you haven't given people a chance to like you.''

''Maybe, Miss McDonald.''

The music had stopped, but Maureen wasn't sure for how long. Out of the corner of her eye she caught a glimpse of white-and-purple hair. It was Shane.

"Brandon!" she said breathlessly. "You look marvelous. I know you've been saving this next dance for me. Lord knows I've been saving myself for you, and nobody else but you . . . as the song goes." Shane grabbed his arm and nearly pulled him away from Maureen.

Brandon seemed surprised by Shane's actions, but he graciously bowed to Maureen and then led Shane in the two-step.

Maureen had the oddest feeling she was witnessing Shane's acting talents at work.

Alexander walked up behind Maureen. "Are you ready to go home?"

"Oh, Alexander. I'm sorry . . . about everything. I should have told you right off . . ."

"Don't worry about it. I guess I just wanted it too much. It's my own fault. No harm done. Not really."

"You're really special, you know that?"

"I hope I am. To you."

As he walked her over to his mother to say their good-nights, Maureen did not know that Brandon's eyes followed her until she disappeared inside the house.

10

♦

AFTER A FORTY-FIVE-MINUTE DRIVE in total silence, Burt
Bean pulled his gold Mercedes 500 to a stop in front of his
three-story house. Lynn got out without waiting for her husband. She unlocked the front door, threw her Judith Leiber
snakeskin purse on the glass console and mounted the white
carpeted staircase. Before she went to her room, she checked
on her children, Brian, who was six, and Stephanie, who was
eight. She peeked in on the slumbering Mexican housekeeper, Rosita.

She tossed her black cowboy hat onto the satin-covered
four-poster bed. She sat in the chaise lounge as she pulled off
her boots.

Burt held a Waterford double old-fashioned filled with
scotch when he entered the room.

"Don't you think you've had enough?"

He glared at her. "Never."

"Shit," she muttered, and went to her closet. Lynn was
proud of her closet. It was eighteen feet long and ten feet
wide. At the far end it formed an L that was entirely mirrored
so she could check every detail before she left her bedroom.
There were floor-to-ceiling cubbyholes filled with shoes,
scarves, hats and costume jewelry. The real stuff was in a
wall safe behind the Picasso over the bed. She owned three
dozen ball gowns, all black and white. She had twelve furs
in the chilled storage closet to the left. Her newest Fendi still
had the price tag on it, just as they'd joked about that evening.
Along the eighteen-foot wall there were three long poles

holding blouses and jackets on the top pole, skirts on the
middle pole and slacks on the bottom one. On the right side
of the L were her street-length dinner dresses, day dresses
and cocktail dresses. Every dress, every shoe, every pair of
hose was designer. Lynn shopped all over Texas for her
clothes, but her favorites were the exclusive boutiques such
as Tootsies and Tucan in Houston and Lou Lattimore in Dallas. The furs were from Koslows and Szor-Diener. The jewels, both real and the fabulous fakes that were as costly as
the genuine article, came from David Webb, William Noble
in Highland Park and Tiffany's.

But with all her possessions, Lynn had a penchant for
scarves. She tied them in her long blonde hair, wore them
around her neck, draped them across her shoulders over simple black knits and wore them around her waist. Lynn was
the only one in her circle she knew of with a five-thousand-
dollar credit limit at Hermes in Dallas. She easily spent that
much in scarves in any given year.

Lynn was Burt Bean's wife. And that meant that she was
"new money." It meant that Burt would do anything, spend
any amount, to show the rest of Texas that he was as good as
any "old money" around. And that included Barbara Cottrell.

Burt had worked on the Cottrell ranch as a hand since the
age of ten. He and his five brothers and sisters lived on a tiny
farm after they were abandoned by their father. Burt felt lucky
to have made it through the eighth grade. The Beans never
had much of anything—until Burt's oldest brother, Rick, told
him about a friend of his who was going to drill a well. Burt
left home with Rick, went to Midland and worked the rig.
Rather than taking pay, they both became investors in the rig.
It struck big. Burt used his money to give him the stake he
needed to invest in other wells.

By the time he was twenty-two he was rich . . . and in love
with Lynn Nelson.

Lynn was Burt's ticket out of the barrio and into society.
When they met, he was the sexiest, most handsome man in
Kerr County. Nobody could fill out a pair of Levi's like Burt
Bean. He could have been a movie star with his dark, sensual
looks and his muscular body.

Lynn remembered being the envy of all her girl friends
when she went to parties with Burt that summer. He had
money, which he spent freely on her, charm and looks. But

it was his kisses that had awakened a passion in Lynn that she had thought existed only in her fantasies. She felt as if she had been the one to strike oil the day he proposed.

Her parents loved their daughter and, though they objected to Burt's background, they knew Lynn was headstrong and would marry Burt with or without their blessing. They gave her the most lavish wedding of the decade.

Because Lynn's family was on a par with the Kerns and Cottrells, Barbara had not only attended the wedding, but had given Lynn her bridal shower. Barbara told Charleen that she approved of the marriage because Lynn seemed happy, but more important, Barbara believed Burt would never be as big or as rich as she was. He was no competition, whereas Brandon Williams was. Burt would always "keep his place."

These days, Lynn tended to believe Barbara's convictions about background. Burt's childhood poverty and low self-esteem always pulled him back and kept him from becoming the kind of man he could be. But Lynn was tired of the struggle. She'd tried for fifteen years to show him that his ego was his worst enemy. And for fifteen years he had continued to declare his undying fidelity to her. She hadn't believed him for a very, very long time.

Lynn hung up the hot pink suede Western dress and pulled the three-carat cubic zirconia earrings out of her ears. She tossed them unceremoniously into one of the cubbyholes. The real earrings were in the safe. In the past year, Lynn had developed a fear about wearing her real jewels in public. Unbeknownst to Burt, she'd been slowly taking her very best things to a jeweler in New York and having them copied. He was a friend of Charleen's, and she knew he could be trusted. Lynn didn't know why she'd developed this new habit, only that she felt compelled to carry out her mission. She wouldn't rest until she had everything, including her wedding rings, duplicated.

Lynn emerged from the closet wearing white satin Chinese pajamas decorated with soft, misty blue French lace. She'd bought them at La Lingere in Trump Tower. It was another of her "get backs."

Every wealthy Texas wife had her own story of when she learned about "get backs." Lynn's initiation had been more cruel than most.

It was when she was twenty-four and pregnant with their first child, a child that died at birth. During her fifth month, she learned that Burt was having an affair with a new barmaid in town. She learned later that it wasn't his first affair, only the first she'd known about.

She was so distraught and miserable that she couldn't eat or sleep. Sadly for her, she was still madly in love with her husband.

She always blamed Burt for the baby's death. He told her she was neurotic and needed a rest. She booked herself for a two-week stay at the Golden Door. She emerged a new woman. She flew to Los Angeles and bought her first mink coat at Bonwit Tellers. She sent all the bills to Burt. He never said a word. That tiny bit of restitution was her "get back." It wasn't revenge. Revenge required risk and courage.

She went now to the bathroom, which was a luxurious thirty-by-thirty room carpeted in white. The walls were covered in beveled mirrors; the moldings and doors were painted in gleaming black auto body paint. There was a raised platform with a black Jacuzzi tub, a separate black-tiled shower and a ten-by-ten partitioned area to the far left that contained the toilet and bidet. All the fixtures were twenty-two-carat gold. She went to the black marble sink and washed off her makeup. When she looked up, Burt was staring at her. He was fully dressed.

Suddenly, she felt the pit of her stomach drop out of her. Her knees felt as if they were made of water. She wanted to throw up. "Don't do it."

"Lynn . . ."

"Don't go, Burt."

"I'm just going for cigarettes."

"There're two cartons in the pantry."

"I checked. We're out. I'll be back in an hour."

"Don't bother," she said, and threw her towel at him. He nearly spilled his drink.

He turned and walked quickly out the door, down the stairs and out of the house.

"Fuck you!" she yelled at him, but he was gone.

Lynn ran to the toilet and vomited.

Charleen shivered and then pulled the shoulders of her Adolfo autumn haze mink around her shoulders.

"Are you cold?" Harry, her date for the evening, asked.

"Yes." She pushed the silver intercom button on the armrest between them. "Luis, turn up the heat, *por favor.*"

"Si," the chauffeur replied, and depressed the computerized thermostat control.

"More champagne?" Harry asked, picking up a bottle of Piper-Heidsieck and filling his own Bacarat glass.

"I think not," Charleen replied, and scrunched down into the folds of her coat. A contented smile crossed her lips.

"Happy?"

"Yes."

Harry leaned back and slipped his arm around her shoulder. "Good."

"I think I made a friend tonight."

"Really? Flattery will get you . . . everything." He began nibbling on her ear.

Charleen twisted away from him. "Not you, Harry. And stop that!"

"What's the matter?"

"I was talking about Maureen McDonald."

"Oh." He withdrew his arm and took a big gulp of wine.

"It's not often I feel this way about someone I've just met, but it's as if I've known her for a long time. Maybe I did."

"You did? When? Where?"

"In another life. Maybe we were friends in a past life—or maybe even sisters. Or brothers."

Harry rubbed his eyes with his fist. "I've had too much to drink to get into all this. Come on, Charleen. Brothers?"

"It's possible. Very possible. Anytime you meet someone and get along right off the bat, chances are that you interacted in a past life."

"Charleen, I'm Baptist. I don't believe in reincarnation."

"Harry, I've known you for five years. You've never once gone to church that I know of."

"I used to."

"Sure. When you were six."

"Okay. I used to be Baptist. But you can drive a person crazy with all your mumbo jumbo stuff about spirits and psychics and past lives. It's all shit anyway."

Charleen rolled her eyes. "That's what I get for trying to talk to an engineer."

"Let's make a deal. I'll run your wells and rigs and you take care of my spiritual side for me. Only let's not talk about it."

"That's fine with me. There's nothing worse than trying to talk to a moron."

The black Lincoln limousine pulled to a stop in front of Charleen's hundred-year-old white painted house. She waited for Luis to open the door for her.

Harry started to follow her out.

"Where are you going?"

"Inside. With you."

"No, you're not. I had a lovely time, as I always do with you, Harry. But 'inside' is off-limits and you know it."

"Jesus, Charleen!"

"Take him home, Luis."

She leaned inside the car and gave Harry a quick peck on the lips. It was no more than she gave any of her friends, male or female. "Take the bottle with you. I bought it just for you." She smiled sweetly and backed away. "I'll talk to you on Monday. And don't forget the Cancer League Ball next Saturday."

Harry slid back in the seat. Sulking, he poured a very full glass of champagne. It was little compensation. But then, he'd been a fool to expect anything more. Charleen was his boss. If job security was priority one in life then one should never sleep with the boss. Harry had to remember that. He was not that big a fool.

Charleen entered the single-story frame house that looked more like it belonged along the Louisiana riverbanks of the Mississippi than it did in Texas. It was a giant square box completely encircled by a covered porch supported by white columns. On each of the four sides were six French doors that opened to the porch, making twenty-four doors in all. The full-length shutters were painted green. On the east side porch were huge wicker planters filled with ferns and flowers. The wicker rockers, settee and side chairs had been in the family since the 1870s. She'd just had her interior designer choose a new English rose chintz for the seat pads.

Charleen crossed the planked wood floor in the foyer, checked herself in the gilded antique rococo mirror and went into the salon. Maria had left the lights on as usual. Everything seemed in order, she thought, as she glanced around the antebellum room. She'd finally had her designer paint the room in a light pink-and-white crackled look that resembled marble. The workman the designer had used was an artist in Charleen's opinion; she couldn't have been more pleased. The fireplace had been newly faced with green marble, and the wood mantel had had its cracks filled, its warped side planed and then been painstakingly painted. All the furniture, glass-ware, bric-a-brac and paintings were family heirlooms.

She passed by the library, with its animal skins on the floor, leather sofas, stone fireplace and heads of African game mounted on the walls. It had been her husband's, Charles's, favorite room.

Charles had taken Charleen on six African safaris. They went to Rhodesia four times and Zululand only twice because the government required special permits to hunt in Zululand. That was why there was only one enyala head mounted on the wall. Charleen's favorite was the eland, an ancestor of the Brahma bull. There were two water buffalo heads on the wall, a sable antelope and one lion. Because her neighbors were mostly cattle breeders, Charleen was envied for her safari trips and her wild game collection.

Charles and Charleen had a perfect marriage, until he died of a heart attack when he was thirty-five and she was thirty. He had loved her and pampered her more than was necessary. When they'd gone on safaris, Charles hired a plane to fly Charleen from the bush into Victoria Falls so that she could have her hair done each week. Charleen had never known want with Charles, and Charles had always been different from other men. He'd never once raised his voice to her. He'd never been unfaithful, stating to her that he didn't understand the concept of ''affairs'' in the first place. He believed that if a man did not believe in fidelity then he shouldn't be mar-ried. Everything was black and white to Charles.

Even more astonishing was the fact that he and Charleen seemed to have lived in a world all their own. Though they had many friends and houses or apartments in London, St. Moritz, Paris, New York and Dallas, they lived their life through each other. Charles had often said they were one spirit, breathing the same air, seeing the same things. And it was true.

Charles was the last of the Sims family, a family even older than the Cottrells. Charleen's family had come to Texas only five years after Barbara's great-grandfather. Because her fam-ily was as influential as Barbara's, Charleen never took any bullshit from anybody . . . including Barbara.

Charleen's only regret in life was that she and Charles never had any children. For that, she envied Barbara. However, she thought as she walked toward her bedroom, seeing Shane's antics tonight, Barbara might just envy her for *not* having any children.

Charleen went into her bedroom and closed the door. And as was her habit, she locked it.

Though all the rooms in Charleen's house were constantly being updated by her designer, this was one room no one—not her maid, her designer, no friend—had ever seen. This room was sacred. This was Charleen's sanctuary.

The furniture, the linens, the draperies, the upholstery and carpet remained exactly the way they were the day Charles died. The antique rosewood bureau on the left still contained Charles's clothes. His bottles of cologne rested next to a fifteen-year-old photograph of the two of them sitting in a Land Rover in Zambia. His hairbrush had never been cleaned; his comb lay in exactly the same position as it had the morning he'd tossed it onto the bureau. Charleen took great pains when dusting and cleaning to replace everything exactly the way he'd left it.

On the nightstand was his coffee cup, ashtray and pipe. The French telephone was the one he'd bought for her in a little shop off the Rue Cambon in Paris. His brass-and-mahogany valet held the Yves St. Laurent suit he'd worn to dinner the night before he died, when he'd flown her to Dallas and they'd dined at the Adolphus Hotel.

There had been only two changes in the bedroom since Charles's death. The longest wall now held five ultramodern storage units of cream-colored enamel and brass that Charleen had had custom-made to hold her shoes. She had one cabinet filled with Charles Jourdans, one with Maud Frizons, one for Gucci, one for El Vacqueros—those opulent, nearly gaudy creations of leather, brocade, net and sequins—and last, a unit for her Ferragamos, of which not a single pair had been purchased anywhere except on the Via Condotti in Rome. Charleen was a "shoe person." She'd read somewhere that her particular idiosyncracy stemmed from a Cinderella complex: the subconscious belief that a new pair of shoes would change her life, just as the glass slipper had for Cinderella.

The second alteration was the stack of books that rested next to Charleen's side of the bed and in the floor-to-ceiling bookshelf next to her nightstand. There were the purple-jacketed Seth books; Martin Buber's *Hasidism and Modern Man; The Unobstructed Universe;* Aldous Huxley's *The Pe-*

rennial Philosophy; The Zen Teaching of Huang Po; The Light of the Soul; and Teilhard de Chardin's *The Phenomenon of Man.* There were the works of Kant, Kierkegaard, Heidegger, Spinoza and Hegel. There were astrology books and charts, and books on mediums, "channelers" and psychics. There were books on time travel, dimensions and every religion on earth. Charleen knew the secrets of Prana, Yoga and Pranayam. She had five versions of the Christian and Catholic Bible, the teachings of St. Augustine and a copy of the Torah.

This room was Charleen's past, present and future. It was her life.

"Charles? Are you here? Or are you resting?" she asked the air as she undressed, put her clothes away and then brushed out her hair. "Charles . . . I'm talking to you," she said in that teasing, singsong lilt she often put in her voice.

"I'm here, darling."

"Good. I missed you today."

"I was here," Charles's voice replied.

Charleen pulled back the sheets and lay on the bed. "Since when have you been shy with me, Charles?"

Suddenly, an incredible light filled the room. Had she not been used to it, it would have blinded her. At the end of the bed stood an image of Charles. To Charleen he was beautiful, for he loved her more than life, more than death. He smiled at her.

"Charles. I love you so."

"And I love you. I always will."

"We'll never be apart, will we, Charles?"

"No, my darling. Never."

"Then come to me." She held out her arms. The light that was Charles moved over the bed and hovered just above her body. She could feel his energy, his light, filling her mind and soul . . . and her body.

Never, she knew, would there be any man for her but Charles. In ten years she had dated many men. The newspapers were constantly linking her with wealthy Venezuelan oilmen. There had been a French movie director, a Saudi prince and a Swiss billionaire. The most eligible men in Texas had tried to woo her, but to no avail. The gossips in Dallas and Houston told tales of all the men she'd bedded because they were jealous, and the list of her admirers was lengthy and impressive.

Charleen had let them have their fun. She never refuted

what her escorts said about her, for they had always been complimentary. Her money kept her beaux in line.

Charleen didn't mind if men boasted of their conquest of her, for she knew the truth. And the truth was that Charles had been her only lover. She was forty years old and she had never been unfaithful to him . . . not even after death.

"Make love to me Charles. I love you . . ." she cried, and then climaxed.

Burt Bean sat in his Mercedes with the lights on, cursing. "Where the fuck is that bitch?"

Just then, a red Toyota MR2 roared up the mountain road and spun on the gravel. The driver's window lowered itself electrically. "Hey, sport. You ready for a good time?" Shane asked, licking her lips.

"It's about damn time you showed up."

"You got the stuff?"

"Yeah, I got it."

"Great!" She rammed her foot against the gas pedal and took off. In two minutes she braked in front of a glass-and-wood "cabin." Burt had built his "getaway cabin" two years ago at the cost of half a million dollars. It had a spectacular view of the valley. It was equipped with a hot tub, sauna, weight room, bedroom, living room and kitchen. It had the latest in state-of-the-art stereo equipment and a wide-screen television in two rooms. The kitchen boasted all the amenities, though Burt never cooked. He was always too busy to think about food. So were his guests.

Shane turned off the car and got out.

Burt was right behind her. He grabbed her roughly and kissed her hungrily.

She shoved her hand down his pants and squeezed him. They broke apart; Burt unlocked the door and they went in. Burt started stripping off his clothes immediately.

"Not so fast," Shane said, and snapped her finger, then held out her hand.

"Jesus! Sometimes I wonder if it's me you want or the coke."

"I'll ease your mind right now . . . it's the coke. But . . ." She moved seductively toward him. "You're the icing on the cake."

"Now, gimme . . ." she said breathlessly, tracing his lips with her tongue.

Like a robot he pulled the cocaine out of his jacket pocket and handed it to her.   —

She smiled, then sprinted for the counter that divided the kitchen and living room. She sat on a bar stool, took out her personal "equipment" that she kept in a suede pouch: mirror, razor blade and glass straw. She snorted two lines. She looked back at Burt. He was naked. And he was hard.

She stood up and whipped her sweatshirt over her head. Slowly, she peeled off the skintight leggings she wore, then slipped off her silk panties. Last, she took off the oversized men's undershirt.

There before Burt Bean stood the most perfect breasts on the face of the earth. Shane knew they were perfect because she'd consulted with Henry Gleason for six months before he performed the surgery. New tits had been the number-one priority for Shane when she went to Los Angeles. There wasn't a single scar that showed, for Henry had gone in through the nipples and placed the implants behind the muscle. All that stuff about women losing sensitivity in their nipples after the procedure was a bunch of crap, Shane thought. They should have gone to Henry. Her tits looked more natural than real ones. Shane had a "thing" about her doctor, and had tried like the devil to get Henry to respond, but he never succumbed.

Shane smiled to herself. Burt was literally drooling as he looked at her. Burt was a tit man through and through. And so damn pliable it was a joke.

Shane did not know that Burt thought the same of her. Her addiction gave him the edge he needed.

"You're gorgeous, baby," He put his hands on her shoulders and pushed her down to the sand-colored carpet.

"I know," she said, now feeling the effects of the cocaine. She was flying. It was going to be a great night.

"Now give me what *I* want," Burt said, and closed his eyes.

11

◆

IT WAS AFTER ONE when Alexander got back home. He'd purposefully not pressed Maureen about the ranch, nor had he pushed himself on her. He knew he must be careful in his strategy. This evening's debacle had taught him that. Alexander couldn't afford another mistake. The cost might be too high.

He started to get out of the car when he saw something shiny in the passenger seat. It was Maureen's lipstick. He smiled and picked it up.

He went into the house and, rather than going to his room, went to his study. He unlocked the drawer where he kept Maureen's lipstick and added the lipstick.

He didn't hear his mother enter the room.

"What do you have there?" Barbara asked.

"Nothing. Maureen left her lipstick. I'll give it back to her next weekend at the ball."

"She's going with you?"

"Yes. Why wouldn't she?"

Barbara's eyebrow raised. "I thought after her encounter with Brandon—"

"Brandon?" Alexander interrupted. "What's he got to do with anything?"

Barbara sat calmly on the love seat. She spread her black suede skirt around her. She pretended to pick a piece of lint off the jacket sleeve. "If you'd been paying attention, as I was, you would have seen it."

"Quit playing games. Seen what?"

"She's attracted to him."

"That's preposterous. They only met for a second. Why, they didn't even dance."

"I don't care. I know what I saw."

"How?"

Barbara couldn't tell her son that she'd seen that same look in John Williams's eyes nearly forty years ago. She hadn't seen that look in a man's eyes since Charles Sims died. He used to look at Charleen like that. It was one of the reasons she envied Charleen, though she'd never admit it aloud. Barbara wondered if Brandon knew what had happened tonight. More important, she wondered if Maureen did.

She tilted her head. "I know what I saw."

"Well, Maureen was fine when I took her home. She never mentioned Brandon at all. There was no reason to." His mother could be exasperating at times. "If Maureen is interested in anyone—it's me. I've known her for years. Something tells me that fact is *very* important to her. She's told me she trusts me because we're friends."

"What about that boyfriend of hers in New York?"

The side of Alexander's mouth quirked up in a triumphant smirk. "I won that match hands down. She's not going back to New York, is she?"

Barbara frowned. *"But* she's not selling to us, as you said she would."

"I know. But on the way home she explained it all to me. She's got some silly idea she owes Mac."

"Owes him?"

"Thinks it's her responsibility to carry out his dying wish."

"She sounds as wacky as Charleen."

"Mother, trust me. One month of trying to take care of that run-down place with no equipment, no help and virtually no money—a fact she slipped into the conversation without thinking—and I'm sure she'll be begging me to take the place off her hands."

"I hope you're right. I want that land, Alexander."

"I know you do, Mother."

He walked over and kissed her cheek. "Maureen hasn't got the slightest idea what to do. She can't even figure out the old man's accounting books, much less get her herd off to market. She's relying on Wes to help her fulfill Mac's Venezuelan contract. And you know what an ass he is."

"Wes Reynolds? He's still over there? How long ago did we fire him?"

"Five years."

"Has it been that long? Well, you're right about him. He hasn't a brain in his head."

"Which is all the better for us."

"What?"

"Never mind. I have some plans for Wes. I thought I might enlist him on our side."

"Whatever are you talking about?"

"I'm too tired to explain it now, but just suffice it to say that Wes could help us persuade Maureen that she and the cattle and the ranch would be better off if she simply sold out."

"Well, that's the truth." Barbara rose. "Waste makes me ill, Alexander. Always has. And having that inexperienced girl over there, wasting potentially good land, is a sin. A sin, Alex."

"I know, Mother." He patted her shoulder. "Now, why don't you get some rest? It's been a long day."

They had just walked out of the study when they heard the sound of Shane's car in the drive. Shane stumbled in the front door and dropped her purse on the floor. Her head bobbed and weaved on her shoulders.

"Jesus!" Alexander gasped. "You look like shit."

"Alex!" Barbara admonished him. But she did not go to her daughter. "Where have you been, Shane?"

"Out." Shane started giggling. "Out of this *world!*"

"Oh, Christ . . ." Alex went to her and caught her just as her knees gave way. "Where are you gettin' the stuff, Shane?"

Lying in his arms, she tried to lift her head but it was too heavy. "What stuff?"

"The coke."

"In the machine. I wanted a Pepsi, but they were out." She laughed uncontrollably.

Barbara scowled. "Take her to her room. I don't even want to look at her." Barbara mounted the stairs and went to her own room.

Methodically, Barbara took off her black suede and carefully hung it on a padded, scented hanger. She put her boots in their proper place and put the jewelry in the wall safe and spun the lock before closing the door.

Since the day she'd found Shane in a very private, very exclusive sanitarium in Los Angeles, she'd never understood her daughter's addiction to drugs. It had come as a shock to Barbara, who neither smoked nor drank. Barbara could not understand anyone whose purpose in life was to lose control when Barbara perpetually sought to gain it.

When Shane made the decision to enter UCLA, Barbara had been furious. She'd wanted Shane to remain in Texas; she'd planned a coming-out party. But Barbara had also expected Shane to get a degree. Shane told her mother she wanted to be more than "just another debutante." Barbara suspected Shane said this only to do as she'd always done . . . oppose her mother.

Once in Los Angeles, Shane changed her major from business to drama. Six months later Shane went Hollywood. She abandoned all plans for a degree. Barbara had not been informed of Shane's new life. She did not know the money she sent Shane for tuition went for acting, diction and dancing lessons until nearly a year later. Then came the few parts on television.

At that point all Barbara could hope was that Shane had found a goal, a purpose to her life, something Shane had never had. She had been popular in high school. She'd always had lots of boyfriends, but even Barbara knew that the boys were as attracted to the Cottrell money as they were to Shane.

Barbara never knew exactly how or why Shane started using drugs in California, only that she had. She had her guesses. Hollywood was a tough playground, even for the strongest psyches. Not many people are prepared for rejections . . . Hollywood style. Shane had not been strong enough.

Barbara knew that her daughter had the blood of her ancestors in her veins. She believed that Shane could kick this habit, find the kind of belief in herself that Barbara had. Barbara also didn't want her daughter in an institution somewhere, locked away like an animal. Shane needed to be at home, where she had the love of her family to guide her, strengthen her.

Barbara eased herself between the cool Irish linen sheets. She would help Shane through this difficult time. She would make certain her daughter chose the proper paths for her life. Shane had simply become confused. That was all. It was up to Barbara to direct her daughter. Barbara felt up to the challenge.

12

◆

MAUREEN STOMPED her boot on the ground and shoved her hands angrily into the back pockets of her jeans.

"What do you mean there are no trucks?" she asked Wes.

"Just what I said. Every truck in the area is already booked. Everybody's haulin' their cattle out before winter. We ain't no different."

"Okay. So now what?"

"The big ranchers fly their cattle to market."

"On airplanes?"

"On gutted-out DC-10s. The Cottrells have a plane of their own. Maybe we could . . ."

"No. I have a feeling it would be 'booked,' too." She was remembering the hard glint in Barbara's eyes. Maureen believed that Barbara would like to see her fail. Barbara was possessive of Alexander in a way Maureen didn't fully understand. It was as if she wanted her son all to herself. It was too complicated to figure out. She looked at Wes, who was waiting for her to come up with answers. "Where else can we find these planes?"

"There's a service in Dallas and one out of Waco."

"I'll bet there's even more than that. Come on. We'll call them all if we have to."

Three hours later, Maureen had just about done as she'd predicted. She sipped lukewarm coffee and held the receiver to her ear as the sixteenth air service turned her down. She hung up.

"Damn! How many head of cattle can there be in Texas?"

Wes laughed.

"Don't answer that."

Maureen picked up the phone and dialed the last name on the list, a service out of San Antonio. Someone picked up on the third ring.

"San Antonio Air Freight."

"Hello. This is Maureen McDonald calling from Kerrville. I understand you have cattle planes."

"Yes ma'am. How many will you be needin'?"

"I've got a hundred and fifty head of cattle I've got to fly to the holding pens in Houston."

"Where you shippin' 'em?"

"Venezuela."

"Hmm. Must be good stuff. Did we ever service you before?"

"No."

"I see. Well, we usually only work our regular accounts. But we could make an exception. When will you be needin' us?"

"Monday."

The man laughed. "Whoa, little lady! Don't you know nothin'? We book three months in advance. Everybody books up ahead."

"You can't help me?"

"Sorry."

"Do you know who can?"

"Naw. Say! Wait a minute. There's a buddy of mine who's just opened a service. He's out of Wyoming."

"Wyoming? That'll be expensive."

"Maybe. Maybe not. It's better than nothin'. Here's his number. Area code 307-444-3313. His name's Bill Handley."

"Thanks."

Maureen quickly dialed the number. Bill Handley was available . . . for a fee.

"That's a lot more than I'd wanted to pay."

"If you're calling all the way from Kerrville, then I must be the only game in town. You gotta pay for the gas from here to there. Sorry. But tell you what I'll do. I'll knock off a hundred and fifty bucks. That's the best I can do. I'd like to do business with you."

Maureen knew he was taking advantage of her, even with the discount. But she had no choice. "It's a deal. I'll expect you Monday."

"Be there around noon. Where's the airstrip?"

"On the northeast side, about two miles from the ranch house."

"See you then."

Maureen turned to Wes. "Well, we got our plane."

He smiled. "That's all that counts."

Monday morning arrived. Wes, Grady and Randy had spent the weekend rounding up the cattle. They were awaiting the arrival of the air cargo plane in the holding pen. On Saturday, they had started adding yeast to the cattle feed to prevent "shipping fever," a respiratory disease brought on by the stress of being shipped. Maureen wanted nothing to go wrong. She wanted to fulfill the terms of her Venezuelan contract.

Bill Handley landed his twenty-five-year-old plane at precisely noon. As Maureen walked up to the patched, welded and rusty aircraft, she wondered if it would make the trip. If she were riding on it, she wouldn't have been half as worried as she was for her cattle.

She shook Bill's hand.

"Glad you could help us out."

"No problem."

"Here's all their papers, your check and the information for the agriculture officials in Houston."

Bill looked through everything and nodded. "Seems to be in order. I'll take the first load now, then I should be back for the second load about three. Then—"

"What are you talking about? First load?" Maureen interrupted.

"Lady, don't you know nothin'? These planes only hold fifty head at a time. And the pens only hold fifty head at a shot. They send the inspector from the Agriculture Department in, he gives the high sign and then I bring in the next load. How long have you been shippin' cattle?"

"About fifteen minutes."

"Terrific."

"You have to make three trips?"

"I thought you knew. It'll take two days."

"No wonder it costs so much."

Bill gestured with his head toward Wes. "Is he your vet?"

"No. The foreman. Why?"

"You gotta have a vet on board each flight to tend the cattle."

"I don't believe this."

"Me either."

Bill was as exasperated as she was frustrated. Maureen's ignorance had cost her time and money already. Why hadn't she asked more questions? Why didn't she know the questions to ask? This was no time for mental debate, she thought.

"Wes, what's the name of the veterinarian you had out here last week?"

"Doc Silver."

"Is he in Kerrville?"

"Yes."

"Go call him and find out if he can fly with these cattle to Houston this afternoon."

"Yes ma'am." Wes bounced up onto his horse and took off at a full gallop.

Maureen turned to Bill. "What else don't I know about this shipment?"

He shook his head. "More than I can tell you."

"Great," she mumbled.

Twenty minutes later, Wes came riding up. He reined in his horse. "Doc says he'll fly out with them. He's on his way."

"Thanks," she said. "By the way, Wes. Why didn't you tell me about the vet? Or the number of trips this would take?"

"I figured you knew that much."

Doc Silver drove up in a tan-and-burgundy Silverado pickup. He was all smiles as he emerged. He shook Maureen's hand. "You're lucky. This is the first quiet day I've had in months. How many head are we flying in?"

"A hundred and fifty in all."

"Three trips, huh?"

"So I'm told."

"Well, I can only help out today. I'm booked up tomorrow."

"What if we made a very early flight in the morning? That way, Bill can get back to Wyoming."

"Wyoming?"

"That's where he's from. I'll let him tell you. In the meantime, I need to get this plane loaded."

Wes, Grady and Rusty began herding the cattle onto the

plane. Bill oversaw the operation while Maureen assured Doc Silver she'd taken precautions with the cattle's feed and other nutrients. Once she was assured that everything was going well, she mounted her horse and watched from a distance. Finally, the last cow stepped onto the plane. Fifteen minutes later they were airborne. Maureen heaved a tremendous sigh of relief. She rode silently back to the ranch house.

Juanita was in the kitchen preparing lunch. "You want to eat?"

"No. I think I'll work on the books."

Maureen went to Mac's study and settled herself in for a long day of computations. She'd just about finished a profit projection for the year. Wes had not been as much help as she'd hoped. His realm of knowledge was limited, but still, he knew more than she did.

By the end of the afternoon Maureen had deduced that Mac's current debt amounted to more than fifty thousand dollars. Within the month she needed to buy a new truck, which at bare minimum would cost ten thousand for a one-ton pickup. They needed a new trailer . . . even a used one would be close to two thousand. For the house she needed to replace the furnace with a new L.P. gas furnace—eighteen hundred dollars for the unit and another fifteen hundred for ductwork. The plumbing estimate was over three thousand for minimum repairs. She had wanted to get everything repaired and buy all new fixtures and finally make the bathrooms truly functional. She needed paint, plasterers, roof work and carpentry. Some things she could do—paint, wallpaper, even make drapes. The rest would have to be hired.

Maureen needed a lot of money. Even the profit from the sale of the cattle wouldn't begin to satisfy her needs.

Now she must focus on building a new herd. She had four cows who would calf before Christmas. If they didn't abort.

Grady had told her they'd found two dead cattle during roundup. They assumed it was from poisonous plants in the pastures. Maureen had quickly learned that such plants cause a three-to-five-percent loss of the herd every year. Plants such as halogeton and false hellebore can cause cows to abort up to two weeks after ingesting the plant. Trying to spot the plants from a pickup was too risky. She would go over the new grazing pastures on foot.

"No wonder Mac concentrated on gold," she mumbled

dejectedly. She thought of Sylvester Craddock's words: "It's a hard land."

"Maybe so. But I'm just as hard."

Just then she heard the sound of an airplane overhead. "They're back!"

Maureen raced out of the house. The plane was coming in for a landing. She jumped into the pickup and blew the horn. Wes came running out of the bunkhouse, jamming his hat onto his head.

They reached the plane just as Bill and Doc Silver climbed out.

"How did it go?" she asked expectantly.

"You got trouble, little lady," Doc Silver said.

"What now?"

"The agriculture officials won't pass inspection. He says he's gonna hold the herd for three days."

"Three days? I can't afford that kind of time! I don't have anyone but Bill here to fly them. I don't understand. What's the matter with the cattle, Doc?"

"Nothin' I could see."

"Then what the hell is going on?"

"I don't know," he said sympathetically. "But if I were you, I'd get up to Austin and talk to the secretary of agriculture about it."

"Austin? Why, that's hours away."

"Not by air it isn't," Doc said, looking at Bill.

Bill threw up his hands defensively. "Oh, no! This old crate wasn't made for passenger flights. No offense, Miss McDonald, but I'm a businessman. I'd have to charge you more than it's worth for a little trip like that."

"But time is money here, Bill."

"Sorry. Don't you know somebody with a smaller plane?"

"I don't know. Do I?" She looked at Wes and Doc.

"Every rancher in these parts has at least one plane. Except you. Haven't you got any friends?"

"Friends?" She immediately thought of Alexander. "Yes. I do."

Maureen jumped into the pickup and sped back to the house. She dialed Devil's Backbone. The housekeeper informed her that Alexander was not at home.

"When do you expect him back?"

"Tomorrow. He in Houston."

"Houston? Well, thanks anyway." She hung up. Then she dialed Charleen's number.

Again she talked to the housekeeper. "Señora Sims is in Dallas with Señora Bean. She come back Wednesday."

Maureen hung up. "My God, doesn't anybody stay around here?"

She was running out of friends. Suddenly she remembered Brandon. She looked up his number in the phone book. As she dialed it, her mouth went dry. She wondered why.

The phone was answered by a woman with a Southern drawl.

"Is Mr. Williams there?"

"He's just out the door. Could I take your name and have him return the call later?"

"Could you catch him? This is very important. Tell him it's Maureen McDonald. We met at the Cottrells' Saturday night . . . in case . . . he doesn't remember me."

Maureen could hear the woman calling Brandon's name. She heard his voice answering. She noticed that the pencil she held shook in her hand. She put it down, then shoved her hand into her lap.

She couldn't understand why she was acting so strangely. She wondered who the woman was. His secretary? Housekeeper? Lover?

"Hello."

"Mr. Williams, this is Maureen McDonald. I hate to bother you when you obviously are in a rush . . ."

"No bother at all. I was wondering when I would hear from me. *If* I would hear."

"I hate to do this . . . I hardly know you . . . but I'm in a jam and need some help. I understand you have a plane."

"Several. Do you need the Lear?"

"You own a Lear jet?"

"It's for sale. You wanna buy it?"

Maureen cleared the astonishment from her throat. "I just need to fly to Austin. Do I need a jet for that?"

"The Cessna will do. When did you need to leave?"

"Well . . ." She hesitated. "Now would be good . . . but I know you had other things to do—"

"They can wait," he interrupted. "I'd rather help out a pretty lady. I'll be there in fifteen minutes. Meet me out at the strip."

"I really appreciate this, Mr. Williams."

"Brandon. See you in a bit." He hung up.

Maureen bolted to her feet. "Yahoo!" She tore down the hall, only barely noticing Juanita's startled look. "I'm going to Austin, Juanita. What does one wear to fight City Hall?"

"No comprendo 'City Hall.' "

Maureen started for the stairs. "Sometime I'll explain it to you." Maureen went to her room, chose a blue silk dress, combed her hair back and stuck an enormous black taffeta bow at the base of her ponytail. She whisked on blush, brown eye shadow and pink lip gloss. She checked herself in the mirror and saw the image of Brandon's face flash across her mind. She picked up the grey eyeliner and carefully placed a smokey smudge beneath her lashes. She used a triple coat of mascara and sprayed herself liberally with Opium. As she left the bathroom, she wondered why she was taking extra pains with her makeup when her intent was to curse this asshole in Austin up one side and down the other.

Maureen was standing at the side of the airstrip with Doc, Wes and Bill when Brandon landed his twin-propellered Cessna. It was a pretty blue-and-white plane, new, and in excellent condition. Dust spiraled about the belly of the plane like smoke curls. Maureen covered her eyes. When she looked up, Brandon had emerged from the plane. He smiled at her.

He was wearing jeans and a Western shirt. She noticed that his boots were expensive black eelskin. He ran toward her, signalling for her to come ahead.

"I thought you were in a hurry!" He laughed as he shook Doc's hand, then nodded at Bill and Wes. He glanced at the cattle plane. "Some problem with your cattle?"

"It's a long story," she said.

"And these fellas couldn't help you? I'm flattered."

Doc chuckled, but his eyes remained serious. "I'll let her explain, but there *is* something fishy about all this. You've got a lot of clout up there in Austin. See what you can do, Brandon."

Maureen's eyes narrowed. She didn't like being treated as if she were a child. "It's my cattle and my problem. I can talk to them just as well as Mr. Williams," she said huffily.

"But you still want my plane, right?"

Humility pulled out Maureen's throttle. "Yes, very much so," she said quietly. "Can we leave now?"

"Absolutely." Brandon bid farewell to Doc and the others

and followed Maureen. He helped her into the plane and gently put his hand on her waist as she climbed into the seat.

"I can do it myself," she said as she buckled her seat belt and locked the door.

Brandon settled himself behind the controls. He revved the engines, turned the plane around and taxied to the end of the airstrip. The airstrip was in disrepair, and he'd found several deep ruts on landing that he wanted to avoid on takeoff. He had a passenger this time. An important passenger.

"You ever fly in a plane this small?"

"Of course. I've been all over the bush in Africa in planes not nearly this modern."

"Pardon me." Brandon didn't know why she was being defensive. He hoped it wasn't him. He decided to chalk up her attitude to tension over the cattle.

The little plane shook as the propellers roared. Excitement glowed in Brandon's eyes as he raced the Cessna down the airstrip and then pulled the controls toward him. In seconds they were airborne. They soared over the hills and edged higher toward the clouds. Brandon made several radio calls to Austin verifying time of arrival and weather conditions.

Maureen scanned the landscape below her. Chills covered her skin as she realized how truly like Zimbabwe this area was. She heard the sound of Brandon's voice as her thoughts took her to other lands, other people. Oddly, however, she felt incredibly safe right where she was . . . in the sky, with an almost total stranger.

"Tell me your problem," he said.

"Problem?"

"Uh, why I have cancelled my meetings and am flying you to Austin."

"Oh." Maureen smiled sheepishly. She related the entire story to Brandon, making certain she illuminated the details with Doc's observations.

"I don't think you'll have much trouble dealing with this office. I think it was just some mix-up, that's all. But you're doing the right thing by going to the top. By the time we get back home, the cattle will be released and you can fly the next group down."

It sounded so easy when he said it, she thought. "I hope you're right."

"I am. Trust me."

The flight was smooth and effortless. Maureen found herself relaxing. She watched the land below her fill with crystal blue lakes and green trees whose leaf tips were only beginning to be outlined in gold. Brandon explained that autumns in Texas were disappointing to those accustomed to the blaze of maples and oaks in New York.

"Here the trees molt rather than flame. They turn a dull brown and then one morning in January you'll find they're naked. Almost without warning."

Maureen liked being in the air with Brandon. She liked the easy sound of his drawl, the depth to his laughter and the manner in which he tried to reassure her about her problems; his piloting capabilities, himself. He seemed different to her up here. Or, perhaps, she was different.

Before she wanted to, they landed.

Two men in overalls ran out to meet the plane. They chatted quickly with Brandon, he giving instructions. Maureen climbed out of the plane and followed Brandon toward a metal building. A young, pretty blonde stepped out of the glass door and waved to him. Her face was jubilant. Maureen decided the girl must know him *very* well.

"Hi, Kitty. Did you get the car for me?"

"Yes, sir. You had some calls." Kitty handed him a stack of pink memo papers. Kitty scanned Maureen with a studied gaze. Kitty moved a step closer to Brandon. She kept her smile in place, but Maureen noticed she was careful to maintain a "professional" distance from Brandon.

Maureen held her purse and briefcase in front of her, looked over at a group of planes closer to the main terminal at Municipal Airport. She didn't want Kitty to think she was interested in either her or Brandon. Maureen was here on business.

Brandon turned to Maureen. "My car's out front." He motioned to her, and as Maureen walked over to him, she noticed that he put his arm on her waist again. She also saw Kitty's smile fade.

They walked through the building and out the front door to a waiting Lincoln Continental. Brandon held the door for her.

"Skip, this is Maureen McDonald. She wants to see the people over at the Agriculture Department."

"Yes, sir, Mr. Williams," Skip, Brandon's driver, replied. He stepped on the gas as soon as Brandon and Maureen were settled in the car.

They drove down Interstate 35 to the downtown area. To

Maureen it seemed as if they were going around in circles, down one-way streets, up Congress Avenue so that she could see the pink granite State Capitol Building that was seven feet higher than the Capitol in Washington. She was impressed. Suddenly, the car pulled to a stop. Brandon started to get out.

"I don't want you to go with me," Maureen said firmly. "I'm fully capable of handling this on my own."

"I think I can help," Brandon insisted.

"Jesus! I wish everyone would stop treating me as if I didn't have a brain! I managed to run my career and my life in Manhattan, which is a hell of a sight bigger than Austin. I really think I'll be fine."

Brandon settled back in the seat. "Have at it—"

"And *don't* call me 'little lady'!" she interrupted. "I *hate* that."

"Furthest thing from my mind." He smiled at her with a grin that made his dimples deeper.

She got out of the car growling to herself. She didn't know why she was suddenly angry at Brandon. On the trip in, everything had been perfect. Once they were on land, however, she had the overwhelming desire to smack him. Sometimes he reminded her of Sylvester Craddock with his patronizing ways.

Maureen entered the marble-and-granite building and took the elevator to the third floor. She found the office and entered the reception area.

"I'd like to see the secretary, please."

"He's not in."

"I'll wait."

The receptionist rolled her eyes. "He's in the Middle East."

"Oh." Maureen felt foolish. "Then I'll speak to whomever is in charge."

"That will be Mr. Plohn. The assistant to the secretary. May I have your name and to what this matter is pertaining?"

"McDonald. Maureen McDonald. I want to know why my cattle are being held in Houston."

The receptionist spoke quietly into the receiver. She looked up. "You may go in. The office to the left."

Maureen opened the heavy oak-and-frosted-glass door.

Seated beneath a large window that overlooked downtown Austin sat a fat man, tie askew, bottom button of his soiled white shirt missing and shirttail half out. His feet were propped on his walnut desk, which was piled with messy stacks of papers. The room smelled of stale smoke. The man burped.

He should be in the Sanitation Department, Maureen thought.

He did not stir as she walked into the room. He continued cleaning his fingernails with a long steel nail file. He pointed to a wooden chair facing his desk.

"Have a seat," he said, then put the nail file into his pants pocket. He folded his chubby fingers over his belly. "What can I do for you?"

"I sent fifty head of cattle to Houston to be shipped to Venezuela." She pulled Mac's contract out of her briefcase. "My buyer expects all one hundred and fifty head to be delivered by the first of next week. Your people told my veterinarian that they would not release the cattle. I want to know why."

Sniffing loudly, he pulled his heavy feet off the desk. "I don't know anything about it. The order must have come from someone else."

"According to these papers Doc gave me, it was your name on the authorization. Now tell me—what do I have to do to get my cattle released?"

"Nothing. I'll release them in three days."

"I can't wait that long. And what do you mean 'nothing'? Why are you holding them?"

"I felt like it." He smirked.

Maureen glared at him. "What kind of government official are you? You have to have a reason!"

"No I don't."

"Okay. Then *I* need a reason."

He glared back at her. "Where are you from?"

"New York."

"Figures."

"What's that supposed to mean?"

"You Yankees are dumb. Well, I'm gonna give you an education. You want your cattle released? I'll do it, and I'm the *only* one who can do it. But it's gonna cost ya."

"Cost?"

"Christ! You're dumber than I thought." He held out his hand. "Cost, lady. About five hundred bucks, the way I figure it. Yep. Paperwork, overhead. All that must be considered these days."

Maureen looked at him for a moment. Suddenly, it hit her. "You're talking about a bribe."

"That's a crass way of putting it, but yeah, I'm talkin' about a bribe. You scratch my back; I'll scratch yours. That kind of thing. Greasing the wheels of commerce. You could say that, too."

"I won't do it."

"Suit yourself. The cattle stay for three days."

Maureen had never been so angry in all her life. Adrenaline shot through her veins. Her jaw clenched and her fists balled. The animal groan she heard came from her throat. In an instant she bolted out of her chair and leaned over the filthy desk. Her face was as close to Carl Plohn's as she could stand. When she spoke, spittle rained on him. She didn't care.

"You're a *pig*, Mr. Assistant. And I can see that you have certainly Peter Principled your way to this position. I'll never give you money—only a hard time. This won't be the last time you hear from me. I'll tell everyone I know about what happened here today—"

"Ha!" He laughed in her face. "You're nothin' here in Texas and don't forget that, *Miss* McDonald. No one will listen to you. This is the way things are done here. Get used to it."

"You make me sick."

"If you aren't gonna give me the money, you can leave."

Maureen stalked out the door, through the reception room and down the hall. She punched the elevator button six times while cursing under her breath. When the elevator doors opened she nearly jumped inside. She tapped her foot angrily as she rode down. She tried to ignore the scowl from the elderly woman standing beside her. After all, what would a sweet little lady like that know of corruption? And would she care?

Maureen's cheeks were flushed when she reached the car. Skip saw her coming and opened the door. She got in. Brandon was not there.

"Where is Mr. Williams?"

"He had some business to attend to. You're to meet him at Grove Drug."

Skip started the car and pulled away from the curb before Maureen could answer. She didn't like the way Brandon made plans for her. She felt as if he were taking over—trying to take control of her. Her accelerated temper shifted into high gear. She didn't want to have a drink in a place she didn't know. She didn't want to spend any more time in Austin at all. She wanted to go home. She wanted to scream at Mr. Plohn, the scum, the creep. And she didn't want to waste any more time with any Texans. That included Brandon Williams.

Maureen watched as they passed one renovated Victorian building after another. Her anger fogged her eyes, distorting her appreciation for the historical district on Pecan Street. She didn't hear Skip's explanation of the area with its Bourbon Street atmosphere. Maureen was too busy fantasizing about how she could get even with the Agriculture Department's scumball.

"Are you getting out?" Skip asked politely.

"Huh?" Maureen looked up to see that they had stopped and Skip was holding the door for her. "Oh, yes."

"I'll be back in twenty minutes with Mr. Williams." He smiled, then gestured with his head toward the Grove Drug Store. "Try the chocolate soda. It's the best in Texas."

Maureen reluctantly went inside. The building was charming and pleasant. The soda fountain dated back to 1902 and was still in operation, though it was surrounded by contemporary diet pills, headache medications and current issues of magazines. As she ordered the soda, she glanced down to see Bitzy's face staring up at her from the cover of the November issue of *Ultra Woman.*

"I'll take a copy of this," she said to the waitress.

"We just got them in today," the flame-haired woman replied. With a wistful sigh she added, "I'd give anything to look like that," and she pointed to Bitzy.

"She is very beautiful, isn't she?" Maureen made a mental note to write to Bitzy that night. Maureen leafed through the magazine, thinking how quickly her life in New York had faded from her mind. It was almost as if it had happened to someone else.

She must have been crazy to ever leave it. Now she was faced with losing all the profit from her sale and all because she refused to pay a bribe. She wondered if principles were all that important when one was struggling to survive. She wondered if this was what Michael had meant—she felt as if she were in the gutter, fighting with the rats. Plohn was definitely vermin.

"How's the soda?"

Maureen would have known his voice anywhere. She turned around. Again, she was stunned by the impact he had on her. She didn't like this strange effect. She didn't understand it, and therefore, to Maureen, if she couldn't logically explain something to herself, it was not to be trusted. Her experience this afternoon told her there was little about Texans to trust.

"The soda's fine. It's cold. I thought it would cool me off."

His expression was puzzled. "Cool off?"

She slid off the stool. "Can we go now?"

"Of course. Did you get everything straightened out?"

She frowned as she laid her money on the counter for the soda. "No." She headed for the door and went straight to the car.

Brandon climbed in behind her. "What happened?"

"The assistant to the secretary of agriculture is a crook. He engineered all this just to get a bribe."

"Oh."

"That's all you can say? 'Oh'? You act as if you *expected* this."

"I'm not surprised. It happens all the time. I thought Doc might have warned you. I thought you knew."

"You must be kidding. If I'd have known, why would I ask you to fly me all the way to Austin?"

"I . . . uh . . ."

Her mouth fell open. "Of all the arrogant . . . conceited . . . You thought I just wanted to see you? Jesus! Give me a little credit. I don't have to go to these extremes. I would have asked you over for a drink and to look at my etchings if that's what I wanted. But I didn't."

"No. You certainly didn't."

"Besides, I thought this was the land of Southern gallantry. You're supposed to do the calling."

"Maybe I should have."

"Don't bother. It won't get you anywhere."

He folded his arms over his chest. "I wouldn't dream of it."

Maureen folded her arms over *her* chest.

"I suppose you *would* still like a lift home," he said.

Suddenly, Maureen remembered how gallant he had been. But then, she realized now, he'd thought there was something in it for him. A quick roll in the hay—a one-night stand. She supposed she could take a commercial flight back to Kerrville, but if the schedule at the Houston airport was any indication of the infinitesimal number of flights to Kerrville, she'd probably be waiting in Austin for two days to get a scheduled flight. By that time her chances of doing anything for her cattle would be lost. Brandon was her fastest ticket home. And right now she didn't give a damn what he thought. "I think you owe it to me."

"I don't owe you anything. But I brought you here, and I'll see to it that you get home safely."

Maureen glared at him. They were at a standoff, and in her mind that was the way it should be.

13

◆

CARL PLOHN WAITED patiently until his receptionist went out for a coffee break. She left the phone recorder on as was her custom. Carl refused to answer any incoming calls himself. He left the inner office door open so that he could see anyone who happened to enter his office. He picked up the telephone and punched out seven digits.

"You can come to my office now. She's gone."

Carl hung up without waiting for an answer.

Ten minutes later, Alexander Cottrell walked casually into Carl Plohn's office. He wore an expensive Italian suit and a satisfied expression.

"Well done, Carl," Alexander said as he pulled a thick envelope from his pocket.

Carl held out his hand, but Alexander did not offer the envelope to him. Carl was confused.

"Not so fast, Carl. How do I know she didn't pay you off and you've already released her cattle? You could be playing us both."

"Mr. Cottrell"—Carl splayed out his hand—"why would I do that? This woman is a nobody. I would never cheat you."

Alexander smiled. "Open the drawers in your desk."

Carl did as he was asked.

"Now the briefcase."

Carl opened the briefcase, then opened his file drawers and emptied his pockets. "Are you satisfied?"

"I can never be too sure."

"Mr. Cottrell. Even if I divested Miss McDonald of a few

dollars, I still would not have released her cattle. That wouldn't be fair to you."

"No, it wouldn't." Alexander handed him the envelope. He watched as Carl greedily counted the ten one-hundred-dollar bills. "Keep up the good work, Carl. I'm sure I'll be needing your assistance in the future."

"Anytime, Mr. Cottrell. Anytime."

Alexander left without another word.

The door had just closed behind Alexander when the telephone rang. The answering machine clicked on, but the caller refused to leave a message. In the subsequent fifteen minutes the telephone rang seven times. There were no messages.

The receptionist returned to a ringing phone. She picked it up and buzzed Carl's office. "It's the governor's office!" she said excitedly. In the eighteen months she'd worked in Carl Plohn's office, Lily Mae Steddham had never gotten a call from anyone in the governor's office.

Carl picked up the phone. "Yes, sir."

"Mr. Plohn. This is Mark Dixon's personal assistant, George Camden, calling."

"Yes, sir. What can I do for you?"

"You can release Maureen McDonald's cattle you're illegally holding down in Houston."

"Sir, I'm doing no such thing. There is a question as to the health of these cows. We suspect Leucaena poisoning."

"Bullshit. Release them by morning or you'll find yourself without a job."

Carl knew he had to cover his ass. "Sir, I want my own vet to check out those cattle. I can't be responsible if we ship diseased livestock out of the country."

"The governor will assume all responsibility, Mr. Plohn. Do you understand me?"

"Yes, sir."

"Good day, Mr. Plohn."

Carl's hand was shaking as he replaced the receiver. For six years he'd been under the impression that he was dealing with the most powerful family in Texas—the Cottrells. But now he realized that there was someone else with as much or even greater influence. *But who?*

Maureen McDonald had powerful friends. Carl Plohn hoped he would never have to deal with her again.

* * *

Brandon drove a bronze two-tone Corvette back to his house from the hangar. He blasted the Bose stereo, hoping to drown out his experiences that afternoon. He punched one button after another trying to find a station he liked. Finally, he gave up and turned it off.

When he parked the car in the drive beneath a huge oak, the sun had already set. The mercury lamps that lit his two-story red-brick house came on automatically. He'd just reached the white painted double doors when Shirley stepped out.

"What happened to you?" she asked, looking at his unnaturally sullen face.

"Nothing."

She shrugged her shoulders. She'd worked for Brandon for eight years and knew that when he didn't want to talk no amount of cajoling could coax him to do otherwise. She had learned to leave him alone. "I left your messages on the desk. I finished the letters and they're ready for you to sign. I'll mail them in the morning."

"You have big plans tonight?"

"Sammie has a soccer game and Billie has basketball practice. Then we're going for a pizza afterward. You wanna join us? You look as if you could use some cheering up."

"I'll pass. I'm beat. Give the girls a hug and kiss for me. I'll be glad when they get out of this tomboy stage and I can call them Samantha and Beth again. You know what they need?"

Shirley shook her head. "Don't tell me . . . a father. Well, we're doing nicely, thank you. You know what *you* need?" she teased back.

"Forget it," he laughed. "I'll see you tomorrow."

Brandon watched as Shirley drove away. He went into the opulently mirrored foyer. He dropped his keys into a turquoise-and-yellow enameled dish. He passed the living room, decorated in cream, white and black with zebra skins on the floor and a black baby grand piano, and went directly to his study, located adjacent to the living room. There were pocket doors separating the two rooms that he kept closed at all times.

The study was ringed by black lacquered bookshelves. The floor was black-and-cream marble with a custom-made area rug in white and black with gold braid trim around the shell designs in each corner. In the middle of the room sat an exquisite black-and-gold rococo desk. His chair was a comfortable misfit with a reclining back and cream-colored raw silk upholstery.

Brandon loved this house. It had been built on the site of his parents' home, which had been nothing more than a shack. But Brandon had been proud of them and the land. His father had died when he was twelve, and his mother when he was eighteen. During those years after his father's death, he and his mother had become very close. They had worked side by side. It was then that Brandon learned that men and women were made by God to complement one another. What qualities men lacked in their makeup, women possessed in abundance. His mother had never treated him as a child, only as her equal.

Brandon considered himself a contemporary man, though he did not understand ''women's lib'' or ''men's lib'' because he'd always lived in balanced and loving surroundings.

Brandon was a self-taught man because there had never been any money for college. At nineteen, six months after his mother died, he'd been out riding his Andalusian horse when he came upon a patch of earth that was unusually soft. The horse had begun to sink into the murky ground. Upon dismounting, Brandon found that the earth was slimy. He knew he'd found oil. He sold his Andalusian to pay for a professional geological survey of the land. His suspicions were correct. His land contained as much, possibly even more, oil than Charles Sims's land that lay to the south.

He married Cynthia Kramer at the age of twenty-three. He was in love and he was a millionaire. Cynthia loved him and not his money. Of that Brandon was certain. Cynthia's dream was to build a fine home, like the ones she'd seen in Williamsburg. ''A house that would give birth to a president,'' she'd said. And so, he'd started construction and Cynthia tried to become pregnant.

Before they'd even started the interiors, Cynthia died of a cerebral hemorrhage. For years Brandon lived in the house, making do with unpapered walls and half-installed floors. In truth, he lived little of his time in Kerrville. He was building an empire. He had the high rise in Houston, the town house in Dallas. He didn't need to submerge himself in memories.

Finally, common sense took over and he hired Sherrie Tucker from Houston to finish the job. Sherrie had designed his apartment in the Warwick Towers in Houston. She had a client list that took her from New York to Palm Beach to Palm

Springs to Paris and back again. Sherrie had designed most of the mansions in and around Kerrville and so she was familiar with the workmen and laborers. They worked well together, and she knew Brandon's taste better than he did.

Brandon realized that this house was never going to breed presidents, and so he had Sherrie use her impeccable taste and sense of style to reflect the life he now led. Brandon felt Cynthia would have been pleased.

He now signed the letters Shirley had typed. He quickly went over his messages. Upon reading the last one, he picked up the telephone and dialed Austin.

"This is Brandon Williams. I know it's late, but does George happen to be in?"

"For you, Mr. Williams, always," the secretary answered a bit too sweetly.

George came on the line. "We're all set, Brandon. I think our little weasel is shaking in his boots."

"Did he release the cattle?"

"I'll get confirmation in the morning. But I threatened him with the full force of the governor's wrath."

"Don't let Mark hear you say that."

"I have a feeling that if Governor Dixon knew the details, he'd have given his full blessing."

"I just hope I haven't gotten you into any hot water over this," Brandon said.

"Don't worry about it. I sort of felt like Superman there for a minute. Truth, justice and the American way."

"Don't let it go to your head. When do you expect the governor back anyway?"

"Monday morning."

"Give him my regards."

George paused for a moment. "Say, Brandon. Can I ask you a question?"

"Sure."

"Who is this McDonald woman?"

"Just a lady in distress."

George chuckled. "Must be *some* lady."

"She is." Brandon hung up.

Brandon leaned back in his chair and crossed his hands behind his head. Maureen was some lady, all right, he thought.

Since the night he'd met her at the Cottrell barbecue, he hadn't been able to get her out of his mind. He'd thought about calling her a hundred times in the interim, but he'd always been on his way to Dallas or Houston or San Antonio. He thought about her early in the morning, in the middle of business meetings, or when he was in conference with his employees at the bank he owned in Dallas. Mostly, he thought about her every night when the sun went down and he was alone. He wondered what she was doing, what she'd had for dinner. Was she seeing friends? Was she alone, too?

Today he'd seen a side to her that he hadn't dreamed existed. Until today, he'd thought Maureen to be beautiful, very, very sexy and smart. He could see that in her eyes. She was the kind of woman he'd want to have an affair with. His intuition told him she'd be fun *and* interesting. They would *enjoy* each other.

But today he'd seen a different Maureen McDonald. He'd seen a woman with principles. A woman with guts and spunk and courage. He'd seen a woman who didn't give a damn about money. He'd seen a woman witnessing the kind of corruption he saw every day and had learned to take in his stride. He'd witnessed something he didn't think existed in the world today. He'd seen innocence scraped from her eyes.

Right now she was angry as hell at Carl Plohn, Texas, the world *and* him. But she would get over it. He didn't blame her. He was mad, too. He despised the kind of greed that made men debase themselves. He'd known what it was like not to have a full meal on the table. He'd known what it was like to have a roof that leaked, a house with no warmth in winter, a father who died because there wasn't enough money for kidney dialysis.

But Brandon had never compromised himself. He'd rather be dead. He was glad his parents had taught him to be the kind of man he was. For if they hadn't, he might never have met Maureen McDonald—and he would never have possessed the moral yardstick to know that *this was the woman he intended to marry.*

14

◆

MAUREEN ROLLED out of bed at seven the next morning thanking God He'd brought an end to her torturous night. She still had Bill Handley on hold, Doc Silver waiting to fly back to Houston and no official word from the authorities that she could proceed.

She'd spent four hours on the telephone last night with the vet in Houston and the supervisor at the pens, trying to persuade them to release the cattle. But until Carl Plohn gave the go-ahead, she was only spinning her wheels.

Maureen went to the bathroom, turned on the shower and watched a spray of rusty water seep out of the shower head. "Damn!" She turned the water off, pulled on her robe and went downstairs. Juanita was dressed and already preparing breakfast.

"There's no water."

"Si. But I bought extra bottle water yesterday."

Maureen smiled. "We have coffee?"

"On the stove. And orange juice."

Maureen poured herself a huge mug of steaming coffee, and had taken only one sip when the telephone rang. "Please, God, let it be a miracle."

She picked up the receiver. "Hello?"

"Miss McDonald? This is Clem Dobson in Houston. I spoke with you last night. I've just gotten the clearance from the Agriculture Department in Austin. You can fly those cattle in anytime today."

"Thank you! Thank you, Mr. Dobson. We're on our way."

131

"What happen?" Juanita asked, seeing Maureen's joyous face.

"A miracle!"

Maureen skipped the shower, jumped into her jeans and plaid blouse, grabbed the keys to the truck and dashed out the back door.

"Wes!" she yelled as she headed for the bunkhouse. "Grady! Randy! Let's get going!"

Wes came to the screen door, tucking his shirt into his jeans. He took one look at her face and said, "Come on, fellas! We're on our way to Houston!"

Maureen called Doc Silver while Wes, Grady and Randy loaded the cattle onto Bill's plane. In an hour and a half she was waving to them as they flew over the ranch house.

It wasn't until Maureen was back in the kitchen with Juanita that she felt it safe to question her "miracle."

"I wonder just who my guardian angel is."

Juanita flipped the sausage patties. "Angel?"

"Somebody got that creep to reverse his orders. I have a feeling it was not my persuasive tactics that did it, either. It had to be Brandon. God! And I gave him such a hard time, too."

"Hard time?"

"Yes, I was riding my high horse a bit too loftily."

Juanita shook her head. "I no understand you. . . . Yankee talk."

Maureen laughed. "Sometimes I don't understand me, either, Juanita. I guess it's time for me to eat crow." She looked at Juanita's puzzled face. "Apologize, I mean." Juanita nodded.

Maureen had just started down the hall when the doorbell rang. She could see a man's silhouette outlined by the morning sun at his back.

"Brandon?"

She opened the door.

"Alexander! What are you doing here?" She smiled at him, not able to admit her disappointment to herself.

"Did you think you could avoid me forever?"

"Avoid you? You're never around. I called you yesterday, as a matter of fact. But the housekeeper said you were in Houston. I needed your help."

"I'm sorry I missed you. So, tell me now and I'll see what I can do."

"It's taken care of now."

"It *is?*" he asked, a bit too stunned, then quickly retrieved his boyish grin.

"I fount out—the hard way—that to get things done in Texas there are a lot of hidden costs. My cattle were being held in Houston. To get them released, the assistant to the secretary of agriculture in Austin demanded a bribe."

"Ah!" Alexander said knowingly. "And so you paid it."

"No, I didn't. But somebody did."

"You didn't pay him?"

"No."

Alexander's mind raced. None of this made sense. Plohn wouldn't have double-crossed him if Maureen hadn't paid him off. Alexander had to think fast. "How long did this guy say he would hold the cattle?"

"Three days."

"Well, you see there? He couldn't really do that. He was just bluffing. He didn't get the money from you and so he had to let the cattle go. It's just the natural course of events that saved you."

"Do you really think so?"

"I know so. Why? Did you think someone had intervened for you?"

"Well, I . . ." She paused, thinking of Brandon. She should have known he wouldn't have been an "angel." She'd been right about him after all. Thinking back on it, she was rather proud of herself for seeing through him. She'd put him in his place. And that was where he would stay.

"Maureen, how did you get to Austin?"

"That's why I called you. I needed a ride. But Brandon flew me up there."

Instantly, Alexander remembered his mother's warning about Brandon. He watched Maureen carefully for any sign that Brandon had usurped his position with Maureen. "I wish I would have known. But I'm glad he did the neighborly thing. I must tell you, I don't like him taking my place." He placed his arm around her shoulders and pulled her to him and chuckled. He wanted to keep the message clear but the mood light.

"You don't have to worry about that, Alex!"

"Promise?"

"I know for a fact his intentions were not 'neighborly' at all. He's the most arrogant man I've ever met. He has the misguided notion that I would be interested in him. But I straightened him out on that score."

"I hope so," he said softly, and then kissed her gently.

Maureen looked into his gleaming green eyes. She put her arms around his neck. "There's nothing more important in life than friends—good friends, Alex. Don't you forget that."

"I won't . . . as long as you remember *who* your friends are."

She nodded and then paused for a minute. "How about some breakfast?"

"Sounds terrific."

They kept their arms around each other as they went into the kitchen. They sat at the table and shared Juanita's thin pancakes. Maureen was reminded of a similar scene long ago. They'd laughed at the same jokes and they'd felt the same camaraderie. Only Mac was missing.

Shane Cottrell pulled the purple satin sleeping mask from her eyes and groaned at the flood of morning sunlight that bathed her room.

"Shit," she muttered as she pulled herself to a sitting position. Her head was pounding to the rhythm of an Ozzy Osbourne song that blared from her ghetto blaster. She slammed her hand down on the controls. The music stopped abruptly.

She started to stand, but painful cramps shot through her thighs and she fell back onto the bed. "What the . . . ?"

And then she remember last night. "Oh, yes. Burt." She smiled to herself. Lynn Bean had been in Dallas all day with Charlene Sims . . . shopping. Burt and Shane had taken full advantage of the circumstances to spend the entire time together. Shane couldn't remember how many times they'd done it. Probably once an hour—she could never get enough of him. Burt could be an asshole at times, but he was the best lay she'd ever had . . . in Texas, anyway.

But the best part about her times with Burt was the coke.

"Where do you get this stuff?" she'd asked him.

"It's the best, isn't it?" he'd said, handing her his glass straw.

"It's incredible."

"I always get the best. You remember that, Shane. Burt Bean is the best." He'd put his hands on either side of her face. "Say it, Shane. Burt is the best."

"You're the best, baby. You really are."

They'd gone through a whole bottle of Dom Perignon. Judging from her headache, maybe it had been more than one. Shane had elicited a promise from Burt to take her to Cozumel before Christmas so she could rev up her tan for the holidays. Her next project would be to coerce him into going to Rio for Mardi Gras. Shane had visions of herself in a string bikini walking the Brazilian beaches, sending all the native boys into a stupor.

Shane had many dreams for herself.

Unfortunately, Shane's dreams and Barbara's plans for Shane clashed like two Roman Titans. Shane wanted adoration. No, strike that, she thought. Craved adoration was more appropriate. Barbara had sent Shane to enough shrinks in her life for her to know that she had lacked some necessary psychological building block in her childhood. It had something to do with never knowing her father, or never feeling her father's love and caring. Shane had never paid much attention to what the shrinks said. She only went because it kept Barbara off her back for a week or two. And besides, psychiatrists were only interested in Barbara's checks anyway. They didn't really care what happened to Shane; how she really felt; what she really needed.

Shane knew what she needed. She needed to have fun.

Burt was fun. Coke was fun. Needling Alexander was fun. Pissing off Barbara was fun. After that, everything was a drag. Major drag. Burt understood her better than any shrink, her mother, her brother . . . better than anybody. Shane *needed* Burt.

Burt understood her. He took care of her. Shane believed that Burt loved her. After all, he gave her anything she asked for. She knew he didn't love Lynn. Shane had listened to his complaints about his wife for over a year. But, like most Southern men, he was reluctant to divorce the mother of his children.

Shane believed that, given time, she could show Burt that he didn't need Lynn anymore. That it was a ridiculous farce for him to be unhappy and remain married to a woman he no longer cared for. It wouldn't happen overnight, Shane knew. But one day she would have everything. She would have the fun, the drugs, the endless days of lovemaking with Burt with no one to answer to. Not her brother. And especially *not her mother.*

Shane stood, went to the window and closed the blinds. The sun was creating a heavy metal symphony in her head.

The walls of Shane's bedroom were plastered with a collage of movie posters. Some dated back to the early thirties. There was a particularly wonderful poster of Garbo that Shane treasured. It had been given to her when she was sixteen by one of her first lovers. He'd been a middle-aged Dallasite. He'd dated her for three months, showering her with all kinds of movie memorabilia, since that's what she had been into those days. But then he'd gone to Phoenix for a face-lift and Shane never heard from him again. Neither had anyone else. She heard a year later that he'd moved to Mexico City, but she was never sure.

Shane loved the movies and for many years had dreamed of becoming part of them. She could act, sing and dance.

What she couldn't do was keep up. She couldn't keep up the energy, the pace and the strong will it took to handle the pressure and the rejection.

God, the rejection. It had been more devastating than anything she'd ever encountered. Shane had expected things to come as easily to her in California as they had in Texas. But she'd learned quickly that her competition in Los Angeles was more talented and gutsier than she would ever be.

Above all, Shane had learned that she didn't *want* to be a star as much as the others did. She'd met young girls with determination that knew no bounds. She'd met boys and girls who would stop at nothing to get what they wanted. Shane didn't want it badly enough. She only wanted to have fun. What point was there to a career or to life if there was no fun?

Shane had tried desperately to keep up. That's when she'd started the drugs. A pill here and there to make her sleep during the day so she could perform at night on-stage. A pill to wake her up; a pill to get her up. It had happened to hundreds of kids in Hollywood from Judy Garland to John Belushi. She was no better and no worse.

Shane had never lost her love for the movies. She still had times when she dreamed she would claw her way out of her mother's web and make it. But, fortunately, the dreams never lasted long and their torment was short.

Shane went to the bathroom, pulled out the vanity drawer and reached for the toothpaste tube that contained her coke.

A hit before breakfast would make her forget Hollywood and things like dreams and plans.

She kept rolling the bottom, but nothing would come out. She squeezed the tube angrily. "Shit! I couldn't have used it all!"

Her mind sped over the last two days. Burt had given her three grams. She had put every grain into the toothpaste tube herself. She knew she hadn't been that bad off that she couldn't remember.

She rummaged through the drawer. Maybe she had the wrong tube. No, it was the right one.

"Then who's taken it?" she asked herself.

Quickly, she went through her things. She opened the medicine cabinet. At first glance it looked as if nothing had been touched, but on closer inspection she realized that everything of value was missing. Gone were her diet pills, the tranquilizers, the Valium, the Seconal, even her diuretics. The birth control pills remained. She foraged through her drawers, her closet, but again everything seemed in order.

Suddenly she remembered one last hiding place. She took out her old set of Clairol electric rollers—now defunct except as a hiding place for her grass. She picked up one of the rollers and then slipped the metal bottom plate over the stems.

"It's gone!"

Shane thought for a minute. There was only one person who would go to such lengths.

"Mother!"

Shane pulled on a pair of kelly green stirrup pants and a huge hand-knit sweater that had cost a small fortune. She shoved her feet into a pair of men's wing tip shoes. Just to antagonize her mother, she drew a black heart on her left cheek. She outlined her eyes in black kohl and went downstairs.

Barbara was sitting at the head of the ten-foot-long Sheridan dining table discussing dinner plans with the cook. In her left hand she held the telephone. There were five incoming lines at the house. Shane noticed that the red hold button was depressed and that two lines were holding.

Shane went to the buffet and poured herself a cup of strong coffee from the George III sterling coffee pot. She put a generous amount of sugar in the coffee and gulped it down. She poured a second cup and sipped it black and never took her eyes off her mother.

"Consuela, I wish to speak with my mother."

Barbara frowned. "When we're finished, Shane."

"*Now*, Mother dear."

Barbara finished her conversation with the cook, ignoring Shane's pacing. She signed off one of her calls, and instructed the second caller to "sell the embryos to the conglomerate in Johannesburg."

"What is so important that you must interrupt my business, Shane?"

"What did you do with it?" Shane hissed angrily.

Barbara peered at her. "I flushed it down the toilet."

"Who gave you the right? Since when do you confiscate my personal property as if you're the KGB?"

"Shut up and sit down." Barbara waited.

Shane did not budge.

"I said, 'Sit down.' "

Shane sat.

"You live in *my* house. That means *my* rules prevail. I dug you out of a sanitarium in California and brought you back here so that you could *try* to clean up your act. Obviously, there's been little progress." Barbara sighed. "I don't understand you, Shane."

"No shit."

Barbara ignored her daughter's foul language. "Don't you care about yourself at all? Don't you want good things for yourself? I do. I love you, Shane. I just wish you loved yourself as much as I love you."

"I do love myself that much. You can see how much love I think you have for me."

Barbara nearly recoiled from Shane's bitterness. But she kept her head high. She would not buckle under Shane's erroneous indictment of her. "I will not have drugs in this house. Period."

"Then I'll move out."

"Do that."

"Push me, and I will."

Barbara cocked an eyebrow. "Make sure your boyfriends are willing to pay for your expensive life-style. I won't."

Shane started to tremble. She took a long slug of coffee. "You can't keep Daddy's trust fund from me."

Barbara's mouth curled upward in triumph. "Without me, you're not entitled to a cent. He left *me* as trustee . . . until I felt you were capable of handling money matters on your own. My attorney is well aware of my attitude about your trust fund. In fact, at this moment, I've written you *out* of my will.''

"You what?''

"You heard me. Until you redeem yourself in my eyes, live according to my rules, which means no drugs, you get nothing. Nothing, Shane.''

"You're treating me like a child.''

"You *are* a child. Until you behave I'll take your toys away. And if you don't change your ways soon I'll take Burt away from you, too.''

"You can't do that! You can't play with people's lives as if we're tokens on a game board! Burt's a grown man. He can't be pushed around.''

"Grow up! Burt will never leave Lynn. That's a fact you won't face. But I can make his life miserable for him. And I'll do it, too. If you won't save yourself, I'll do it for you.''

"No, Mother, you're wrong. Only I can do that.''

Shane pushed herself away from the table and stalked out of the room. She grabbed her car keys and slammed the front door behind her. As always, she and Barbara were stalemated.

15

◆

MAUREEN FOLDED a shawl-collared sweater and placed it in the suitcase. She packed only one dress, her jeans and a work shirt. She was glad there was lots of room left, because she would be bringing back more clothes than she was taking. She placed her plane tickets in the pocket of her tote bag, grabbed her makeup case and the paperback copy of Steven Birmingham's newest novel.

Juanita was waiting for her at the bottom of the stairs. "Señora Sims is here."

"Thanks. Now, you have my number in New York if you need me."

"Si," Juanita answered despondently.

"Would you quit worrying? I'll only be gone a few days."

Juanita's eyes were huge round pools in her face. "You come back?"

"Of course I will. My life is here now." She glanced out the window next to the door. She could see Charleen sitting in the back of her limousine. Luis, the chauffeur, was mounting the front steps. "I've got to go. I'll call you when I get in."

Maureen handed Luis her luggage. She sat next to Charleen. "I really appreciate your taking me to the airport."

"I'm glad to do it. Besides, it gives us a chance to get to know one another better. I heard about your problem with the cattle."

"How . . ." Then Maureen remembered. "Your maid, right?"

"And my pilot. He's friends with Brandon's mechanic.'

"Oh." Maureen indulged herself in the vision of Brandon's face, the remembered gentleness of his voice.

Charleen's merry brown eyes danced in her face. She could tell that Brandon meant something to Maureen, though she doubted Maureen was fully aware of it. Charleen's curiosity was tickled. "He's one of the nicest men I've ever met."

"Who is?"

"Brandon. I didn't know him very well when we were growing up. I went to school in Switzerland. But I knew Cynthia, his wife."

Maureen remembered the woman's voice on the phone when she'd telephoned him asking for help. "Why didn't anyone tell me he was married?"

Charleen smiled coyly. "I didn't know it was important to you. He's just a neighbor, isn't he?"

"Yes, of course."

"To ease your mind, he's a widower. She died years ago. Brandon has kept to himself—he's a workaholic."

"I know the type," Maureen said, thinking of Michael. As far as she was concerned, she didn't need to know any more about Brandon. She was glad she'd put her trust in Alexander.

Charleen saw the closed look in Maureen's eyes. She changed the subject. "How long will you be in New York?"

"Not long, I hope. I'm putting the apartment up for sale, having my furniture and things shipped to me, moving bank accounts . . . things like that."

"I'm sorry you have to sell your apartment."

"Me, too. But I didn't make as much from the cattle sale as I'd thought. By the time I paid the air shipping . . ." She sighed. "I don't want to bore you."

"It's okay. Is there anything I can do to help?"

"You've done enough already."

"Nonsense. When you fly back just call and I'll have Luis pick you up. I like you, Maureen. I *want* to help. I couldn't help noticing that your house is in need of repair."

"No kidding. That's one of the reasons I need more money. I barely have running water."

"Tell you what. Let me call some friends. I know the best plumbers and carpenters in the area. I'll make sure they give you a good price. I could get all the bids for you while you're out of town."

"I've gotten bids. They're astronomical."

"Then let me negotiate some of them for you. They all know me."

"Are you sure?"

"I've been running my husband's oil business for years. I haven't made very many wrong decisions. But then, I have a lot of help myself."

"Help?"

"Yes. Whenever I'm in a jam, I ask my psychic what I should do."

Maureen wondered how far her jaw had fallen. "You consult a fortune-teller about business decisions?"

"Not a fortune-teller. That's carnival sideshow stuff. My advisors are very knowledgeable. I've found the best in Texas.'

"I don't believe this," Maureen whispered to herself.

"I know. Everyone is skeptical at first. I understand that. I'll be patient with you until *you* can learn how to listen to your heart."

Luis pulled up at the entrance to the Kerrville Municipal Airport.

Thankful the trip and her bizarre conversation with Charleen was at an end, Maureen bounded out of the limousine with a bit too much exuberance.

Charleen hugged her. "You'll have a good and safe trip. I know. I already asked my guides. But don't see the boss man. It won't be a good experience."

"What boss man?"

"The man you used to work for . . . the man who used to be your lover."

"How do you know about Michael?"

Charleen smiled. "My maid."

"Right."

Once on the plane, Maureen leaned back and looked out of the window. She was almost relieved to be away from Charleen. Psychics, guides . . . what a bunch of mumbo jumbo, she thought, and quickly dismissed their conversation from her mind.

Maureen had called Bitzy from the ranch and told her when she'd be flying in. Bitzy had to finish an assignment in Chicago and had told Maureen she would see her around nine and they would have dinner together.

Maureen rode in the taxi through the streets of Manhattan. She'd never felt claustrophobic in her life, but she did now. Everything seemed to be pressing down on her, and in on her. The city sounds were intensified a hundredfold from what memory had served her. She looked up and was surprised at how grey the sky was . . . what little of it she could see, that was. Complaints about the city she'd heard from visitors over the years suddenly had new meaning. For the first time, Maureen felt like a *visitor*. And already she wanted to go *home*.

Maureen paid the driver and greeted Eddie, the doorman, fondly.

"I didn't know if you'd ever come back."

"I'm only back for a few days, Eddie. I'm . . . selling the apartment."

His face fell. "I'm sorry to hear that."

"It can't be helped."

Maureen took the elevator to the eighth floor and unlocked her door. Though it was unusually cold in New York for November, the apartment was warm and stuffy. She cracked a window open to allow the air to circulate.

Maureen did not unpack but went straight to the telephone, making the necessary arrangements for the sale of the apartment. She booked a ten o'clock meeting the following morning with a real estate agent, and hired a moving company to come in the following day and pack. They would return the next day and move everything out. Maureen changed into her jeans and Western shirt, then began the business of cleaning out the kitchen.

She was glad she'd bought the large almond-colored refrigerator three years ago. Juanita would love it. The other appliances were built-in and would have to remain. She hoped they would help her get a better price for the apartment.

She'd just tossed out a molded jar of applesauce when Eddie buzzed her from downstairs. But it was Bitzy's voice she heard.

"I'm on my way up!" Bitzy said excitedly.

When Maureen answered the door and looked into Bitzy's beautiful, smiling face, she was more depressed than elated.

"You don't look happy to see me!"

"Oh, Bitzy!" Maureen flung her arms around her friend. "I just realized how much I missed you." She closed the door. "You got my letters?"

"Every one. This is only the second time I've been back

in the city in weeks. You were lucky you caught me the other day. I wouldn't have missed seeing you for the world.''

Bitzy eyed Maureen from head to toe. ''What is this?'' She picked up the end of Maureen's shirttail.

''Work clothes.''

''Spare me.''

''I'm serious. I was cleaning out the refrigerator. Come talk to me while I finish.''

''I don't believe this.'' Bitzy tossed her long wool cape and Gucci tote bag on the sofa. ''So, you're really going to sell this place and go off to Mecca.''

''I wouldn't call it Mecca—but there's something about it. I feel, well . . . I feel good about it. Despite the problems.''

''Such as?''

Bitzy bit into a cold apple while Maureen told her everything about life on the ranch, the people she'd met, the injustice, the hard work and her hopes. Bitzy was stunned.

''I know you like challenges, Mo. But don't you think you're biting off more than you can chew here?''

''Jesus! You, too?''

''You've heard this before?''

Maureen nodded. ''I can't decide which is working against me most, my being a Yankee or a woman. At least Alexander doesn't patronize me . . . not like *some* people.''

''Me?''

''No, not you. Brandon.''

Bitzy's ears pricked up. ''This is a name we have not heard.''

''And you won't either. He's just a neighbor. He did me a favor once.''

''Yeah?'' Bitzy was intrigued. Maureen was trying to dismiss Brandon's importance for some reason. ''How good a neighbor is he?''

Maureen didn't like the Cheshire cat grin on Bitzy's face. ''Not that good. I don't trust him.''

''Why not? What did he do?''

''Uh, nothing.'' Maureen remembered too easily how he'd used her misfortune to his advantage. He could be conniving when he wanted to be, she told herself. She also remembered how she turned to a mound of jelly whenever she saw him. He did a lot of things to her and none of them inspired confidence in herself. She'd found the best way to keep her wits about herself was to not think about him and definitely to not be around him.

Bitzy scrutinized Maureen's expression. Bitzy had known Maureen for . . . forever it seemed, and she'd never seen her act like this. Until this moment, Bitzy had thought Maureen was doing the wrong thing by moving to Texas. Now she changed her mind.

"No, change your clothes."

"What?"

"I'm starving and I'm going to take you to dinner. Lutèce, I think."

"Isn't that a bit outrageous?"

"Not at all. We're going to celebrate. I want to send you back to Texas in style."

Late night at Lutèce was coveted by New York's social elite like a showgirl hankering over her first follies revue. It was not only the place to be . . . it was being.

Maureen McDonald and Bitzy, the reigning queen of the cover girls, arrived along with the theatre crowd, dressed to the teeth in designer frocks. Maureen sensed it would be a long time before she got to again wear any of the Patou "samples" she'd bought for a pittance upon the conclusion of an *Ultra Woman* assignment.

The maître d' escorted them to their reserved table. Every head in the restaurant turned to watch them. They passed the table where the Kissingers were seated with two foreign dignitaries and their wives. Maureen saw Merv Griffin and two men from his staff. And there was Helen Gurley Brown, Geraldine Ferraro, and Norman Mailer, who kept shaking his head at the woman he was seated with.

When they sat down, the waiter began pouring the French champagne Bitzy had ordered over the phone.

"Here's to you, kid," Bitzy said, and raised her crystal flute. "I hope you know what you're doing."

Maureen smiled. "I hope so, too."

Out of the corner of her eye, Maureen saw a man approach the table.

"Oh, shit."

"What's Michael doing here?" Bitzy asked.

"You didn't tell him?"

"Me? Never! He's one good reason for you staying in Texas."

Michael smiled at Maureen, bent down and kissed her on her mouth. She felt nothing. And it surprised her. Shouldn't there have been some kind of residual feelings?

Michael signalled to the waiter. A chair was quickly brought to the table for him. When he sat next to Maureen, he took her hand and kissed it.

"Please don't," she said, retrieving her hand. Bitzy sipped her wine and looked away.

"My spies told me you'd be here." Maureen remained silent. "Eddie told me."

"I should have known."

He looked around the room, hoping for inspiration. But Michael wasn't a man to mince words. "I want you to move back, Mo. There's no reason for you to sell the apartment. Unless you want to. That is . . . after you move in with me, you might feel it impractical to pay two rents."

Maureen was stunned. "I don't understand, Michael. It's over between us."

"I've had a lot of time to think about all this. I've missed you . . . more than I thought I would. Not just the working together, though that's a wonderful, fulfilling facet to our relationship. I love you, Mo. And you were right. We were miserable together. But things can change. I can change."

"Michael . . . so much has happened since I saw you last. I . . ."

"I don't care. You don't belong out there in the middle of nowhere. Look around you, Mo. These are your kind of people. This is where you belong. You belong with me."

She looked at him. She wanted to believe he was sincere, but there was something missing. It was that same something that had always eluded them. "Michael, when did Eddie tell you I was here?"

"Tonight."

"And all this time you never picked up the phone to call me, you never jumped on a plane to come tell me this?"

"No, I . . ."

"Michael . . . It's like I said before . . . I'm convenient. And that's all. You only seek me out when it doesn't put you out. It only took a few minutes for you to get here from your office. I know I'm right."

Michael was fuming. His ploy wasn't working. He wondered if he would ever be able to accept the fact that Maureen was incapable of bending to his will. "Forget it. Forget the whole damn thing. It was a mistake my coming here. I thought I could reason with you, Mo. But you've always been unreasonable. You're right. You *do* belong in Texas."

"I know, Michael. I know."

Maureen watched as he stood and walked out of the restaurant. He stopped twice to pay social courtesies to friends in the business. Michael was an expert at saving face.

Maureen's spirits were completely deflated. Suddenly, she remembered something that sent chills down her spine. She shivered.

"Are you all right? What is it?" Bitzy asked.

"I have a new friend who warned me not to see Michael."

"Warned you?"

"Yes. I should have listened."

"Is that new friend named Brandon?"

"No. Charleen. But why would you think it was him?"

"Because he's important to you. I only have to mention his name and your entire attitude shifts. You get defensive and at the same time there's this look in your eyes . . ."

Maureen put her glass down. "This is the most ridiculous thing I've ever heard. I hardly even know him—"

"But you want to," Bitzy interrupted.

"Would you stop? You're always doing this to me. I don't trust people I don't know, especially arrogant, conceited men, to which group Brandon belongs."

"Jesus! Okay already. So, tell me about Alexander. You said in your letter he was gorgeous."

"He is. And he's been a friend to me just like I knew he would."

Bitzy listened while Maureen rambled on about Alexander, but her praise was a bit too profuse. there was no softness to her eyes, no tingle to the edge of her voice the way there was when Brandon's name came up. Bitzy's intuition told her that Brandon was nowhere near the asshole Maureen portrayed him to be. She guessed that Brandon must be hellfire on wheels to get to Maureen the way he did. Bitzy was convinced that Alexander could never be anything more than a brother figure to Maureen. But she didn't like the way Maureen was attaching so much importance to him. Bitzy was afraid Maureen was positioning herself for another go-around like the one she'd had with Michael. It was a waste of time.

"And so, I think that Alexander is in love with me."

"You don't know?"

"He's certainly alluded to it, dropped enough hints. But he hasn't proposed, no."

"Be careful, Mo."

"Alex would never hurt me."

Bitzy's eyes were intensely serious. "I think he's wrong for you. And before you say anything, hear me out. You always pick men using some kind of intelligence ruler that you think is more reliable than love. You made a mistake with Michael. This Alex was a friend when you were young, but don't let that cloud your head and your heart this time around. I wish you could hear yourself, see yourself, when you talk about Brandon. I don't know who any of these people are or what they are. But I do know you—even better than you do, I think. You are headed for disaster if you keep trying to push Brandon out of the picture and put Alexander in."

It took several minutes for Bitzy's words to sink in. Bitzy was younger than Maureen, but a hundred times more wise, especially when it came to men. Bitzy had never been sheltered the way Maureen had. She had come up the hard way and had learned things Maureen might never know. Maureen would be wise to listen to her.

"I'll think about what you said."

Bitzy smiled. Coming from Maureen, that meant a lot. "I couldn't ask for more."

16

♦

Maureen climbed out of Charleen's limousine not watching her footing as she kept her eyes fixed on her ranch house. "What the hell is going on?"

There were two carpenters on the roof tacking down an entire new section of tiles. Another carpenter was planing the front door jamb while the door lay astride two sawhorses on the front lawn. Maureen could hear the sound of electric drills and saws coming from the inside of the house.

Maureen stumbled forward as if in a daze while Luis took the numerous boxes and suitcases from the trunk.

She entered the foyer and dropped her purse and tote on the floor. There in the middle of the living room stood Charleen dressed in skintight Guess jeans, high-heeled black Charles Jourdan shoes and a black-and-white zebra print silk blouse with at least fifty thousand dollars worth of diamond jewelry clamped around her throat, wrists, fingers and ears. She turned her perfectly coiffed head around and saw Maureen. Her face lit up.

"Maureen! You're back!" She rushed over and hugged Maureen tightly. "Did Luis get you in time? How was your trip? Did you get a good realtor? . . . One can never be too careful in choosing reliable people, I always say. Did you see your friend Bitzy?"

Charleen's happy eyes glowed so brightly, Maureen found it impossible to be angry with her—almost. "Just what do you think you are doing?"

"I told you I was going to get things going for you. I got

such a good price from these men I couldn't wait for you to get back. Besides, they had a few weeks open. I hope you don't mind.''

"Mind?'' My God, Maureen thought, this woman is taking over my life and I've got to stop it. ''You should have consulted me. These were my decisions to make.''

"Please don't be angry with me. I called you several times, but there was no answer. You said you had a recorder.''

''I packed it,'' Maureen said a bit sheepishly.

Charleen was all smiles again. ''I haven't had this good a time in ages! And I've only started the things that couldn't be put off. You have running water now. And the roof doesn't leak anymore. And the furnace is repaired. With the cold weather expected for Thanksgiving, I thought you'd enjoy the holiday more. I only wanted to help.''

Maureen felt a warmth spread throughout her body. It was the same feeling she had when she was with Bitzy. She felt more than comfortable with Charleen—and her decisions, despite her personality quirks. She wondered what Charleen would say if Maureen told her she'd been right about the meeting with Michael. Charleen was going out of her way on many fronts to be kind to Maureen. Perhaps she shouldn't be so critical, so skeptical.

Maureen looked up at the patched and repainted living room ceiling. ''No leaks?''

''None.''

''And real running water? No rusty showers?''

''No,'' Charleen said.

''Sounds like heaven.''

Charleen chuckled. ''Believe me, it's going to take moving heaven and earth to make this place a home. You've really got your work cut out for you.''

''I know. But that's what I want—a home.''

''When does the van arrive?''

''Next week. I'll sort through everything then. I hate to get rid of any of these things.''

''Why don't you have them reconstructed and then recovered? I'll call my designer in Houston, Sherrie Tucker. I'll fly her out here for you and she can get this place whipped into shape in no time.''

''I couldn't ask you to do that.''

''Then don't. It'll be my housewarming gift. Welcome home, Maureen. I'm glad you're back.''

Maureen looked around, at the sawdust on the floors, the new ceiling, the warped walls. She put her arm around her new friend. "It's good to be back.".

Alexander telephoned Maureen and made a date for lunch on Friday. He told her they were going someplace "special." Maureen had no idea he meant Baby Routh's in Dallas. They sat in the "power dining room," the one to the right, in full view of the bar. And their seats were the "power seats" . . . the ones against the wall flanking the minimalist fireplace, Alexander explained. Maureen ordered the fried chicken and whipped yams. She avoided her cool white wine and instead drank in the pastel vanilla interior, the long expanses of glass, and wondered just how the designer had lit the interior so that every nook and cranny seemed to glow.

Since meeting with Sherrie Tucker, Maureen was paying attention to every detail of interior design these days. In fact, she was paying attention to everything except Alexander.

"I'm over here," he said.

"Oh, I'm sorry," she replied. "I was just thinking about the work I'm doing on the house."

"I know. Could we talk about something besides your ranch, my ranch . . . could we talk about us?"

"Us?"

"Maureen, you do know that I care a great deal about you."

"Well, yes. And I care for you . . . I always have."

He smiled, and when he did Maureen noticed that the two chic young women at the next table whispered to one another. Maureen could see desire written across their faces. She wondered why she didn't react the way they did.

"We're a lot alike, you and I," he said. "We like the same music, the same books. I want a family." He said the last words carefully, placing the proper pause at the end.

"You do?"

"Of course I do. The Cottrells and my mother's family, the Kerns, have always been important Texas families, Maureen. I'm the only one left to carry on the name. I'd like to have at least two sons."

"What about daughters?"

"Those, too." He chuckled and kissed her hand. "I know you have dreams for your ranch, Maureen. And I don't want to stop you in the pursuit of those dreams. But I want to be part of your dream, that's all.''

"Alexander, just exactly what are you saying?''

"Nothing more than this for right now. I don't want to press you. I just want you to know that I want us to be more than friends. I believe in fate, Mo. I think it's more than coincidence that all this time your land and mine has been joined. I think it's destiny that we grew up together. You were brought back to Texas for a reason. I think that reason is me.''

"Oh, Alex.'' She peered into his green eyes. "I know I always feel good with you, safe and cared for. But I'm confused about so many things right now. I feel like I'm being pulled in a thousand directions. I want to do the right thing for the ranch, what Mac wanted and what I want. Although now I'm just not quite sure what that is.''

"I know. Just remember, I'm not going to let you go. That guy in New York was a fool. I've never been accused of being a fool. We were meant to be, Maureen. And I intend to prove it to you.''

"You're getting nowhere with her,'' Barbara said coolly, stating the facts as she saw them. She and her son were seated in Barbara's office, which encompassed the entire far left wing of the house. It had stucco walls and Mexican tile floors spread with thick Persian rugs that had belonged to her grandmother, who had purchased them in Indonesia in 1842. Barbara sat in a red upholstered Spanish high-backed chair. It was very old and very, very expensive. It had belonged to Queen Maria Louisa, who died in 1714.

Alexander's temper flared within him, but he kept his emotions reigned in. He'd fought with his mother too many times not to have learned the rules by now. "I disagree. If I suddenly slam-dunked a marriage proposal on her, she'd turn tail and run.''

"She's all alone, struggling with that ranch. Why, Wes told me that she'd ordered a third more feed than was necessary. It'll rot before she uses it. Mistakes like that add up.''

"You should be happy. Then she'll give in.''

"I wish I had more confidence in the fact that *you* will be the one to pick up the pieces.''

"I will be.''

"I'm not so sure. But you're right . . .'' Barbara mused.

"About what?"

"She is making mistakes. Perhaps it's time she was shown that she's made the biggest mistake of her life. She hasn't got the talent, the knowledge, not even the guts, to run that ranch."

"I'm not sure about *that*. Maureen is no wimp." Alexander remembered the incident he'd engineered in Austin . . . another of his failures he had been fortunate in keeping from his mother. If she had known, he never would have heard the end of it.

Barbara picked up the receiver to the new, computerized telephone system she'd had installed the week before. She could automatically dial over two dozen numbers with the touch of one button. If Barbara had a weakness, it was for mechanical devices with buttons. She glanced at Alexander.

"What is Maureen's number?"

"444-4568. Why?"

"You'll see." She punched out the numbers and paused only a moment before the line was picked up. "Maureen? This is Barbara Cottrell. How are you today? Alexander and I were just making plans. . . . I was wondering if you were free for Thanksgiving dinner? You are? Would you do us the honor of joining us? Fine. Fine. We'll be eating around three. I'll tell Alexander to pick you up at two for cocktails. See you then."

Barbara replaced the receiver and watched the red light go off, signalling that the line was once again clear. Then it beeped rather than rang. Before she answered her call she dismissed Alexander with a wave of her hand.

"See that you're on time for dinner, Alexander."

Alexander was indeed on time. He had no idea what Barbara was planning for Maureen. He only knew how mixed his emotions were over the issue. Half of him wanted Barbara to succeed and the other half of him wanted her to fail, which would give him the time to place *his* plan into action. Alexander needed a victory in his daily power struggle with his mother. If Barbara won, that would mean that he had lost.

Maureen felt pretty in the tea-length black silk skirt and white angora sweater with rhinestone appliqués she wore. She stood next to the blazing fire trying to warm herself. The heater in Alexander's Jaguar hadn't been working, and it was unseasonably cold for Texas.

Shane entered the living room with her usual theatrical flourish. She was wearing a pair of blue jeans with holes in the knees, black-and-white Converse high tops, with brilliantly striped socks she'd pulled up to her knees. Her thin wool cardigan sweater, complete with a detachable Peter Pan collar, was from around 1955. Her hair looked like a teased blonde sunburst. She wore four shades of pink eye shadow on her lids and had glued rhinestones to her cheeks and along her eyebrows. She glanced from Maureen to Alexander. She did not offer a greeting.

"Where's Mother?" she demanded.

"I see you decided to dress conservatively for dinner," Alex said. "Aren't you going to say hello to our guest?"

"Hi," she muttered. "Where's Mother?"

"Right behind you," Barbara said as she glided past her daughter. Barbara was handsomely dressed as always, wearing a Bill Blass hostess gown. For the first time Maureen was struck by the physical resemblance between Shane and Barbara. Shane was a cookie cutter version of her mother. Maureen wondered if the tension between them was Shane's jealousy toward her mother or fear on Barbara's part over growing old. Something, however, told Maureen that Barbara feared nothing and was jealous of no one.

"What did you want, Shane?" Barbara asked politely as she sat on the antique Hepplewhite sofa.

"Nothing. I just wondered where you were."

Alexander scowled at his sister, but he was glad to see that Shane was apparently drug free today. He hoped there wouldn't be any heavy scenes. Although now that Shane had an audience in Maureen, he wouldn't breathe freely until dinner was over.

"I'm delighted you could join us today, Maureen," Barbara said.

"Thank you for inviting me. It would have been a difficult day for me . . . my first Thanksgiving alone."

Shane sat on the sofa opposite her mother. She fidgeted constantly, gulped her drink and took a handful of black olives as if they were peanuts. She listened intently as Maureen talked about her relationship with her uncle. The more Maureen spoke of the affection Mac had had for her, the more Shane came to realize she *hated* Maureen. Shane couldn't understand what there was about the too-tall, thin, black-haired girl that was so damn lovable. What did Maureen have that she didn't have? Shane never had anyone treat her like that. She didn't have any uncles—she looked at Alexander—or brothers that loved her. All she had was Barbara—her nemesis. And that was another thing. How come Barbara wasn't mad as hell at her? She'd spent two hours putting this ridiculous outfit and makeup together and the old witch barely batted an eye. She must be losing her touch. She was going to have to find something else to annoy her mother, something else to get a rise out of her. For Shane knew that as long as Barbara was angry with her, it meant her mother still cared.

Barbara listened to Maureen, but just as Maureen was deep into her favorite anecdote about her uncle, Barbara rose and cut her off by saying "Shall we go in to dinner?'''

Maureen was stunned at Barbara's lack of good manners, but equally, she was amazed at how quickly Alexander took both their drinks and put them on the coffee table and walked her into the dining room. No one, not even the rebellious Shane, balked. It was a strange bond of power and struggle that adhered one Cottrell to the other. And Maureen didn't understand it one bit.

Over the traditional American Thanksgiving feast, Barbara's manner was easy, nearly familiar. There was nothing of the cold, restrained woman Maureen had met at the barbecue almost two months ago. Something had changed her attitude. Maureen guessed it was Alexander's growing attachment to her that had much to do with it. And yet, as she glanced from one to the other, seeing an almost imperceptible taut edge of unrest between them, she realized that nothing had changed at all.

Barbara's invitation carried motives Maureen could only guess at.

Shane was unusually quiet during the meal, and Maureen saw none of the open hostility she'd displayed at the barbecue or upon their first meeting today. She wondered if this passivity was the real Shane or if she was simply acting. More important, she wondered if Shane knew the difference.

The maid had just poured the coffee and was offering a silver tray filled with antique dishes of whipped cream, chocolate shavings, lemon peels and cinnamon dust, when Shane stood abruptly.

"May I be excused now?" she asked in a childishly high voice.

"We aren't quite finished," Barbara said icily.

"I've done as you asked and stuck around for your holiday party. Can I go now?"

To avoid a scene, Barbara acquiesced. "Yes."

Shane stopped at the doorway, pivoted and looked back at Maureen. She didn't like her, but only because she could tell that Maureen was a lot of the things she was not. She didn't like the way Maureen made her feel inferior. And yet, she pitied her. Shane knew more about her mother's and Alexander's methods than they thought she did. Shane wasn't the smartest girl on earth, but she wasn't stupid, either. At that moment, as she looked at Maureen, she saw a victim entangled in a well-constructed web that offered no freedom, no choices. Shane had firsthand knowledge about the Cottrell web. She'd been trying to escape it all her life.

The trio finished their coffee in near silence. When Barbara rose, Alexander and Maureen followed.

"I thought perhaps you might enjoy a tour of my ranch, Maureen," Barbara said. Then she chuckled lightly. "Not the acreage, of course. I thought you might like to view the essence of Devil's Backbone."

"I'd love it." Maureen looked to Alexander, who nodded eagerly.

They donned coats and drove in an enclosed Jeep down the paved road behind the house to two metal buildings that sat to the left of the road. To the right were four barns. They entered the blue-and-white metal building first.

Maureen thought she'd stumbled into something from *2001: A Space Odyssey* rather than a cattle barn. Along the right wall, instead of stalls, were glassed-in research rooms. There were three technicians dressed in protective clothing. Obviously, holidays were unimportant to them, or maybe to their employer. In a center section were huge stainless steel drums that looked like giant pressure cookers. On the left were long stainless steel cabinets and more rows of the round drums. Maureen counted twenty-five drums in all.

Maureen could tell that Barbara was in her element. She strutted with a masculine, authoritative gait rather than her elegant glide. Her voice was stripped of any cordiality. She was strictly business.

"This is the heartbeat of my ranch, Maureen. You are

witnessing the zenith of cattle breeding. I have purchased the finest bulls from all over the world . . . South Africa, the Brahman from India for its durability in hot climates and its resistance to disease; the Friesian dairy cows from Britain, which produce ninety percent of all the milk in England. I also have imported the Normandy breed from France.''

She walked over to one of the steel drums. ''In here we store the straws of semen from the breeder bulls in liquid nitrogen. Each straw contains one milliliter of semen. Depending upon the bull and the breed, a straw can sell for as little as eight dollars or as much as a hundred. Possibly more.''

''How long can the semen be frozen?''

''Years. I had a prize Santa Gertrudis I paid over two hundred thousand for six years ago. He died two years ago. But I'm working on a deal now for his semen that will net me fifty thousand more than I paid for him in the first place.''

''Who do you sell the semen to?''

''Australians have had to import all their cattle. They are a large market. India uses only one percent of all the semen produced in the world. They aren't technically ready for artificial insemination, but there is a ground swell going on that, fortunately, I've been quite instrumental in creating. I'm one of their main suppliers. I expect that ten years from now India will be a good source of revenue for many American breeders. Israel and Finland put almost ninety percent of their cows to artificial insemination. It's the wave of the future. There is no room for archaic practices anymore,'' Barbara said pointedly.

Maureen did not miss the inference. ''What's in the next building?'' she asked, hoping to chase away the vibrations of intimidation Barbara was laying.

''That's Mother's pride and joy,'' Alexander said proudly.

''And this isn't?'' Maureen murmured as they left.

The next building was outfitted with offices. There was only one man on duty here. He wore corduroy pants and a flannel shirt. No protective clothing for him. As they walked further into the interior, Maureen felt as if she'd entered an IBM showroom. There must have been twenty-five computers, along with computerized scales, sensor devices, electronic disease detectors and even a computerized climate control for the barns across the road.

"Everything on this ranch is computerized," Barbara explained. "I not only know when each cow is going into heat but also their weight, carcass composition and body temperature by using electronic sensors. In the next few years we'll make great strides with this sensing technology. My computers also tell me how much grain to buy according to the foliage on the pastures they grazed that week. I can judge the development of calves during each month of gestation—"

"Just like ultrasound for humans?"

"Yes."

"This is truly incredible," Maureen said appreciatively. "But is it necessary?"

Barbara raised an imperious eyebrow. "Your ignorance is greater than I had imagined. Of course it is. We live in a technological world. The kind of ranch your uncle ran was outdated at the turn of the century. Perhaps he confused himself with the cowboy legends of the Old West."

Maureen was quick to discern Barbara's gambit. Her voice was even more stern than Barbara's. "I think you've been cooped up with your livestock too long, Mrs. Cottrell. Instead of buying all this fancy equipment, maybe you should have invested in a few books about human psychology. You would have learned that not everyone is as pliable as your . . ." She looked at Alexander and realized that she must not let her anger take charge. She must be careful not to hurt his feelings. ". . . as you might imagine. I don't care what you thought of my uncle or what you think of me. But I will tell you that you can't intimidate me. I am very well aware of the odds I face in running my ranch. But I should at least be given the chance to *try*."

"You misunderstand me," Barbara said calmly. "I only wanted to help you—show you what a tough time you're going to have and spare you that misery."

"I don't need 'sparing.' "

Barbara's eyes were inflexible. "For thirty years I've had to kowtow to men who had half my intelligence. I had to make business deals with men who weren't good enough to spit on. I've faced ridicule, injustice and prejudice every step of the way. I was the first woman in Texas to become an international breeder. I was the first woman to sit at the auctions in New Delhi and outbid other breeders—men—from Texas. I've been blackballed, slandered and sued. If I refused to go to bed with a man to make a sale, I was not only shunned by him but by his wife, too. I'm sure there are more women in Texas who hate me than men. I've tried to keep my principles high and my morals intact, and it hasn't been easy. There's always been some good ole' boy waiting to topple Devil's Backbone. I've won the game so far, Miss McDonald, because I've *had* to.''

"I sympathize with you. I don't know a woman who wouldn't. But just because I won't sell my land to you doesn't mean I'm not doing the smart thing. I have reasons of my own for wanting to stay here, Mrs. Cottrell. I intend to win this fight—just like you did. I have to. And if nothing else comes of today, at least you'll know that even the strongest woman in Texas couldn't make me back down.''

Maureen turned on her heel and headed for the house before she said anything more. She didn't want Barbara Cottrell for an enemy—she only wanted her to understand.

Alexander sped down the two-lane country road that led to Maureen's ranch. He kept his eyes on the road and his mouth shut. Maureen hadn't spoken a word, and he knew that now was not the time for casual conversation.

"I'll have the heater fixed next week." He smiled at her as they drove up to her door, but she kept her eyes glued on the dashboard. "It *is* the cold weather that's keeping your lip buttoned up, isn't it?''

Slowly she turned to him. "You and your mother think I'm a fool, don't you?''

"No, I don't. I *do* think you're trying to do too much by yourself. I won't deny that I'd like to be the one to help.''

"Did you help set up that little show-and-tell display today?''

Alexander dropped the smile and the convivial tone in his voice. "No. I did not. That was all Mother's doing.''

"Well, you can tell her for me that she went digging in the wrong quarry this time. I'm not used to being told I'm inadequate, Alex. It grates on my ears whether it's candy coated out of your mouth or whether it comes from her—''

"Hey! Don't get me confused with *her*. . . .''

"Right now I don't know who to believe. All I know is I'm pissed at both of you." She threw off the lap blanket he'd provided for her.

"Maureen, wait. . . . I don't want us to be like this . . .''

She opened the door. "Leave me alone, Alex. I need some time to myself." She got out and closed the door.

Alex started after her, but she was inside the house before he'd even gotten out of the car. He slid back into the seat and started the engine. Maybe it was best he let her cool off.

"Damn!" He rammed his fist against the leather-wrapped steering wheel. Barbara had really botched things this time. If there had been any chance to talk Maureen into selling, it was gone now. Knowing Maureen as he did, she would stay on the ranch just to prove Barbara Cottrell wrong.

Alexander was going to have to devise a new strategy for dealing with Maureen. But he knew he'd come up with something. There were many ways to skin a cat, he thought. Many, many ways.

As he thought about Maureen, his foot pressed harder on the accelerator. For months now he'd told himself she was just another woman. She was no different, no better. But each time he saw her or talked to her on the telephone, he realized she was becoming increasingly important to him. Maureen, both the woman of reality and the woman of his fantasies, was occupying a great deal of his time. Since the day she'd arrived back in Kerrville, he dreamed about her every night. His dreams were highly sexual, and he'd awaken with a throbbing erection. Alexander didn't know how much longer he could go on playing the "nice guy" role. He wanted Maureen badly.

But Alexander was no fool. If he pushed himself on her, he would jeopardize his chances of winning her total trust. He had learned many lessons from his mother, and one was how to manipulate people. He wanted Maureen, but he also wanted her as his wife; then he would also have her ranch. Alexander wanted it all.

He clutched the wheel and made a quick left-hand turn and headed toward Kerrville. He jammed his foot against the accelerator and watched the speedometer jump to ninety-five. He loved racing his Jag on these quiet country roads. He felt the adrenaline fill his body as he thought of Maureen.

He envisioned himself peeling off her clothes at an achingly slow pace. He knew her body would be perfect in every way. The palms of his hands began to sweat as he gripped the leather steering wheel. She would want him as much as he wanted her, he knew. He could almost feel her long black

hair as it fell over his chest when she kissed him—deeply—
again and again.

Alexander moaned aloud. He felt his erection get stronger.
There was only one place to go when he felt like this . . . to
Jennie Sloan.

17

◆

JENNIE STOOD in the huge master bedroom of her three-bedroom apartment checking her tan in the wall of mirrors that surrounded the room. She'd just purchased a tanning bed and put it in the same room with her Nautilus weight machine, slant board and Lifecycle. The salesman had been right. For the first time in her life, she'd gotten a perfect tan . . . all over. She'd been worried about her breasts burning, but she'd used the thin, blue lotion he'd supplied and it had worked. She was overjoyed.

She walked over to one of the mirrored walls and pressed her hand against it. A door-sized section popped open to reveal floor-to-ceiling shelving containing fabulously expensive lingerie in every color of the rainbow. Each color section contained bras, panties, slips, nightgowns, teddies, peignoirs, satin mules with rhinestones or ostrich feathers, Moroccan slippers or simple silk slides. There were garter belts, hose, lace bed jackets and hair ribbons all to match. The labels were impressive: Odette Barsa, Christian Dior, Georgio Armani, Calvin Klein, Yves St. Laurent. Most of them came from La Lingerie in Dallas. Some were by unknown designers, and frankly, Jennie thought they were the most well made and the most lavish.

Jennie draped a short nightgown of apricot and deep cream lace over her perfect body. She looked at herself again in the mirror. She liked the way the lace let her nipples show through and she liked the deep cut that allowed her breasts to billow over the edge of the gown. She smiled.

"And they didn't cost a penny." She laughed to herself, thinking of Shane Cottrell's expensive boob job. She slipped on a pair of French mules to match. She twirled in front of the mirror. She liked the way the gown barely skimmed the top of her buttocks, letting all of her fabulous legs show. Jennie was tall, too. Another bonus God had given her. Another cause for Shane to envy her.

Jennie Sloan and Shane Cottrell had gone to kindergarten together, but that had been the end of it. Shane had been sent off to one boarding school after another. They'd seen little of each other after that, except during summers, at the movies, or parties, or summer dances at the high school when mutual friends would bring them together. Jennie hated Shane and Shane hated Jennie. Jennie had all the natural beauty one woman could contain without blowing up. She had a head full of wavy, coppery auburn hair that grew over an inch a month. Her skin was not like that of most redheads, but was smooth, even and flawless. It tanned perfectly. Her eyes were such a brilliant blue she'd often been accused of wearing colored contacts. She was five-foot-nine, and weighed in at a hundred and twenty-five pounds. She was only sixteen percent body fat. And what little fat her body contained was in her breasts. There was many a Texas man who would swear in a court of law that Jennie's body was more perfectly proportioned than Cheryl Tiegs's the year she did the fishnet swimsuit cover for *Sports Illustrated*.

Jennie could have been on every cover of *Cosmopolitan* since the age of fourteen—if she'd had the money to get to New York. But Jennie didn't.

Jennie had been born poor. She had never met her father; in fact, she wondered if her mother even knew who her father was. Jennie's mother had been only sixteen when Jennie was born. She'd dropped out of high school to have Jennie. She started waiting tables at the Denny's in town, and she was still there. Jennie had always wished her mother had put her up for adoption. Then she might have had a chance at a better life. She'd wanted to go to college and have a career as a model. But it had taken her too long to figure out a way out of Kerrville. Now, at twenty-five, it was too late.

Perhaps it had all worked out for the best. Look at Shane Cottrell. Shane had broken out of the house and gone off to California, and look what happened to her. But then, Shane was stupid. Jennie was smart.

Jennie pressed against another section of mirror and was presented with rows of velvet-lined drawers, each with a combination lock. She twirled a lock back and forth, then pulled out the drawer. She took out a four-carat emerald ring surrounded by diamonds. She put it on her right hand. It was the ring Alexander gave her last Christmas. In the drawer next to it was the ruby ring Burt Bean had given her the same holiday season.

Jennie was a "professional girlfriend." She was a vital part of "the good old boy system" that many Texas men revered. Texas men had always been known to lavish their money on their homes, their wives and their mistresses. It took a lot of money to keep it all going and to placate everyone. Jennie, like other professional girlfriends, and even some of the wives, kept her mouth shut and continued to manipulate the foolish, egocentric males. As long as these men believed that spending ridiculous amounts of money on women was a sign of masculinity, a display of power, Jennie, and those like her, would reap incredible rewards.

Jennie liked being a professional girlfriend. She had stature, for she was a cog in the wheel of a "system" that dated back a hundred years. She was a step above a call girl. Although, if anyone called her that, she wouldn't mind. She didn't like "hooker" or "prostitute" only because such women didn't charge enough.

Jennie was more than expensive; her price was astronomical. And therein resided her allure. Jennie was beautiful, and it cost money to buy beauty. She had many men fighting over her, but she'd learned at a young age never, never to sell herself too cheaply. She would never make the same mistake her mother did.

Jennie had a small fortune stashed away already. She owned over a dozen fur coats, each from a different man. She had half a million dollars in jewels alone, but lately Jennie had a new obsession—real estate.

Jennie couldn't buy enough of it fast enough. She owned the condo she lived in. Her Mercedes had been a gift, but she'd used it as collateral for a small down payment she'd needed for duplexes she was buying on the outskirts of town and that she rented out to Mexicans. In the past year she'd bought twenty of these duplexes. Jennie was a slumlord. And she loved it. She hired the best accountant in Dallas to guide her. She bought a small strip shopping center in Fort Worth, and the rents from her five tenants paid her basic living expenses. Her clothes, jewels and trips were always paid for by men. She paid little in taxes every year because she had only her rent income. Jennie worked hard, but not at anything that was reported to the IRS.

Jennie liked working with her accountant. She thought it a fascinating field. Someday she intended to go to college and get a degree in finance and accounting. Jennie had learned to love the power that her beauty gave her. But like the demi-mondes of the Belle Epoch in France, when her beauty faded—and it would—so would the men. When that time came she would be prepared.

Jennie knew that owning her own company, perhaps a brokerage house or CPA firm, would give her a measure of control. But there were other paths to power. Jennie had been travelling them for years.

Jennie was also a drug dealer. Her client list was small, but it contained wealthy men who "used" heavily and also believed in providing their guests with all the pleasures their money could afford. At the top of her list was Burt Bean. Jennie felt enormous satisfaction at knowing that through Burt she was supplying Shane Cottrell. Jennie had always dreamed of a time when she and Shane would be on the same level. Now they were.

Cocaine could strip anyone of their wealth, their social standing, their mind, their soul. Jennie knew Shane couldn't make it through a day without a hit. Jennie liked the power she had over Shane.

Jennie only wished she had the kind of power that her suppliers had. They were the real giants. She didn't know who they were, what their real names were or where they were from. She had a telephone number she called in Houston so she could talk to one of the higher-ups called the "vice-president." She had only met two "lieutenants" face-to-face. She thought it was funny the way they had code names. She didn't really care. She was just thankful they had found her and allowed her to become part of their organization. As always, she invested her profits wisely.

Jennie closed the mirrored doors, went to her Louis XIV dressing table, doused herself with hundred-dollar-an-ounce Chanel 19 perfume and waited.

As if on cue, the doorbell rang. She walked to the door, past the white kid Roche Bobois sofa, the thirty-thousand-dollar Lalique tulip coffee table and the sheer white silk draperies. She wet her lips, fluffed her hair and tugged at her nightgown so that even more of her breasts showed.

"Alexander," she said seductively. "I knew it would be you."

"How could you?" he said, feeling his heart race as he looked through the sheer fabric at Jennie's body.

"I'm psychic."

"Then you'll know I can't wait," he moaned as he kicked the door shut and grabbed her.

He ravaged her with hungry, impatient kisses. He bit her earlobe and flicked his tongue over her satin-smooth neck. His hands eagerly roamed her body, squeezing her buttocks, grasping her, kneading her breasts. "Take this off!" he commanded as he fought the layers of expensive lace.

They tumbled to the floor, Jennie's head making a "thunk" on the wool carpeting. Alexander stripped off his clothes in such haste he popped two buttons on his Brooks Brothers' white shirt. He flung his pants angrily over a turquoise-and-pink enameled jardiniere. Just as he plunged himself into Jennie, he looked into her eyes. But the woman he saw was Maureen.

Fury and passion battled within him. He sought only his own pleasure, his own release. He clenched his teeth as the muscles in his buttocks tightened with his penetrations. He broke out in a sweat. He didn't hear the sound of his own voice as he burst with his climax. He collapsed on top of Jennie.

Jennie pushed him off her. "Next time you're mad at that bitch, don't come here!"

"What are you talking about?" he asked breathlessly. He felt as if he'd run ten miles.

Jennie stood, still in her high-heeled mules, her magnificent body gleaming with his sweat. Her eyes glared at him as she looked down on him. "You called out her name. Maureen."

"I didn't."

"I don't give a shit whose name you use. Just don't be so goddamn rough! I don't need you, Alex, baby. Let's get that straight."

He looked at her. She *didn't* need him. Jennie chose her men. Everybody knew it. "I'm sorry." He reached for his pants and pulled them on. He went to the bar, poured himself a tall scotch and flopped on the sofa.

"She's really gotten to you, hasn't she?"

"Yeah."

"So what's the big deal? Marry her. It won't change anything between us."

"It's not that simple. She knows I want to buy her ranch. I have to be very careful with her. I don't want her to think I'd marry her for her land."

"But you would."

"Yes. No. Yes."

Jennie smiled coyly and eased herself next to him. She made certain her breasts touched his arm. "So little Alex has finally fallen in love. Is that it?"

"Oh, I want her. I want her so bad I can taste it." He slugged his drink down. "God. It would all be so perfect. I'd finally have that land. Mother would come crawling to me—begging *me* to run the ranches for her. You don't know how I dream about that."

"Then quit dreaming and *do* something about it."

Alexander stared into his drink despondently. He sighed. "I'd give anything to finally be one up on Mother. I know what it's like to see that look of respect in her eyes. I saw it once—the night of the barbecue. It was just a flicker, but I never felt as good as I did then."

"You can do it, Alex. I know you can."

"I'm trying. If I can get Maureen to give up on this stupid idea she has of running the ranch by herself, then I have a chance." He turned to Jennie's earnest face. She was truly on his side. That's what he liked about her. That and the fact that she kept her mouth shut. He could confide in Jennie. She was a good friend. She was the *only* friend he had. "I'm paying Wes Reynolds to be a little less careful with her animals and her money. Once she realizes she's in over her head, maybe she'll be more willing to listen to a marriage proposal."

"Hmmm." Jennie wasn't so sure his idea was strong enough to produce the results he wanted. "Maybe you shouldn't be trying to do this alone."

"What do you mean?"

"You need more muscle. You know, I'd like to see you get the best of your mother. That old bitch has had it coming for a long time. I've got a score to settle with her myself."

He touched her chin playfully. "Yeah, she never liked you. White trash—that's what she called you."

Jennie's eyes narrowed. "Snooty bitch. Her kind needs to be brought down a peg or two. I've got some friends who just might be willing to help you. *If* you're interested."

Alexander considered her offer. He had a pretty good idea who Jennie was talking about. For the first time in his life, he was very close to a victory over his mother. But he hadn't been able to make things happen on his own. He was at a standstill and he didn't like it. He had to move forward, and maybe this was the way to do it. Maureen, the ranch, besting Barbara could all be his. He would bargain with the Devil himself to get what he wanted. Alexander *had* to gain self-respect. If he didn't, he was doomed.

"I'm interested."

18

◆

BRANDON WILLIAMS SAT at the head of a beveled-glass conference table atop his glittering tower of steel and glass known as the First Bank and Trust of Dallas. Brandon owned not only the skyscraper in which the bank resided but four branch banks as well. It was a fact that gave him little comfort.

Since 1982 Brandon had seen a softening in the Texas economy due to the inflation-fueled double-digit interest rates and sky-high drilling costs. Since June of that year, Brandon had systematically begun to sell off his liabilities and some of his assets. Wisely, he'd realized that even in the best of times he had more than he could handle.

Brandon's empire brought revenues from oil, gas, ranching and banking. He was grossing over a billion dollars a year, and his personal fortune was nearing four hundred million dollars. It was time to get out. Because he was nearly five hundred million in debt, he cut back drastically. He sold over half his oil production and slashed the work force from a thousand to two hundred. He shut down a pipe supply company; shucked almost two and a half million acres of ranch land he'd acquired all over the state and in Wyoming. He sold twelve hundred head of Brangus cattle at auction for nearly six million dollars. He kept his bank, his personal ranch and just enough oil wells to start up again when times looked better to him. Today he signed the papers ridding himself of his Lear jet, a Porsche, a town house in Houston and the last of his oil leases.

Brandon had diversified his interests in the past month with the purchase of a telecommunications company that would link most major Texas cities. He expected the company's revenues to be in the red for only a year or less, and after that, he projected by the end of 1988 to reach a gross of seventy million.

Brandon listened attentively to the last of his bank board members as they gave their reports.

"If that's all, gentlemen," he said as they nodded in unison, "I have a plane to catch."

Everyone filed out of the room except Ed Pierce, the executive vice-president and Brandon's right arm.

"Why don't you stay in Dallas and spend Christmas with Loretta and myself? The kids would love it."

Brandon smiled. "I suppose Loretta has someone she wants me to meet."

"Well, you know Loretta. She doesn't think anyone should be alone for Christmas."

"I won't be."

"Oh?" Ed paused and looked at Brandon. "Anyone I know?"

"No."

"Come on. Don't be so tight-lipped about all this. Must be someone special—you always keep to yourself at holidays."

"She is special. Only she doesn't know it yet."

"What?" Ed's face contorted in confusion.

"Never mind. It would take too long to explain."

"Okay." Ed shrugged his shoulders. "Did you want to take any of these files with you?"

"Yes. I want to look over some of these applications we've got. Now remember—I don't want any major loans granted to any oil companies for six months. Just hang tight for a while. I want your personal assurance you've scrutinized everything on these apps."

"You know I have."

"We can't be too careful."

Ed shook his head. "You really think something's going to happen, don't you?"

"I do. All the signs are there. I'd be a fool if I didn't pay attention to them. We're headed for a fall—and a big one."

"But Texas has never had a depression."

"*That* is the kind of thinking that gets people into trouble. Overconfidence will kill you every time."

"Okay. You're the boss."

Brandon left the building and got into his black Lincoln limousine. He'd had two offers on it this week. He'd have to find a job for Skip, his driver. The only part about cutting back that Brandon disliked was laying off his employees. But it couldn't be helped, although when possible he'd found them all other jobs.

Since the day Brandon had flown Maureen McDonald to Austin, he'd kept himself on a whirlwind of business meetings. He'd been to Saudi Arabia twice, Mexico three times and had hopscotched across Texas every week. But no matter how hard he worked, he couldn't get her out of his mind. Every time he called the house and asked Shirley for his messages he hoped there would be something from Maureen. There never was.

It was time he took matters into his own hands. Brandon sent her a Christmas card and followed it up with a formal invitation to a Christmas party on the twenty-third. As soon as he got to Kerrville, he would call her and make certain she planned to attend. He would not tell her the guest list was small . . . very small. Other than Charleen Sims, Lynn and Burt Bean, Shirley and the kids, he'd invited no one else—except Maureen.

Brandon hadn't given a party in years. And he'd found to his delight that the preparations had been fun. He'd bought toys for Lynn's children and Shirley's girls. He'd bought enormous holiday food baskets and Godiva chocolate Santa Clauses for everyone. He'd even hired a Santa Claus to distribute the gifts. Shirley had attended to all the arrangements for the dinner and decorations. Except for the tree. He would buy it and decorate it himself.

Brandon had great plans for this Christmas. He only hoped they worked.

Maureen crouched down and ran a soothing hand over the cow's head.

"What do you think, Wes?"

"It's a breech birth. It's gonna be tough."

"But Doc Silver has left for California."

"We gotta have a vet, Miz McDonald. This heifer is in a lot of pain. You could call the vet over to the Cottrells'. Mr. Cottrell would be glad to help."

"I know he would," Maureen said. *But Barbara wouldn't*

lift a finger to help. Maureen envisioned a laughing Barbara in her mind. Maureen couldn't live with herself if she went running to her. Submission was not in Maureen's vocabulary. "But we're not going to ask him."

"Why not?" Wes was dumbfounded.

"Because I'm going to ask someone else."

Maureen left Wes with the moaning cow and went back to the house. She didn't tell Wes that the real reason she didn't want to call Alexander was because she wanted to see Brandon.

For weeks as she worked the ranch, fed cows, painted walls, inspected pastures and juggled her accounting books, she tried to make herself not think about Brandon. She told herself the same things she'd told Bitzy in New York . . . that he was arrogant, he was conceited—but she'd been foiled in her own fencing match. Brandon invaded her waking thoughts and her dreams. He was everywhere. And then she found that she *liked* keeping him in her thoughts. But as the days went on, fantasies were not enough.

She kept remembering Bitzy's warning that Alexander was simply safe and that she was afraid of Brandon. Once she'd accepted that observation as fact, Maureen decided to face the problem dead-on. However, she had no reason to call Brandon. She didn't want to appear forward, especially since their last encounter had not ended on the best of notes. Too, she'd heard from Charleen that Brandon had been out of the country for almost six weeks. He'd been anywhere but at the ranch. Maureen blessed the day she'd met Charleen. There wasn't much news that escaped her.

Today was the first time Maureen had a good reason to call Brandon. She wanted to see him and she hoped he would want to see her. She picked up the telephone and dialed the numbers quickly, before she lost her nerve. She felt like a schoolgirl calling a boy for the first time. It was silly. But it was true.

The phone was answered on the third ring.

"This is Maureen McDonald. Is Mr. Williams in?"

"I expect him around seven this evening. He's in Dallas today at his bank. You could reach him there."

Maureen wondered why he would have to go all the way to Dallas to do his banking. But then, Brandon probably had more to worry about than deposits and withdrawals like she did. "Would you ask him to call me when he gets in?"

"I surely will," Shirley answered, and hung up the phone.

Disappointed, Maureen went back to the cow barn. As she slid back the old, warped, wooden door, she thought of all the equipment the Cottrells had. She remembered Barbara's warnings on Thanksgiving. Then she heard the painful moan of her best cow. She couldn't afford to lose this cow or her calf. She'd been mated with the best bull on the ranch. It was imperative to Maureen that the herd grow. She wanted to show everyone, including herself, that she could be just as good a rancher as anyone else. She wanted to make the McDonald name important. She wanted to make Mac proud. "It's not fair," she mumbled to herself as she joined Wes in their already five-hour-long vigil.

Brandon arrived at his ranch forty minutes ahead of schedule. Shirley was all smiles as he walked in.

"How did it go?' she asked.

"Good," he said in his usual terse manner. He didn't need to tell Shirley the details because she'd see them next week when the papers were sent to her for his final signature. Shirley knew *everything* about his life. "Any messages?"

"Only one that matters," she said, and handed him a stack of pink message slips. The one from Maureen was on top.

"When did she call?"

"Around five. Do you want me to get her on the phone for you?"

"No. I'll do it."

"I figured you would."

Brandon had started for the study, then stopped short. "What do you know about it?"

"I work here, remember? It doesn't take a genius to know what's going on in your head. Ever since you met Miss McDonald you've been whacko, as my Billie would say."

"I am not."

"Yeah? Did you know you doodle her name on your telephone pad? You must have asked me a hundred times if there'd been any calls from her. Or mail."

"I never mentioned her name."

"See what I mean? You men think you're so cagey. You're all transparent as glass. I knew who you meant. I know what you did for her up in Austin. You're a pretty classy guy, Mr. W."

"Thanks," he said, and went in to make his call.

* * *

Maureen waited anxiously for Brandon to arrive with his veterinarian. She tapped her unpainted nails on the steering wheel of the old rusty pickup. She should have gotten a manicure. She checked herself in the mirror. And put on some makeup. Changed clothes. She smelled like cows.

It was too late now, she thought, as Brandon's helicopter landed. After all this time, she was still amazed at how fast these people came and went from each other's houses. They all owned high-performance cars that ate up miles of highway in minutes, helicopters that brought ranches within seconds of each other and prop planes that kept huge cities available morning, noon and night. Whatever one's whim or fancy, they could have it all.

Tonight she was glad it was this way, because she needed this friend and his vet.

Brandon emerged from the helicopter with a young, light-haired man who carried a medical bag. They rushed over to her. She got out and shook hands.

"Maureen, this is Joe English. He's a good man."

"I'm so glad you're here, Joe. She's very weak and there's no sign of the calf."

Joe smiled, revealing uneven teeth that were blindingly white. His dark eyes were leveled on hers, and she got the feeling that he was a man to be trusted.

"Let's get to it," Joe said.

Maureen drove them back to the barn, and Joe dashed out of the truck and went straight to the cow. Wes stepped aside and allowed the doctor to do his ministering.

Joe conducted his examination. "She hasn't dilated much, but I'll have to turn the calf. We've got a long night ahead of us. Have you got any coffee? I could sure use some."

"What about supper? Have you had anything to eat?"

"That would be real nice," Joe said.

"How about you?" She turned to Brandon.

"I'd love it."

Maureen felt unsteady, suddenly wondering if she had been wise to call on Brandon. "It's the least I can do for you for helping me. I guess I'm getting into a bad habit . . . always asking you for something."

"I don't mind," he said, stepping closer to her, allowing his eyes to bore into hers.

"You should. I could be taking advantage of your good nature."

"It's okay. . . ." He started to lift his hand . . . he had an overwhelming desire to touch her hair. He stopped himself. "Should I come with you?"

"Huh?"

"To the house. I don't think we'll be much help to Joe, do you? I make a great Caesar salad."

"Oh, no. I mean yes. You're absolutely right."

They walked together toward the ranch house. Maureen thought it strange that they weren't holding hands. Somehow it would have seemed more natural.

Maureen entered her newly renovated kitchen first. Juanita was pouring cold water into the Krupps coffee maker. She turned around and smiled broadly.

"*Buenas noches,*" she said to Brandon.

"*Buenas noches,* Juanita," he replied.

Maureen looked from one to the other. "You know each other?"

"Si, for a long time," Juanita said. She wiped her hands on her soiled apron. "I fix supper. You sit."

Maureen motioned for Brandon to sit at the new white pickled-pine table and chairs. "I've just had the kitchen modernized and Juanita likes to show off. The only thing she hasn't mastered is the Cuisinart. For two weeks she thought the Jenn-Air was cursed because there was no smoke when she grilled chicken."

Brandon laughed. "I know all about Juanita's ghost stories. My cook believes that Juanita can predict the future. She's always giving me warnings, but nothing has ever come true."

"She's harmless, really." She looked over at Juanita as she took out a package of okra and defrosted it in the microwave. Maureen was proud of her new kitchen. All of the small appliances had come from her apartment in New York. She'd only had to buy the stove, dishwasher and garbage disposal. She loved the bleached wood floor, the pastel Navajo printed wallpaper and the recessed lighting in the ceiling. There was plenty of counter and cabinet space. It was the prettiest room in the house. And it was the only room that was completed.

Juanita handed them each a cup of coffee, then called the bunkhouse on the new telephone and had Grady take coffee to Wes and Joe.

Brandon watched Maureen as she helped Juanita with the

jambalaya they were preparing. He liked how easily she moved about the room, speaking in broken Spanish to her maid, making the effort to absorb some of Juanita's world into her own. He noticed that every so often she looked over at him, smiled and then carried on with her work. Each time their eyes met, he felt a sudden flash of magnetism drawing him to her. It was as if she were weaving a bond between them. He wondered if she was aware of what she was doing. Brandon had always been an optimist. He hoped he was reading her signals correctly.

"Will you be coming to my Christmas party?" he asked as she set a plate of rice and jambalaya in front of him.

"What party?"

Brandon nearly choked on his food. "I sent you an invitation. You didn't get it?"

"I got a lovely card, but no invitation."

"On the twenty-third . . . I'm having the neighbors in. . . . I can't believe it got lost in the mail. I'm glad I mentioned it."

"So am I." She smiled happily. "It sounds like fun."

Brandon watched her as they ate. They conversed, but he wasn't certain what the topic was, for there was another exchange going on in their heads. Brandon was a firm believer in mental telepathy. He'd used his powers of persuasiveness both in thought and in speech many times to sell an investor on one of his projects. Brandon believed his will was stronger than most people's. He'd seen himself able to sway argumentative, stubborn opponents to his way of thinking hundreds of times. But that was business—this was more important.

Brandon and Maureen went back to the barn and relieved Wes and Joe while they went to the house to eat.

Maureen sat on a soft mound of hay, wishing her cow were not in so much pain.

Brandon looked around at the antiquated barn. It reminded him of a time he'd tried to forget but couldn't. He knew what it was like not to have the money to properly run a ranch, much less adequately care for his animals. But he also remembered how close he had been to his parents. How his mother had worked herself to death for their land, for their ranch. He remembered her pride.

"Why are you doing this?" he asked.

"What?"

"Why aren't you back in New York, carving a path to fame

and fortune? I heard you were pretty good back there. You don't need this . . . scraping for every dime of profit, worrying all night about one cow . . ."

Maureen didn't know whether to hit him or burst into tears. The past months of frustration and setbacks had relieved her of tolerance for anybody or anything. Like strobe lights, the images of Sylvester Craddock, Barbara Cottrell and the agriculture assistant nearly blinded her. Her patience melted.

"Not you too! Somehow I thought that you would be different, but I guess I was wrong!" She bolted to her feet.

Brandon was quicker than Maureen. He grabbed her by the shoulders and peered deeply into her eyes. "I didn't mean to upset you and I'm sorry for the way I phrased my question. I think you're doing a hell of a job and I admire you for it. It takes a lot of courage to do what you're doing. I just wondered if you really knew what you were in for."

Maureen didn't try to wrest herself from his grip. His hands felt more comforting than intimidating, more friend than foe.

"I know I must look like a fool to you. I don't have your money or the proper equipment. And every calf is vital to me. I *care* about my herd. I've got names for almost every one . . . which isn't hard to do since it's a small herd. But they're mine. I want the McDonald Ranch to be *something* someday. I want what Mac wanted. But I also want it for myself. I'm going to make everyone who ever doubted me eat their words." She sighed, feeling suddenly deflated. "I don't know. Maybe I won't make it, maybe the odds *are* against me . . ." This time tears stung her eyes and she couldn't fight them. She looked up at him. She was stunned at what she saw.

It was more than sympathy. It was as if he had pitched himself into the middle of her fight with her. He hadn't said a word, but she *felt* it . . . she *knew* it somehow. She'd never had a sensation like this before. She tried to understand it, but her brain was not programmed for this feeling.

"You'll make it," he said softly. "If you love it, you'll make it."

"I do love it."

"Then never give up. Never give in. Don't let anyone tell you otherwise. Keep your eyes on the future. It's all there for the taking."

"How can you be so sure about me? Even *I'm* not sure."

"I know what I know. If you believe in yourself, it will come to you."

"Don't give up the ship?" She laughed hollowly.

"Something like that. I watched you in Austin, and now here. I wasn't always rich, like you may think. I remember when I didn't have as much as you have. If I can do it, anybody can."

"Even a woman?" she said, testing him.

He laughed, ran his hand down her arm and up again. He liked the way she felt . . . soft, with firm muscles beneath the skin. She *had* been working hard. "Are you kidding? Women are naturally superior to men."

"What?" She was shocked. This coming from a Texan?

"It's a matter of scientific fact. Their chromosomal makeup is better, they are more disease resistant, the skull is more evolutionarily advanced and women are constitutionally stronger than men. Men only have muscular superiority—not very comforting if one happens to be a male."

"Jesus . . . where did you get all that?"

"I've lived on a ranch all my life. Nature tells you plenty if you listen."

"Oh," she said, smiling, noticing that he still kept his hands on her shoulders.

Brandon kissed her. It was a soft, gentle kiss, much like the ones friends exchange upon arrival and departure. He pulled back and let his eyes delve into hers. It was not the kiss but his eyes that rendered her motionless and stripped her of all thoughts but those of him.

"Maureen," he said quietly, in a way she'd never heard her name uttered before. As if it were a prayer.

This time when he kissed her he pulled her body next to his, then clasped his hands around her waist and pressed her closer until she could feel every inch of him from his knees to his shoulders. His lips were possessive, as if marking her, this place, this time for eternity. She felt as if there was no beginning and no end to them. It was as if in her mind they always were and always would be—together.

She felt her arms slide around his neck, though she was not conscious of making the decision to do so. She was suspended on the edge of a tempest that raged only within herself, and yet she felt its power from without.

In those moments, only seconds really, as Brandon claimed Maureen for himself, she felt incredible faith in him, herself and the world. She found herself kissing him back, claiming him as her own. For an instant, she did not consider or discern or dissect the issue. She was *feeling*.

He kissed her cheeks, and eyes, and ears and neck. He held her close and willed her not to speak, not to destroy this moment for him. It was Joe who did that.

Joe burst into the barn exuberantly. "How's it goin'?" he said before he realized what he was seeing. Sheepishly, he hung back a moment for Maureen to regain her composure. He felt like the proverbial uninvited guest.

The cow groaned loudly.

Joe rushed past Brandon and Maureen. "Looks like this is it."

Joe went straight to work, greasing his hands and arms up to his elbows. Brandon went to the head of the cow and held her, while Joe turned the calf. The cow moaned repeatedly, while Maureen winced in empathy.

Maureen named the calf Claudia. She'd always liked that name, but she didn't know why because she'd never known a Claudia. Brandon liked it, too; she could tell from his smile when she said it aloud.

"This is a special calf," Maureen said as they sponged the calf clean.

"It's a special night," Brandon replied and paused for a moment to watch Maureen.

She leaned back on her heels as she knelt by the calf's side, "Very special."

As they looked at each other, they forgot about the calf, or Joe or the cow. At that moment the world consisted only of the two of them.

19

◆

IF A CHRISTMAS WERE TO BE MAGICAL, Maureen thought, snow was required. But then she drove up to Brandon's house the night of his party and her opinion was forever changed. Thousands of tiny clear lights hung on the dozen and a half ancient oaks that lined the curved drive to the house. They had been strung from the top branches straight to the ground so that they resembled icicles. The effect was startling. On the low-growing ligustrums that hugged the huge red-brick house were more lights. They were so many and so brilliant, Maureen could not look directly at them without squinting.

Maureen was greeted at the door by a Mexican butler dressed in formal attire. He took her coat and motioned for her to enter the living room to the left. She had only stepped to the doorway when she saw Brandon already walking toward her.

"I knew it was you," he said, kissing her cheek.

"You did?" she said, seeing only the Beans, Charleen and a woman with two children whom she hadn't met.

"You're the last to arrive," he said.

Maureen was surprised, but happily. Somehow, she should have known he wouldn't throw one of those pretentious affairs like Barbara Cottrell. This was Christmas, after all. She'd always felt the holidays were meant for friends who were almost like family. She was glad to see he felt the same.

Brandon introduced Maureen to Shirley and the girls, Billie and Sammie.

Shirley shook Maureen's hand. "You're even prettier than

I heard. But then, adjectives aren't used much around here. Just the facts and bottom lines, if you know what I mean. The girls have been dying to meet you for weeks."

Maureen was surprised. Obviously, Shirley knew something she didn't. "I'm happy to meet them."

"Do you really have gold on your ranch?" Billie asked. "I heard at school that you did."

"I'm afraid not. My uncle looked for a long time, but he never found any."

"Oh. Too bad. That would have been pretty cool to dig for gold."

Sammie grabbed her sister's arm. "Let's get some more cookies."

They walked away and Shirley followed them.

Just then Lynn and Charleen came over to greet Maureen. Charleen was her usual effervescent self. The holidays seemed to have infused her with even more high spirits—if that was possible, Maureen thought. Except for a couple of chance meetings in Kerrville, Maureen hadn't seen Lynn since the Cottrells' barbecue. Charleen had mentioned that Lynn had been staying close to home the past few weeks. There had been concern in Charleen's tone at the time, but Maureen had so many problems of her own that she'd dismissed it.

Now, as Maureen saw Lynn again, she was struck by the incredible pain in the other woman's eyes. It was more pronounced than the last time, and her mask had begun to slip.

"That's a beautiful dress, Lynn," Maureen said, hoping she could find a way to erase even a fleck of Lynn's sadness.

"Thank you. I got it in Dallas," she said morosely. Then, suddenly, she brightened. "Say! Maybe you'd like to go with Charleen and me for the after-Christmas sales. I get a kick out of digging through those racks. What do you say?"

"I don't think I can take the time."

"Oh," Lynn replied. There was unquestionable despair in her voice. She glanced around the room quickly, her eyes darting in her head like a caged bird when it readies for flight but knows it can go nowhere.

Maureen got the impression that Lynn's emotions were riding recklessly beneath a thin, easily penetrable surface. Maureen felt compelled to help her. "On second thought, maybe I could manage a day or two."

"Really?" Lynn said excitedly. "We'll take our plane. It'll be my treat. I'll get rooms at the Mansion. Don't worry about anything. It'll be so much fun. It'll be fun, won't it, Charleen?''

"Of course. We always have fun, dolly."

This time, when Lynn's eyes scanned the room, Maureen followed her gaze. This time, she saw what Lynn saw.

Burt was on the other side of the room talking to Shirley, who was standing next to the baby grand. Burt casually laid his hand on Shirley's hip and then moved it seductively lower. Shirley was indignant. She stepped back and slung some nasty words at him under her breath. Maureen was able to make out a few of them. Shirley obviously knew how to handle herself in such situations. When Maureen looked back at Lynn, her friend's lips bore a harlequin's stage smile.

For the first time, everything made sense to Maureen. Suddenly, she understood the "code" Charleen and Lynn used. Burt was a womanizer, and Lynn was struggling to maintain her family, her personal dignity.

Charleen had not been oblivious to the drama that had been taking place in the room. She took Lynn's arm protectively. "Let's check out that lovely buffet in the dining room."

"Sure," Lynn said, her anger hissing through her lips. Maureen followed them, wanting to say something, do something to help, but she didn't know what.

Though the buffet was Cajun food, an unusual departure for Christmas fare, Maureen's appetite was not what it should have been. She was genuinely concerned about Lynn's plight. Just as she was about to fill a small gold-rimmed bowl with red beans and rice, Lynn burst into tears. Charleen was first to take matters in tow.

"Come on, dolly, it's okay. You can get through this."

"I want to kill him," Lynn sniffed, and whisked away the tear on her cheek. Her eyes went pleadingly to Maureen. "I didn't want you . . . of all people . . . to know."

"Why not? I want to help."

"Because . . ." Lynn's face broke and crumbled, but quickly she flicked her hair back and forced herself to be calm. "You don't know how much I envy you . . . your independence. You can come and go as you please. You can do anything with your life you want. I know you're struggling with your ranch . . . but do you know how wonderful your life seems to me?"

"Then get rid of Burt and don't put yourself through all this."

"It's not that simple."

Maureen was astounded. "Divorce is even easier than getting married these days. This man is making you miserable. I wouldn't stand for any of his crap. You shouldn't either. You're better than this, Lynn. You deserve so much more."

Lynn tried to smile. She couldn't. "I *am* worth a whole lot more than this. But I have to think about my kids."

Maureen glanced into the living room and saw Brian and Stephanie playing with a video game under the Christmas tree. "They seem very well adjusted to me. I don't think a divorce will be as tough on them as you think."

"That's not what I'm talking about. I couldn't go on living if I couldn't see my kids every day."

"Why shouldn't you see them? You're their mother. You'd have custody."

Lynn's eyebrows rose to a cynical peak. "Ah, that's not the way it works here. Burt would get custody. He would make it so that I would never see them again."

"That's ridiculous! You're a very good mother. Even a blind man could see that. No judge in this world would give Burt custody."

"That's where you're wrong. This isn't 'the world.' This is Texas. This is Burt Bean's Texas, where he can buy any judge he wants. And the judge makes the rules to suit Burt Bean."

Maureen was in shock. "He would *ransom* your own children?"

"You got it."

"My God! How long has this been going on?"

"Fifteen years. Burt has the kind of money that can buy him anything he wants. He has professional girlfriends in three cities I know of. He used to keep Jennie Sloan, but she has a new sugar daddy now. I heard it was Alexander Cottrell." Suddenly, Lynn remembered how close Maureen had seemed to Alexander. She'd heard about their lunches in Dallas and dinners in town. She bit her lip. "I can't be sure, of course. I didn't have him followed."

"This is just unbelievable!" Maureen looked to Charleen. "Are all the men like this?" She was now thinking of Brandon.

"No, of course not," Charleen assured her, knowing what and who was on Maureen's mind. "Charles wasn't like that at all. I would have known. A wife always knows. But, unfortunately, there are too many like Lynn who married young not knowing about this double standard—and now, they're caught.''

"All I know is . . . if it were me, I'd find a way to get out. I don't know how, but I'd get me and the kids and get the hell out.''

"Yeah?'' Lynn's bitterness rattled in her breath. "When you think of the way, you let me know.''

Maureen's eyes were steady. "I will, Lynn.''

Brandon went over to Burt, who was plunking out a carol on the keys of the baby grand.

Burt picked up his straight scotch and belted it down. He saw Lynn going into the dining room with Charleen and Maureen. "Nice party, Brandon.''

"Glad you're having a good time. Just don't make it too good a time.'' Brandon was as protective of Shirley as she was of him.

Burt glared at him. "Keep your nose out of my business.''

"When it concerns Shirley, it *is* my business.''

Burt backed off. "Okay.'' He decided to change the subject. "I heard you sold your Lear. What gives with you? Everybody is talking about how fast you're dumping your wells, company shutdowns. Are you sick?''

"Nope. Just cautious.''

"What the hell are you talkin' about? Things couldn't be better. By the end of next year, I predict oil will hit fifty-five a barrel.''

"I don't think so.''

"I'm makin' a million dollars a month—*profit*—right now.''

Brandon noticed the edge to Burt's voice, as if he didn't believe his own good fortune. There had always been an insecurity to Burt. He was the kind of man who in most cases usually did destructive things to himself to stop himself from coming out on top. Burt was careless about many things. One of them was the way he treated his wife. Brandon believed it would all catch up with Burt. Sooner or later. Brandon sensed that later was almost here.

"I'm probably wrong about all this. But I know that I have let things get out of hand. I can't manage it all—even in the best of times.''

"Yeah? Well, I *can.* ''

"I was in debt for over five hundred million. That's a lot of jack.''

"You think so? I've got almost that myself. But I also have a chance to double my money in three more years if I can keep it all afloat. After all, there's only so much oil in the earth. The Saudis aren't as big as they think."

"I was just over there a few weeks ago, Burt. These guys mean business. I think they are going to go through with their boasts and flood the market. They'll drive the price so low—"

"Horseshit!" Burt interrupted.

"Burt, just because you don't want it to happen doesn't mean it won't."

"I refuse to listen to negativism. Think positive, that's what I've always said."

"I hope you *are* right, Burt. Lord knows, I don't want to think what will happen to Texas and its economy if it all falls apart. I guess I'm just ready to slow down. Ready for my life to take a new direction." He looked over at Maureen, who had just entered the room with a full dinner plate.

"She's a looker," Burt said. "Better keep close tabs on her before somebody else takes her. She's fair game, you know."

Brandon folded his arms confidently over his chest and smiled. "I'm not worried, Burt. Not at all."

Burt watched as Brandon rose and went to Maureen. He looked at Lynn and saw her incriminating eyes lock with his. He felt oddly little, weak and small when she looked at him like that. And he didn't understand it. He was doing nothing different than his father had done and his father before him. He was *rich*, damn it. Why wasn't she happy? Why wasn't *he* happy?

Maureen awoke Christmas morning to a pounding at the front door. The bell turned anxiously three times before she was able to jam her arms into her robe and race downstairs.

"I'm coming! I'm coming!" she shouted.

Juanita rubbed the sleep from her eyes. "Señorita?"

"It's all right, Juanita. Go back to sleep."

But Juanita remained at the top of the stairs, curiosity keeping her yawns at bay.

Maureen opened the door and found a man with a white beard wearing a red suit and a black patent leather belt. He had a sack flung over his back.

"Santa Claus?"

"Alexander to you, little darlin'. Merry Christmas!" He pulled his fake beard down and kissed her soundly on the mouth.

She was in shock. She hadn't seen or heard from him since Thanksgiving, and she hadn't particularly cared to see him.

He bounced into the living room and looked around. "No tree, I see."

Maureen had to laugh at him. "You look ridiculous," she said.

"I go to all this trouble, and that's all you can say?"

"Sorry. I didn't mean to sound ungrateful . . . but it's"— she glanced at the clock on the mantel—"it's seven in the morning."

"You should have been up hours ago. Still too much of a city girl, I see."

"Only on Christmas."

He sat on the sofa. "Come sit on my lap and tell me what you want from Santa."

He was like the Alex she'd known as a child. She wanted to pretend that nothing had changed so she did as he instructed. "I want a million dollars."

"Done!" he said, and pulled out a large box from his sack.

"You shouldn't have done this."

"I wanted to," he said softly, seductively.

"Just a minute," she said, and went to the marble-topped chest and took the brown-foil-wrapped package and handed it to him.

"I hope it isn't a tie. I hate women who pick out ties. They're usually very boring people."

"It's not a tie."

"Good." He opened it and found a pair of leather driving gloves. They were from Italy. He'd seen a pair in New York and hadn't had time to buy them. He loved them. "How did you know?"

"You like them, then. I thought they were appropriate."

"Now you open yours."

She ripped open the green paper with reindeers printed on it and found a charcoal fox jacket. "Oh, Alex, I can't . . ."

"You can. Put it on."

"This is much too expensive," she said, letting her hand glide over the incredibly wonderful fur.

"Put it on," he urged, holding it for her as she slid her arms into the satin lining.

She noticed that her initials were already embroidered on the inside. She fingered the expertly sewn glove pocket on the inside of the coat.

"You see? You can't take it back."

He pulled out another box, smaller this time, suspiciously like a ring box. But to her relief it was an enameled pillbox. There were three more gifts to follow. A bottle of Joy perfume, the same he'd given Jennie Sloan; a set of lace pillowcases from Belgium. In the last box was the jewelry . . . a diamond bracelet. It was tasteful, beautiful and costly.

"Alexander, I can't accept any of this. It's too much."

"I want to spoil you. I have no one to spoil. I had a wonderful time picking out all these things. And I won't let you ruin my Christmas for me. Now here." He took another gift out and handed it to her.

"No more!"

"It's for Juanita."

"Oh."

"I'm off to finish my rounds."

"You're leaving? Just like that?"

"Santa's job is a weary one." He rose and went to the door. "You could pay me back, you know."

"How?"

"Come to dinner today . . . at the ranch."

Maureen remembered Barbara at Thanksgiving. "I don't think so."

"I understand. But I'll call you tomorrow. Maybe we could have dinner in town."

"That sounds better."

Before he turned to leave, he pulled her to him and kissed her. Though he probed her mouth with his tongue, she felt nothing.

He dashed out the door and sped away in his Jaguar.

Maureen watched him go, thinking about his kiss . . . their evolving relationship. The past few weeks had taught her a great deal about Alexander, and most of it she didn't like.

She was still convinced that he'd had something to do with Barbara's educational "ranch tour." Even if he hadn't known about it, he did nothing to sympathize with Maureen or side with her. He had wanted Maureen to see the futility of her quest. He'd even said so. Maureen had no doubt that Alexander wanted to marry her. But now she wasn't sure why.

She remembered Bitzy's warnings about him. She remem-

bered Lynn's slip two nights ago about his girlfriend Jennie
Sloan. Maureen wondered how all of it could have escaped
her. But it made perfect sense.

Alexander had been a friend to her—a perfect gentleman.
In fact, he'd been a bit too perfect. She felt his attraction to
her. She'd even thought his restraint a bit uncalled for. At
first she'd chalked it up to his empathy for her grief over
Mac's death. And then there'd been the problem of Michael.
But once Alex had known Michael was out of the picture, he
still had not made any sexual move. Alexander had done
nothing that would jeopardize his standing with her. It was
all too calculated.

Analyzing everything from the standpoint of pure logic,
Maureen was able to see many things. Alexander wanted to
buy her ranch. Barbara thought that she could intimidate her
off the land. There was an obvious power play between mother
and son that Maureen didn't understand, but she knew it existed.

Was it possible then that Alexander was courting her so
that he could marry her land?

She shook her head. No. She wouldn't think that. He
couldn't have changed *that* much. Or could he?

Alexander was ambitious. His dream was to own the largest
cattle-breeding ranch in Texas. With the addition of her land,
he'd meet his goal. It made sense. And it frightened her.

She went back to the living room and looked at the lavish
gifts he'd brought her. She was right. It was too much. She
realized then that Alexander was trying to buy her. Just like
Burt bought his wife and his girlfriends.

She wondered what Alexander gave Jennie Sloan for
Christmas. But as the thought passed through her mind she
realized that she didn't care.

Maureen was so deeply into her thoughts that she didn't
hear the phone ring, nor did she hear Juanita enter the room.

"Señorita, the phone. . . . It is for you."

"What?" Maureen felt as if she'd been in a drugged stupor.

"The phone," Juanita said. She leaned over the newly re-
upholstered sofa to the library table behind it and handed
Maureen the receiver. "It is Mr. Williams!" The Cheshire
cat grin on Juanita's face told Maureen she'd not been discreet
enough about her feelings toward Brandon.

"Merry Christmas," he said. "I wasn't sure if you'd be

up yet. I'm making my Christmas rounds and wondered if I could drop by for a minute.''

"Of course you can," she said, touching her unwashed face, looking down at her robe. "Anytime."

"Great! I'll be there in fifteen minutes." He slammed down the phone without saying good-bye.

Maureen looked up at Juanita. "Fifteen minutes . . . he'll be here."

She immediately replaced the phone and bolted for the stairs, whisking off her robe as she ran upstairs. Juanita laughed aloud.

"Yo creo que esto Santa Claus es muy bueno."

Brandon landed his helicopter near the spreading oak in front of Maureen's house. He pulled a Douglas fir tree out of the back, grabbed the four brown paper bags from the seat next to him and a Neiman Marcus shopping bag.

He hadn't told Maureen about his surprise the night of his party. He'd wanted it to remain a surprise. But he had conspired with Juanita, who told him Maureen had done no decorating at all.

Maureen was waiting on the front porch. He could tell from the look on her face that his surprise had worked. She looked like a little girl with her hands clasped in front of her face, wide grin beaming at him and her eyes filled with expectancy.

"You brought me a tree!"

"I can't believe you didn't have one."

"I've been so busy with chores and all. But how did you know? Oh, Juanita told you."

"Of course." He stopped on the top step. "It isn't very big. Only five feet—I had a tough time fitting it in the 'copter.''

"You could have driven over . . ."

"That would have taken too long." He moved forward and kissed her. He let his lips linger on hers, feeling their softness, feeling their surrender. "Merry Christmas."

"Merry Christmas," she whispered, not wanting to move. She wished they could just stay like this . . . suspended in a moment where there were no fears. She wondered if it would be like this again. Or would she find something about Brandon that would distort the dream, shatter the expectations as had happened with Alexander?

"Shall we go inside?" he asked.

"Oh, sure. Yes," she said, wondering how idiotic she'd seemed to him, standing there just looking at him.

Brandon moved an overstuffed chair away from one of the windows and set the tree in a stand. He pulled out strings of colored lights he'd bought, and two packages of blue glass ornaments, one of green and one of red. Juanita brought in a canister filled with iced cut-out cookies, each with a string attached. It was her contribution to the tree. They popped popcorn and strung cranberries. Brandon handed Maureen her own box of tinsel to hang.

When they were all finished, Brandon stood back and said, "It's tacky as hell. Isn't it great?"

"I think it's wonderful."

"I forgot the angel. It's gotta have an angel." He turned toward her. "And I think you'd be uncomfortable sitting up there."

"Too boring . . . and you'd be down here," she said as he came to her and cupped her face in his hands.

He kissed her, and this time Maureen was more stunned than the last at the jolt that surged through her body. She felt his arms around her. She felt the power of his body and the power of his emotions as he drew her into the vortex with him. She felt his lips on her neck and down farther on the cleavage between her breasts. She wanted to peel off the open-necked silk blouse she wore, but she didn't. Her consciousness spun around in her head seaching for a place of prominence. She felt as if she were falling off the planet.

She was breathless. Her heart was at warp speed. Something had to make her stop.

"I love you, Maureen," he said.

At first she thought she was hearing things. But then he said it again.

"I love you. And I wish I could stay around to really show you, but I don't have much time."

"Time?"

"I have to go."

"Why? You could stay here for dinner." She didn't understand. Where could he be going on Christmas? He didn't have any family. And why were they talking anyway? Why wasn't he kissing her?

"I have to leave Texas. I'm going to be out of the country for a month. Maybe longer."

"Where are you going?"

"Saudi Arabia. It's very important."

"Can't you go tomorrow?"

"No. You forget. Moslems don't stop for Christian holidays. It's business as usual over there."

Maureen remembered how Michael had been about his work. Charleen had even told her that Brandon was a workaholic. Could she be making the same mistake twice? Was she getting into the same routine as she had with Michael?

"You'd go off on a business trip on Christmas? Don't you think that's carrying things a bit too far?"

"Believe me, I'd much rather stay here with you. But it can't be helped. Just so you understand, though, I'm going to have to trust you with something that no one else must know."

"I won't say anything."

He smiled and traced the outline of her lips with his finger. "I know you won't. I'm being sent there by Washington. They want me to check out a few things for them."

"Washington? Are you in danger?"

"No. Nothing like that. I'm going to sit in on a few meetings, make a couple of reports and then come home. That's all."

"I'll miss you," she said, thinking it a risky statement.

"I'll miss you, too. More than you know. But I'll call as often as I can."

She smiled. "It's very expensive to call overseas . . ."

"Screw the money," he said, and kissed her again.

Maureen held him, wishing she could find some new scientific device that would allow their bodies to meld. But even Barbara Cottrell didn't own anything like that.

When she walked him out the door and to the helicopter, he kept his arm around her waist. He recited a litany of instructions that were meaningless, but were only meant to ease the sting of departure. He wanted her to take care of herself, to sleep, to be safe from harm. He wanted her to be there waiting for him when he returned.

He kissed her again and then got into the helicopter. A funnel of dust spun beneath the helicopter as it whirled into the sky and then zoomed out of sight. Maureen thought it looked like the ascent of a god back to heaven.

20

♦

BRANDON WILLIAMS WALKED silently out of the last OPEC summit meeting he would attend for a long time. He'd known this day would come, but he'd always hoped his hunch was wrong.

He went to a pay phone and dialed the American Embassy. His call was answered straightaway.

"It's Williams. Let me talk to him."

He waited only a few seconds before he heard his contact come on the line. "It's over. A debacle, really."

"How far will they go down?" the voice on the other end asked.

"Under ten dollars a barrel."

"That's ludicrous."

"There are too many in OPEC who want to drive the British and the United States out of the oil business. Nobody can keep a lid on it."

"Did you talk to King Fahd?"

"I've been to his palace in Riyadh three times. I've been here in Geneva so many times even the doormen know me. Of course I've talked to him. I was in meetings with Saudi's ambassador to Washington, Prince Bandar. I thought he could get to King Fahd and maybe that would push prices back up. But Fahd's oil minister, Yamani, believes in the old rules of supply and demand. So do I. However, if the rest of OPEC wants to glut the market, there's nothing left to do. We're on a skid now. I just never thought it would be this bad."

"And Iran?"

"They need higher prices to finance their six-year war with Iraq. They're going to lose just like we are."

Brandon heard a sigh of hopelessness on the other end of the phone. "That's it then. I guess you might as well pack and go home."

"That's the only good news I've heard in weeks."

"We appreciate this, Brandon. I don't know anyone else who would have given us so much time. I guess sometimes we forget that everyone has lives to lead. . . . I know I get too caught up in these things. . . ."

"Maybe you should pack up and go home, too."

"*This* is home."

Brandon shook his head. "Sorry I couldn't have been of more help."

"It was a shot in the dark. We needed a miracle . . . something we're all fresh out of."

Brandon hung up the phone. The oil ministers were filing out of the conference room. He watched as they were bombarded by questions from news-hungry journalists. There were Minicam crews, still photographers and microphones everywhere. He eased his way through the wave of noisy reporters and worked his way to the open doors. He emerged into the sunlight. He wondered what Maureen was doing at that moment.

Alexander Cottrell had decided on New Year's Eve that the tactic he was using with Maureen wasn't working. His mother had done nothing more with her strategy than to give Maureen renewed strength of will to continue her fight for her ranch. And in the week between Christmas and New Year's, Alexander had called Maureen four times for a date and she'd turned him down each time.

Alexander wasn't certain what had happened, but he intended to find out. Alexander met Wes Reynolds at the pool hall in Kerrville the following Saturday. He'd found Wes to be a wealth of information and as greedy as he'd remembered.

To his surprise and pleasure, Alexander had found that Wes did the majority of the supply purchases for the ranch and had check-writing privileges on Maureen's corporate account.

It took Alexander only five minutes to concoct a plan that would drive Maureen to frustration and near bankruptcy.

Then, once she was down and out, crying on his shoulder for help, perhaps then she would come to him. She would get her mind off the ranch and back to him, Alexander thought. He would propose—and she would accept.

For a thousand dollars, Alexander hired Wes to start siphoning money off the corporate ranch account. He told Wes to write phony checks and pocket the extra money, but to try to make it look as natural as possible. Alexander wanted Wes to skim everything he could in the next thirty days.

Wes gladly agreed. He asked no questions other than to keep his instructions straight. Alexander was not worried about Wes keeping his mouth shut. He was already prepared for the day when Wes would come to him and threaten to go to Maureen with his information. Alexander figured that, for another five thousand, Wes would not only leave town but would never come back again.

For the first time in months, Alexander felt more confident than ever about his future. He would succeed where his mother had failed. And he would never, never let her forget it.

21

◆

PANIC SPREAD like a black, diseased cloud over Texas. Nothing in the state's experience had inoculated her against its ravages. First there had been disbelief, then denial of the facts, then the fear began to fester. No one was immune. Rich and poor felt the effects. Jobs were eliminated, companies shut down. Millions of dollars that existed one day vanished into thin air the next. Names of multimillion-dollar drilling, supply and exploration companies were erased from computers and logbooks.

Middle management was eliminated in nearly every energy company in the state, or its ranks were so drastically reduced that its members were rendered useless. The rig count dropped from the thousands to seven hundred.

On January 28, the *Challenger* exploded. Texans viewed the disaster as a personal loss and their grief was visible. Many believed that God was punishing Texas for their former flamboyant ways. The rush was on by the rich to extricate themselves from the entrapments. Gone were the Mercedes, BMWs, and Rolls. Used-car lots popped up along the freeways in Dallas and Houston. There wasn't a Chevy to be found. Texans went to New York and Los Angeles trying to find buyers for their condos in Aspen, Palm Springs, Palm Beach and Paris. They looked to movie stars and Wall Street stockbrokers to buy their Lear jets and Cessnas.

Pawnshops hit their zenith as "the ladies who lunch" hocked their diamonds, fur coats and heirloom silver.

Throughout the winter, the jet-setters from the East Coast,

the West Coast, the south of France, St. Moritz and London bemoaned the empty seats at their dinner tables for the Texans who had brought their laughter, their glitz and their naive charm. The parties that winter of 1986 weren't quite the same without them. They were genuinely missed.

The pall that enveloped the state grew as the weeks dragged on and the price of a barrel of oil plummeted to Brandon Williams's predicted ten dollars.

The disease infected real estate, both commercial and residential. Hundreds of families walked away from houses that had become homes, left their friends and their children's playmates.

Banks were flooded with defaulted loans, and they absorbed mortgages by bankrupt homestead companies and savings and loan institutions. Then the banks began to crumble and fall.

Insanity embraced the land.

High-powered corporate men jumped from the windows of Houston skyscrapers. Oil drillers shot themselves in the head in Dallas. Charities had to beg a hundred times harder for half the donations they'd received only months earlier. Starved children, with their desperate fathers and mothers, huddled under bridges in Laredo, El Paso and San Antonio. The mission houses closed. There was no place to turn.

Houston
April 14, 1986

Four black Cadillac limousines ringed the curved drive in front of Three Allen Center in downtown Houston. Six impeccably dressed middle-aged men finished the last of their lunch at the Heritage Club, located high in the sky above the city, above the turmoil.

The silver-haired man with his back to the window rose first. The others followed suit. It was his meeting. He made the rules.

He snapped his fingers and the maître d' appeared. He whispered something to the maître d' and then motioned for everyone to follow him.

He showed them to the elevator. Once everyone was inside, he pressed a button and the doors shut. When the doors opened, they were standing in a white carpeted room with a long walnut conference table.

The silver-haired man sat in the blue leather chair at the head of the table as was his due as chairman of the board.

They sat in order of rank from the president on his left, followed by the vice-president, and then three lieutenants under them. It was an ancient pecking order utilized in every civilization since the beginning of time, since the day when man realized there must be harmony in life.

"This is a momentous time in the course of our history, gentlemen," the chairman began. "For decades we have wanted to implement our plans, but have been unable to do so. Fate, timing and the rig count have been against us."

Everyone laughed. It was expected of them when the chairman made a joke. Even a rotten joke.

"The Texas Plan, gentlemen, is about to become reality." He paused. "As you know, we have purchased several small banks in the past weeks. By the end of the second quarter, I expect that number to treble. We will continue our pattern of foreclosing on oil companies, developers, land companies and cattle ranches."

He sipped his water, then continued. "If you will look at the notes I have placed in front of you, you will see that the map I've included is one of the Kerrville area. We have recently acquired two small ranches in this area here," he said, pointing to the map. "This large parcel of land is the one we most desire. Note the long airstrip. It needs repaving, but that's minor in light of all the requisites this land fulfills. It is quite scenic as these photographs show. There is an abundance of water and good irrigation. It is the perfect place to build our own Las Vegas. On this parcel alone we could build a half dozen hotels and casinos. Once we acquire this land, we'll move more aggressively toward the procurement of other land parcels in the area. Now, as you know we already have our people working up in Austin on the pari-mutuel betting and gambling bill. Everything there looks fine. I am quite pleased."

He put the map down. "Mr. President," he said to the man at his immediate left.

"Yes, Mr. Chairman."

"I want you to send your people to Kerrville and establish themselves. You know our contact there, Jennie Sloan. She informs me that she has someone who could be of great use to us. He is as anxious to speak to us as we are to recruit him."

"Would that be Alexander Cottrell, sir?"

"Yes. It would be quite a coup for us to have use of the Cottrell name, especially in Austin."

"I have looked at my notes and I don't seem to find the name of this ranch anywhere."

"I did not include it for a reason. *Tracks*, Mr. President. We never leave any tracks."

"Yes, sir, of course."

"The name is McDonald. I want you to get me the McDonald Ranch."

"Yes, sir."

Brandon Williams strolled into Bobby Mac's Restaurant on Hill Country Drive. It was a beautiful spring day, and though he would have rather spent it with Maureen, he had agreed to meet Joel Konner, the president and founder of Kerrville National Bank.

Joel was already seated when Brandon walked in.

"How's it going?" Brandon said as he put his napkin in his lap.

Joel's face bore a trace of desperation that Brandon had thought he'd never see. Joel was a strong man, a decisive man. Brandon almost wished he hadn't come. "Terrible. I don't think things could be much worse."

"Never say that. Murphy's Law, you know?" Brandon tried to keep it light. He was not succeeding.

"I'm glad you came. I was hoping you could help me."

"No promises. But I can try."

"How's your bank in Dallas?"

"Holding our own. It could be better."

"You're not bailing out then?"

"No. Why should I?"

Joel looked at Brandon aghast. "In case you haven't noticed, we're in the middle of a depression here."

"Bailing out isn't the answer." Brandon sipped a glass of iced tea. "Joel, I told you two years ago to tighten up restrictions on your loans. Did you do that?"

"Well, no."

"Christ!"

"Hell! How was I supposed to know? I can't tell the future."

"Damn it, man. The signs were everywhere. How bad is it?"

"I've had a 'run.' A small one, but everyone pulled out. I've had to foreclose on ranches and businesses already. I have a feeling this is the tip of the iceberg."

"What else, Joel?"

"I want to know if you'll help me shore up some of these losses."

"Why don't you ask me to cut off my arm? I can't do that. I wish I could. But I've got just as many problems as you do."

"No you don't."

Brandon sensed that Joel wasn't telling him everything. "What is it, Joel?"

"I've had to go to some . . . private investors to prop up the bank."

"Oh, Christ." Brandon felt Joel's panic seeping through the air, invading the space between them. "What *kind* of investors?"

"They're from Houston."

"Loan sharks."

Joel laughed tensely. "No. Nothing like that. Just investors. They were very willing to help."

"I'll bet."

"I needed them."

"You're really in it now, Joel. I don't know how to get you out. I don't think anybody can."

"There's always a way out, Brandon."

"Not always," Brandon said, and then realized what Joel was thinking. "Don't, Joel. Think of Martha and the baby. Don't do anything stupid. Promise me."

"I promise," Joel said, but Brandon feared he didn't mean it.

Charleen Sims sat across the table from Mira, her tarot card reader. Mira was from New York City, born in Little Italy, and had come to Kerrville when she was a teenager. She was over fifty now, and though she wore Western garb, she had retained her Italian dialect. Charleen believed that Mira kept the dialect only for theatrical reasons. It made her sound mysterious as she told the future.

Charleen kept her eyes glued to the cards as Mira turned them over and interpreted their meaning.

"What about the oil wells? Should I shut them down?"

"No. Keep them open. Once they are capped they cannot be reopened again."

"That's true," Charleen agreed. "My employees. What about them?"

"You must get rid of all but the most essential."

"Oh, no. There are so many families that depend on me for their jobs."

"It cannot be helped."

"What else?"

"Do not be afraid. You will always have plenty of money. You will never go hungry and shall always be happy. Keep your friends around you. Trust in a new friend."

"A new friend? Is that Maureen?"

"Maureen. Yes. She will be important to you in the months to come."

"She will help me?"

"Yes. And then you will help her."

"How could Maureen help me?"

"She has many lessons to teach. Lessons that you must learn."

"How long will this depression—this economic problem last?"

"Until 1988. Then, in January, you will open your company again. There will be much need for oil and gasoline."

"Really? Why?"

"I see a war, but you will be safe here."

"Where is the war?"

"In the Persian Gulf."

"I hope you're wrong, Mira."

"The future can always change."

Burt Bean considered himself a lucky man. He'd just lived through the most devastating day of his life. He turned around and looked at the tall, green-tinted-glass-and-steel building that bore the name of his company, B. Bean Oil Company. For seventeen years he'd gotten an ego boost every time he'd so much as looked at his name on the company letterhead. When he built this structure, ten years ago, he'd felt a surge of pride, a sense of accomplishment. He'd finally felt that he'd put the past behind him.

Burt's greatest fear in life was poverty. He'd struggled all his life to cut a wide chasm between his roots and himself. But now his nightmares were reality. He was in jeopardy of losing it all. He felt as if he were hanging on the edge of a cliff by his fingernails, and slowly they were being ripped off.

The meeting today with his accountant and lawyer had told the tale. If he could not find another source of income in the next ninety days, he would be bankrupt.

Burt walked to his car and unlocked the door of the Mercedes. As he caressed the smooth leather on the steering wheel, he began to formulate a plan. Burt had come too far and worked too hard to lose it all now. He *liked* his fancy cars, his mansion, the Savile Row tailor-made suits he wore and the planes he flew. It was important to him that his wife be the best-dressed woman in Kerrville, if not Texas. He wanted his children to go to private schools and have the best clothes, the best toys, the best friends. Burt refused to give up any part of his life-style.

It was essential to Burt that he find a way out. He refused to be beaten. He wasn't going to let the Cottrells and people like them have fun at his expense. He knew that they still thought he was "trash"; that he would never fit in; that he could never be part of their world. But he would prove them wrong. He was better than they were and twice as smart. He was a fighter. And a survivor. His childhood poverty had taught him how to turn the odds in his favor.

It was the old landed Texans who were shooting themselves, he thought—like Sam Railson in Dallas. He had been a friend of the Cottrells, and guys like him had never known a day of want in their lives. Burt wasn't like that. He was more interested in getting it all back. Burt would do anything to get it all back.

Burt pulled away from the curb and stepped on the gas. He raced through yellow caution lights and took shortcuts. He knew exactly where he was going. He pulled into the parking area designated "For Residents Only." He got out of the car and unlocked the gate with a key he kept on his key ring. It was a key he hadn't used for a long time.

He pressed the doorbell. The door opened.

"Hi, Jennie. We need to talk."

Shane Cottrell left messages at Burt's office and even tried to call his house. Fortunately, Lynn had been gone and the maid answered. "This is crazy," she said to herself, remembering Burt's warnings never to telephone his home. But she was desperate.

Shane bit her nails and twirled a piece of hair around her finger. Burt had only seen her twice in the past six weeks. It was business, he'd said. But she didn't care. All she knew was that he was always too busy or not in town. She'd had to find other sources for her drugs. There *must* be something she could do to reach Burt. She'd tried everything, but she was running out of options.

She asked several old boyfriends for drugs, but she'd only gotten an ounce of coke and some crack. She didn't like crack. It didn't last long enough. She'd gone into Kerrville to one of those sleazy little bars where construction workers and cowboys hang out. She'd found a young drifter who was more interested in a lay than her money. The cocaine he had wasn't as pure as Burt's, but there was plenty of it. She saw him regularly for two weeks before he disappeared.

Then she'd gone to Dallas and hit the discos. She stayed gone for a month. On Saturday nights she danced to the Cure and the Clash at the Starck Club. She was with friends who understood her needs. She wore her wildest punked-out clothes, white lipstick and her black kohl eyes. She told herself she was cool and her friends were cool. She popped tablets of X, which cost a mere fifteen dollars, and sailed off into delirium for hours. It was a cheap and fantastic high. Sex was better on Extasy than on cocaine, and at bargain basement prices.

But the morning after was a killer. Blood turned to sludge and her brain felt like a truckload of bricks. Motor skills were something she only remembered having in kindergarten. After four weeks of racing from the Tango and Club Clearview at night and days of begging God for a release from mighty X, she went back to Kerrville. After all, she wasn't trying to punish herself. It was Barbara she was after. Shane knew her limitations.

It had only taken a week of living without drugs and without Burt to know that she wanted them both back. She'd even decided she could live without the drugs if she had Burt. It was a revelation. And either choice was *still* enough to get Barbara's goat.

On that Wednesday afternoon, Shane had decided to get in her car and physically search for Burt. She would turn Kerrville upside down until she found him. And then the phone rang.

"How's my little darlin'?" Burt said.

"You son of a bitch. Where the fuck have you been?" she stormed.

"Missed me, huh?"

"You asshole! I want to see you. . . . Now!"

"I want to see you, too. How about my place in an hour?"

"I'll be there. And bring some stuff."

"Bring some money."

"What?"

"You heard me. Times have changed, little darlin'. You gotta change with them."

"I'll bring the fucking money."

"See that you do." He hung up.

Barbara Cottrell sat in her office and looked out the huge glass window at the acres of spring bluebonnets behind her house. Never in her life had she felt this confident, this powerful.

For twenty-five years she had dreamed—prayed for the day when she would see her opponents toppled like dominoes. That day was here. Ranchers who had tried to blackball her from cattle sales back in the sixties because "she was a woman" had been forced to sell their ranches. Bankers in Houston and Dallas who had refused her loans or made the stipulations so high that she would have been crazy to agree were fighting for their last breaths. And the oilmen—that group of self-righteous, egotistical chauvinists who'd tried to buy her land at ten cents on the dollar when she'd had hard times—were now out of business.

Barbara believed that God had wrought His retribution.

Barbara didn't owe anybody anything. She had made all the right moves. Her land was paid for. The cattle, the equipment, the barns, the plane were all paid for. Her reputation would keep her business alive, for she'd been smart enough never to fall for tricks, or flashy deals. She'd always given her clients hard work and an honest trade.

She was a smart businesswoman, and now the world was proving her right.

Everything was going her way. Even Shane was towing the line. She knew Shane was going through some rough times—Burt Bean hadn't been around for months. He was nearly bankrupt and had problems of his own. Barbara had predicted he'd be one of the first to fall. He'd taken loans out at Kerrville National Bank that were based on thirty-dollar-a-barrel oil. Joel had told her—in confidence, of course—that Burt's interest rate on his real estate alone was over twenty-two percent.

Barbara had discovered Shane's cowboy boyfriend who had supplied her with drugs. Barbara paid him off, and he left with a very wide smile on his face. Other than her trip to Dallas, Shane had stayed close to home. Barbara believed that if Shane could stay clean for just a few more weeks she would beat the drugs. It was obvious it had been difficult; Barbara had never seen Shane this tense, this anxious or this sullen. It was a good sign.

Even Alexander suddenly seemed happier. She knew he was seeing less of Maureen, but she believed he was doing as he said: "Biding his time." The downturn was doing Maureen no good at all. Barbara knew the bank would not extend her credit. Perhaps Alexander was simply waiting until it became too much for Maureen and then he would make his move. Barbara believed him when he told her that he and Maureen had a "special" relationship. It was obvious even to her that Maureen had a soft spot where Alexander was concerned.

These days, Barbara was not even worried about Brandon Williams taking Alexander's place. With the collapse, Brandon surely had to be hurting as badly as the others. She knew he'd cut his empire almost in half. It took a lot of time and a great deal of energy to reshuffle the many ventures Brandon owned. Yes, Brandon had other things on his mind than romancing a poor rancher like Maureen.

Barbara seldom smiled to herself, but today she did.

She was on top of the world. And God had seen fit to put her there.

Alexander Cottrell checked his tie and the buttons on his white oxford shirt before entering the Riviera, a posh supper club on Inwood Road in Dallas. The single dining room was airy, but sumptuous. Alexander realized that though times were bad there were many familiar faces as he walked to the back table. He was surprised the meeting would be held here. He would have picked someplace less conspicuous—but then, the choice had not been his.

He shook hands with the men he'd never met.

"It's good to meet you . . ." He stalled, realizing Jennie

had never mentioned any names. "Lieutenant?" He chuckled, thinking he'd make light of their strange code names.

Their expressions were mechanical. They looked like ro-
bots, he thought. Both had brown hair, cut the same length,
parted on the right exactly alike. One was about thirty years
old. One about forty. They wore the same Brooks Brothers
suits—Alexander recognized the cut and fabric. Even their
ties were similar. They stared at him. Obviously, they were
not going to give their names.

Alexander sat down. "I heard the grilled veal chop is good
here."

"We've already ordered for you. It saves time."

"Thank you. I think," he said, and discarded his smile.

"We understand you have problems and that we might be
of some small aid to you. We also believe this partnership
will be mutually beneficial. We think we can help you gain
the McDonald Ranch," the older of the two lieutenants said.

"Really, how's that?"

"We will put up the money so that you can purchase it."

"I have enough money. I've already tried that approach
with Miss McDonald. She doesn't feel like selling."

"Everyone has their price, Mr. Cottrell," the older one
said.

"I have a plan now that I think is working very well."

The man on the left, the older one, clearly held more rank.
He was cautious with his words. "Tell me about that plan,
Mr. Cottrell."

"Could you call me Alexander?" He noticed the young
man never spoke.

"Of course."

"Maureen is trying to prove something to herself with this
land. She wants to make the ranch a success. I am paying
her foreman to skim money off the accounts. Once she's out
of funds, I think she'll give up and sell to me."

The two men shifted their eyes toward each other, but their
heads did not move. Alexander was reminded of the puppets
that ventriloquists use. It was an eerie-looking exchange.

"What is this foreman's name?" the older man asked.

"Wes Reynolds. He worked for me a few years back. A
greedy son of a bitch."

"I don't like this plan," he replied, without looking to his
younger partner.

"No?" Alexander was defensive. "Why not?"

"Loose ends, Mr. Cottrell. You must get rid of Mr. Reynolds. He can be traced to you. That's not good. There are other ways to drive Miss McDonald off her land."

"And I suppose you have these other ways?"

"Yes. We do."

"Would you share them with me?"

"Not today. We are here simply to confirm to you that you may rely on us to help you. Whatever it is, we will help. We would like to see you buy this land or to come into possession of it."

"When Maureen comes to her senses and realizes she's in over her head, I think she'll take me up on my proposal."

"She would marry you?"

"Absolutely," Alexander said confidently. He'd spent so much time thinking about her he was convinced she must be spending equal amounts of time doing the same.

"That *is* good news."

"There's always more than one way to skin a cat, I always say." He smiled. They did not.

"When you come into possession of this land, Mr. Cottrell, we would like to lease or buy a portion of it from you."

Alexander's back became more straight. "You would?"

"We'll give you twice what she's asking."

Alexander's eyes were saucers. What a coup this would be! He would not only obtain the land his mother wanted so desperately, but he could render a final killing blow by telling her he'd sold it to outsiders. In one single transaction he would best his mother *and* become rich in his own right. It was the answer to all his problems. Jennie had been right. He *did* need these men.

"Gentlemen, you have a deal."

Stunned at Alexander's swift decision, the older lieutenant said, "Don't you want to know why we want the land?"

"I don't give a shit what you do with it, as long as you don't sell it to my mother. If that's understood, I'm in."

For the first time during their meeting, the older man showed expression on his face, but Alexander wasn't sure if it was respect or disdain. Alexander chose the former.

22

◆

LOVE TASTED BITTER, Maureen thought, as she kissed Brandon. Since the day he had proclaimed his love for her, they had spent more time apart than together. And she missed him—more than she would admit to him or herself. She blamed her restlessness on money worries, but she was lying to herself. She'd lost five pounds because she spent so much time analyzing their compatibility. Charleen told her to listen to her heart. But then, Charleen was a kook. Loveable and well meaning, but still a kook. She worried about Brandon, if he was safe, if he was overworked and if he thought about her. He called her nearly every night from wherever he was. He always gave her a number and a hotel address, but still she worried. Was she the only woman in his life? She'd picked the wrong man before. How could she be sure?

She wondered if their relationship could ever progress. If it wasn't her work, her ranch, her problems, it was his work, his problems that interfered. Now they were dealing with his patriotism.

The oil crisis had brought unemployment, heartbreak and complications to nearly every family in Texas. For some reason, Brandon had determined that he should be a champion to the people. He had sound ideas for legislation that would aid the state in picking itself back up. Maureen knew that he had the political connections to make himself heard. However, she didn't understand why he was so compelled, so possessed with taking on the problems of a state that was bigger than half of Europe.

"Don't go," she pleaded, feeling his arms around her.

"I have to."

"No you don't. You just think you do. We've only seen each other for a few hours."

"I promised Blane Arlington I'd be there for this session. I want to know more about this gambling bill . . . and who's behind it."

"You make it sound like there's some kind of sinister plot in all this."

"Maybe there is." He kissed her again. He sank his face deep into her shoulder and inhaled her perfume. He knew when he awoke in the morning he wouldn't forget how she smelled, nor the particular softness of her body. . . . He was torturing himself. They would be hundreds of miles apart.

"You're beginning to scare me with talk like this."

"Don't be scared. It's probably nothing. But that's why I want to check it out. I need to know how much of a fight I have in front of me."

"Fight?"

"I'm not going to let this bill go through. It's not the answer. It's a quick-fix kind of idea and it's a lousy one. Texans don't need Band-Aids; we need solutions."

"Okay," she said, and smiled. "That soapbox you're standing on is getting higher all the time."

He ran his hand through her long black hair. "Too preachy?"

"Yeah. You better watch it."

"I wish you could go with me."

"Me, too. But I've got bills that are a month overdue. I've got plenty to keep me busy till you get back."

He took her hand and they walked to his truck. He kissed her one last time, and though he told himself he would not look back as he drove away, he did. He always did. If he spent the rest of his life sitting in a chair staring at her, it wouldn't be enough.

"Some day . . ." he said to himself as he reached the gates to her ranch and looked back at her standing on the porch, the thin silk of her skirt molded by the wind against her slim legs, "some day we'll have all the time in the world."

It took over two hours for Maureen to concentrate on her bookwork. She was too busy thinking about Brandon. As usual, she fantasized about making love with him, to him.

Circumstances were all that were to blame for their lack of opportunity. It certainly wasn't because there was a lack of desire. But time had been a depleted commodity in the McDonald household. Brandon had told Maureen that he'd slowed down his pace from two years ago. She didn't believe it. He still did enough to keep a dozen men busy from dawn till nightfall. She was glad they hadn't met back then.

She sighed and stacked all the bills to be paid on the left and then took out the two envelopes of cancelled checks and her bank statements from the Kerrville National Bank. She glanced over them and then suddenly did a double take.

"Jesus Christ! This can't be right!"

Her hands were shaking. She checked her balance. It was under two thousand dollars.

"This should be over fifteen thousand! Even after paying all the bills."

Quickly she scanned the checks. The first few were correct. She found many with her signature. Then she found clumps of four, five, six checks made out to cash or to the feed store, for hundreds of dollars worth of goods that she didn't remember buying. They were signed by Wes.

She found a check for two thousand written directly to the bank. It, too, was signed by Wes.

She bolted from Mac's desk and headed for the bunkhouse. She wanted explanations.

It was afternoon and she knew that Grady and Rusty were tending the herd to the north of the ranch. Wes had been due back from town at noon. Two hours ago. She opened the screen door. She saw no one. The bunks were made, there were Pepsi cans and Coors cans on the chest next to the portable television. She glanced to the far corner, where Wes usually hung his antique holster set and Colt 45's. He'd told the more impressionable visitors to the ranch that they'd belonged to Wild Bill Hickock. She knew he'd bought them in San Antonio at a pawnshop. The guns had pearl handles and had been made in 1910. The guns were gone.

Gone, too, were Wes's alarm clock and portable radio. Maureen checked the bureau where he kept his clothes.

"Empty! Goddamn empty!"

Maureen raced out of the bunkhouse and back to the kitchen. She picked up the phone and punched out the sheriff's telephone number.

Juanita rolled out her flour tortillas. She paid no attention to Maureen until she heard her employer say, "I want to file charges against Wes Reynolds for embezzlement."

Maureen signed the papers at the police station in Kerrville that would give her restitution. She listened as the police sergeant put out an APB for Wes Reynolds. She heard a squad car report in over the radio as she turned around and left. She was told she must be patient.

Maureen was back at the ranch only an hour when Sergeant Mailer telephoned her and told her they'd found Wes.

"Where was he?" she asked.

"At a pool hall. He was still drunk from last night, and the owner said he'd been flashing a big wad of bills around."

"How long before I can get my money back?"

"The courts will decide that. But, Miz McDonald, there didn't seem to be more than five or six hundred dollars. He made some pretty wild bets on his pool games last night. The owner said he was a lousy shot."

"God, a lousy shot . . ." Maureen thought of all the money she'd hoped to recapture. Those hopes were quickly dying.

"We'll keep you informed, Miz McDonald."

"Thank you for your help."

Wes Reynolds woke up in a jail cell. His head felt like the inside of a cement mixer. His memory of the previous night was fuzzy, but as he rubbed the stubble on his face and opened his eyes wider, it all came back to him. He remembered the two bottles of Cuervo tequila he'd downed.

His head pounded as if it were being trampled by a thousand mustangs. Maybe it had been three bottles of tequila.

He remembered winning at pool. Then he remembered losing.

But most of all he remembered Sally. She'd sidled up to him when he'd first come into the pool hall. She had long blonde hair she wore in a braid. She wore tight jeans that showed off every curve in her hips, even the crack in her butt. He liked that. She had a tiny waist and huge tits. He liked that even better. He remembered how large her brown eyes had gotten when he flashed his roll of money.

Somewhere between the first and second bottles of tequila, he and Sally had gone out to her pickup truck and screwed in the flatbed. There had been no blanket beneath them, no sheet to shield them from any onlookers. But neither of them cared. Sally had wanted it more than he had. Just thinking about her now made him horny.

Sally had stayed with him all night. He remembered giving her some money to buy a new dress she'd told him she wanted. But he didn't remember how much. He also remembered telling her that he'd stashed a large amount of money in a San Antonio bank.

"Oh, shit," Wes mumbled to himself.

As his mind became clearer, so did the conversation he'd had with Sally.

"Which bank, Wes?" she asked sweetly, sitting back on her haunches, letting the moonlight fall on her naked breasts.

"The State Bank, near the River Walk."

"I know it."

"No kidding," he said, filling his hand with her breast. He liked the big pink nipples and the way they instantly hardened with his touch. He was getting turned on again.

"I grew up in San Antonio."

"I've been there a few times. It seemed like a safe place."

"Yes. Safe." She pushed her breast into his mouth. "We could go there together, Wes. I have a friend who would rent us a house on the west side of town. We could have lots of fun, Wes." She picked up his other hand and placed it on her left breast.

Wes was going crazy. He was in heaven. Booze, tits, money. He had it all. "Yeah. We'll drive there in the morning. We'll take your truck."

"Sure, honey. Anything you say."

Wes shook his head. Had they driven to San Antonio? Or was he still in Kerrville? He wondered just how much trouble he was in.

He started to stand, but his knees gave way under him. He sat back down on the cot. Now he remembered. It was three bottles of tequila.

Just then the guard walked in.

"Sleeping beauty is awake," he growled indignantly.

Wes frowned. Even that hurt.

The guard opened the cell door. "Come on."

"Where are we going?"

"Your attorney's here."

"I don't have an attorney."

"You do now."

Wes followed the tall, overweight guard to the windowless

meeting room. The man sitting at the interrogation table was well dressed, young and neatly groomed. In fact, he was a bit too neatly groomed. His nails were professionally manicured and his haircut was the kind that cost thirty bucks easy.

"You ain't no court attorney."

"No, I'm not."

"Who sent you?"

"Mr. Cottrell thought . . ."

For the first time that day, Wes smiled. "Mr. Cottrell sent you. That's good. I'm practically a free man."

Maureen was informed by Sergeant Mailer over the telephone the next day that Wes had been released.

"Released? Why? How?"

"Bail was posted and he was freed on his own recognizance."

"He's a criminal. He stole from me!"

"It's his first offense. The judge will take that into consideration."

"You sound as if he were harmless, as . . . as if everything was all right."

"I understand, Miss McDonald," the sergeant said.

Again, Maureen heard that same patronizing voice she'd heard so many times since coming to Texas. Why was it that she'd never heard it in New York? Or perhaps she had—it just hadn't been so *loud*.

"You don't understand anything. He's a cowboy. He'll leave town within the hour. Why would he stick around to go to trial?"

"Why, Miss McDonald, he has to remain in town. That's the law."

"How stupid do you think I am?" She slammed down the receiver. "Jesus! Why do I even try? Why did I ever come here?"

It didn't take a Harvard law degree to figure out that someone was protecting Wes, Maureen thought, as she went back into her study. But who? And why?

Did Wes have friends on the police force? Maybe that sergeant was an old buddy of his. One thing she'd found out since moving here, Texas men stuck together. The more she thought about it, the clearer the situation became.

Wes had stolen a great deal of money from her. There was no way he could have gambled away all of it in a pool hall.

In Las Vegas it was possible. Wes obviously had put some of it away. Maureen had heard of convicts buying all sorts of things from behind prison walls. For the right price, the sergeant and anyone else, even the best attorneys, could have been hired.

Wes was no dummy. And now more than ever she was convinced that he would never be in Kerrville to go to trial.

Wes Reynolds shoved the last of his jeans and old work shirts into a duffle bag. He looked around the motel room to see if he'd missed anything. He lifted the cheap, thin bedspread and found the pair of socks he'd worn last night. Wes's feet were always cold—it had something to do with his circulation. He put the socks in the bag.

Wes had nearly a thousand dollars of his "fun money" left. It was enough to get him and Sally to San Antonio in style. Once there, they would rent that little house and for a few months they'd have a hoot. Maybe later they would go on down to Mexico, where his dollars would stretch out for years. What a life they would have, living on the beach, drinking Cuervo and screwing.

Suddenly, there was a knock on the door.

Wes knew it was Sally. She'd told him on the phone she only had to gas up the truck, pack a very small suitcase because she intended to buy new clothes in San Antonio, and then she'd be there.

"You're right on time, honey," Wes said with a grin as he opened the door.

The man at the door wore an expensive Brooks Brothers suit. His brown hair was parted on the right side. He wore no smile, no expression at all. Wes thought he looked like a robot.

Wes knew the man had the wrong room. Hell, he had the wrong damn motel. Wes was just about to tell him so when the man pulled a black Magnum with a silencer out of nowhere, aimed it at Wes's forehead and pulled the trigger. Wes heard a faint "pop" sound.

Wes dropped to the floor, his eyes wide open. There was a bullet hole in his forehead, but there was little blood.

The man shut the door on Wes and calmly walked to the waiting blue Ford that his partner drove. Both "lieutenants" drove away in silence. They didn't see Sally drive up behind them and take their parking place. They did notice that someone's car radio was playing much too loudly. They both disliked loud music.

Alexander Cottrell sat in his office fondling Maureen's head scarf. He'd bought a bottle of Opium so that he could spray the scarf. Then it would always smell like Maureen. Then he could pretend they had just been together. As he knew they soon would be. He looked forward to the end of pretense with her.

Alexander heard the doorbell, but he paid no attention because he was not expecting anyone. He heard the Mexican maid repeating herself and he heard the sounds of two male voices. One of the voices sounded familiar.

Alexander bolted to his feet. He rushed into the foyer.

"Gentlemen, come in, come in," he said with profuse politeness. He waved the maid away as if everything was in accordance with his plan. "Don't mind her," Alexander said as he indicated they should seat themselves.

They stood. "She wanted our names to announce us. You know how we feel about that."

"Yes," Alexander said uneasily. He didn't like the way they showed up without warning. He also didn't like the way they looked at him—with eyes like black ice.

The older of the two lieutenants did most of the talking, as usual. "We don't like the way you handled the Reynolds man."

"Pardon me?"

"You were counselled about 'loose ends.' You not only paid for his attorney, but you let Sergeant Mailer know that you were helping Wes Reynolds. That's not good. It's expensive."

"Expensive? How?"

"We found it necessary to cover your tracks, Mr. Cottrell. Soon the attorney will be leaving town."

"I don't understand."

"He has been wanting to move to Chicago. Nearer his wife's family. A handsome offer will be made to him that will enable him to make his wife happy. We found it necessary to eliminate Mr. Reynolds."

"Eliminate?"

"Yes. He is no longer a threat."

"Jesus." Alexander sucked in his breath. What had he gotten himself into? Who were these men? Alexander wondered momentarily if defeating his mother and possessing Maureen were worth this. Sickeningly, he knew the answer was yes. Alexander would do *anything* to get what he wanted. "And the sergeant? I know he can be bought. I do it all the time."

The two emissaries from the chairman of the board glanced at each other. "Yes, he can be bought," the older man said.

Alexander sighed with relief. He wouldn't want to see anything happen to old Mailer. He was a likable guy. Alexander had known him since he was a child. Alexander had told himself—each time he'd offered Mailer a bribe and each time the man had taken it—that he was simply supplementing Mailer's income, which was far, far too low.

"I understand."

"We're not sure you do. But to make certain—the chairman wants you to act only when he gives the orders and in the manner he so chooses. You are *not* to act on your own accord. We know more about these things than you do. You were told your plan was not a good one and to abandon it. Wes Reynolds was a liability. See that you incur no more liabilities."

"I won't," Alexander said, trying to control his shaking hands.

The men turned, and without further word they left through the front door.

Alexander collapsed into his desk chair. "My God. What have I done?"

Maureen read about Sergeant Mailer's heart attack and the upcoming funeral in the *Kerrville Daily Times*. There was a tribute article to him on the front page with a color picture of him at his desk in the station house. On the wall behind him were rows of black-framed commendations, awards and plaques that he had acquired over the years for various services and duties he had rendered to the County of Kerr. She noticed that the photograph had been shot to the left side in order to allow a third of the composition to be taken up by the American flag. When she first glanced at the picture, it had even seemed to her that the man, Sergeant Mailer, was an incidental in the picture.

If it hadn't been for the horrendous rains that day, Maureen would not have indulged herself in a second cup of coffee at the kitchen table. She also would not have spent so much time reading the paper. On the very back page, in a narrow column where the obituaries were listed, was a listing of the police calls, the break-ins and the false fire alarms.

She hadn't recognized Wes's obituary because he was listed under his given name of Harrold Reynolds. However, under the police arrests and reports were the details of Wes's death. He had been shot at close range by a Magnum. There were no witnesses, no clues. The police suspected robbery as a motive because he had no money on him when he was found. The only report given by the motel manager was that a pickup truck with blaring music drove past about the time of the murder. He could not describe the driver.

Maureen decided she'd been wrong about Wes. He didn't have any friends at all. And he'd had no money on him when he died.

"No money." Maureen said it to herself matter-of-factly. "No money. Wes had no money." She got up and poured herself another cup of coffee. She looked out the kitchen window at the rain.

"*I* have no money!"

Brandon Williams sat in the upper gallery of the Senate Hall in the Capitol Building in Austin. He rested his left arm on the back of Blane Arlington's seat. Brandon was trying to listen to Blane over the sound of filibustering on the floor below him.

Blane Arlington had been a friend of John Williams since the Williamses first came to Kerrville. Brandon's father had wanted to be a rancher and had supported Blane Arlington when he'd first run for congress in the late 1940s. Blane had always liked John Williams—had thought that John—and, later, Brandon—were good, honest people he could trust. When Brandon hit oil and became rich, Blane had reaped the rewards of keeping in touch with the Williamses; if it hadn't been for Brandon's generous contributions to his campaigns, he knew he would have lost the election in 1984. It had been tough being an old man in a young man's world. Brandon had helped him show all the young men that an old man could be just as tough.

"You're a fool," Blane's scratchy voice croaked. "Nobody in this state wants to hear what you're saying."

"Mark Dixon does."

"Yeah? And look at his ratings in the polls. He's slipping faster than the price of crude."

"A gambling bill isn't the answer."

"Nobody said it was. The way I figure it, we'd only get a billion, maybe a billion and a half, out of it the first year, and we're five billion in debt. But"—Blane stuck his crooked, arthritic, stubby finger into Brandon's chest—"you go out and tell that to the guy on the street and you know what he'll say? A billion's better than nothing. And what if it brings in more?"

"It will bring in more—that's what I'm worried about. It'll bring all kinds of things. Prostitution, drugs, numbers, loan-sharking."

"You don't think we haven't got all that now? Course we do."

"This would be on a grander scale." Brandon leaned closer. "I've had bankers in Kerrville and Dallas tell me that they are selling out to the mob. I know for a fact that land is being foreclosed on, bought up and auctioned off by the mob all over the state. I think the situation is the worst in Houston. Of course, they were hit the hardest. Something has to be done. I can't run the entire banking industry for the state, but I sure as hell can do something about this gambling thing before it goes any further."

"You're right."

"Then why are you fighting me?"

"I'm not. I think you're right. We need to pare the budget drastically, trim out the dead wood and raise taxes. It's drastic medicine, but necessary. However, if I went on the air and said that I'd never be reelected. People don't want to hear that shit, boy. And if I don't get reelected, I can't help you. You gotta learn how to play the game."

"So you won't help me?"

"Did I say that?"

"Well, no."

"Of course I'll help you. Do all I can. But I'm gonna do it *my* way. It's worked for forty years. No sense upsetting the applecart now, is there?"

"No, sir." Brandon smiled.

Brandon left the Capitol Building and went straight to his waiting car. They were pulling away from the curb before he realized that this was not Skip, his chauffeur.

"What's the meaning of this? Where's Skip?"

"He got sick," the young lieutenant said. "He'll be back

tomorrow. I'm taking you to the airport. That *is* where you want to go, isn't it?''

"Why, yes. How did you know?"

"Skip gave me explicit instructions. He even told me about the little dirt road behind the airport to take to get to your private hangar, sir.''

Brandon felt as if he should be reassured, but he wasn't, and he didn't like it one bit.

They rode in silence to the airport. The driver adjusted the air conditioning twice to make the temperature perfect. They pulled to a stop. The driver got out of the car and opened Brandon's door for him. Just as Brandon was about to step away, the driver grabbed his arm.

"What . . . ?"

There was a gun stuck in his back. The man's grip was tight.

"Forget your meeting with Senator Arlington today, Mr. Williams. If you pursue that course, you'll find the price very high."

Brandon turned just enough to look the man in the eye.

"You don't frighten me. If you had done your homework you'd know I don't respond to threats. If you want to stop me, you'll have to shoot me.''

Brandon wrenched his arm out of the man's grasp and started walking away. He never once looked back. He kept his eyes on the Cessna, which his pilot had begun to rev the minute he'd seen the car pull up. Brandon waved to the pilot. The pilot waved back.

Brandon kept walking, wondering when he would hear the gun go off, or if there was a silencer on it and he would never hear anything at all—he'd just drop dead.

He swore he heard the trigger pull back.

He thought of Maureen. He could see her face in front of him. He wanted just one more night with her before he died. He kept walking. He heard nothing. There was no gunshot, only the sound of his car engine starting and then driving away.

As his adrenaline dropped back to normal and relief filled his veins, it was all he could do not to piss his pants.

23

◆

MAUREEN CUT the tags off the new China-blue silk dress she'd bought. After the fiasco with Wes, and realizing she hadn't any money left, she'd still gone into Kerrville to have lunch with Lynn and Charleen. They'd had a wonderful day, all of them pretending that everything was right with the world when, in fact, everything was wrong. Maureen had felt guilty buying the dress, but she was more depressed than guilty, and she did look lovely in it. She thought of Brandon and what he would think of it.

Maureen had found the dress on sale for only fifty dollars at a small dress shop. Even Lynn agreed it looked like three hundred. Maureen had put it on her MasterCard. She wondered absentmindedly when she'd handed the card to the clerk if she could use her credit cards to buy farm machinery.

"Aren't you going to buy anything?" Charleen had asked Lynn.

"No."

"Not even a 'get-back'?" Charleen teased.

Lynn laughed. And this time, Maureen noticed that Lynn's laughter was genuine, unrestrained. Something had changed.

"I'll get back at him, but not this way," Lynn said as she looked at Maureen.

"Can I help?" Maureen asked as they walked outside.

"Yes, you can. But not yet. It's not time."

Maureen was intrigued. "You'll let me know?"

"You'll be the first."

"What about me?" Charleen pouted.

"You'll be the first and a half to know."

Charleen was confused, but Maureen was not. She knew exactly what Lynn was going to do. She was going to divorce Burt. Lynn was wise to plan carefully.

Maureen believed that if Burt had resorted to threats of keeping Lynn's children from her, he was the kind of man who would do anything to get what he wanted. It was obvious Burt wanted to remain married, but she didn't understand why. Maureen had never seen any sign of affection from Burt toward his wife or his children. Maureen believed that Burt only saw his family as status symbols. To a man like that, the well-being of his children and his wife's feelings were easily discarded. Burt was the kind of man who could make a nun turn into a women's liberationist.

Maureen was more thankful than ever that she'd found someone like Brandon. His list of good qualities was endless, she thought, as she checked herself in the mirror. Suddenly, her brow crinkled.

"Nobody is that perfect. There's gotta be something wrong with him."

Just then she heard the doorbell ring and Juanita's voice as she greeted Brandon.

Quickly, Maureen picked up her gold beaded evening bag and rushed down the stairs. She didn't want to waste a single moment. They had so little time together.

"You look fabulous," he said a bit too breathlessly. But he couldn't help the effect she had on him. It didn't matter to him if she was wearing blue jeans and cowboy boots or designer silk and rhinestone-studded shoes. She was beautiful in both and comfortable in both. Everything suited her. To him, she was perfect. He pulled her into his arms and kissed her hungrily. He caressed her back and allowed his hands to travel to her hips. She leaned into him.

"You've lost weight," he said.

"You can tell?"

"Yes. And I don't like it."

She smiled. "That's number one. You're too critical."

"What are you talking about?"

"I've decided that while we have dinner tonight I want you to tell me all your faults. I can't find any."

"Is that right?" He pulled her closer and cupped her breast with his hand. "I'm impatient. Number two: sometimes I forget my manners. Right now, I'd rather take you upstairs than take you to dinner.''

"Think we should?'' His eyes were smokey with passion. Her brain was being cancelled out by her desire. She was just about to turn toward the stairs when she saw Juanita watching them from the end of the hall.

Brandon saw her at the same time. "I guess we'd better go.''

"I think so.'' They started out the door. "By the way, where *are* we going?''

"Houston.''

"Just for dinner?''

"There's a special place I want to take you.''

Maureen shrugged her shoulders. "How much better can steaks be in Houston?''

"There's no comparison. So is the champagne, the violinist—and the owner is a friend of mine. It's all arranged, so don't fight it. Come on. They were gassing up the plane when I left the house. I thought we'd start with a bottle of Dom on the plane and some caviar. I had a new compact disc player installed so you could listen to soft jazz on the trip over. Then the limo will pick us up at the airport. We'll have the Piper-Heidsieck en route.''

They walked out of the house, and as she got into his Corvette she looked up at him and said, "I've just found another one of your faults.''

"What's that?''

"You're too unorganized.''

La Colombe d'Or was one of Houston's most renowned restaurants. Nestled in the heart of Montrose, near River Oaks, the European-style hotel had been host to kings, presidents, movie stars and millionaires from all over the world. It was romantic, lush and quiet. Maureen fell in love with it on sight.

They met Brandon's friend, Steve Zimmerman, the owner, who had recently been in *Time* magazine and on national news programs for his ingenious marketing idea of regulating the luncheon prices to the commodity price of a barrel of crude oil each day at noon. With a computer hookup to the commodity exchange, Steve was able to quote his guests the fluctuating West Texas Crude prices at any given moment. In a town where restaurants were closing their doors daily, Steve Zimmerman was having his best year yet.

Steve showed Maureen and Brandon to their table. Brandon had ordered a beautiful arrangement of roses, ruberum lilies and white tuberoses.

"Is this a special occasion and I don't know it?" she asked.

"Every night with you is a special occasion," he said.

"You're too gallant."

He held her hand. "Actually, that's the truth. It's been so long since we've had a moment to ourselves, I thought the best thing to do was take you away from your ranch where no one can disturb us. And I didn't want to go to Austin or Dallas, where I could be found. It just made sense to me to come here."

"I'm glad we did. I like this place."

They ordered cream soups, the veal chops and fattening chocolate mousse cake. But it wasn't until Maureen lifted her after-dinner brandy balloon to her lips that she found the courage to tell Brandon about Wes.

"I know I'll never see that money."

"I agree."

She looked at him, a bit stunned. "I was hoping you wouldn't. I need it desperately."

"Not too desperately, I hope."

"You know what I mean."

"I think so." He leaned over and kissed her cheek. "You know, I'd be glad to advance you anything you need."

"No," she said emphatically, and perhaps a bit too loudly. The woman at the next table looked up from her Caesar salad. Maureen's eyes focused on her brandy. She gripped the glass firmly. "I want to do this on my own. It's not the same if you just take over for me. Then all I'd be is an extension of Williams Enterprises. I don't want that."

"It wouldn't be all that bad," he teased, trying to cheer her up. She looked so forlorn. He knew the feeling. He knew she didn't like it any more than he did. At this point, however, Brandon was more worried about Maureen's safety than he was her pride or her need to accomplish goals. He didn't like the way Wes Reynolds had died, almost as if he'd never existed. He couldn't tell Maureen that he suspected a "plan" in Wes's death. In fact, he didn't know what he suspected, only that something was not right.

His incident in Austin with the mysterious chauffeur had

told him that someone was watching him. He'd brought Maureen here because he'd asked Steve to keep his whereabouts secret. Together they had picked this evening because it was the least busy for La Colombe d'Or. There were no journalists here, no oilmen, only a few couples celebrating anniversaries. There was no one in the bar.

More than ever, Brandon felt an overwhelming need to protect Maureen. He didn't know how a drifter like Wes could fit into anyone's grand scheme, but Brandon doubted that Wes had come up with the idea of embezzlement all by himself. Someone had been helping him, but Brandon didn't know who. Or why.

Even more frightening was that someone wanted Maureen to lose her money. Someone wanted her to be desperate, just as she'd said she was. He wanted her to know that he would help her financially. It was important that she come to him for help—for many reasons.

Brandon wanted to think that she felt the same about him as he did her. But he wasn't sure. She had not told him she loved him. At least not yet. About most things he was impatient. About her, he would bide his time. The rewards were too precious to risk.

"This has been a lovely evening, Brandon," she said, letting her hand slip into his. "I'll never forget it."

"It won't be the last. I want you to know me better. You can trust me, you know."

"I can?" Trusting never came easily for her. She always seemed to get hurt when she trusted. She wanted to trust him. More than anyone before or anyone now, she wanted to trust Brandon. But because her feelings for him were so intense, so all consuming, she knew he could hurt her more than anyone she'd ever known. She was frightened of him. She wondered if he knew it.

"You can." He kissed her hand. "I know it may take some time for that to happen, but you will one day. I know it."

Maureen didn't say anything. She was afraid she'd crumble into an emotional heap in his arms. She was overworked, scared that she'd never get the ranch on its feet again, and she was afraid she had disappointed Mac. She loved her ranch so much sometimes she wanted to burst when she looked down on her valley. She couldn't fail. She wouldn't fail. And until she knew that her land was secure, she would not allow herself to fall in love.

Her eyes flashed with blue fire when she looked up at him. "You're going to have to wait. I have a lot to do."

"I know. Just remember that I'm behind you a hundred percent."

She scrutinized his face carefully. She saw only caring, honesty and sincerity. "I believe you."

"That's a start."

24

◆

MAUREEN HAD JUST STUCK a bright red begonia in the ground next to the front steps when she heard the sound of a car. She wasn't expecting anyone. She pulled off her gardening gloves when she realized it was not Charleen or Lynn or Brandon or even Alexander, who still managed to see her two or three times a month.

The car was a rental, a 1985 blue Buick Le Sabre. She didn't recognize either of the two men, who dressed alike and even wore their hair exactly the same. They smiled mechanically.

"Miss McDonald?"

"Yes? Do I know you?"

"No. But we hope to change that."

"What can I do for you, Mr. . . . ?" she asked the older of the two men.

"Jameson. Bruce Jameson. And this is Clint Sanderson. We have a business proposition we'd like to discuss with you, Miss McDonald."

His smile was pleasant and he had an easy way with him. Maureen had no reason to distrust him. "Are you interested in buying my cattle?"

"In a manner of speaking. Could we . . . go inside? And I wonder if I could bother you for a drink of water."

"I apologize, Mr. Jameson. How rude of me. Of course. It's rather warm out here today, isn't it? I'll have Juanita prepare us some iced tea. How would that be?"

"Wonderful," he said with a broad grin. "It's quite a drive out here."

"Are you from Kerrville?"

"No. From Houston," he said as they followed Maureen into the house.

They sat in the salon, which she had filled with baskets of white begonias on the Plexiglas tables. The room looked fresh now that everything had been painted eggshell white. Maureen loved this room the best.

Juanita put sprigs of homegrown mint and floated lemon slices on top of each tumbler of tea. Both men drank deeply. Maureen liked that.

"About my cattle, Mr. Jameson."

"We're interested in more than just the herd."

"Oh?"

"We would like to purchase the herd, the ranch and all its acreage."

Maureen felt the hair on the back of her neck stand on end. "You don't look like cattlemen."

"We aren't. We represent the Culbertson family in Houston. They would like to buy your ranch."

"I see. Well, it's not for sale."

The older lieutenant, who was calling himself Bruce Jameson today, reached into his pocket for an envelope. He was smiling as he did. Maureen had the distinct impression of a cabaret club magician as he made the gesture. She decided she didn't like this man at all.

"Not at any price, Miss McDonald?"

"No."

"Please, take a look at this before you turn us down."

He rose and handed Maureen the envelope. She opened it and withdrew a check written out to her for four million dollars. Her hands instantly began to shake.

"Is this a joke?"

"Hardly." He was still smiling. "That's a cashier's check."

"I see that." Her eyes were wide. She knew her jaw had fallen to her chest. "Why?"

"Pardon me?"

"Why would you offer so much?"

"We . . . my employer believes it is a fair price."

"This is almost twice what it's worth."

"Think of all you could do with that kind of money."

"I'm thinking. I'm thinking," she said, her wide, surprised eyes travelling from one man to the other. She could pay off all her bills. She could go anywhere. Do anything. But as her mind raced, she realized she only wanted to be here. She had no place to go but here. She didn't *want* to go back to New York. Her world was in Texas. Brandon was here. Her promise to Mac was here. This was her life.

"I can't accept this."

Bruce Jameson noticed she was reluctant to hand back the check. It was a good sign.

"With that kind of money," he said, "you could make dreams come true. It's a generous offer. I doubt you'll see another like it."

"I doubt I will, either. But I can't."

This time, she gave him the check.

"Is there anything I can do to change your mind, Miss McDonald?"

"No. I don't think so."

"Nothing?"

"Mr. Jameson. This is my family's home. Or at least what there is left of my family. My uncle is buried outside under that tree. I can't leave him."

"It's a great deal of money. . . ."

"I know that. And I could use it, believe me. I've just recently had a downturn that was devastating."

"Then make it easy on yourself. Take this offer."

She smiled at Bruce Jameson and his partner. She rose. "I'm very sorry, gentlemen. I'm staying."

"Very well," he said, putting the check in his breast pocket and rising. "We'll be leaving then."

She showed them to the door and watched as they drove away.

"How odd," she thought aloud, "that they should come to me right when I need the money so badly." She walked back to the salon and picked up the tea glasses and placed them on a tray. She was on her way back to the kitchen when suddenly she stopped.

They had offered her *twice* what the ranch was worth. Even if she worked the ranch for a decade and built the herd as large as Barbara Cottrell's, the ranch still wouldn't be worth that kind of money.

"There must be something else!"

Her mind whirled. What would make an investor want a piece of land so badly he was willing to double the price for

it? Was it oil? Was it natural gas? Did people in Houston
think the end of the oil crisis was near? What did they know
that she didn't? Did they have some kind of information from
Washington? Had OPEC altered its policies?

It could have been any one of a million answers.

She raced into Mac's study and put the tray down on his
desk.

"Somewhere in here I'll find the answer. The only reason
someone would pay so much for this place is because they
know something I don't. And I'm going to find out what that
something is . . . if it kills me."

Patriotism demanded more than courage from mortal men,
Brandon thought as he drove up to Barbara Cottrell's house.
And he probably wasn't the first patriot who'd had to kiss a
little ass.

It hadn't taken Brandon long to connect the mob to the
zealous push behind the sudden reappearance of the gambling
bill in Austin. If he could see it, so would others. The only
problem was that not enough people would come to his conclusion unless he did something about it.

Brandon had connections in Texas. But he didn't have the
kind of clout he would need to wage a campaign of the magnitude necessary to defeat this bill.

For the first time in his life, Brandon Williams needed Barbara Cottrell.

His biggest surprise had been when Barbara agreed to see
him. His gut told him the whole idea was an effort in futility.
Barbara had never liked him—had never liked anyone in his
family. She probably wanted the titillation that turning him
down would give her. But Brandon didn't care. There was
more at stake than her need for control, or his pride.

A Mexican maid answered the door. He waited in the huge
vestibule while he was announced. He watched as the maid
disappeared into the room at the left.

Barbara Cottrell had taken great pains that day with not
only her appearance, having her hairdresser come to the house
to comb out her hair, but also with the carefully chosen St.
John knit suit she wore and the Ferragamo shoes in darker
charcoal grey. She had had the two huge wing chairs removed
from her office and replaced with smaller, Spanish wooden
side chairs. Because Brandon physically was a big man, she
was certain he would feel uncomfortable. It would put him

at a disadvantage. Barbara had always believed in stage setting.

She sat regally as the maid showed Brandon in. She did
not rise or smile as she greeted him. She noticed he did not
offer his hand. He merely sat opposite her in one of the small
chairs. He crossed his legs comfortably and folded his hands
in his lap. She was disappointed that he held as much com-
mand as she. They were evenly matched. Barbara was ready
for the challenge.

"Why did you want to see me?" she asked directly.

"I need your help."

Barbara almost laughed. Instead, she kept her eyes leveled
on him. She didn't miss a beat. "For you to come to me, it
must be serious. I can't believe you need a loan," she said
hopefully.

"I don't. And you know it."

"I do."

He didn't flinch. He knew the game she was playing. They
were two and two, the way he scored it.

"I don't have much time to spend, and I'm sure you don't
either. So I'll be direct. You know of the pari-mutuel and
gambling bill that certain factions are pushing for in the state
congress."

"I do."

"I can't prove it in black and white but I've reason to
believe the lobbyists are being bought by mob money."

Barbara's eyes narrowed. For the first time that day, she
listened to what he said. Curiously, she didn't doubt his word.
"Go on."

"I have friends in banking who have been selling out to
the mob. It hasn't come out in the papers yet, but it will. I'm
seeing a steady, carefully orchestrated takeover going on. It's
all being quietly done. If this bill passes in Austin, the doors
will be open for even more criminal elements to move in. We
already have drugs, prostitution and protection rackets, but I
believe it will get worse if we legally allow the mob free
rein."

"You think you can stop them?"

"Yes."

"Your ego seems limitless, Mr. Williams."

"My ego has nothing to do with it. I know you have some
kind of twisted hatred for men. I've heard that about you
since I was a kid. But, you know, I never believed it." His

hands were clenched now as his emotions surfaced. He uncrossed his legs and planted his feet firmly on the floor. He leaned closer to her. His eyes were blazing. "This thing is bigger than anyone's ego—yours *or* mine, Barbara. I'm trying to save my home, my state, and if you can't see that, you're blind."

Barbara's hands were trembling, but she kept them tied in a ball under the desk so he couldn't see. She didn't want him to know what she was thinking.

At that moment, with his eyes filled with rage and passion, and his voice pinched with conviction, he had never in his life looked and acted so much like John Williams, she thought.

Barbara felt herself softening. She felt her heart opening as it once had. She wanted him to convince her to join forces with him. She wanted him to prove to her that she was not only worthy of the fight but that, win or lose, she would come out on top because they had done it together.

She remembered the kind of political passion and idealism that had spurred John. She remembered that it was John who had been committed to his beliefs. She had not been. Barbara had always known that she could rely on her background, her wealth, to see her through the rough times; to line her patriotism with shiny silver. Barbara had never had to commit herself in the way John had or, now, as Brandon was doing.

Brandon was putting his money and his reputation on the line for a belief. He could easily lose. The mob could buy newspapers, television and radio. They could buy off and were buying off people every day. Desperate people oftentimes took the easy way out.

Brandon was offering her the hard way. She was smart. She had a lot to lose.

"Do you know what you're asking?"

"Yes. Do you?"

Her eyes widened. "I think so."

"It could be very dangerous, Barbara. For both of us."

"I've never been afraid of blowhards before."

"These men are playing for keeps."

"I know. But this is my Texas. My family has been here for over a hundred years. I don't have anywhere else to go. It's always been a good life for the Kerns and the Cottrells. I can't let anyone deprive me of the future. Of my children's future."

"Then you'll help me?"

She looked at him. Suddenly, she was seventeen. And his name wasn't Brandon. It was John. She had never stood up to her father back then. Perhaps she should have. Perhaps there might have been a future for her and John. Maybe everything would have been different. For a split second she allowed herself to imagine what it would have been like to have a life filled with love. The pain was excruciating.

"I'll do everything I can."

She didn't smile and neither did he.

Brandon had an overwhelming urge to go to her and put his arms around her. For an instant she'd looked so vulnerable, so fragile. For the first time he understood everything about Barbara that any living man could know, for he was certain no one had ever seen this side of her. He knew she was a woman of her word—that was her reputation. He pitied her the troubles she'd had with her children and wished he had the power to erase her distress. But that was not within his realm. Only God could do that. Somehow he knew that she had made a new beginning in that room. They both had. He saw her with clearer eyes. He believed he had begun the foundation of a friendship that would last the rest of his life. He was glad. He stood, and this time he offered his hand. She took it.

"I'll give a rally next weekend. I'll invite everyone I know in the state. We'll have the strongest Texans on our side. Then I know we will win."

"I appreciate this, Barbara."

"I'm doing it for Texas."

"I know," he said, and walked out.

Barbara quietly went to the door of her study and watched him as he walked out the front door. Then she went to the living room window and watched him drive away until he was out of sight. She was reminded of the day John walked away. She had the overwhelming feeling that life had completed its plan.

She and John had come full circle.

Maureen had spent three days rummaging through every nook and cranny of Mac's study and the library shelves. On the fourth night, as thunder rumbled over the West Texas hills, she found an old, battered, leather file folder. She untied the strings. Inside the first few pouches were clippings from magazine articles about conquistador gold. She found Xerox copies of stories on mining in the Kerrville area over the past three hundred years.

In the fourth pouch she found a very old map. She turned it around and around, trying to decipher it, for it covered a small area. She followed the creekbed with her finger and then recognized two peaks that sat on the northwest side of her property.

"I know where this is!" she said to herself excitedly. "But then, Mac should have known, too."

This must have been the map that had spurred him to needlessly spend his profits on gold mining gadgets. Deflated, she flipped through the remaining file pouches. In the last file she found a piece of cardboard with an arrowhead taped to it. On the back of the cardboard was a small sheet of paper with typing on it. It explained that this was the route to an old Spanish mine. It had been mined until the mid-1700s, then abandoned.

Mac had scribbled a notation on the side. It read: "Dead End."

Maureen turned the card over and examined the arrowhead. The carvings on it matched the map. She examined the map again and then the arrowhead.

She knew she should be putting all this aside; obviously, Mac had already investigated the mine. She got out a magnifying glass to inspect the finer markings on the map and the arrowhead.

At the very tip of the arrowhead was an arrow pointing backward. Without proper lighting and the magnifying glass she never would have seen it. Excitedly, she searched the map. Then she saw it.

"The same! The arrow is pointing in the same direction."

It was faded so much on the map she felt certain Mac had *not* seen this marking.

"Is it possible?" she asked herself, feeling chills trickle down her back. Had she found something Mac had missed? Was it possible there had been a gold mine on the land all this time? Could Mac have been right? Perhaps he hadn't been such a kook after all.

Maureen looked down at the map. There was a reason those men had offered her so much money. Perhaps they knew about the gold. It was a shot in the dark, Maureen knew, but she didn't care. She needed that gold. Not so much to pull her out of her financial troubles, but because if she found it, she would vindicate Mac.

Maureen didn't believe in hunches. She told herself she was using common sense, empirical data and an old map to form her conclusion. She wanted to be right. She *had* to be right.

25

◆

THEY CAME in caravans of limousines and flocks of private planes, banding together so that no one would be lost. From San Antonio, El Paso, Fort Worth, Abilene, Dallas, Wichita Falls, Amarillo and Austin they came. From as far east as the tiny towns of Tyler, Longview and Texarkana they rode in air-conditioned Cadillacs and Lincolns. They were the politically astute and wealthy of Texas. They were the ones who cared. They were the ones who counted.

Barbara had expected four hundred, but six hundred and twenty people showed. It made her happy.

The caterer went nuts. There wasn't enough food, they were a hundred tables short and two hundred chairs were desperately needed. Everyone was baking in the sun. They should have had another tent. Possibly two. More bartenders, waiters and cooks were needed. The flower arrangements were too few and spread too far out. The "decor" had been mutilated with all these changes.

Barbara turned a beaming face to the caterer, a frail-looking Austrian man from Fort Worth. "I don't give a damn if you have to rope a steer and roast him yourself, you feed these people. They are my friends."

Never in the fifteen years Herbert Hansberg had been working for Barbara Cottrell had he seen her so lackadaisical about a party. Something had changed. But because she was his wealthiest client, he beamed back at her. "Yes, ma'am. I'll take care of everything."

"See that you do."

Barbara entered the gardens, making certain she spoke to everyone as she passed. She knew all their names, the names and ages of their children. She inquired with concern about their lives, their flagging businesses, their health. As she went from clique to clique, everyone commented on the change in Barbara. She was still tough as nails; the familiar glint was still in her eye. No one would dare cross her. But something was different, they whispered to each other in wonderment. Very different, indeed.

Maureen's stomach housed a gross of butterflies. The last place on earth she wanted to be was Barbara Cottrell's political rally. She knew how important it was to Brandon that she accompany him, but still, though he squeezed her hand when they entered the mansion, she couldn't help but remember the past Thanksgiving. She didn't know whom she wanted to see least, Barbara or Alex.

Though she was incredibly uneasy, she never said a word to Brandon. She held her head high and smiled as they walked through the vestibule and into the gardens.

They had been there nearly thirty minutes before Maureen saw Alexander. It was while Brandon was introducing her to Martin and Nina Mayor from Houston that she spotted Alexander standing beside the pool. He wore a white silk linen suit and white shoes. His blonde hair was two shades lighter and his skin was three tones darker. He looked like Don Johnson as he pushed his Ray Bans off his face and to the top of his head. He raised his tonic glass in tribute to her. But though he smiled winningly, she noticed that he had not taken his eyes off Brandon's arm, which was placed possessively around her waist.

She didn't realize Brandon was speaking to her.

"I said, this is Henry and Judy Smith, Maureen. They're also from Houston."

"I'm sorry." Maureen shook the beautiful brunette's hand. "I'm pleased to meet you."

"You and Brandon must come visit us at our new beach house in Galveston," Judy said.

"I'd love to," Maureen said, letting her eyes glance back at Alexander. But he was gone.

This time, everyone in the group from Nina to Henry followed Maureen's eyes. And so did Brandon.

"I think we should say hello to our host," he said.

"You don't mind?"

"No. He's the one who's worried. You're with me."

She smiled. "I sure am."

They walked over to Alexander, who was speaking with Charles Smitt, Fort Worth's renowned polo player, and Trammell Crow, the Dallas developer.

Maureen started to give him a friendly kiss on the cheek, but his eyes glared at her with such force she felt as if she'd been physically rebuffed.

"It's good to see you, Alexander," she said.

"Is it?" he said bitingly, his eyes darting to Brandon.

Maureen could almost feel the heat of Alexander's anger. She understood, but she didn't. At first she thought it was because she was with Brandon, but something told her there was more to it than that.

"Alex, could I speak with you in private?" She looked to Brandon, who nodded his approval. She liked how he was so easy with himself, comfortable with the situation. He wasn't threatened by Alexander. She wondered what he knew that she didn't.

Alexander excused himself and followed Maureen to a small wicker settee.

"What's the matter with you, Alexander? It isn't like you to treat me as if I were an enemy."

"What do you know about what I'm like—really? What do any of us know about each other?" he said, thinking of his mother's recent change of heart.

Maureen was puzzled. She was definitely missing something. But she didn't know what. She still believed that his anger was directed toward her. "I want us to remain friends. We were always friends, Alex. Don't throw all that away."

Alexander looked over to Brandon. "What exactly is *he* to you, anyway?"

"I don't know—yet. But I want to find out."

"You aren't in love with him?"

"I don't know."

"You could have fooled me."

"He's in love with me."

"No shit." He leaned very close to her. His green eyes sparkled with earnestness. "Well, I'm in love with you, too. But you never give me two minutes time. Oh, a lunch here and there or a quick phone call."

"A lot's been going on."

"Not that much."

"Look, Alexander. I don't even see Brandon all that much. He's forever off on a meeting—going here, going there."

"Yeah? Sounds to me he's not doing such a swell job of romancing you." His voice softened. "I could do better." He was hoping, he knew, once again—like a fool. But when it came to Maureen . . .

"How can I say this without hurting you?"

Alexander felt his heart crack. It was going to be the last time. "You can't. There's no pleasant way of kissing someone off. I could do it for you, but that would make it too easy for you. And *that* I don't want to do."

He bolted to his feet. When he looked down at her, his eyes were white-hot with anger and bitterness. "Be careful what you wish for, little girl. You just might get it."

Alexander stalked off. He felt like smashing a few heads—he wanted Brandon's to be the first.

Jesus Christ, how he hated the bastard!

He pushed his way to the bar and pounded his fist on the counter. "Give me a double scotch on the rocks," he demanded.

He bolted the drink and then plunked the glass down for the waiter to refill. He marched off.

Alexander felt as if he'd just faced the guillotine—twice.

It was bad enough that Maureen had dumped him in favor of Brandon, but he'd seen it coming for months. Today was simply the validation of what he already knew. He'd been trying to sway her to his side, using the force of their past history together as a wedge. But it had fallen flat in the face of true passion. On that score, Barbara had been right. Brandon was in love with Maureen and she with him. He wasn't sure why she wouldn't admit it to him—or to herself—but it was fact.

But the crowning insult had come from his mother. They had been in her office over a week ago when she broke the news.

"I'm joining forces with Brandon Williams on this issue," she had said matter-of-factly.

"You're not serious!"

"I am. He needs my help."

"So let him go to his buddies in Houston."

"He came to me."

"And you jumped in there without even consulting me?"

She looked at him. He saw what he perceived as disappointment in her eyes. He thought he'd go insane on the spot. Was there nothing he could ever do to please her?

"Perhaps I should have talked to you before giving him my answer. Would it have made any difference?"

Alexander's mind flew. Difference? He had joined forces with the men his mother intended to fight. He *needed* that bill to go through in Austin. He stood to gain everything he wanted if he could only get Maureen's land and then sell it to the mob. He still had time to convince her she'd chosen wrongly by siding with Brandon.

"Of course it would make a difference. What makes you think you can trust Brandon all of a sudden? I grant that it's flattering that he has come to you with his wild story, which I don't believe in the first place, but you seem to have thrown all your judgment aside. Where's his proof?"

"He doesn't have any."

"I don't believe this."

"I'm sorry I hurt your feelings. . . ."

"You're sorry . . . ?" Alexander couldn't believe his ears. He'd never heard his mother tell *him* she was sorry. Something had happened in this office when Brandon came to see Barbara. He only wished to hell he knew what it was.

"It's a mistake, Mother. Mark my words. There's still time. Call off the rally."

"No. My mind is made up."

"I have a bad feeling about all this. No Cottrell ever sided with a Williams."

"Perhaps it's time," she said wistfully.

Alexander had been more confused than ever.

Alexander knew that till the day he died he'd replay that scene and try to understand it. Unfortunately, it didn't matter whether he understood or not. The bottom line was that on two counts Brandon had defeated him. Once with Maureen. Once with Barbara.

Alexander didn't take defeat easily.

Barbara had just finished her speech urging her friends and neighbors to join with her and Brandon to lobby against the gambling bill. She was applauded. But when Brandon stood center stage and began his even more earnest appeal, the crowd went wild.

Maureen was proud of him. She found herself being mesmerized by his energy, his spirit. She'd always known he was
doing the right thing in this fight. But as she watched the
faces around her, she knew he would win. His sincerity was
evident in his face, in his voice and in the words he used. He
didn't rely on a written speech; he spoke from the heart. He
wanted the best for Texas, and it showed. He would be wonderful on television, she thought. She wished she had brought
her camera so she could catch him on film for herself.

When his speech was over, everyone wanted to talk to him,
shake his hand. Maureen had wanted to go to him, hold him,
absorb his energy. Instead she stood aside, letting those who
would fund his campaign, who would place his articles in
their magazines, who would editorialize in his favor in their
newspapers, be the first to touch him.

Charleen was the first to find Maureen in the crush of the
crowd. "He was magnificent, Maureen. And he's right. If we
all band together we can fight this thing."

"I think so, too."

"In the morning I'm having my cards read. Why don't you
come with me and we'll ask the psychic if Brandon will win?"

Maureen sighed deeply. "Charleen. You have to stop this.
Ever since the oil crunch you've been going to her too much.
I don't need a psychic to tell me that Brandon is right."

"But it's better to know."

"Sometimes it isn't."

"Like when, Maureen?" Charleen's eyes narrowed as she
peered at Maureen. "Are you afraid of what she might tell
you about you and Brandon? Are you afraid of him? Or
yourself?"

"What do you mean?"

"Only that maybe you should listen to your heart a little
more. You're in love with him and you won't let go."

"It's not the right time to be falling in love. I have the
ranch to think about . . ."

"Good God! I don't believe you're saying this. And I
thought you were a smart girl. Maybe you aren't so smart at
all. If all you can see is what your mind tells you, your life
is going to be very barren. It's the heart that makes us happy,
Mo. The heart. Not the head."

"If your heart was doing such a good job ruling your life,
how come you always have to see a tarot card reader to find
the answers? What's missing, Charleen?"

Maureen knew she'd been too rough on Charleen when she saw her friend's dark eyes sparkle with tears. But at the same time, she didn't like Charleen picking off parts of her as if she were a puzzle.

Charleen, still fighting tears, said, "I just wanted to help you." Then she turned her back on Maureen and walked toward the house.

"And I wanted to help you. . . ." Maureen mumbled sadly as she watched her leave.

Charleen went into the house and walked directly to the front door. She had the valet signal for her chauffeur.

She rested her head on the back of the seat as they drove away. All she wanted was to go home, back to her retreat. She would tell Charles about this day. He would know all the right things to say to ease her bruised feelings. He would show her how to put Maureen on the right path. And in the morning she would see her psychic just as she'd planned. She had no reason not to. But as she looked out the window at the brilliant blue sky, she wondered if perhaps Maureen could be right.

Did she rely too much on her psychic? Was she listening with *her* heart, *her* head? Or someone else's?

She would ask Charles what to do. He would know. Wouldn't he? He'd always guided her correctly before. She had no reason to doubt him now. Nothing had changed. Or had it?

By midnight most of the guests had left. Those who had not made a pledge of money or time or favors to Brandon did so to Barbara. Between them they had raised half a million dollars for the campaign. During the boom years that would have been a pittance. During the crunch, it was manna. Brandon was still enlisting aid from the guests as they walked out the door. Barbara thanked each and every person. She was smiling—broadly. It was a night many Texans would talk about for weeks to come.

Maureen sat with Lynn beneath an umbrella table near the pool. There were still fifty or sixty people who were reluctant to leave. One of them was Burt Bean.

"Burt doesn't believe in any of this, you know," Lynn said.

"So I gathered."

"He thinks the gambling bill will get the state back up on its feet."

"What do you think?"

"I think I want a divorce."

Maureen was surprised only that Lynn had finally admitted her intentions aloud. "Are you sure?"

"Very. I just want to handle it the right way. I don't want my kids to get hurt."

"I understand."

"I need your help."

"Anything."

"I want to ask Brandon to arrange for his lawyer to see me. He's got the best. But I can't ask him myself. I'm afraid Burt would suspect something. If you do it and he finds out, he'll dismiss it. Burt thinks that women have no brains. Only pedigrees and pussies."

Maureen burst out laughing. "I'm glad you see the humor in this."

"I have to laugh. Otherwise I'd want to slit my wrists for waiting so long." She was silent while a uniformed waiter refilled her glass with white wine. "I'll tell you, Maureen. There are days when I think God has brought this entire recession on us so He could strip Burt Bean naked and allow me to get the hell out of this farcical marriage."

"That's one way of looking at it."

Lynn smiled. "Personally, this is the greatest thing that ever happened to me. It sure as hell has separated the men from the boys."

Maureen thought instantly of Alexander and Brandon. "Yes, it has done that, hasn't it."

On the far side of the pool, hidden by a clump of Barbara's English hedges, Shane Cottrell was raping Burt Bean.

Though he protested, she'd stripped him of his beige linen summer slacks in less than three seconds. The instant she grabbed him, he was hard.

"Jesus! This is insane. My wife is only fifty feet away!"

"Shut up, Burt. I've been wanting you for weeks. And I'm getting what I want. I could give a shit about Miss Goody Two Shoes."

Shane went down on Burt, and he thought he'd scream from the pleasure that shot through his body. She was right.

It had been too damn long. She was the best. He wanted her even more than she wanted him.

Burt knelt on the ground and pulled Shane's gauzy tangerine-colored cotton skirt over her head. He nearly ripped her panties off as he fell on top of her and entered her. Sweating and moaning, in less than two minutes they both climaxed.

"Shit! We must be nuts!" he said, realizing what they'd done.

"I hope she heard," Shane hissed.

"I just bet you do. You'd like to see me and Lynn bust up."

"Damn right. Then I'd have you all to myself."

"Forget it. She's my wife."

"She's nothing to you. She doesn't love you. *I* love you! How long is it gonna take for you to figure that out?"

He pulled on his pants and dusted off his knees. "You don't know what love is." He stuck his hand in his pocket. He pulled out a small packet of white powder. "Here, Shane. Here's what you love."

She glared at him. She looked down at the cocaine—then back at Burt. "I don't want it. I want you."

He snickered at her. "Yeah? Well, you won't be seeing me for a week. I gotta go to Monterrey. Think you can go a week without this?"

Shane thought about the agony she'd been through waiting till she could see him tonight. She could make love to him at least a half dozen more times. This little romp had only whetted her appetite. He was right. She'd go crazy. A whole week with no sex and only her mother and brother for company.

"I'll take it," she said, and shoved the packet into her pocket.

"I knew you would," he said. She calmly walked back to the party and blended in with a group discussing the hot spots in the south of France and all the rest of the places they could *not* go that summer.

Lynn saw Shane as she emerged from the garden. She also saw Burt appear only a minute later. She had suspected many women in Burt's life, but Shane Cottrell was a low blow. She was young enough to be his daughter. Lynn felt that familiar nausea.

"Tell Brandon to make that appointment as soon as possible."

"I will," Maureen said.

Lynn sipped her wine and looked over at her husband. She was finally going to be rid of Burt. The nausea faded.

Everyone had gone and the house was finally quiet. Alexander sat at his desk, his tie draped over the back of the chair, his gold-and-diamond cuff links tossed carelessly on the coffee table so that he could roll up his sleeves. He sipped his eighth scotch. He was incredibly depressed.

He had watched Brandon and Maureen very closely as the night progressed. He'd noticed the way they caught each other's eye as they stood on opposite sides of the garden. Brandon was earnestly seeking supporters, but he never became so absorbed that he forgot Maureen. He would go to her, put his arm around her waist, sometimes kiss her cheek or just hold her hand. But it was the lack of pretense, of flourish, that bothered Alexander.

They seemed too familiar with each other, too comfortable—as if they'd known each other a hundred years. People in love were usually unable to hide their passion. People in love were possessive of each other to the exclusion of anyone and everything else. Passion, Alexander knew, could be fickle. Brandon and Maureen showed none of the signs to tell him their love would die.

Alexander felt doomed.

He took out the key that unlocked the drawer he'd filled with his fantasies. Carefully, he pulled out Maureen's scarf, the lipstick, the bottle of Opium he'd bought.

His hands were steady, but his eyes burned with angry tears. He squeezed them back.

"You were meant to be mine, Maureen. Not his."

He sprayed the perfume into the air and filled his nostrils with the scent. The vision of Maureen's beautiful face floated in front of him. He ground his jaw. He felt a lump in his throat.

Alexander believed he'd asked little of life. All he wanted was his mother's respect. And a marriage with the one woman he'd *thought* he could trust.

"We were fated to be together, Maureen—since childhood—you were meant to be mine. . . ."

His hands were trembling as he picked up her lipstick. Angrily, he ground the pink-colored wax into the silk scarf. Suddenly, he could contain his temper no longer. He picked up the gold letter opener and jammed it into the silk, tearing and shredding the scarf. Alexander felt jilted, cheated out of what he thought was rightfully his. He wanted to hurt Maureen as she had hurt him. He didn't understand her. Why didn't she love him as he loved her? How could it have happened? How could he have ended up with nothing? It wasn't fair. It wasn't right. Fate was playing a trick on him. Yes. That was it. And he must put himself in the right again. He must take revenge. He must balance the scales again so that he could go on with his plan. He must even the score with Maureen.

Rage scalded his cheeks with silent tears. His mind went haywire.

"He can never have you. No one will ever have you!"

26

$\blacklozenge$

MAUREEN CHEWED her thumbnail as Grady maneuvered the backhoe into position. The minute the mechanized shovel dug into the ground, she felt her heart skip a beat. "It's there," she mumbled hopefully to herself. "I know it's there."

The old map and the arrowhead with its strange carvings had led her to this place two days ago. She hadn't wasted a minute renting the backhoe.

Grady had dug down about two feet when suddenly he stopped and climbed off the small rig.

"What is it?" she asked excitedly.

"This isn't natural."

"What isn't?" She stared into the shallow hole with him.

"It looks like layers to me. I ain't seen nothin' like that before. Look . . ." He crouched down and brushed sand and silt off the bottom of the hole. He revealed a flat rock.

"What do you think?"

"I can't be sure. We'll dig some more."

Grady got back on the backhoe and began again. Half an hour later they were down nearly eight feet. A strange pattern to the earth was exposed.

Grady scratched his head as they looked at layers of carefully placed rocks and sand. "Mother Nature didn't lay this stuff. That's for sure."

Maureen's eyes were wide. "Someone was covering something up."

"Absolutely. Someone a long, long time ago."

Maureen was so excited she thought she'd burst. "Keep digging, Grady. Keep digging!"

"Yes, ma'am!" He hopped back on the backhoe and went to work.

"This is it, Mac. This is what you were looking for. . . ."

Maureen had no more than said the words when Grady's shovel hit the earth and, suddenly, the ground caved in.

"Back up!" Maureen yelled. She rushed to the edge and lay down on her belly on a pile of excavated sand and rock. She motioned for Grady to hit the ground again with the shovel. Again, the thin layer of rock fell away, this time revealing a gaping hole.

"It's a shaft! A mine shaft!" she yelled excitedly. "We found it, Grady!" She jumped up and watched as he continued digging.

Maureen thought of Mac and all those years he'd spent looking for gold. It had been here, just as he'd known, only he hadn't looked at the map carefully enough. He'd been digging in the wrong place. If there was gold here, then Maureen knew she had her explanation as to why the men from Houston had offered her so much money.

An hour later, Grady had revealed the huge opening of a mine. Using flashlights they could see the mine walls and the wooden timbers that formed the beams along the ceiling. Maureen was ecstatic.

"I hope it isn't mined out," Grady said, wiping the sweat from his face and neck with a blue bandana.

"Mined out? What do you mean?"

"Lots of these old mines were closed down because there was nothin' left in 'em. All the silver and gold had been stripped out." He shined his flashlight on the walls. "See that? No sparkle. Wouldn't surprise me if there was nothin' here but just more of the same stuff we been diggin' up."

Maureen looked down into the dark tunnel. Her heart sank. She hadn't thought of that possibility.

"Well, I'm not giving up that easily. I'm getting a professional opinion before I make any decisions."

Maureen took a last look at the shaft. "There's gold down there, I just know it. Mac knew there was gold on this ranch. That's why he didn't want me to leave." But she wondered if that was only wishful thinking.

* * *

Barbara Cottrell began campaigning for her new cause early on the Monday morning following the rally on Saturday night. It was a beautiful early June day. The blue skies stretched over the rocky hills, and she could see her cattle grazing in the distance. A blue jay chirped in the pine tree outside her window. All the signs were positive, she thought as she donned a pair of brown gauchos, her brown boots and a brown, olive and camel Western blouse.

She'd made an appointment with Jessie Durham, a wealthy rancher and oilman who lived thirty miles to the north of Devil's Backbone. Jessie had been in London on Saturday and had been unable to make the rally. Barbara both wanted and needed his help. Jessie was the kind of man who, if he believed even half as much as she did in the cause, would write a check for half a million on the spot.

That kind of money could buy a lot of votes.

Barbara went downstairs and found Shane and Alexander in the dining room, sharing barbs rather than breakfast.

"Lay off, Shane," Alexander growled.

"Why should I? If it was me with the hangover, you'd be outside my room banging a gong. Besides, you slept all day yesterday. You should be over it by now."

"I'll never get over it," he mumbled, his mind on Maureen.

"What?" Shane poured herself a second cup of coffee. She needed the caffeine because she was out of coke. She intended to see Burt today.

"It's none of your business," he nearly yelled, but the effort sent new shock waves of pain pounding through his skull. He rested his forehead in his hand.

Barbara wondered if any brothers and sisters lived in peaceful coexistence. Her children forever seemed to derive perverse pleasure out of continually needling each other. How many times had she lain awake at night trying to decipher her actions; trying to understand what she'd done that was so wrong to create these two unhappy children.

She looked at Shane. She wore a disgustingly sheer blouse that clung to her body like a second skin, with no bra. Today her hair was cellophaned blue. She looked as if she hadn't washed her face since Saturday night. Perhaps she hadn't, Barbara thought.

She sat at the head of the table, and as soon as she was settled the maid scurried in silently and placed a fruit plate in front of her, then went back to the kitchen, returning with a silver pot of steaming coffee. Barbara waited silently until the maid was gone.

"Have you any plans for today, Shane?" Barbara asked.

"No."

Barbara sighed. "I didn't think you would."

Shane chewed her lip, searching for a nasty retort. "Well, actually I do, but I'm sure you don't want to hear about it."

Barbara looked her dead in the eye. "You can bet on it."

Shane was taken aback and found herself speechless. She'd been ready for the daily breakfast lecture when Barbara would list her Ten Best Ways to Clean Up Your Act. Today, she was saying nothing.

Shane looked at Alexander. His face was just as puzzled as hers.

Barbara continued with breakfast. The phone rang, and as usual she began taking her calls right at the table.

Alexander scrutinized his mother carefully. What was the deal? Barbara wasn't reading either of them the riot act. It was as if . . . as if she'd given up on them. As if she didn't care. Alexander panicked; nothing could be worse.

"Are you all right?" he asked.

"Of course. I've just got a million things on my mind. I'm going over to Jessie's today."

"Durham's?" Alexander asked, surprised.

"Yes, why?"

"You hate his guts, that's why."

"I need his money."

"He blackballed you back in seventy-four. Have you forgotten?"

"Alexander, you know I never forget anything." She looked at Shane. "But times have changed. I think he'll come around. He's an old man now. I heard his heart's very bad. I'm hoping he's softened a bit since the old days. Maybe I can make him feel guilty."

"You'd be *real* good at that," Shane remarked snidely.

Barbara ignored her daughter and finished her breakfast. She called her pilot to make certain the helicopter was ready. Assured that everything was in order, she drank the last of her coffee and rose.

Alexander was still in a quandary over the change in his mother during the last week. He didn't like it. He didn't know the rules anymore and how he should play the game.

"Alexander, would you see that the contracts for the embryo sale to Mr. Marchand in Le Havre are in order and send them off for me?''

"You want *me* to do *what?*" Alexander couldn't believe his ears. His mother *never* allowed anyone to handle her precious contracts.

"You heard me. I don't have the time." She walked out.

"I don't have the time . . ." Alexander looked at Shane. Her jaw was hanging just as much as his.

"What the hell is going on?" Shane asked.

"I don't know.''

They both rose and went over to the French doors, watching as Barbara strode confidently out to the helicopter pad. Within minutes, she was airborne. The helicopter rose like a shiny silver-and-blue bird against the brilliant sky. It moved away from the house toward the north.

Suddenly, as they watched, the silver bird vomited up a stream of black smoke.

"Jesus!" Alexander cried.

Shane grabbed the door and flung it open. They were both running at breakneck speed toward the downward spiraling helicopter.

"Mother!" Shane screamed as a thin flame of fire erupted from the helicopter.

Alexander raced faster and faster. He thought his heart would never keep up with his legs. Gone was his hangover. Gone was his pain.

The helicopter spun against the sky, down, down. Then as Alexander and Shane watched in horror, it crashed against a low hill. Black smoke billowed into the sky, marring its early morning beauty.

Flashing red-and-amber lights struck against Shane's mesmerized eyes as she watched the paramedics load the remains of the pilot's body into a black Visqueen bag. The sound of the zipper on the body bag sounded so impersonal, so final, she thought.

The helicopter, twisted, burned and mutilated, looked like the gutted carcass of some prehistoric bird. It seemed impossible that her mother could have survived the crash, but she had—barely.

The ambulance driver came over and put his hand on Shane's shoulder. "Do you want to ride with her to the hospital?"

She nodded and, trembling, climbed into the back of the ambulance with the young paramedic. She wanted to be anywhere but here. She tried to turn away from her mother but she couldn't. With only morbid curiosity motivating her, Shane looked down.

Barbara's arms were burned and her hair was badly singed. No hairdresser in the world could right the havoc her silver hair had endured. Entire patches of hair had been burned off. Shane wondered if it would ever grow back.

Barbara's face looked untouched, even though the paramedic had said some of her facial bones had been cracked.

The real damage was internal. In her chest, in her lungs, in her brain. Barbara was unconscious.

She was hooked up to oxygen and an IV. One paramedic was taking blood pressure, pulse, temperature.

"Is she going to live?"

"We have to get X rays . . . the concussion was bad . . . the ribs crushed. It's too soon to tell. . . ."

Shane felt as if she were watching some medical show on television. This couldn't be real life, could it? Could this happen to a Cottrell? To her invincible mother?

Shane looked out the door and saw Alexander talking to a man. They were about to close the ambulance doors.

Shane panicked. "You're not coming?" she nearly screamed at her brother.

"You go ahead. I have to take care of some things here."

Shane saw the deputy sheriff, Alan Barstow, walk into view. He tipped his hat to Shane. "Sorry to hear about your mother, Shane. I hope she'll be all right. . . ."

There was despair in his eyes and Shane saw it. "Alex!"

He spun around and looked at her. "What?"

"Is Mother going to die?" She was more afraid of the question than the answer. If she didn't ask, she wouldn't know. Why had she asked?

"I don't know," he said, and suddenly the doors slammed shut.

Shane was alone with her mother.

Alexander turned to Alan Barstow. "I don't care how you do it, Alan, I don't want this to hit the newspapers. Write up the report any way you see fit."

"Jesus Christ, Alexander! You must be crazy. Don't you want to find the bastard who did this?"

"I want my mother spared the investigation—that's more important. She's fighting for her life. I don't want some god-damn cops badgering her with a bunch of exhausting questions that could be more deadly than the crash. You got that?"

"Alex, this is a clear case of sabotage. Those instruments were tampered with. Somebody severed the rudder lines and shorted the electrical system. Somebody wanted your mother dead."

"It was just some kook, Alan. I have to believe that. Mother doesn't have an enemy in the world. At least not someone who would want her dead. Now, please, do me this favor. I'll make it worth your while."

"I don't know . . ."

"*Very* worth your while."

Alexander had been known over the years to be quite gen-erous to law officers who would look the other way. But this was the first time Alan Barstow had ever been in a position to benefit. Because he was first on the scene, Alan *could* falsify reports and state that it had been simply a mechanical failure. He would have to pay off the two investigators from the Texas aviation board, but that was okay. It would just cost Alexander a bit more was all.

Alan thought of the new roof they needed on the house. The carpeting his wife wanted and the braces his son would need next year. Life could be a bit sweeter with a "gift" from the Cottrells.

"I don't come cheap." Alan began the bartering.

"No good man ever did. Ten thousand seems like a nice round number."

"Fifteen is rounder."

"Come with me to the house. I'll make out a check."

"After the check clears, I'll write my report."

Alexander's eyes narrowed. Then he smiled. "I like you, Alan. I think we may do business in the years to come."

"I should think so," Alan said with a greedy grin.

Shane stood outside the doors of ICU. They wouldn't let her in to see her mother. And she wasn't so sure she wanted to see her anyway. Shane was frightened. She was terrified.

For two hours she'd seen doctors and nurses running in and out of the swinging doors. She'd heard that Barbara had been taken to surgery. There was internal bleeding. She knew about the punctured lung. The plastic surgeon hadn't been to see her yet.

Shane wondered what her mother would think of that. Had Barbara been conscious, she would have demanded the plastic surgeon first. But she was in a coma.

Just then the doors opened again. A surgical nurse scurried by. Shane noticed that the woman kept her eyes straight ahead. She didn't want Shane to see what she was thinking. But Shane knew.

Shane felt icy cold tears fill her eyes. They weren't the hot, angry tears she normally associated with her bouts with her mother. These tears were different. They were tears of hopelessness. Tears of death.

Shane paced back and forth. She couldn't go back to the waiting room. There was a family in there she couldn't face. They had been told their father would die today. Shane had to think positively. She wasn't going to let Barbara die. Her mother *had* to live. Shane believed she could will her mother back to life.

Shane wondered why it was during times like this, when fate wrenched the fabric of one's life, that people turned to introspection for the answers. Shane had never found comfort from within. She'd always avoided herself—at all costs.

She leaned against the wall, thinking of her mother. Remembering a time when she was very small. A time when her father was still alive, when her mother had plenty of time for her. Time for Alexander, too. They had done many things together. She remembered smiling a lot.

It was when she was four that the arguments had begun between her mother and father. She recalled standing on the staircase late one night. The sound of their voices had wakened her.

"You bastard!" Barbara yelled.

She heard the loud crack of a hand as it hit a cheek. She heard her mother scream.

"You don't hold a candle to her!" her father said drunkenly.

"Then get the hell out. Leave us alone."

"Maybe I will."

Shane had raced off to bed, covering her ears with her hands. Her father loved someone else. He never left them, though, because a few weeks later he died.

Shane had always wondered why her father had not loved

her mother enough, and had never loved *her*. She had loved him. Shane had done everything she could to get his attention. She was as perfect as she could be. But it didn't matter. Her father didn't want her.

Shane remembered, too, that after his death her mother had thrown herself into her work. There never was enough time for her and Alex, for fun, for being a family. Barbara was always exhausted, worried and angry at the men who tried to keep her from doing business. Her mother's happy smile faded. It was replaced by a cool facade that enabled her to work with those who tried to thwart her.

Shane wondered now why she'd failed to see all this before, why her mother had not seen what she needed. But then, how could Barbara have known when she had not known herself?

Shane had hated her mother all these years. She had blamed her for not being the woman her father had wanted. She had blamed her for her father's death, for robbing her of what she needed most—another chance to win his love.

Shane was trembling. She felt her knees give way and she sank to the floor. Did she love her mother? Was it her father she truly hated . . . or herself?

Alexander came racing down the hall, his coattails flying behind him. His golden hair was windblown.

"Where the hell have you been?" Shane demanded.

"I had a lot to do at the house with the police."

"There was a lot to do here," she scolded.

"How is she?"

"Still in a coma." Shane's eyes filled with tears as she looked at her brother. They'd never been close. She felt a rush of emotions . . . guilt, sorrow, anger, grief. Like a volcano they all seemed about to spew forth at once.

Alexander didn't understand the pathetic look on Shane's face. He did something he'd never done before; he held her.

Shane put her head on his shoulder and let a silent stream of tears slide down her cheeks. She said nothing. She had never felt so alone in all her life.

Awkwardly, they broke apart. Neither of them understood what was happening. Neither knew how to comfort the other. They were confused.

"I'm going to get a cup of coffee. Do you want any?"

"No. I'll just stay here."

Alexander went to the cafeteria and filled a giant styrofoam tumbler with strong coffee. He sat at a table for two by the window and looked out at the brilliant day. A wind was kicking up. It was hot and dry and strong. A Santa Ana wind, he thought.

Alexander felt confident he'd be able to keep this whole matter quieted down. The last thing he needed was a full-scale investigation. If it should come out that Barbara's helicopter had been tampered with, the reporters would never stop. Sooner or later, his link to the mob would be discovered. He'd be a dead man.

There was no doubt in Alexander's mind who was behind the crash.

What he didn't understand was why. Obviously, these men felt Barbara's power was something to be reckoned with. It gave Alexander chills just thinking about it.

It was one thing to knock off a drifter like Wes. Even Sergeant Mailer's death was understandable, if a bit difficult for Alexander to swallow. But his mother . . . If they would do this, there was no stopping them.

However, it was also obvious to him that they believed, perhaps even more than he did himself, that he could get Maureen's ranch from her. He was necessary to them. He liked that.

He knew he would have to be more than careful in dealing with the mob. One slip could be the end of everything for him. He must make certain they never knew how important Maureen was to him personally. The mob turned a cold shoulder to affairs of the heart. His plans meant nothing to them except as they would benefit their goals.

Alexander was no fool. He would play their game, no matter how deadly they stacked the deck. But he still believed he would come out on top. He had to think that way . . . to stay alive.

Brandon heard about Barbara's accident from his cook. Maureen heard about it from Juanita. Underground communications of household employees were faster than UPI, Maureen thought as she dressed for the hospital visit she and Brandon would pay on Barbara.

Brandon picked her up in his Corvette. For a long time they rode in silence.

Brandon didn't think for one minute the helicopter crash

had been an accident. He would have loved to conduct his own investigation with some really good people. Not some half-wit deputy who was not mentally equipped to handle his job. Brandon believed that someone was trying to kill Barbara. He just prayed to God she would pull through this and show them up.

Brandon was terrified as the ramifications of the incident sifted through his brain. He'd been threatened at gunpoint himself. He was realizing that his campaign to stop the gambling bill had a great deal to do with these events.

Maureen had told Brandon about the two men from Houston who had offered her so much money for her land. He'd allowed her to think that it was the gold they were after. He didn't want her to know the truth. He didn't want her to know that she might be a target for the mob, too.

Brandon was certain of one thing. He was not about to let Barbara suffer for nothing. Though he feared for Maureen's safety, he knew he must take the risk. He must go through with his plans. If he didn't stop this takeover now, there would never be an end to the killing.

Brandon's face was lined with concern when they entered the hospital and rushed down the corridors. They saw Shane slumped on the floor outside the ICU. When she looked up her face was tear-streaked. Maureen thought she seemed very, very young. And very frightened.

"We came as soon as we heard," Brandon said, placing his hand on Shane's shoulder. "How is she?"

"In a coma. There's a punctured lung. She had surgery. I saw her about half an hour ago . . . you won't believe it . . ." Her voice trailed off. "They won't tell me much. Maybe it's because all the news is bad. . . ." Shane's voice croaked.

"She'll be all right," Maureen said, trying to comfort her. "She's a very strong woman."

"I know," Shane replied, thinking how weak she was in comparison. She never could have done the things her mother had done. She didn't even know if she'd want to. There seemed no point.

"Can we see her?"

"I don't know. You have to ask the nurse. Ring the bell."

Brandon depressed the buzzer on the wall. The door opened to reveal a fresh-faced young nurse.

"May we see Barbara Cottrell?" Brandon asked.

"Are you family?"

"No."

"Sorry."

She started to shut the door. He held his hand against it. "Please."

"We make no exceptions. It's too disruptive to the other patients. If we bent the rules for you, we'd have to let everyone in. It's impossible."

"I must see her," Brandon insisted.

"You and half the state. The switchboard operator has been flooded with calls for the past hour. The nurse at Receiving said the lobby is filled with truckloads of flowers. I kept the cops out. I can't let you in."

Brandon grabbed her hand. "You don't understand. It's vital. Just for a minute. Please . . ."

She gazed at him as the sincerity of his plea crackled through her. Perhaps she'd been working here too long. As she looked at him, she remembered she'd once vowed not to become jaded. But she had. And she was only twenty-three.

"Three minutes."

"You can time me." He smiled.

He took Maureen's hand as they walked to the second curtained stall in the ICU.

Maureen didn't understand what all the fuss was about. There was more noise, more commotion and confusion inside the ICU than outside. Phones rang, nurses shouted orders to each other and machines bleeped and beeped.

When Maureen saw Barbara lying prone on the hospital bed, she gasped. Barbara looked like another person. Her beautiful silver hair was more black than anything else, and sprouted in ugly patches from her head. Her arms were burned and covered with salve, as was her neck. But her face looked nearly untouched, except for some swelling on her left cheekbone. What was most frightening were all the tubes coming out of her. There was a huge chest tube, an IV, a catheter, a heart monitor and a pace monitor. She wore an oxygen mask on her face. Her breathing was incredibly labored.

Maureen could hear Barbara's pain. She said a quick prayer.

Brandon leaned down and whispered something into Barbara's ear.

Though Maureen strained, she could not hear what he said. She watched as he carefully inserted his hand under Barbara's burned one. He did not touch her, nor cause her pain.

He leaned down again.

"Barbara. It's me. It's Brandon. Maureen and I are both here. You're going to pull through this, Barbara. I need more than just your help, Barbara. I need *you*. We aren't going to let them get away with this. I promise you that. I'm not going to let you suffer in vain. We'll stop this. I want you to live, Barbara. Do you hear me?"

Brandon straightened.

Just then the nurse came up from behind them to tell them they must leave. Maureen turned around to answer her, and as she did, she missed seeing Barbara's little finger press down on Brandon's hand.

When they walked out of the ICU, Brandon's face was once again filled with hope.

27

♦

BURT BEAN FLIPPED OFF THE TELEVISION after the newscast on the morning after Barbara's helicopter crash. He'd never liked Barbara, and she definitely had never liked him, but he always felt sympathy for anyone when tragedy struck.

Burt never once thought of his "associates" in connection with Barbara's accident. He'd believed both Alexander and the deputy sheriff when they stated emphatically that there had been a mechanical failure. Burt had no reason to think otherwise.

Burt was flying high. Just last week he'd received the first of many large checks to come his way. A quarter of a million dollars went a long way in keeping his corporate doors open.

Through Jennie Sloan, Burt had met the men who had put him into the drug-smuggling business. And it had been easy. Nothing was asked of him except the use of his airstrip for late-night drops. All he had to do was keep his eyes, ears and mouth shut. Only once was he asked to oversee a shipment. He'd shown the driver of the U-Haul truck where to park, then watched while the pilot and the truck driver loaded duffle bags of marijuana and a small crate of cocaine onto the truck.

For this little amount of work, Burt was handsomely compensated.

At a time when his oil buddies were losing houses, cars, planes and companies, he was staying afloat. He was proud of himself. Damn proud.

Neither he nor his family had to suffer. Lynn was still

able to shop the way she always had, and he was able to keep Shane happy.

It was obvious to him that Lynn appreciated his accomplishments; she'd argued very little with him lately. He'd been able to come and go as he pleased of late. He was able to see Shane a bit more often, too. He liked that.

Lynn had gone off with Maureen McDonald and Charleen Sims to Dallas to shop. He could spend the whole day with Shane. Considering the strain she was under, she would like the "uppers" he had for her. He hoped he had to spend hours "consoling" her.

Burt had another reason for seeing Shane. He had a little "business" to discuss with her.

The night before, while Burt had been finishing his work at the office, he'd gotten a call from Jennie. She'd told him that his "associates" wanted to meet with him. She gave him the time and an address off Harper Road. He went to the appointment willingly. He was told that he could make an extra fifty thousand dollars by enlisting Shane Cottrell's aid.

"What for?" Burt asked.

"Her brother is causing us some consternation. We only want her to check on him. Make certain he's doing as he's been told. However, she is *not* to know about us. Drug addicts have loose tongues."

Burt was surprised. "Alexander is working for you, too?"

"As we've said before, only the finest people are in our employ."

"I'm beginning to see that."

"Promise her everything she wants if she spies on her brother for us."

"You can count on me," Burt said.

"Of course we can."

Burt now leaned back in his easy chair. He was a lucky man. He had the perfect life. He was winning when his friends and business colleagues were dropping like flies. Nothing in his life had changed for him since the crunch. In fact, it was better. Burt had it made.

Lynn Bean wasn't at all nervous when she walked into the attorney's office high atop a Dallas skyscraper. She'd been waiting for this day for weeks. Brandon had arranged not only the appointment for her but had given herself, Maureen and Charleen the use of his plane and pilot to fly to Dallas.

John Kimberley shook her hand and closed the door to his office behind them. The attorney saw a striking brunette and a pretty blonde in the waiting room. He guessed the dark-haired girl to be Maureen. Brandon had told him a lot about Maureen. She looked special, indeed.

"I'm so glad you could see me," Lynn said.

"No problem. Brandon briefed me a bit, but I'd like to ask one thing before we proceed."

"Sure."

"Is this a recent decision? I don't want you to be hasty."

"I've wanted to leave Burt for fifteen years."

John was taken aback, although he shouldn't have been. He'd been a divorce attorney for twenty-one years. He'd heard every story in the book and then some. Not much surprised him anymore, but recently there'd been a rash of divorce filings. A lot of women were filing because the money was gone. He wanted Lynn to be sure.

"Why now all of a sudden?" he probed.

"Burt has been stripped of his money so he can't hold my kids over my head anymore."

John nodded knowingly. "I understand."

"Burt's always told me he could hire a judge to keep me from the children and any of the property. Now he can't."

"What makes you so sure?"

"What?" Lynn felt that familiar nausea creep through her stomach.

"I did some preliminary investigations. Your husband seems to be hanging in there somehow."

"That's impossible."

"I could show you the reports."

"I've hired investigators before. Unfortunately, they've always been accurate." She sighed. "How can he be doing okay?"

"On paper, it looks like he's simply cut back, laid off a few employees, shuffled monies around, but he's far from broke . . . yet."

Lynn's forehead knotted. "I heard him on the phone only six weeks ago begging his banker not to foreclose. He told his attorney he was washed up."

"That's quite possible. Is there someplace where he could have borrowed money? Family?"

"You must be kidding. They're poor as church mice."

"Well, it's coming from somewhere."

"Then, I . . . I can't file yet?"

"I wouldn't let it stop me altogether. We can fight him every step of the way."

"But it could be ugly, couldn't it?"

"For the children . . . it could be difficult. I won't lie to you."

"Oh, God. Where do we go from here?"

"It's up to you. I'd like to find out if the papers I saw were accurate. That would be a start. If he's falsified information, then we've really got a case."

Lynn brightened. "I could get that information for you."

John hesitated. "I can hire—"

"No. I'll do it myself. I have ways . . ."

"I'm sure you do."

Lynn rose. "I'm going to get this divorce if it's the last thing I do."

"I think you should. No one can live forever in tyranny."

"Tyranny. Yes. That's exactly what it's been."

They shook hands and Lynn left. She walked out of the building explaining the situation to Maureen and Charleen.

Lynn was disappointed that things had not gone as smoothly as she'd hoped. But this was only a setback. She was *not* going to give up. She was right and Burt was wrong. She had her friends to help her. She was going to be free. And it wouldn't be much longer.

28

◆

MAUREEN WAITED outside the excavated hole while the geologist took samples. Brandon had found him in Austin. He was young, just out of the University of Texas two years, but he was smart.

Ryan Lassiter heaved himself out of the hole. He was tall, thin and light-haired. He had bright blue eyes, a high forehead and a big smile. There was nothing about him not to like.

"I could see the shafts that radiate from this opening. Once it's excavated properly, you'll be able to walk right in and go to three tunnels. I'd clear out the bottom of this slope. I think that's where the original opening was."

Maureen nodded her head. He wasn't telling her anything she didn't already know. "What did you find?"

"I took over a dozen samples. I'll have them assayed properly for you."

"How long will it take?"

"Usually a couple weeks to be sure. But I've got a friend in Washington who was just hired at an assay office. He could go in at night and speed this up for us."

"That would be great!"

"Yeah," he said, looking down at the mine. "I'd like to find out how close I am in my guess."

"Close to what? You're either right or wrong."

Ryan scratched his head. "I already know I'm right. I'm certain there's gold down there. Silver, too. And I'm sure this

271

is platinum in this rock.'' He started digging in his backpack for the sample.

Maureen couldn't believe her ears. And he was being so calm about it. *"Gold? And* platinum?''

"Yeah. If there's enough platinum, you could make a killing selling it to space companies . . . NASA. You know.''

"I do?'' she said breathlessly.

"Look, Miss McDonald, I can't give you an accurate count right here and now. There's calcite crystals in all this stuff. You gotta have point-oh-one troy ounces of gold per ton to make it profitable. There's some heavy mining over at Presidio Mine in the Trans-Pecos area. But the Bureau of Economic Geology has never tested this area.''

Maureen was stunned. "I just can't believe there's even a trace here.''

"What?'' Ryan looked at her askance. "You mean you brought me all the way down here and you hadn't even seen this much?''

"Pretty stupid, huh?''

"Man, you're what I call a believer.''

Maureen wondered what Charleen would say to that. Perhaps she was using her heart—her hunches, her dreams—more now.

"I'm hoping this is micron gold,'' Ryan continued.

"What's that?''

"It's the kind of gold where the veins have not been played out. But it's expensive to mine. You have to crush the rocks containing the gold and then leech the mineral out. I have a strong hunch that's what we're going to find.''

"If it's so expensive to mine then why would I want it?''

"Because that's the kind of gold that would not be only in one place. It would be running through all these hills.'' He spread his arm over the area, his eyes wide. "Think of it. . . . By the way, who owns all this?''

"I do.'' Maureen smiled widely.

"No shit?'' He gasped and looked out at the hills again.

"No shit.''

"I'll make sure you get an answer this week.''

Shane rested her chin on her hands as she lay nude on the carpeted floor of Burt's cabin. It was a sunny day, the kind of day she normally hated because she was usually battling a hangover. Not today. She just wanted some time to think. She was finding it a painful process. She thought about her mother, her life, her future. All of it looked dim, fuzzy, and yet was edged with gruesome black outlines. Shane's entire existence was a nightmare.

"What's the matter, baby?" Burt asked as he watched his hand lazily graze the surface of her back and then move down to the smooth mound of her buttocks. Shane had the most perfect body he'd ever seen. And Burt had seen many.

"You got any more coke?"

"It sure takes a lot to get you high these days."

"I've got a lot on my mind."

Burt laughed. "Sure you do, honey."

She rolled over and sat up. "What's so funny?"

"I've known you a long time. There's only one thing on your mind." He touched her breast.

She pulled away from him. She was straight at the moment, and she didn't like the condescension in his voice. She didn't like his patronizing. He was treating her as if she were . . . someone like Jennie Sloan. The thought was a bitter one. She was Shane Cottrell, not some sleazy whore; not some "white trash," as her mother would say. Shane shook her head, trying to get rid of all these depressing thoughts. The world was a much happier place for her when she was stoned.

"Fix me up, Burt." She stood. "And where did you put that grass?"

"On the counter." He pointed. "I guess maybe you do need something at that. You haven't been yourself all day."

Shane rolled a joint and lit it. "I wonder what 'being myself' is," she mumbled. She waited while Burt prepared six lines. She did four. He did two.

Immediately Shane felt better. Much better. She put her arms around his neck. "I just wanna be happy, Burt."

"We all do, sugar. And that's what I'm here for." He kissed her deeply. They sank to the floor, and he caressed her gently.

"Shane, honey. Did you do as I asked you?"

"Do what?"

"Check on Alexander for me? Is he being a good boy?" He slid his hand between her thighs.

"As far as I can tell. He's busy running the ranch now that Mama . . ." Shane felt tears, but fought them. "Burt, I don't understand what you want me to find out about Alexander." Her thoughts, her words, were coming more slowly. Her vision was fuzzy. Even as she asked the question she'd almost forgotten what it was.

"Oh, just anything unusual you might see. Who he's seein'. If there was anything that might disturb you. I'm just thinkin' of you, darlin'. I know this is a terrible time for you . . . with your mother bein' so close to death and all. . . ."

Shane looked into his sincere eyes. "You're so sweet to me, Burt."

"You know I always have your best interests in mind."

"I do know that. Don't I?"

"Of course you do. And Alex, well, sometimes he can get on his high horse and he doesn't think of anyone but himself."

"That's true. But you'll take care of me, won't you, Burt?"

"I sure will. I promise. I won't let Alex take advantage of you. But you gotta tell me what he's up to."

"I'll do it." She lay back on the floor. She thought of what would happen if her mother died. There would only be her and Alexander left. Shane wondered where she'd find the courage to face each day. For years she'd lived only for the opportunity to make her mother angry. It was how she knew her mother cared. Barbara got mad at Shane's behavior; Alexander merely considered his sister a pest. He didn't really care. He didn't love her. If her mother died, she would have no one to love her. There was Burt . . . but he was still married to Lynn.

Shane put her forearm over her eyes. Her thoughts were too much for her to take. "Can I take the rest of the coke home with me, Burt?"

"Sure, darlin'."

"And I don't have to pay for it?"

"Not if you tell me about Alexander."

"I will. I'll do anything you say."

"I know you will, darlin'. I know you will."

Alexander picked up the phone in his study. It had rung eight times.

"Goddamn Mexican women! Where is everybody?"

Alexander had a lunch date in town with Jennie. He was late. And he was horny.

There was no greeting from the man on the other end of the line. But Alexander knew the instant he put the receiver to his ear who it was.

"Yes?" Alexander said.

"This is your last warning, Mr. Cottrell. *Do not* interfere with our plans again. You have been told that you must obey orders. This is a rule that we strictly enforce."

"What did I do?"

"You bribed another law official."

Alexander's anger pressed on his skull. "You son of a bitch! What the fuck did you expect? *You* try to murder my mother and you're pissed because I wanted to keep it out of the papers? A good investigator would have traced everything back to me. Or . . . was that the point?"

"No. It was not. We did not try to kill your mother. There was not supposed to be a crash. Only a malfunction on taking off. It was unfortunate about the pilot."

"I'm sure you won't lose any sleep over it."

"No need to be flippant. The warning still stands. Follow our rules. And our orders."

"And if I don't—?"

"You won't see morning."

"Okay. You made your point."

"It is crucial that your mother not be involved in this lobbying campaign."

"I don't believe it. You mean you're worried?"

There was silence on the other end of the phone. Alexander had struck a chord. He thought it valuable information that he could use to his own benefit. He was smiling.

"If you think you can do as you're told . . ."

"Jesus! You think I'm a kid or something? Of course I can."

"We have a job for you. You must do the work yourself. Do not hire someone else. Loose ends, Mr. Cottrell."

"I understand."

"Very well. We are most interested in persuading Miss McDonald to sell her ranch."

"So am I."

"Good. Then we understand one another."

"Perfectly."

* * *

It was Sunday so Maureen was not expecting a call from Austin. But Ryan Lassiter was too excited to wait. The receiver nearly vibrated when he spoke.

"My friend went in on Saturday night and did the run. I'd done a few tests myself, but his equipment is more accurate than mine. Jesus, Miss McDonald. Oh, 'scuze me. But this is pretty big."

"Tell me exactly what the report says."

"There's point-one-eight ounces per ton of gold; point-one-six of platinum and six-point-one of silver."

"Then it's worth mining?"

"I should think so. If this runs through even a tenth of your land . . . say, five hundred acres, you'd be looking at an estimated worth of over three hundred million."

"Dollars?" Shock buckled Maureen's knees. She sank into the chair. "Oh, my God!"

"I want to do more surveys for you. There's got to be gold in the creekbed and the hills behind where you've excavated. My bet is there're mines that aren't as old as the one we found."

"How old is it?"

"That mine was probably constructed by the Spaniards in the late sixteen-hundreds."

"Spanish gold . . ." Maureen whispered, stunned. Mac had been right! Chills coursed her entire body. She looked out the window to the oak tree where she'd buried him. She couldn't believe this was happening.

"You've got a lot of work ahead of you," Ryan was saying. "It's gonna cost plenty to mine all those minerals out of the ground."

"How much?"

"Seventy-five . . . maybe eighty million."

Her heart sank. "Where am I going to get that kind of money?"

Ryan laughed. "That's total outlay over a decade's time. I should think it would cost about three million to get started. Then you can pay for more equipment out of the profits."

"Only three million . . ." She sighed. Where was she going to get that?

"I'll send you a copy of the report in the morning, Federal Express. Then I'd like to arrange another trip down there if I can."

"Sure," Maureen said, then said good-bye and hung up.

She looked out at the oak tree. "I found your gold, Uncle Mac. But it looks like there's little I can do about it. Very little."

29

♦

A SUMMER SUNDAY NIGHT in Texas was lazy, quiet and un-
eventful, Maureen found. Ranch hands, once recovered from
their hangovers brought on by rowdy Saturday nights in
honky-tonks, went to town to visit girlfriends who would cook
fried chicken dinners and then beg for a sad song accompa-
nied by guitar. They were nights of front porch swings, lem-
onade and children playing hide-and-seek. Like a trip back
in time, a Texas Sunday night lost none of its allure, none of
its magnetism. Sunday nights were beyond tradition, a way
of life. They were a religion.

Maureen sat on a wicker rocker on her front porch, peeling
peaches for a pie, while Juanita droned on and on about the
friends she'd seen at Mass that day. It was the same friends,
in the same situations, doing and saying the same things they
had every Sunday since Maureen moved to Texas. In that
sameness rested their appeal. It was appropriate that Juanita
only spoke of them on Sunday night.

Juanita slid her knife into a juicy, perfect peach. She placed
the slice on her knife blade and inserted the fruit into her
mouth. Maureen smiled. Now she knew why it was taking
them so long to make this pie—and why it was taking so
many peaches.

Juanita kept talking in the same tone. She was lulling Maureen to sleep, and so Maureen did not realize that Juanita had
changed the subject.

"What did you say?" Maureen asked.

"Mr. Williams. He be here for dessert?"

"No. I don't think so."

Juanita heaved an exaggerated sigh. "He is gone again. No?"

"Yes, to some ranchers to the south of here. I'm not sure if he'll be up to a visit. It's been a tough week for him."

Juanita ate two more peach slices. "I think he be here."

"It's getting late. The sun's almost down. Maybe tomorrow."

"He be here." Juanita chuckled to herself. She knew a man in love when she saw one. Brandon saw Maureen every chance he could. Tonight would be no exception.

Juanita began a tale about two young Mexicans who were very much in love. Maureen listened as her maid moralized about the girl who would not allow herself to love the boy, even though he'd poured his heart out to her.

Suddenly Maureen thought she smelled smoke. She sniffed the air.

"Juanita? Did you turn the oven on already?"

"No, Señorita."

"You're sure there's nothing in the oven?"

"Si. I'm sure."

Maureen sniffed again. "I thought I smelled smoke."

Juanita sniffed. "I no smell smoke. . . ." Juanita stood and started for the front door, sniffing the air. Suddenly, she screamed.

"Señorita!" She raced down the front steps and pointed to the horse barn behind the house.

Maureen felt dread shoot through her veins before she even saw it. She knew she smelled smoke. And she smelled death.

Maureen stared with shock-filled eyes at the blazing fire that was devouring the horse barn.

"*The horses!*" she screamed as she sped toward the barn. She was halfway there when she remembered that both Grady and Rusty were in town. There was no one to save the animals "Esprit!"

Juanita had never moved her fat body so quickly in all her life. She went to the bunkhouse and returned with buckets. She started filling them from the water spout on the outside bunkhouse wall. Juanita had seen fires before, as a child in the barrio in Mexico City where a blaze could devour a shack in less than twenty minutes. She remembered hearing the screams of two of her playmates who'd been trapped inside one of those ramshackle huts when she was only four. She'd prayed all her life she would never see another fire.

Juanita did not let reason tell her that her tiny buckets were no match for the monstrous flames. All she knew was that she had to put out those screams she was certain she was hearing again.

Maureen dashed into the bunkhouse and ripped a blanket off one of the cots. She soaked it in water and wrapped it around her head and body. It was inadequate protection, but it was all she had.

Maureen could hear Esprit whinnying from outside the barn. In some metaphysical way, Maureen felt the horse was her last link to the past. It was more than just wanting to save an animal. Maureen did not feel she was foolish for risking her life for her mare. If Esprit died, then everything would somehow end for her, and Maureen couldn't and wouldn't let that happen.

Juanita looked up to see Maureen racing toward the inferno.

"No! Señorita! No! You be killed!" Juanita could hear the screams in her brain. Now they were Maureen's screams. Juanita was certain she'd just seen the future.

Maureen ran into the barn. The flames were on the far left side of the barn and the horses were on the right. But the summer had been dry and hot. The wallboards had not felt rain in weeks. The fire moved fast, gobbling up inches of roof and walls, then seeped down to the ground and ignited the flooring.

Maureen tried not to listen to the growl of the flames as they ate up the structure. She kept her eyes on her horses. She told herself the fire was far enough away to give her the time to get her horses out.

She unlocked the stall to the new filly who had been born only six months ago. Next to Esprit, this horse was closest to her heart. Brandon's face flashed into her mind as she remembered the night the filly was born.

The horse was frightened. She knew she should trust Maureen, but she backed away.

"Easy, girl. I'm here to take care of you. Come with me."

Maureen patted the horse's nose and moved closer, soothing her with words she used everyday. She won the horse's confidence and was able to lead her out of the stall. As they approached the open doorway, the filly snorted. The heat was incredibly intense and still building.

Maureen was stunned at how fast the fire had moved. She pulled the blanket farther over her head to shield her face.

The filly reared and punched at the air and flames with her forelegs.

"It's okay." Maureen tried to calm her and get her closer to the door. It was a battle. She threw her blanket over the horse's face so that she could not see the flames anymore. Maureen was able to get the frightened filly to the doorway. Then, quickly, she pulled the blanket off the horse's face, whacked her flank and yelled, "Get going, girl! Go!"

Maureen watched as the horse raced through the flames to Juanita, who was waiting for her. Maureen sighed with relief. She pulled the blanket over her head again and disappeared into the flames.

Juanita stood on the outside, screaming at Maureen, filling buckets and tossing water on the barn doors. She knew she must keep the entrance from collapsing. She hustled back and forth, constantly trying not to cry, knowing she couldn't stop her tears any more than she could stop this fire.

The flames crept over the roof and sucked up the dry wood shingles. The fire was like a crazed demon, spreading its claws over everything in its path. The roof now consumed, the rafters caught fire. One by one, they fell like dying kamikazes to the hay-strewn floor. Flames shot up from the floor like stalagmites. The remaining rafters and the main beam leaked long fingers of fire that met those from the floor, creating a blazing cage of death.

Maureen could hear Juanita screaming at her from outside the barn to leave now before it was too late. But there were two more horses and Esprit. She had to save them.

Brandon had taken the helicopter to Willis Blake's ranch. He'd hated like hell to book a meeting for Sunday, when he could have been with Maureen, but Willis was a busy man. He had no other days free. And Brandon needed his support. They had both talked about Barbara's accident.

Brandon was surprised that he had no trouble convincing Willis of the truth. Willis promised his full endorsement. It had been a great day.

Brandon headed the helicopter toward the McDonald

Ranch. He'd had dinner with the Blakes and he was hoping to simply relax with Maureen. He could use a rest.

Brandon had chosen a low-flying route. He liked how the setting sun painted pink, mauve and blue streaks across the hills. There was nothing like a summer sunset in Texas, he thought. It was the one time he was reminded how vast was the world, how great God's power. As he flew over the scraggly hills, watching the colors of sunset turn to the silver-gold of twilight, he noticed an odd orange light coming from behind the last hill.

"What the . . ."

He flew in closer. The hairs on the back of his neck stood on end. He'd seen that color only once before . . . when he had been nine years old and Shelley Larson's house had burned to the ground.

He topped the hill. "Damn . . ." It was true. It was coming from Maureen's ranch. Luckily it wasn't the house. Maureen would be safe. It hadn't rained in forty-six days, and everything in this part of Texas was a tinderbox. He hoped she wouldn't try to fight the fire. Everyone knew that anything would be burned to the ground before the fire department arrived. Everyone knew there was no fire department in the country.

He flew the copter in close to the house, but as he did, he saw Juanita standing outside the barn, much too close to the fire. She was waving her arms about frantically. At first he assumed that she was signalling to him. Then he realized she hadn't seen him at all. She was shouting at someone *inside* the barn.

"Jesus Christ!" Suddenly, he knew Maureen was in that barn. He landed the helicopter and in seconds he was racing toward the horse barn.

"Oh, Señor Williams! She loco! She crazy to save that horse."

"What?"

"Esprit!"

The flames had formed a wall at the entrance. But as he screamed Maureen's name, he saw her appear at the opening, a blanket wrapped around her. Two horses came galloping toward him, their eyes huge, frightened saucers in their heads. Miraculously, they were unharmed.

Brandon doused a blanket in water, just as Maureen had. He knew she would not come out until her horse was safe.

Brandon entered the inferno with prayer as protection. His pant leg caught fire, but he beat it out with the blanket.

"Maureen!"

She was at the far stall, struggling with a panicked Esprit, who was whinnying and fighting her.

"Brandon!" Maureen screamed over the roar of the blaze. "Help me!"

He rushed to her, and just as he did a huge rafter fell from the ceiling, narrowly missing him. He didn't even look back.

"You're crazy! You know that? What the hell do you think you're doing?"

"Bitch at me some other time. Save my horse!" There were tears in her eyes and her voice was filled with terror, but she kept trying to cajole Esprit out of the stall.

Brandon went into the stall next to Esprit's, climbed up on the four-foot-high wall and perched himself over Esprit's rump.

"Get out of the way, Mo!"

Maureen stepped aside as Brandon whacked Esprit on the flank. The horse reared back once, then took off down the aisle and out the door.

Brandon jumped down and grabbed Maureen. He put his blanket over them both. "Come on!"

They raced for the door. As they left Esprit's stall, a rafter fell and ignited the hay. A curtain of flame enveloped the far end of the barn.

Maureen could hear timbers cracking and falling. The flames roared like a great wind, and waves of heat nearly knocked her down.

Smoke billowed and curled overhead. She choked and coughed as she kept her head bent down low. She felt like a rag doll being dragged along by Brandon, who sidestepped one bank of flames after another.

They zigzagged to the entrance and outside. Maureen sank to her knees, coughing and wheezing. She wondered if the insides of her lungs had been burned.

Juanita rushed toward them.

Brandon's face was sweaty and black with soot. "Are you all right?" he asked Maureen.

She nodded because she couldn't find her voice. Had it been burned away? "Esprit . . . ?"

"She okay. I go get her," Juanita offered, and then went off to find Esprit, who had galloped out past the gates.

Brandon knelt beside Maureen, gently taking her face in his hands. "You could have been killed! Do you know that? Don't ever do anything that stupid again!"

"Why are you yelling at me?"

"Because I could have lost you!"

She stared at him. They both could have died, she thought. And slowly, the magnitude of what had happened, and what had *nearly* happened, sunk into her brain.

She turned back to look at the fire. There was not an inch of the barn that was not covered in flames. The countryside looked as if it had been lit by dawn. It was brilliant and hot and deadly.

"Brandon . . . I . . ."

She fell against him, seeking solace in his embrace. She held him closer and tighter than she ever had before. How like him to simply appear when she needed him. It seemed that life was constantly throwing them together, placing them in each other's lives. For so long she'd fought the feelings within her, the need to love him completely. She'd been frightened. She'd been afraid that if she loved him he would discover the challenge gone and he would leave her.

She'd been through that kind of thing before with Michael, and men before that. But none of them had mattered. Not really. That was the discovery she'd made. Brandon *did* matter. He had the power to break her heart if he wanted to. And she was the one to give him that power—because she loved him.

"I love you, Brandon," she whispered tentatively.

He cupped her face in his hands. He peered into her blazing blue eyes. Finally, she had said it. There had been days when he thought she would never admit it to him.

From the first moment he'd met her, he believed they had been fated to be together. He'd never told Maureen that, sensing instinctively that she could be frightened away easily, terrified of being hurt. The man she would choose would have to be very special to her. She would have to trust him first and then love him.

But Brandon had never worried about that. He knew he could never hurt her. He felt he'd always known her, as if they'd been together in another lifetime, in another world, another galaxy. He also knew that they would always be together. Nothing and no one would ever pull them apart after tonight.

"I love you, too," he said. "I waited a long time for you."

"You never said anything . . . you never pushed me."

"I loved you from the first moment I saw you. And you've loved me. There was no need to push you."

He kissed her deeply, probing her mouth with his tongue. She smelled of smoke, fire and danger. Her hair was singed around her face and her skin was red. He gently peeled the collar of her shirt from her neck. Already, a smattering of tiny blisters had raised. Gently, he held her, wishing he could crush her to his chest. He kissed her ear and outlined the pink rim with his tongue. He felt his heart slam against his chest. He was growing hard and his passion shortened his breath. He closed his eyes and kissed her again. His brain thundered with desire. His emotions ran wild through his body, making him feel as if he'd been pitched off the face of the earth. Tonight they would be one. Tonight they would seal their destiny.

Forcefully, she clung to him. She felt as if she had been branded by hundreds of tiny irons, but her need for him was greater than her pain. Suddenly, she was more frightened than she had been inside the barn, fighting for her life. At that moment Maureen realized she'd never loved a man before. What she felt for Brandon could never be put into words. It could only be felt. It couldn't be reasoned, and so she feared it. But tonight, she would succumb to him, to her love for him. She locked her fears into a tiny chamber in the far recesses of her mind where they belonged.

Her fingers clutched at his shoulders as she tried to pull him closer. He kissed her again and again. He sprinkled her cheeks, eyelids, chin and ears with kisses. She tried to stop crying but she couldn't; her emotions were flooding her with gratitude, joy and relief.

Her sobs were muffled only by the pressure of his lips on hers.

"Take me away from here, Brandon. I don't want to see any more of this," she said, glancing at the blazing barn.

He nodded, understanding what she meant. The fire was an end. This was a night for beginnings.

He lifted her in his arms and carried her into the house and never looked back on the flames.

He carried her to her room, shut the door and laid her gently on the bed. She kept her arms around his neck, reluctant to let him go. She wondered how she'd been able to spend so many days without him. She thought of all the time they had wasted—and it had been *her* fault.

"I could have lost you," she said. "Don't leave me . . . not tonight."

"I won't," he said.

Slowly, he peeled off her soot-streaked blouse. There were tiny holes the size of pinpricks where sparks had burned through the fabric and onto her skin. She was peppered with blisters and black smudges all over her arms and chest. Reverently, he kissed her breasts, thanking God she'd been spared real harm. Tenderly, he touched her, wanting to ease her pain, to make her well again. He kissed an ugly red patch on her neck, but she winced and pulled away from him.

"Maybe we shouldn't . . ." he said breathlessly, thinking he could not hold his passion another second.

"No . . . please . . . I want you. . . ."

She unbuttoned her skirt and lifted her hips while he slid it down her legs. As he stripped off her sweat-soaked slip, he noticed burn spots on her legs. She was streaked with soot.

Quickly, he stripped off his clothes and lay next to her. He looked at her, thinking that even burned and sooty she was the most beautiful woman he'd ever seen. He could see the soft lights of love and passion in her eyes. And as she gazed up at him, he saw those lights become more intense than the barn fire. She put her arms around him and pulled him to her.

She felt his hands on her back. She knew her skin was hot, but it was passion now, her need for him, inflaming her body and her heart. His hands felt cool as he gingerly touched her breasts, stomach and thighs. She knew he was afraid of hurting her, but she was numb to her pain. All she felt was pleasure as she lay beneath him. He had magic in his hands, she thought, as he touched and caressed every inch of her.

She heard him moan as he kissed her breasts and teased her nipples. It excited her to hear his voice as he played her body. She heard him whisper her name over and over—like a prayer.

Carefully, he eased himself over her, kissing her, whispering into her ear over and over that he loved her. She noticed that he did everything to avoid her burns. She kept hearing his voice penetrating her brain—marking her soul as his territory. When he entered her, her pleasure was so intense she felt as if she were sinking through the bed, through the earth and falling down, down into eternity to a place where they would never be apart.

They were joined forever as lovers had been since the beginning of time. No ceremony, no paper could be more sacred, more blessed than their union.

He penetrated her slowly, but as his passion rose and overtook him, he followed her guidance, increasing the tempo, sending shock waves of desire through her body. Maureen moaned and pressed her head backward into the pillow. She tilted her hips toward him. She squeezed her eyelids and bit her lip. She had never felt anything so intense, but she didn't want to scream.

Brandon saw her restraint. "Don't hold back. Not with me."

She groaned loudly as he penetrated her again. She flung her legs around his hips, bringing him in closer and deeper. Somehow she must find a way to fuse them together.

She felt as if she were soaring on a winged, sturdy steed. She could see the hills and valleys of her ranch. It was like flying in the plane with Brandon for the first time. He was taking her to the sky again. She screamed and flew higher.

Their bodies were soaked with sweat as she gyrated her hips beneath him. She called his name. He moaned when he spoke hers.

Like a whirling pinwheel Maureen spun through the sky. She lifted her head and kissed his throat in that vulnerable spot where the head meets the body, where intellect meets heart. She could feel his heartbeat; she could feel his love.

Suddenly she climaxed, and as she did she cried his name.

Brandon could hold himself back no longer. He groaned as he came inside her. "I love you," he said. " I love you . . .''

Exhausted and spent, they held each other. Both were reluctant to have the moment end. They wanted to go on forever.

Brandon held her hand. "I'm not leaving."

"I want you to stay tonight."

"I meant . . . ever. I'm never leaving you."

She rolled onto her side and looked at him. Suddenly, she realized what he was saying. So much had happened that night; she felt as if she'd crossed over into someone else's life. Perhaps it was because she was understanding herself for the first time. He still frightened her—his sureness of his love, the demands his love made on her. It was still difficult for her to trust. But she trusted him more than anyone else on earth. It was herself she had distrusted. All along, the answers to her fears had been within herself.

"I don't think I could leave you, either. Not now."

"Good." He smiled and pulled her next to him. He smoothed her hair and kissed the top of her head. He'd been right to wait for Maureen to come to him, he thought. He'd never believed in second best and he'd never compromised. All those lonely years had not been erased.

He looked down at her and was surprised to find that she'd fallen asleep. He could see the slow rise and fall of her chest as she breathed. He wrapped his arms around her. Maybe, if he prayed hard enough, God would give him a miracle. Maybe he could protect her from those who were trying to kill her.

Morning dawned in a blaze of sunlight that reminded Brandon of the fire the night before. He'd slept fitfully.

Maureen awoke, and smiled when she saw him looking at her. But then she realized that his eyes were filled with concern and dread.

"What's the matter?" she asked.

"Maureen, darling. I want you to think seriously about what you said last night. . . ."

"You mean that I love you? Well, I do . . . love you." She smiled. But he didn't.

"Maybe we should use more caution. Maybe we shouldn't see each other."

Maureen felt as if he'd lanced her heart. "What are you saying? I thought you loved me. Are you saying you don't?"

She tried to pull away from him, but he grabbed her hand. "Jesus! Is that how it sounded?"

"Was it supposed to sound any different?" She snatched her hand back. She felt icy cold.

"Yes." He tried to hold her. She inched away. "Mo, listen to me. It could be very dangerous for you to be involved with me right now."

"What?"

"That fire last night. I think it was set intentionally."

"That's preposterous! Who would want . . . ?"

She looked at him. Suddenly, her mind was on the same track as his. There were many dark and ugly thoughts that had seeped into her mind since Brandon told her about the mob and its machinations. He'd never said anything about

Barbara's accident to her, but she knew without his saying it that he suspected mob interference.

"You think they're trying to stop you by getting to me?"

"Yes, I do."

"What else do you think, Brandon?"

"I've been threatened myself. I didn't say anything because I didn't want you to worry. Now I think we should talk about it. I'll conduct my own investigation out here. It's arson. I know it. I also think that the men who made the offer on your land have something to do with it, but I don't know what."

"I'm not afraid of them. And I'm not going to be bullied into living my life according to someone else's rules. I won't do it, Brandon." Her eyes were stern as she looked at him. He traced the outline of her lips with his finger.

"I just wanted you to know what you were in for."

"I know. Honestly, I do. As for those men, I think they knew about the gold. . . ."

"You don't know for sure if there's anything there worth having."

"I do now."

"What do you mean?"

"I got the assay test results yesterday. There's a strong possibility that there's more gold here than we could count. I think somehow they knew about the gold. Three hundred million is a lot of money."

"Good God!"

"Ain't that a kick in the pants?" She smiled. "Only problem is, I need three million just to start digging it up."

He touched her hair and brushed it off her shoulder. "Sweetheart, I can advance you three million."

"Oh, no! I'll find the money myself."

He rolled his eyes. "Are you going to start that again?"

"Brandon, you know how I feel about this. If I don't do something on my own, for myself, I'll never feel right about anything again. I *have* to do this. Please, don't stand in my way."

"I wouldn't dream of it. I know that feeling. I've had it all my life. I still have it. I guess it's no different for women. Okay, you dig your gold. But if it gets really tough and if using my money is the difference between doing it and not doing it at all, then I want you to promise you'll come to me."

"Okay. But only as a last resort."

His lip curled upward. "You know, I think you're being shitty about all this."

"Thanks a lot!"

"You'll offer your profits to any investor you meet, but to me . . . the man who loves you . . . what do I get?"

"You get me."

"Yeah," he said, pulling her to his chest again. "I do get the prize, don't I?"

30

◆

Houston
July 23, 1986

A TROPICAL DEPRESSION sat out in the Gulf of Mexico, causing no serious threats to life or property but inundating the
city with torrential rains. It was a nuisance to the thousands
of commuters who were streaming into the city at seven-thirty
this morning. Interstate 10 was backed up to Highway 6 near
Katy. Interstate 45 coming in from the north was worse because of the heavy construction. Highway 59 from the south-
west was the same. Uncannily, there were no accidents, no
stalled cars. Even the Metro Network helicopter reporter
commented on that fact to his listeners. Houstonian commuters had learned patience.

In the meeting room at Three Allen Center, the chairman
of the board had lost *his* patience. It was unlike him, and he
became even more frustrated when he realized his composure
was dissolving.

Rain pounded against the wall of glass, and thunder rattled
through the room. But no one was aware. The committee sat
in rapt attention as the chairman spoke. Mother Nature's
power could be awesome and deadly, but the chairman's
power was more swift.

"I find it hard to believe that Miss McDonald has not been
persuaded to sell out."

The older of the two lieutenants was spokesman as usual. "When Mr. Cottrell made her an offer of three million she refused. We returned ourselves and repeated our offer. She referred to the fire as 'unfortunate.' We could see that she had gone into the barn herself—she was still badly burned when we saw her."

The chairman's eyes narrowed. "What kind of woman is this? She has a harrowing experience like that, she has no money and she still won't sell."

"No, sir."

"Then we must find another way. There are loopholes in everything. I want you to call our attorneys and have them find a way we can *legally* divest her of that land. If she won't leave willingly, we'll simply take it from her. We've tried to be fair with her, but she has refused us. In the meantime, we'll hear the vice-president's report."

The vice-president glanced down at his leather folder, closed it and addressed the group, sounding like the Harvard law graduate he was.

"Brandon Williams's lobbying campaign must be stopped immediately," he said. He'd learned in speech and debate classes to use an emphatic opener. That way he kept everyone's attention while he went through his boring statistics. He preferred and trusted people who gave him the bottom line first. He didn't have time for superfluous bullshit in his life. But the man sitting across the table from him did. And he wanted to please his superiors. He wanted their jobs someday.

The chairman's head inclined only slightly, giving the vice-president the assurance he was looking for.

"Our privately conducted poll has revealed that the issue is evenly divided. If Williams's efforts continue, by November he will win. We must not only increase our air time on television, our newspaper coverage and efforts in the private sector, we must curtail Mr. Williams.

"We have devised a plan that will give us the results we need. At this juncture, I believe all of us will agree that any overt action is too dangerous. On the heels of the Cottrell crash and the fire at the McDonald Ranch, action of that nature could easily backfire."

The chairman sipped his water. "You have worked out all the details?"

"Yes, sir."

"Proceed."

The vice-president outlined his plan. It took him twenty-one minutes to do so. When he finished the chairman was smiling. The vice-president knew that if his plan succeeded he would be promoted to president. God, how he loved the merit system.

The chairman looked at his board of directors. "We'll vote on this action. All in favor raise your hands."

Every hand at the table went up.

"It's unanimous. Proceed, Mr. Vice-President."

Charleen raised a bejeweled hand to shield her eyes from the setting sun. "There's nothing left!"

"Not a board," Maureen said as they walked around the debris and remains of the horse barn. She kicked at the ashes with her boot and a tiny black cloud billowed out. For two weeks she'd come out here every morning and just stared at the destruction. Brandon's investigation revealed arson, but there were no clues, no leads. She had not expected there to be any. The insurance company wouldn't pay her until they were convinced she had not set the fire herself. Her books revealed her to be in very difficult financial straits. No one had said anything about criminal charges. Maureen thought that the insurance investigator believed her. He simply couldn't put anything in his report that would convince the company to pay. Maureen had wondered if *he'd* been bought out, too.

Maureen did not want to say anything to Charleen about who she suspected was the real arsonist. She was afraid that too much information might put Charleen in a vulnerable position. She thought of Barbara Cottrell, still fighting for her life. She too easily remembered the heat of the flames. Her burns had been many, but they were minor. She could have been scarred for life, but fortunately she was healing quickly. Maureen had to protect Charleen. She didn't want anything to happen to her friend.

"The insurance company won't give you anything?" Charleen asked.

"Not until they're convinced I didn't set the fire."

"That's ridiculous. You nearly lost your life trying to save those horses. Anybody who knows you knows you're not capable of such a thing."

"They *don't* know me."

"No, they don't." Charleen sighed. "Tell me what I can do."

Maureen smiled warmly. "Just be my friend. I need you now more than ever."

Charleen put her arms around Maureen. "That's a given. But you know me, I have to *do* something."

"You're already housing the horses. And thanks for bringing Esprit over today—I missed her. Anyway, I just have to rebuild the barn."

Charleen's face brightened. "Let me build the barn for you."

"Oh, no!"

Charleen glared at her. "You know, Maureen, one of these days your pride is going to pinch you in the ass!"

"Charleen!"

"I mean it. You take the defensive before you hear the play. I meant I would loan you the money to rebuild. You can pay me later, when you get things going again."

Maureen's eyebrow rose. "Ha! Now there's the part I'm most worried about."

"I can't believe this is you talking. You're one of the most positive people I know. Don't tell me you've started wallowing in this mire of gloom and doom like everyone else in Texas?"

"It's not that . . ." Maureen paused, mentally debating the wisdom of telling Charleen about the gold. If Charleen *was* truly her friend. . . .

"What is it?" Charleen asked.

"I think I've found Uncle Mac's gold."

Charleen's eyes ballooned open. "What? How?"

Maureen told Charleen the whole story; about the map, the arrowhead, the excavation and finally the geologist's report. "I've got the complete report in the house."

"I can't believe it. You know, I always believed Mac knew something. A person doesn't go around his whole life chasing a phantom. At least not someone as smart as Mac."

Maureen smiled at her. "You always liked him, didn't you?"

"I told you that the first night we met."

"Yes, you did."

"So, tell me what the report said."

"In essence, there's a great deal of money to be made. The geologist has estimated over three hundred million."

"My God! And how much will it take to get started?"

"That's the rough part. Three million. Obviously, I don't have that kind of money."

"But I do!" Charleen grinned widely.

Maureen gasped. "You can't be serious."

"I want to see that report."

"Sure. Let's go up to the house."

As they started walking toward the house, Maureen's excitement rose. She'd come to the conclusion days ago that she needed a strong investor. Charleen was not only financially capable, she was also a friend. Because of that, there was just as much to lose from the business union as there was to gain.

"Wait, Charleen. You know, this could be very risky for you. What if his findings are inaccurate and you've put up all this money? I'd never forgive myself."

"I'm not worried, why should you be?"

Maureen peered at her. "How can you be so sure?"

"I've always had a gut feeling about Mac. When everyone in Kerr County was laughing at him, I defended him. I don't know why. I hardly knew him, but I knew he was right. It was strange."

"No kidding."

"Besides, I'll just take the report to my psychic and have her tell me what I should do."

Maureen felt like throwing up her arms. "Forget it."

"What?"

"I mean it. I'm not about to have you let a fortune-teller decide the fate of my future."

"Jesus! Are you going to start that again?"

Maureen put her hands on Charleen's shoulders. Her voice was stern, yet sincere. "I'll make you a deal. I'll let you have the report if you promise to take it to real experts to look at. Accountants, attorneys—people with credentials. I want you to make this decision with your *head*. You're a good businesswoman, Charleen. Maybe you could be even better if you really trusted yourself."

Charleen considered the proposal for a minute. She didn't know why Maureen was so intent on all this. Everyone knew that especially in business one had to listen to one's gut, to one's heart. She'd gone through many years of taking books, files and reports to so-called experts, and then having them all come back with a dozen different recommendations. When all was said and done, she'd still been faced with the same decisions. She'd had to ask *herself* what to do. Charleen knew that someday Maureen would learn this lesson. In the meantime, she would indulge her friend.

"Okay. I'll take it to my CPA and to my attorneys. I'll even have my banker look at it. Anybody else?"

"No. Just as long as it's not a tarot card reader."

"I promise. But I can tell you what the answer will be."

"What?"

"They'll all tell me not to do it. But I will anyway, because I believe there's gold here. It's as simple as that."

Maureen was dumbfounded at how simple Charleen made life seem. She was never confused and struggling with herself the way Maureen often was. Maureen found it difficult to make many of the decisions in her life. She'd agonized for years over her decision about Michael. Even now, she knew she loved Brandon, but there was still a lingering fear that gnawed away at the insides of her brain. She knew there were steps she needed to take with him—she was only just beginning. But she was hesitant. Sometimes, it all seemed so overwhelming.

Charleen, on the other hand, had no problems with men at all. She seemed to enjoy her many dates and she spoke almost reverently about Charles. Charleen was always Johnny-on-the-spot with advice for Maureen when the subject turned to Brandon. And yet she had no one of her own . . . and didn't seem to want anyone. Maureen couldn't help but wonder. . . .

"Charleen . . . may I ask you something personal?"

"Shoot."

"You're always telling me that Brandon and I were made for each other. And I think now that you're right. But don't you ever want someone for yourself?"

"What Charles and I had was very special. It would be almost impossible for anyone to take his place. And besides, he . . ."

"What?"

"I don't know if I should tell you this. . . ." She glanced at Maureen and saw only the concerned look of a true friend. She decided to trust Maureen with her most private secret. "Oh, what the hell. I guess I have to tell someone sometime. You see, I'm not lonely at all. I talk to Charles every night."

Maureen wasn't sure what Charleen was telling her. "You mean like when you're praying or something?"

"No. I mean I *talk* to him. And he talks to me. I can see him. Touch him."

Maureen physically took a step back. "He's dead, Charleen. That's impossible. I've heard of ghosts reappearing from time to time. I can understand mental telepathy and energy and spirits speaking from the other side. But once someone is dead you cannot touch them."

"I can. He even makes love to me."

"Are you sure? Are you really, really sure, Charleen? Or do you just think you touch him? Is all this happening because you imagine it?"

Charleen folded her arms across her chest. "I knew I shouldn't have told you. How could you understand something as rare as what Charles and I had when you don't even understand your own heart?"

Maureen was incredibly sympathetic toward Charleen. She was even lonelier than Maureen had guessed. She had concocted some kind of dream world that made her able to function in the real world. It was psychotic. Or was it?

"I think you were supposed to tell me, Charleen. Maybe Charles wanted you to tell me. Maybe he wanted me to talk to you for him."

"I doubt it," Charleen said through tight lips. She'd made a big mistake confiding in Maureen.

"No. I think it's very possible that he does speak to you, just as you say he does. And you're not the first person who has ever told me that."

"I'm not?"

"I did a story for the newspaper one time on this subject. I was supposed to take pictures of poltergeists and ghosts. But when I developed the film, all kinds of crazy things happened. The film got gobbled up by the processor. Some of the pictures were totally blank. Even the real furniture in the room didn't photograph. And yet, when I was standing there, I could feel something there. I couldn't see it, but I could feel it."

"Yes. That's exactly what I'm talking about." Charleen was becoming excited.

"But, Charleen," Maureen's voice was filled with empathy, "you can't touch him. You can feel him, but you *can't* touch him, or he touch you. When you talk to him tonight, ask him these things. Ask him to tell you the truth.''

There were tears in Charleen's eyes. ''I don't think I want to know the truth.''

''You see? You almost have your answer there.''

Charleen was shaking. She didn't want to even think of what life would be like without Charles. She didn't want to be a lonely widow, living out her days alone. She didn't know if she had the courage to do as Maureen asked. It would be too much for her. She was too frightened. ''I can't do it.''

''Maybe you shouldn't just yet. Think about what I said, though. Will you at least do that?''

''Yes. But no more. I can't.''

Maureen put her arms around Charleen. ''You were the one who told me that everything happens for a reason. Maybe I was brought into your life to help you just as you are helping me. I'm seeing things much differently since I met you, Charleen. You've given me a great gift.''

''But now you're asking me to go through a great deal of pain.''

''Maybe not. Maybe there's something even better waiting for you.''

''I never thought of it like that.''

''Try. Just try. Don't rush yourself. I only want the best for you, Charleen. You do know that, don't you?''

''Yes. I know that.''

''Good. Now let's take a look at that report.''

Maureen tossed and turned all night thinking about Charleen, wondering if she was all right, praying she had helped, not hurt, her friend. She thought of Brandon and wondered why he had not telephoned her all day. He was in San Antonio corraling more votes for the cause. Ever since the fire, he'd been twice as torn about his work. He wanted to stay in Kerrville and protect her. But they both knew, as difficult as it was to be apart, that her best protection was for Brandon to continue his campaigning.

It was hot, and the ceiling fan overhead was keeping Maureen agitated rather than lulling her to sleep. She rose and, barefoot, went downstairs. In the kitchen she found a piece of the chocolate cake she'd baked and poured herself a tall glass of milk. Because it was still hot in the kitchen, she went to the front porch. Absentmindedly she wondered how much central air-conditioning would cost.

It wasn't much cooler outside, but a breeze kept the air moving. She had just finished the last of her milk when she heard the sound of an airplane. She rose, leaned over the balustrade and scanned the starry skies.

She quickly realized that it was not an airplane; the sound was a sputtering, like wings thumping against the wind. "It's a helicopter. It must be Brandon!" she said aloud. She scurried down the steps and looked to the north where the noise originated. She waved, then suddenly she stopped. It wasn't Brandon at all. This helicopter was much larger and painted dark army green. She'd seen army surplus copters like this in Africa and other parts of the earth, but not in Kerrville, not in Texas at all. It was flying very low, which was abnormal, and toward Brandon's ranch.

Maureen raced back up to the porch. Her white lace nightgown would look like a beacon from the helicopter, and instinctively, she didn't want anyone to see her. She stood behind one of the stone columns. She didn't know why she was hiding, only that she felt she should.

As she watched the helicopter fly back around and then scan the area around her house, bunkhouse and front lawn, she knew something was very wrong. She crouched behind the column. It was a ridiculous thing to do, because it was her property and they were the ones who weren't supposed to be there. But the past weeks had taught her well.

The helicopter moved slowly. Then she saw a spotlight flip on. It looked like a laser as it swept across the top of a hill. The light was turned off as the copter flew on to the west.

Maureen raced inside the house, whipping her nightgown over her head as she bounded up the stairs. She jumped into a pair of jeans and pulled on a cotton shirt. She jammed her boots onto her feet. She started to leave the bedroom and then went back to the closet immediately. She squatted down and pulled out the huge black box filled with her cameras and lenses.

For years this equipment had been her link to fame, her security. It had brought her travel, income and even friends. Since moving to Texas she'd almost forgotten it existed. How odd it was, she thought fleetingly, that something that was once so vital had become forgotten.

Something told her that tonight she would need the best lenses . . . even her infrared lens.

Maureen didn't bother with searching for logical reasons or data to back up the quick decisions she was making. She was responding to intuition. She knew it and she accepted it as if it were factual material. Many things were changing for Maureen and changing very quickly.

She had tethered Esprit in back of the bunkhouse near an old water trough. The horse snorted when Maureen came running up.

"Happy to see me, girl?" Maureen patted the mare's head and then saddled her.

Maureen didn't want to take the truck, knowing she must be as quiet and unobtrusive as possible. Headlights were too dangerous.

Maureen mounted Esprit and they took off at a gallop, heading for Brandon's ranch.

Just as she came over the last set of hills that divided her land and Brandon's, she heard the helicopter again. She dismounted and took her camera and lenses with her. She could see the helicopter circling above her, but it was five hundred yards away. It hovered over one spot, shined its spotlight on a flat area of valley, then the light was turned off again.

Slowly, she saw something being lowered out of the helicopter, but she couldn't make out what it was. She quickly assembled her camera and fitted it with the infrared lens. She placed a fresh roll of film in the camera, then focused.

"What in the hell is it?" she said to herself as she clicked off shot after shot.

There were two men in the back of the helicopter. She photographed them, but knew she was too far away to get their faces. They were lowering an elongated bale to the ground that had four protrusions that almost looked like legs. She wondered if this was some kind of drug drop.

The crane dropped the object onto the grassy earth, then retracted the cable. The helicopter moved on to an area near the next set of hills. The procedure was repeated exactly. This time, Maureen was much too far away to get any clear pictures. She waited patiently until they finished and then flew out of sight.

Maureen mounted Esprit, racing toward the first drop. As she rode near, she couldn't believe what she saw.

It was the half-rotted carcass of a steer. Its head was eaten away and the bones in its ribcage showed. She clicked off half a dozen shots, then rode toward the next drop.

This carcass was in worse shape. Again, she took her pictures and moved on.

For two hours Maureen followed the helicopter around as it strategically placed the cattle carcasses. Maureen was careful to keep in the distance. She tethered Esprit in a clump of oak trees while she went in close for her last shots. She wanted to get the faces of these men on film. Even though the lens saw them clearly, their faces were smeared with black camouflage paint and they wore army camouflage fatigues. They could be CIA for all she knew.

Maureen snaked back down the hill on her stomach as she heard the helicopter whirl back up into the sky, whiz overhead and then fly back toward the west. She waited twenty minutes to make certain they did not return to the area. She didn't want to be caught riding the hills at two in the morning by these men. They would know why she was there.

Esprit carried her safely back home. Though she was exhausted, she went straight to the bathroom and began setting up a makeshift darkroom. She had all the proper chemicals stashed in her closet. It had been a long time since she'd developed pictures. But never had she photographed anything as sinister-looking as this.

She wasn't sure where all this was going to lead, but she did know she had the kind of evidence that could stop these people. She also knew these same photographs could get her killed.

31

♦

MAUREEN NEVER SLEPT that night. By dawn she'd developed all the pictures. She telephoned the Four Seasons Hotel in San Antonio, but the front desk told her that Brandon had left by cab at six-thirty. They didn't know where he was headed.

Brandon had told her he would be flying back at noon. She knew he had appointments this morning, but she didn't know with whom or where. She left messages at the airport for either Brandon or his pilot to phone her. She was desperate.

At nine o'clock Juanita started a second pot of coffee. "You need something to eat. All that coffee make you sick."

Maureen nodded. "I don't suppose there's any melon or peaches left. . . ." She smiled, knowing how Juanita loved summer fruit.

"Si, we have plenty," Juanita said defensively as she flipped on the portable television.

Maureen buttered the toast. At the same time that the phone rang, Grady and Rusty came to the back door.

"We need to go to town and pick up that roll of wire we ordered," Grady said.

Maureen nodded while telling the pharmacist on the other end of the telephone line that Grady would pick up Juanita's sinus prescription.

The kitchen was a mass of confusion and noise as Rusty teased Juanita and stole a peach. Maureen's eyes glanced at the television while she was saying good-bye to the pharmacist. She gasped.

"It's Brandon!"

He was still in San Antonio, and he was being hounded by a pack of news reporters as he was trying to get into a cab. He was standing in front of an enormous Spanish-style mansion.

"I have no comment," he said sternly.

"Mr. Williams," the commentator from CBS began, "cattle abuse is a serious crime. We have documented videotape of your ranch in Kerrville that substantiates the accusations. Surely you know about these cattle."

"I know nothing because I have not a single misused steer in my herd. I don't know where these carcasses came from, but they don't have a Williams brand on them."

A young, dark-haired female reporter shoved a microphone in Brandon's face. She nearly hit him with it. He backed away and laughed.

"Your enthusiasm, young woman, is not as attractive as you are."

Maureen watched as the girl became completely undone and was won over by his charm. She stuttered for a moment and then pulled back. Maureen clasped her hands in front of her face excitedly.

"Score one for our side."

Juanita, Grady and Rusty huddled around the set as they watched the badgering continue. Brandon fielded a few more questions, but he remained calm and patient with the reporters, who all knew they were onto the hottest story of the summer.

The local San Antonio news anchorman followed up the live report with a commentary.

"In the midst of a heated battle over the gambling issue, Brandon Williams, who is underwriting the less attractive of the two sides of this debate, has now found himself in a very damaging situation. There seems no doubt with the evidence we've seen that formal charges will be filed today. We wonder what bets Mr. Williams is putting on his future."

Maureen hated the sickeningly plastic smile the anchorman wore as he took his last barb. She snapped off the set.

Grady, Rusty and Juanita stared at her with shock-filled faces.

"He didn't do it."

"We know, Miz McDonald. But it looks like somebody's got him dead to rights," Grady said.

"Somebody . . . yes." Maureen's mind was racing at warp speed. Someone had set this plan in action weeks ago. And whoever it was had a master criminal mind. What she had witnessed last night was obviously the latest step in their plan, not the first.

Someone high up in the telecommunications network in Texas was on the take. All those reporters had not had enough time to investigate the story, or come to Kerrville and shoot pictures. She'd been on enough news assignments to know how long it took from the break of the story to air time. There had been careful orchestration to make all this happen so quickly.

Maureen also knew that Brandon's ranch was probably overrun by reporters this morning.

"Grady, when you go to town, I want you to buy me the *Houston Post,* the *Dallas Morning News* and any other papers you can find. I don't care if you have to go to all the news-stands in town. Oh, and get me a *Wall Street Journal,* a *USA Today* and the *New York Times,* too."

"Yes, ma'am."

Grady and Rusty left immediately.

Maureen wondered if these people had been able to put the story on the UPI or AP wires as yet. By tonight, she knew, it would have made the national papers and television. But it was important to her to know if they'd been able to garner national press this early in their plan. It would tell her how powerful they were. In a way, she thought, she didn't really want to know.

Now all she had to do was find Brandon and let him know that she held the key to his vindication.

Brandon had flown to Austin rather than coming home. He needed to enlist his backers. He knew exactly what was happening to him. The mob hadn't been able to stop him by threats and violence, but if they discredited him, ruined his reputation, he could be beaten. It was a sweet setup.

He needed to see Blane Arlington. Then he needed to see his ranch and the so-called evidence.

Blane was in his office. The air-conditioning was at full blast but the older man had two oscillating fans going as well. He was waiting for Brandon.

"Son, you got a pot full of troubles this morning."

"I do."

"I knew it was going to get rough, I just didn't know how rough."

"There must be a lot of illegal money to be made in Texas if these guys want me out of the picture so badly."

"What are you going to do?"

"I'm not sure yet. Other than I need you now."

"I'm behind you. What do you want me to do?"

"I need you to go on television and endorse me personally. Not just the campaign. I know I've been set up. I just have to prove it."

"That's going to be hard to do. But you know the right people. I think you can get it done."

"Oh, I know I can vindicate myself—eventually. That's the part I'm worried about. If it takes too long, which I have a feeling it will, the elections will be past history before I'm cleared. I think they know that all they can do is keep my hands tied for a few months."

"That's all the time they need."

"I can count on your endorsement?"

"I'll phone my people at the newspaper today. I'll get my statement to the UPI. Don't worry."

Brandon stood and shook the old man's hand. "Give 'em hell."

"I intend to."

Brandon raced out of Blane's office, checking his watch. It was nearly one. He should call the ranch and talk to Shirley. He should call Maureen. He should call his friend at KQUE in Houston and get some of the press on his side. He should call his attorney in Dallas and the private investigator he'd used before.

"Hell, I should do a lot of things."

He caught a cab, wishing for once he hadn't cut back so much. He used to have a phone in his car. He used to have a good reputation.

Maureen called the *Kerrville Daily Times*. She spoke to the news reporter there and told him to meet her at one o'clock at her ranch. "I'm gonna give you the hottest scoop of this decade."

The man seemed reluctant, but she finally convinced him.

She called Steve Zimmerman. He was the only person in Houston she knew who might help her out. He had connections. All she needed was his introduction to some news people. It was an extraordinary request to make of a restaurant owner, but Steve did it.

Houston's Channel 2 news was sending Terry Anzur, their five o'clock anchor, and a cameraman to meet with Maureen.

In Dallas she found a reporter and a photographer from the *Dallas Times Herald* who would also meet her. She persuaded a reluctant journalist from the *San Antonio Light* to make the trip.

Most of them arrived by air and landed on her airstrip.

At one-thirty Maureen and her pack of skeptical but courageous reporters set out in her pickup truck and Charleen's Jeep. They were equipped with Minicams, tape recorders, portable microphones, still cameras and mobile phones. Each person wanted to be able to call his or her station or paper to relay the news—if indeed there was a story.

Most of them were convinced they would only see what they'd already seen on television and in their own newspapers that morning. But under the seat of the driver's side of her pickup was a stack of eight-by-ten glossies that chronicled last night's events. Maureen was glad her camera engraved both date and time on each photo. She brought her equipment to verify its accuracy. She wanted no room for discrepancies.

They stopped at the first carcass. As they all got out of the truck and investigated, Maureen withdrew her photos.

"It's disgusting!" Terry Anzur said.

"If you look closely, you can see that the underside of their steer has black mud caked on it. There's no black mud around here. This carcass came from someplace else," Maureen said.

"You mean it was planted here?" Terry asked while signalling to her cameraman to start rolling.

"Yes I do. And I can prove it."

Maureen pulled out the stack of photos.

"This shows you how these carcasses were dropped by helicopter. You'll note the time and day. Last night to be exact. I used an infrared lens. I've gone over these photos a hundred times since I developed them. I noticed that there were no markings, no numerals, on the helicopter."

Terry looked at Maureen. "It can't be traced," she said with astonishment.

"No."

Maureen showed them the pictures of the other drops. "I'll take you to each carcass. I have photographs of them all." Maureen turned to the running Minicam. "I can prove beyond a doubt that Brandon Williams is innocent of the charges against him. Someone wants Mr. Williams's name sullied.''

Terry stuck her microphone to Maureen's face. ''Why do you think that?''

''Because Mr. Williams is successfully fighting the gambling bill that was introduced in Austin. He believes that criminal forces will move into Texas and become more powerful than ever. Obviously, he is a threat to those people.''

Maureen took the band of reporters to each site. Afterward, they all made calls to their home bases, arranging air time for that night's news, holding front-page space. They had been promised a scoop and they got it.

By three o'clock they were all on their way back home. To a man, they'd agreed that no one would ever be able to trace the original phone call that had ''broken'' the story to the press. Phantoms were easy to hire.

Maureen was exhausted when she entered the house and heard the phone ringing. She picked it up. It was Brandon.

''Where have you been?'' she asked. ''I've called half the state trying to get hold of you.''

He was tired and strained. His temper was short-wicked. ''I had a lot on my mind, okay?''

Maureen realized how she must have sounded. ''Are you at home?''

''Yes. I just got here. I'm going to take a short nap, a hot shower and fly to Dallas tonight. I'm really in it now, Mo,'' he said despondently.

''I don't know about that. I thought you looked kind of cute on TV this morning.''

''So you know.''

''Yes. And you handled those reporters really well. Listen, I think I'll get cleaned up and come over there. We can watch the evening news together.''

''Please . . .''

''I'll be over in an hour. Get some rest.''

''I'm leaving for Dallas at six-thirty. I've got a dinner meeting at nine. Why don't you come with me?''

''I promise I'll dress for the occasion.''

Brandon was asleep on the sofa in the den when Shirley let Maureen in. He had his Rolodex sitting on his stomach; the phone was on the floor next to the sofa.

"He must have fallen asleep in mid-conversation."

Shirley laughed. "You want to wake him?"

"Not yet. Does he have a television in here?"

"There's a portable in the kitchen."

"Great. I want to move it in here. By the way, does he have cable or get the Houston stations?"

"There's a satellite dish. . . . We get everything. What's going on?"

"Let's get some iced tea. I'll tell you everything."

Shirley and Maureen sat in the kitchen while Maureen explained. Shirley called Dallas and cancelled Brandon's dinner engagement. She told the cook to prepare dinner and chill champagne.

Shirley left at six to pick up her daughters at a swim meet.

At six-thirty, Maureen had the portable television in place, the dining table set, the candles lit and the champagne uncorked. She poured two glasses and went into the den to wake Brandon.

She woke him with a kiss. The Rolodex fell off his stomach. "What are you doing here?"

"I invited myself, remember?" She turned on the television and saw Terry Anzur's face as she began her special report.

"You're on television . . ." he said.

Brandon watched in amazement as Maureen vindicated him—to the reporters, to Texas and to the world.

"I can't believe this! I saw those carcasses myself—we must have just missed each other."

"Yes. We seem to do that a lot lately." She smiled and kissed him.

He peered into her eyes. "You're really something, you know that? It was a dangerous thing for you to do. It frightens me what they are capable of. I'm glad I didn't know anything about it. I might have tried to stop you."

"You think you could have?"

He smiled. "No, I don't." He smoothed her long, dark hair and then touched her cheek. "I love you."

"I love you, too." She kissed him deeply and felt that familiar fire flare up inside her. She put her arms around him.

"We should celebrate," he said.

"I've got champagne ready and a great dinner."

"Hmm." He looked down at her jeans and shirt. "I thought

we were going to Dallas. You're not dressed for the occasion like you promised."

"Oh, yes I am."

Maureen went to the wing chair and pulled out a small box. She took off the top and withdrew a slinky black silk negligee.

"What occasion were you speaking of?" she asked, moving toward him. "You and I together is all the occasion I need." She knelt beside him and kissed him.

He held her close. "Together . . . always."

32

◆

AUGUST CONTINUED TO BE HOT AND DRY. Farmers and ranchers complained of the drought that seemed to have lasted for years. There were more defaulted loans at the banks. Between the bad oil loans and the farm foreclosures, the Texas banking system was set on a downward spiral that would last through 1987. Oil wells continued to be capped. The momentum seemed to be sapped out of everyone in Texas. Giants of the oil industry and huge commercial developers toppled over themselves. The end of the summer brought dire predictions from every economic projector across the country. Texas had been beaten.

Psychologically, the state was fertile ground for the mob to plant their schemes, to grow their industries and harvest their profits. With only a little over two months until the election, Texas searched desperately for a leader, a Moses to deliver *it* out of bondage. Texas found Brandon Williams.

Brandon sank a million dollars of cold cash into his lobbying campaign. It was money he knew he'd never see again. But he'd never felt so positive, so certain he was doing the right thing, in his entire life.

Brandon arranged air time on every talk show in Texas. He was booked through October. He flew around the state doing radio shows, mall openings, theatre galas, charity balls and private parties. He was constantly "on stage." It was the first time he realized the gruelling life movie stars led. Obviously a job for the very young, he thought, as he crammed an airport hamburger down his throat and raced to make his flight.

Leaders are hard to find even in the best of times. And not always are they male.

Barbara Cottrell had been in a coma for months. The respirators and oxygen had long ago been removed. All that remained was an IV and a catheter. There was nothing more the medical world could do for her.

The doctors all foretold brain damage and the loss of memory, speech and motor skills that was common with coma patients. They told Alexander and Shane about the physical therapy, nurses and care Barbara would need and about the long months and even years of rehabilitation ahead. It was a gloomy picture they saw. They didn't understand that Barbara was not an ordinary woman. Barbara was a leader, and Texas needed her.

It was eleven-forty-three in the morning when she opened her eyes. The austere, sterile room looked fuzzy to her as she focused her eyes to the light. Her neck was stiff. She wondered why.

She saw someone sitting in a chair . . . a blonde woman. "Shane? Is that you?"

Startled, the nurse jumped up, dropping the new issue of *People* magazine on the floor. "Mrs. Cottrell . . ." She smiled broadly. "So, you decided to wake up."

"Who . . . are you?" Words came slowly, and Barbara noticed that her voice was scratchy, dry and at least an octave lower. She didn't like it.

"I'm Miss Ames, your nurse."

Barbara tried to think. She was in a hospital. But she didn't know why. She wasn't in pain. Unless they'd doped her up with something. "Why am I here?"

"You had an accident. In a helicopter. Do you remember that?"

"Helicopter . . ." Barbara did remember—vaguely. She remembered she had agreed to help Brandon Williams. There was the party she gave, and then she had taken off in the helicopter. She remembered her screams and those of her pilot, Larry. "My pilot, is he all right?"

"He's dead, Mrs. Cottrell," the nurse informed her sadly.

"Oh, no," she whispered. "He was such a nice boy. I must send flowers to the funeral home."

The nurse realized quickly what was coming next. "You rest for a minute. I know Dr. Teague will want to see you now."

The nurse hurried out of the room. She returned in ten minutes with the doctor, two interns and the head floor nurse.

Barbara thought it odd that everyone was huddled around her so. They marvelled over her ability to speak. They pinched, poked and prodded her legs, arms and trunk. They stuck needles into her. They tested her reflexes, her pupils, and examined her toes. They wanted more tests and more scans. She felt like a specimen on display. They oohed and ahhed at how well she had recovered. Barbara thought them ridiculous, especially since she had such a horrid headache.

"I think you're making too much of this," she said to Dr. Teague as he instructed the nurse to remove the IV. He handed written orders for solid food to another nurse. Everyone was smiling at her—a bit too widely.

"Not at all, Mrs. Cottrell. You may become famous for this."

"What are you talking about?"

"Why, we've all been tracking your progress here. It's amazing that you have all your faculties about you after such a long time in a coma."

Barbara's forehead crinkled with puzzlement. "What do you mean . . . 'a long time'?"

"Why, Mrs. Cottrell, I thought you'd been told. You've been here for over three months."

Shock registered in Barbara's brain. *Three months,* she thought. The whole world could have changed in three months. The ranch . . . who was running her business? She wondered how Brandon had fared with the campaign. And as her mind grew more clear and returned to its normal sharpness, she thought about the accident.

Larry was the best helicopter pilot in Texas. He inspected his planes scrupulously before every takeoff. Larry would have seen any discrepancies—if there had been any to see at the time of his inspection.

Barbara realized someone had tried to kill her. She didn't know their names, but she knew who they were. They were the ones she was determined to defeat.

"I want a telephone," Barbara requested of the nurse.

"We've already called your family," she said with a placid smile.

"Fine. But I need to talk to someone else. I need to talk to Brandon Williams."

* * *

Brandon was in Houston when he received Barbara's phone call. He was overjoyed to hear her voice.

"This is wonderful, Barbara. Why, you hardly sound tired."

"Of course I'm not tired. I've had ninety days' sleep. I'm ready to go to work. Just tell me what you need me to do."

"Have you talked to your doctors about this?"

"I never listen to doctors. It's a waste of time."

"I appreciate your enthusiasm, but I'd hate like hell for you to have some kind of relapse. Look, I'll be back in Kerrville tonight. Maureen and I will come see you in the morning and we'll talk about it then. How's that?"

"Fine. Just as long as you don't treat me like an invalid. I'm ready to go to work."

Barbara hung up the phone. The call had exhausted her. She felt tears prick her eyes. *Three months.* Someone had robbed her of three months of her life. She'd had some rough times before, and she'd had to deal with some real sons of bitches, but no one had ever taken time away from her. No one had ever tried to take her life from her. She didn't like it one bit. And if it took the last breath in her body, she was going to fight them with everything she had.

Barbara was convinced there were more people in Texas who would listen to *her* than would listen to them.

Alexander was stunned when the doctor called to inform him of his mother's recovery. Somehow, in his head, he'd imagined his life would go on as it had. He'd learned to run the ranch, make business decisions and negotiate foreign sales even better than his mother ever had. The one thing this time had taught him was that she didn't appreciate his talents at all. She never had, and probably never would.

When he entered her hospital room, he saw that she looked awful. She had lost over twenty pounds from a frame that had always been slim. His hopes soared. She might have recovered consciousness, but it was going to be a long time before she regained her strength. The best thing that could happen to him was for Barbara to have a relapse. If she stayed in the hospital, she would bounce back in no time. But he knew his mother was not a good patient. She hated being sick. She was the kind of woman who would push herself until she dropped. He would use that idiosyncrasy of hers against her. If he played this right, he'd be running the ranch for many months to come.

And if he could stretch his reign to the end of the year, he would have won Maureen to his side, married her and gained the McDonald land. Yes, he thought. If Barbara would just lay low for a while, until he gained more power . . . then everything would be just as he wanted.

"Mother, you look wonderful."

"I do? I haven't seen a mirror yet. They won't let me up till tomorrow."

"You don't want to push it. . . ."

"Alexander, don't you coddle me, too."

He had to fight his satisfied grin. She was falling right into his plan. "Who's doing that?"

"Everybody." She waved her arm and then let it fall heavily on the bed.

"Well, I for one can't wait to see you back home and running things again."

"You're having problems?"

"Not at all. I can handle the ranch. It's not that tough." Alexander spoke the truth. He'd found it nearly child's play to run Devil's Backbone, just as he'd always thought it would be. It was simply that Barbara had never given him the chance, never given him the control he needed to do things his way. He was making money and had cut some very good deals. "Mother, I know how much it would mean to you to get back to work. It's where you belong."

She smiled at him. "You do understand, don't you, Alexander?"

"Of course I do." He patted her hand. "We want to get you home as soon as possible."

Shane heard Alexander as he entered the house. She had poured a deep glass of vodka. He came into the living room where she was seated on the grey silk sofa.

"You saw her?" Shane asked.

"Yes," he said, pouring himself a glass of scotch. "Aren't you going?"

"I can't." She looked down into the booze, wondering why her life wasn't as clear as this drink.

"Hmmm." He flopped into an overstuffed chair, his legs stretched out in front of him. He watched his sister. She didn't look stoned, but that didn't mean anything. Shane was becoming expert at hiding her inadequacies.

"How did she look?" Did she ask about me?"

"Do you care?"

She glared at him. She'd revealed too much to Alexander in just those two sentences. She must be careful. After all, she was supposed to be observing him, not the other way around. "No, I don't care. I just didn't want her thinking I'd come running up there because she was conscious."

"Yeah, why start now?" he said, needling her.

"Cut the crap, Alex. You were no better. You weren't going to the hospital every day, either."

"I went once a week and called every day to talk to the doctor."

"Only because you didn't want her to wake up. She's spoiled your little paradise now, hasn't she?" Shane grinned maliciously. She loved being able to get to Alexander like this. He visibly squirmed in his chair.

"Once she comes home, it won't be so easy for you to see Burt as often as you do."

Shane didn't allow her shock to show in her face. She turned a cool eye to him. "You know about that?"

"Hell, everyone in Kerrville does except his wife."

"Too bad."

He looked at her. "That's what you want, isn't it?"

"She doesn't love him."

"And you do?"

"Yes. I'd be good for him."

"Right." Alexander downed his scotch. "I've got better things to do than to sit here discussing your lovers."

Shane laughed uproariously. "At least I have one!"

Alexander wanted to throw his glass at her. Instead, he bolted out of his chair and went straight to his study and closed the door. He took out Maureen's picture, her shredded scarf that he'd never found the heart to discard and poured himself another drink from the bottle he kept in the bottom drawer.

Shane tiptoed across the foyer to the door of her brother's office. Since the day she'd promised Burt she would spy on Alexander, she'd become expert at listening at doors, eavesdropping on phone conversations and going through Alexander's mail. But she'd found nothing of interest. She didn't know what Burt was looking for, only that so far she hadn't found it.

Alexander was talking to someone. She went to the phone in the alcove in the hallway. She got a dial tone. Alexander was talking to himself! She went back to the door and gently, gingerly, turned the knob and cracked it open. This she wanted to see and hear.

Alexander raised his glass to Maureen's picture.

"To you, my darling. Until we are together . . ." He leaned back in his chair, still looking at the picture.

"I'll show them all, Mo. Mother . . . Shane . . . the bastards who want to take your land from me." He started laughing. "Doesn't that beat all? Imagine . . . anyone thinking that they could keep us apart. Keep us from joining forces. It's just a matter of time. I know that . . . you know that."

He flung his forearm over his eyes.

Shane saw that he was crying.

He laid his head on the desk. After a few moments, he raised his head, wiped his eyes and held her picture in both his hands. He was shaking.

"I know you understand about the fire. I had to do it. They made me. I never thought you'd go in there. . . . Oh, God." He had to put the photograph down in order to steady his hands. Alexander was being ripped apart by guilt that sought to shred his fantasies. "I know what you're doing with Brandon—using him as a smoke screen so they won't know. But you can't hide your love from me—you never could. Time, that's all I need, Mo. Then we'll show them all. We'll use *them* instead of them using us. We'll show the bastards, won't we?"

Shane watched as her brother succumbed to a flood of tears. Gently, she closed the door, knowing somehow she'd seen more than even God would allow. It was incredible, she thought, as she went quietly up the stairs, but Alexander's demons were more destructive than hers.

33

♦

THE DOUBLE-EDGED SWORD of introspection had sliced through Shane's life with a vengeance. It was an unrequested intrusion, and Shane resented its presence tremendously.

Life had been simple in the days before her mother's accident. Shane had known the rules, fought them, bent them and lived just outside them. But they had been there, and they had given Shane's life meaning.

But life had taken a serious turn in the days and months since the accident. Shane had always known she loved Burt. But now that he wanted her to spy on Alexander, she had begun to question that love. It wasn't that she cared that deeply for her brother; after all, he didn't love her, did he? It was that she was seeing a side of Burt she didn't like.

Family loyalty had never been strong with Shane. However, no one had ever tested her before, either. No one had ever asked her to choose. Burt was forcing her to make hard choices . . . and Shane didn't like it.

For the first time, Shane was beginning to see Burt as her mother saw him. He was an outsider. He would never be part of the Cottrells' world. It was not because he was from a poor family or that his background was not as patrician as hers. It was because Burt believed himself to be an unworthy person. It was a failing Shane understood completely. That was how she felt about herself . . . most of the time.

Burt's lack of self-esteem had driven him to achieve success at any cost. He would do anything to keep his perfectly manufactured world intact.

Shane was beginning to realize that she *did* have scruples. They'd been dormant for a long time, but they were there. Her choice now was whether to activate them or not.

All these things Shane mulled over and over in her mind as she drove to Burt's house. Lynn had taken the children to enroll them in private schools in Boston. She would be away for four days. Shane had looked forward to this time with Burt for weeks. Now that it was here, she wasn't so sure anymore. Confusion rattled through her head like an angry inmate.

He was waiting for her at the front door. He'd dismissed the servants so that they could be alone. He kissed her after closing the door behind her.

"Anything wrong?" he asked, noticing her odd restraint.

She looked at him. For a very long time she'd told herself that this man was her world. She'd done everything to win his affection. Things she probably shouldn't have. She knew precisely how to manipulate him to get what she wanted. The only trouble was, he knew her buttons, too.

"It's been a rough week. Mother has regained consciousness."

"That's good news."

"Is it?" She went into the living room, straight to the black, marble-topped bar. She sat on one of the black kid and brass bar stools Lynn had had custom-made in Italy. Lynn had exquisite taste. Funny, she'd never noticed before.

Burt poured Shane a Stolichnaya. He pulled a packet of cocaine out of his pocket and eased it onto the marble. He withdrew his suede pouch, containing the two familiar glass straws.

Shane peered at the coke. Then she looked at him. "What do you want, Burt? A fuck? Or are we just gonna get high?"

"Jesus, what's gotten into you?"

She sighed and rested her forehead on her hand. "I don't know. Everything. Nothing."

He was sympathetic and came around to her side of the bar and put his arms around her. "We don't have to do anything. We can just talk."

"We can?" Shane looked up at him hopefully. Perhaps she'd been wrong. Perhaps she'd been analyzing something that didn't need dissection. "I love you."

"I love you, baby." He smiled seductively.

Shane melted, as she always did when he threw her these

crumbs of affection. She put her arms around him and kissed him. She found herself clinging to him, needing his love. She needed to know that someone, somewhere, adored her . . . that it didn't matter what she said or did, only that she *was*. She needed to be loved without reservation. Shane believed that was how Burt loved her.

"Let's go upstairs."

"Okay." He smiled. He helped her off the stool. "You want your drink?"

"No . . ." She hesitated. She thought of the heights of passion they'd been able to achieve. "But bring the coke."

They didn't sleep all night—there wasn't enough time. For the first time, Burt did more coke than Shane. It gave him incredible staying power, and she loved every minute of it. It was almost dawn when they finally rested.

He smoked a cigarette while she lay naked across his chest. He was clear-headed, despite the drugs. She was not.

He stroked her shoulder. "How's everything at home, honey?"

"F-fine."

"Anything particular about Alexander you want to tell me?"

"Do we have to talk about him?"

"Only if there's something to talk about."

Shane raised her head. The whole room seemed to be spinning. As always, she feared that if she didn't do as Burt asked, he would reject her. All her life she'd felt rejected—by her father, her mother, Hollywood, Alexander. . . . It would serve him right, she thought. Alexander shouldn't be the only one in the family to get what he wanted.

"Alex thinks he's a big shot now that he's running the ranch. He thinks he can push me around like one of the servants. But he can't do that."

"No, he can't, darlin'."

Shane propped herself on her elbow and tried to focus her eyes. Her eyelids were heavy and wanted to droop. Her head swayed a bit on her unsteady arm. "Alexander thinks Maureen's going to marry him. I heard him talking to himself in his study."

"Talking to himself? Does he do that often?"

"He has lately." She yawned.

"Did he say anything else?"

"Some stuff I didn't understand. Must be nothing."

Burt was instantly alert. "Like what?"

"That he was going to outsmart everybody. I guess he meant Mother. Said he was gonna marry Maureen and get her land and be more powerful than anybody. Said nobody was gonna boss him around. Or something like that. He kept lookin' at her picture and crying. And he's got some of her stuff in a drawer in his desk. I looked."

"What kind of stuff?"

"A torn-up scarf and a lipstick and some perfume. It's weird."

"It's obsessed," Burt mumbled to himself. Burt knew Shane had changed some of the words around, but the point was that Alexander was still intent on playing by his own rules. It was the kind of attitude that could get a man killed. It was a shame, Burt thought. He'd always liked Alexander. But, if Alexander had his own plans or was allowing his obsession with Maureen to be his conscience, Burt knew the results would be disastrous. Ultimately, the mob would find out that Burt had known about Alexander's plans, and then it would be Burt's ass on the line. And when all was said and done, Burt looked out only for himself.

He caressed Shane's arm and breasts and let his hand rest on her waist. "You look beat. Why don't you get some sleep?"

"I think I will."

Burt rose and started for the bathroom.

"Where are you going?"

"It's almost six. I've got a meeting to make this morning."

"You must be kidding. People really work at this hour?"

"Sure. Especially if they have to fly to Houston."

"Oh," she said, and passed out on the cream-colored satin sheets.

It was two o'clock in the afternoon when Shane awoke. Burt had not returned, and because she didn't know when he would, she showered, dressed and drove home.

Shane did not notice that, as she turned left outside the gates to Burt's ranch, Lynn was coming in from the west road.

Lynn didn't have to take down the license plate number on the red sports car to know that Shane Cottrell had just left her house.

Lynn had not cut her trip short. She had intentionally lied

to Burt for precisely this reason. She had wanted to catch him off-guard, and she'd succeeded.

Lynn went into the house and headed straight for the bedroom. The bed was a wreck. She stood there numbly as she thought about her husband and Shane in bed together. She waited for the familiar nausea to overtake her. But it didn't. Lynn felt nothing. No anger, no sorrow, no pain.

It was over.

Slowly, her eyes travelled to the nightstand. And there she saw it. She nearly pounced on the evidence. There was a mirror, a razor, two glass straws and a few powdery dregs of cocaine.

She knew Shane Cottrell couldn't make it through a day without this stuff, but for the first time she wondered if Burt was using it, too. Funny, she'd never thought about it before. Burt had always been a heavy drinker, and she had assumed that was *all* he used.

Lynn gathered up the paraphernalia and placed it in the suede pouch. She would use this against him somehow. But it was that somehow that puzzled her. Where was she supposed to go from here?

Lynn picked up the phone and dialed Maureen's number. Her call was answered on the third ring.

"I need to talk to you. Can I come over? Great. I'm on my way."

Maureen had just finished a late lunch of fruit and one of Juanita's raisin-and-cinnamon muffins when Lynn arrived. Maureen could tell from the consternation in Lynn's face and the anxious tone to her voice that something was terribly wrong.

"What is it, Lynn?"

"Could we go into the living room and talk?" Lynn asked as her eyes glanced at Juanita.

"Sure."

They sat on the sofa that flanked the fireplace. Lynn opened her purse and pulled out the suede pouch.

"Look what I found when I got home."

Maureen didn't have to open it to know what it was. "It's Burt's?"

"I'm not sure. I saw Shane driving away from the house. I know she uses this stuff."

"But you think Burt is, too."

"Yes. And I also think I've found what I need to keep my children from him. No court in the world would let two kids live with a drug addict."

Maureen looked at her friend intently. "Burt doesn't impress me as an addict."

Lynn's eyes narrowed. "Of course he is. He's just got to be," she said a bit desperately.

"Lynn, I don't mean to frighten you, but have you thought about other possibilities?"

"Like what?"

"That Burt isn't the addict, but the dealer?"

"My God . . ." Lynn's mind backtracked over the last year, then fast-forwarded to the past week. There were all kinds of things she didn't understand about him, his comings and goings. There were things she couldn't explain. But she'd been so embroiled in her own problems she'd tried not to pay attention to him.

"Is it possible?" Maureen asked.

"Yes, it's possible. But how did you think of that? Do you know something I don't?"

"Just a hunch. I've thought it strange that Shane, who is an addict, is so . . . well . . . enamored of Burt."

"It's okay, Maureen. You can say it. It doesn't hurt me anymore. I just want to get out of it. I want my kids to be all right."

"Then I think you'd better be very, very careful. I can tell you, I don't like this at all. It's dangerous."

Lynn smiled at Maureen. "Dangerous? Look who's talking! You've been walking on the wild side a lot lately and you're telling *me* to be careful?"

Maureen laughed. "I see what you mean. But drugs, Lynn . . ."

Lynn took a deep breath. She knew what Maureen was saying. She'd seen enough television, movies—hell, even the news—to know that drug rings involved all kinds of people. It was ludicrous to think that she, Lynn Nelson, the most sought after debutante of 1967, could be involved in anything so seedy, so frightening, as this.

Lynn put her hand over Maureen's reassuringly. "I'll be okay."

"You're goddamn right you will, because I'm going to call Brandon and tell him about this. You can step away and he'll take over."

"I can't let him do that! He hasn't got time to see you, much less take care of someone else's wife! I'll be careful. Besides, I'm still Burt's wife, and there ought to be things I can find out that no one can."

"Are you sure?"

"Positive. I'm going to get my freedom, Maureen. But I want you to promise you won't tell Brandon anything about this. I don't want him calling the cops or anything like that. I don't want my kids to see their father in jail. I'll handle this my way. Okay?"

"I don't like it, but . . . okay."

Maureen walked Lynn to her car as they elicited promises from each other that both knew only the fates could keep. Both women were taking incredible risks with their lives and the lives of the people around them. Neither had asked for these challenges, which had been delivered to their doorsteps by the desperation of hard times. Neither of them could foretell the outcome. They could only wage the battle.

34

LYNN HAD BEEN HOME for two days before Burt breathed easy again. She'd surprised him by coming back early, but when he arrived home nothing seemed out of order. She was busily dictating orders to her household staff. They were to host a barbecue over the Labor Day weekend, and Lynn, as was her custom, made certain not a single detail was overlooked. Lynn ordered the pool company to clean the pool. She had the gardeners plant fresh begonias and geraniums around the terrace. She had the black wrought iron fence painted. She told Burt she'd ordered a red-and-white-striped marquee, two dozen floral arrangements and had hired a fantastically expensive caterer out of Fort Worth to prepare the food.

Burt smiled, downed a scotch and let her have her way.

Burt wasn't quite certain what had happened to his suede pouch. He assumed that Shane had taken it. Since his trip to Houston, he'd had a lot more on his mind than trivialities.

For the first time in a long time, he was being asked to handle some of the drug drops. There would be five in all. This was more than simply allowing someone to use his airstrip. This time he felt like a criminal. It didn't settle easily on him.

Lynn watched Burt as he sank his knife into his steak. She picked at her salad. She kept up a light banter of conversation about the forthcoming party. It conveniently covered her nervousness.

Lynn had devised the party as a cover-up for her real purpose—that of gathering evidence against her husband. She'd

329

had the maids strip every room in the house. She told them she was having the rugs steam-cleaned. The draperies were yanked down and sent to the dry cleaners. It was not at all odd, then, that she would have Burt's study cleaned also. But this room, she told them, she would clean herself. She said she didn't want his papers to be misplaced by the staff.

They understood.

That very afternoon, Lynn discovered exactly what she knew she would find. A wall safe. She didn't know when Burt had had it installed. It couldn't have been during construction. Lynn had been so excited about the house she'd been on the site every day. No, it had to have been later. How much later she would never know.

Since Lynn was not a safecracker, she went to someone who was.

His name was Eagle Eyes. He was Comanche and had lived in the area all his life. Lynn had remembered that he'd been tried for bank robbery when she was in high school. She'd been fascinated by the story. His family was starving, and Eagle Eyes believed he was entitled to the money that would save his brothers and sisters. The judge had been harsh and sentenced him to ten years in prison. Eagle Eyes wrote his story down and sold it to *Penthouse* magazine. For a short time he was a celebrity. Today he was just as poor as he had been then. She knew he would welcome the money.

He lived in a shack up in the hills ten miles to the west of their ranch. The road leading to his home was no more than two ruts in the hard earth. He was sitting in a broken rocking chair on his porch. Though he was only two years older than Lynn, he looked to be seventy. The sun and wind seemed to have carved caverns in his face, but his eyes were merry and twinkled as she walked nearer. She knew now where his name came from.

"I came to ask your advice, Eagle Eyes."

"It's going to cost you."

She was surprised at his directness. She must have seen too many old Western movies. "If it's good advice, I'll pay for it."

"What do you want?"

"I need to crack a safe."

He scanned her with his penetrating dark eyes. He took in the new Mercedes, the size of her diamonds and the emerald studs she wore in her ears. "A thousand dollars."

She laughed. "That's a lot of money."

"Yeah? I could live a year off that kind of money. I bet you couldn't make it last a week."

She laughed again. "I'll pay it."

"What kind of safe is it?"

"A wall safe, with a combination lock."

"Not one of those new computer jobs?"

"No."

"What's next to the safe?"

Lynn thought a minute. "Just some book shelves."

"Perfect. Do you want me to do the work?"

"No. It might be too risky. We have laser security systems, alarms. If I do it, I can make sure my husband is not around."

"Okay. Have it your way. Same price either way. Get one of those tiny tape recorders and place it on the bookshelf as close to the safe as possible. What I want to do is listen to the dial as it's spinning. Make sure the volume is turned up all the way. Then bring me the tape and I'll decipher it for you."

"I'll bring the money when I come back with the tape."

Eagle Eyes nodded with a smile and watched her drive back down the hill. Taking this woman's money was easy. He wondered if there were others like her who wanted to spy on their husbands. He'd have to think about it. Maybe he'd just found himself a new career.

Lynn was in bed when she heard Burt drive up to the house. She heard him get out of the car, come inside and then climb the stairs. He looked in on her and she feigned sleep. Then he shut the door and went back downstairs.

Lynn crept out of bed and went to the balcony railing. It was just as she thought. She could see the light from the study. She was certain he was putting something in the safe, or getting something out. Just then the study door opened. Lynn dashed back to the bedroom and slid beneath the covers.

When Burt came into the room she listened to every sound he made, tracing his steps as he prepared for bed. She noticed that he spent at least four minutes in his closet that she did not understand. Was he drunk and unable to unbutton his shirt? Or was there another safe, another hiding place she didn't know about?

Lynn carefully regulated her breathing to simulate sleep.

Burt climbed into bed, never touched her and went instantly to sleep. Lynn remained awake till dawn, her curiosity greater than her fatigue.

It was ten o'clock before Lynn had the opportunity to inspect Burt's closet.

On the far right side, beneath the three rows of slacks, she found a discrepancy in the carpeting. She ran her hand over the surface and saw the corner edge was not completely tacked down. She yanked it up and peeled it back.

"Another safe!" she gasped out loud. "How many are there?"

Lynn took the tape recorder and put it inside the pocket of a pair of slacks Burt no longer wore. Rather than throw them out, he was forever protesting that he'd lose the two inches in his waistline and "get back into shape."

Lynn next overturned furniture, checked drawers for false bottoms and looked behind every painting in the room. She tore the bed apart, mattress and box springs. She checked the back of the headboard, the underside of the chaise and the walls of the armoire.

Her efforts bore fruit. In the armoire she found a false wall on the left side. What puzzled her most was when and how Burt had made all these installations. Obviously, he was a man of many secrets. She could only guess at how many more secrets he kept.

Lynn found over ten thousand dollars in the armoire. She found a key, more money and two phone numbers scribbled on a piece of paper hidden under the scented liner in one of the bureau drawers. She found five thousand-dollar bills taped behind the round brass mirror that hung over Burt's sink in the bathroom.

Lynn did not alter a thing. This was only a reconnaissance mission. She would make her move later.

Three days later, Lynn went back to Eagle Eyes with two tapes. It took him only fifteen minutes to decipher them both. She paid him with money out of her own account.

That night Burt stayed out till after three. Lynn didn't know where he was and didn't care. In fact, she was glad. It gave her plenty of time to go through the contents of both safes.

There was an incredible amount of cash in both. There were also passbooks to accounts that were registered under false names. She found three safety-deposit box keys. Most important of all, she found a logbook of drug drops.

Lynn couldn't believe what she was reading. There were dates, times and the amounts of heroin, cocaine, crack and marijuana in each drop. It was all written down in black and white. At the first opportunity, she would photostat the logbook. It was the kind of evidence she needed to keep her children.

Burt was planning a two-day trip to Houston at the end of the week. While he was gone, she would find her way to each of the safety-deposit boxes and the savings accounts. Maybe Eagle Eyes could help her on that score, too.

Carefully, Lynn replaced everything just as Burt had left it. She didn't want anything to look suspicious or cause him to question her. She could afford to be patient a while longer. She needed to make certain she had the power when their day of restitution came.

35

◆

ALEXANDER COTTRELL WAS STILL LAUGHING a month later at the "carcass fiasco," as he called it. The ineptitude of the Houston bullies was cause for hilarity, he thought. They no longer intimidated him in the least. Alexander knew the time was right for him to make his move.

Not a day had passed that he was not working on bringing himself and Maureen together. And that meant finding a way to overtake her land. When the answer had come to him, he'd thought it childishly simple. He'd gone to the Kerrville County Courthouse and investigated the county records. He made copies of what he would need. He hired a highly recommended attorney in Waco and asked him for his comments. Alexander heard what he wanted to hear.

The orchestration of his plan took three weeks. He made calls to every family friend of account in Austin, Dallas and Houston. He knew, to a man, every person who owed his mother a favor.

To his credit, Alexander had always been aware of the power of the Cottrell name. In recent history that name had not been employed for personal gain. Barbara had never seen the need. When it would benefit others, or when used in the context of charity, she invoked it often and with great force. Alexander needed the foundation his mother had built. Manipulating it to benefit himself would be child's play.

He camouflaged his plan under the guise of a campaign for increasing state revenues. He hired accountants and statisticians to draw up graphs and numbers that would show the state legislature exactly what they wanted to hear in these trying financial times.

Alexander figured that when it was over he'd be a hero.

Blane Arlington saw the recommendation, as did the other senators, when the proposal crossed his desk. It was the kind of revenue-raising measure he liked. He did not know that Alexander Cottrell was behind it, but he'd heard it kicked around that Barbara Cottrell was in favor of the measure. Blane knew from Brandon Williams that he and Barbara were on the same team.

"It makes sense to me," Blane said to Bill Archer, who was on his way back to Washington. "If we could collect some of the back taxes due the state, we could start to clean up this mess."

"I'd rather see a federal repeal of the windfall profits tax and deregulate natural gas and fill the Strategic Petroleum Reserve with domestic oil."

"Jesus, son, that sounds like a fairy tale. But more power to you. You work on those boys in Washington and I'll do what I can here."

"That's a deal," Bill said.

Blane walked with Bill to the steps of the Capitol Building. They said good-bye and each went his separate way. Blane had tried to call Brandon Williams several times ever since he'd heard about the bill that had been presented in the house. But his friend was jogging around the state, enlisting aid for the cause.

Blane shrugged his shoulders as he headed into the House of Representatives. His gut told him this was a good measure. He intended to vote in favor of the law that would collect back property taxes from delinquent landholders.

Barbara Cottrell was sent home to Devil's Backbone the first week in October. Alexander had pressed her doctors mercilessly to allow her to recuperate at home. They had been obstinate. She was too weak to be moved, they insisted. Throughout the month of September, she regained her strength, her color and her spirit.

Barbara was ready to fight. It was her anger against those who had tried to kill her that spurred her on.

Alexander had been afraid that once she returned, Barbara

would want to take over the ranch again. For months, Alexander had been riding high on his ego. He liked being the boss, having control of the business, and most of all, he liked knowing he could use his mother's name and reputation to get anything he wanted. And what he wanted most was Maureen and her ranch.

The fact that he could not flaunt his victory over his mother bothered him tremendously. He couldn't tell her about the legislation that had been passed and signed by Governor Mark Dixon. He couldn't tell her that soon, very soon, Maureen would be defeated. She would be forced to come to him and take his offer to buy her ranch. Maureen would be at his mercy. Then, when she was at her weakest, he would convince her to marry him. And she would accept. For above all, Alexander believed that Maureen loved him, had always loved him—since childhood. *And they would be together.*

Alexander thought about these things as he watched his mother prop herself up in bed. The nurse, Miss Hayes, who was a thin, narrow-eyed woman with a critical tongue, snapped orders to the two orderlies who had helped Barbara to her room.

Barbara seemed exhausted by the confusion and noise around her. Alexander was glad. It would be a while before she was physically capable of running Devil's Backbone.

"Please, Miss Hayes, I'm perfectly fine." Barbara sighed as the nurse tucked and pulled and stretched on the sheets and blanket. Miss Hayes reminded her of an army inspection sergeant. She was too meticulous for Barbara's taste.

"Is there anything I can get you, Mother?" Alexander asked.

"No. But come and talk to me."

He pulled up a side chair as Miss Hayes clucked her tongue and went to the windows. She pretended to inspect the ranch. Alexander felt as if he were being watched by the Gestapo.

"You look tired. Maybe I should go."

"Nonsense. Tell me about the ranch."

"Everything's running smooth as silk. I've got it all under control."

"In the morning I want to see the contracts you signed. And the books. Bring me the bank statements, the projections for the fall and I want to see—"

"Hold on!" Alexander's anger flew to the surface. "Don't

you trust me? Don't you think I'm capable of making competent decisions?''

She looked at him and realized she'd hurt his feelings. "Of course. It's just that I've been away from everything for so long . . . I want to get back in there and work myself." She took his hand.

He was surprised at the strength in her grip.

"I've lost four months of my life now. Somebody cheated me, Alex. I can't get it back. Ever. I want to live again. I will not spend any more time in this bed than I have to. Miss Hayes notwithstanding." She looked over at the nurse's keen eyes that were leveled on her.

"I . . . I think I understand that."

"I hope so. Because I'm back now, and I've got a lot to do."

"*We've* got a lot to do."

"That's what I said."

Alexander did not smile. He felt as if his Camelot had just turned to ashes. "I'd better let you get some rest." He rose. He must think about his victories to come. It wouldn't be long before all that he'd planned so carefully would fall into place. Then he would crush his mother. She would see then that he was better than she. Then she would respect him.

Barbara watched him as he left the room. She couldn't understand why she was so tired. All she'd done was ride in an ambulance. She was supposed to be well now. Why wasn't everything the way it used to be?

"Alexander . . .''

"Yes?"

"Thanks for keeping it all going while I was . . . away."

He was stunned and so he remained speechless. She'd never acknowledged him like that before. It was as if she did respect him and the hard work he'd done in her behalf. He nodded.

She smiled wanly. It seemed such an effort . . . she was so very, very tired. "I always knew you could do it."

"You did?"

"Of course."

Alexander walked out of the room and shut the door. Every nerve in his body was shaking. Had that really happened? Had his mother actually given him what he wanted? Had he finally pleased her?

"Impossible," he mumbled to himself. "It was too easy. It's never been easy."

Alexander walked down the plushly carpeted wide hallway, his mind so clouded with revenge that he was oblivious to the real victory he'd just achieved. He had been expecting fireworks, accolades and awards. No one had ever told him that the biggest victories are always small.

36

◆

MAUREEN WALKED BACK from the mailbox that stood by the side of the road, through the iron gates to the ranch, thinking it had been over a year now since she'd come to Texas . . . since she'd come home. She paused for a moment by the oak tree and looked down at the modest bronze marker she'd finally had made for Mac. He would have liked its lack of ostentation. It was right for him.

She took a deep breath, feeling relaxed and wondrously at peace with herself and the world. The air felt light, and faint beginnings of autumn tinged the edges of the leaves. It was her favorite time of year . . . especially now, because it had been in the autumn that she'd met Brandon.

She continued toward the house as she flipped through the mail. There were half a dozen Christmas catalogues, which each year arrived a week earlier than the year previous. The light bill, the phone bill and an official letter from the state comptroller's office in Austin.

Once she was at her desk, she opened the letter from Austin. In stunned silence she read its contents:

Dear Miss McDonald,

As a Texas resident and citizen, you are well aware of the difficulties this state government has been incurring in these economic hard times. The state budget has currently a deficit of over five billion dollars.

Your state legislature and government is doing all it can to rectify this problem with both just and necessary legislation. In an effort not to raise taxes which would place a burden on all Texans, at the end of last month, the state legislature passed a new state tax law that enables the state tax assessor to review and collect all negligent taxes due the estate.

Upon investigation, this office has found that no state taxes have been paid on your property, the McDonald Ranch, since 1955. We have found that taxes were paid from 1948 until that year. As calculated by this office, you have a property tax bill due on the original ranch land purchase. We have also found that there were four subsequent land purchases since 1978.

The bill due on these last four parcels is $20,000; a sum that has been delinquent for only the past four years.

The total tax bill due for the original purchase is $780,000, which brings the grand total to $800,000.

This sum is due in this office within ninety (90) days.

If payment arrangements need to be made, please call for an appointment.

Very truly yours,
Sam Dennison

Maureen read the letter three times before its full impact hit her. She slumped into the old leather chair, her eyes filled with disbelief. Reflexively, she picked up the telephone and dialed.

"Hi. It's me. I need you," she heard herself say with a cracked voice. She was numb—making movements like a zombie. She wished she'd fallen into a netherworld, then none of this would be real. "I think I've just lost the ranch."

"Never," Brandon said reassuringly. "But I'll come right over."

"Thank you," she whispered as she lost her voice trying to choke back a sob.

Brandon arrived by helicopter. It was Saturday, and because he'd given his pilot the weekend off, he flew alone. Maureen waited for him at the landing strip, still clutching the letter in her hand. She was shaking when she threw her arms around him and buried her head in his shoulder.

"It's not the end of the world," he said.

"It is this time. . . ."

Maureen didn't want to say it aloud, but she believed the

mob was still riding her back. She knew in her heart that she would fight them again, because she had to. They'd tried to crush her and Brandon and they would keep on trying until the election was over. But still, she was tiring of the war.

Brandon kissed her, and when he did he could tell this setback had been rougher on her than the others.

"Tell me."

She handed him the letter. "This says it all."

He quickly read it. "They never quit, do they?"

Maureen was surprised. "You're thinking the same thing I am."

"Yes. And because I am, you should know that somewhere they've slipped up. All this is too suspicious."

"You think the tax is too high?"

"Actually, for a delinquency that's over thirty years old, it's probably on target. No, what I'm talking about is the swiftness of this legislation. Somebody with a great deal of influence is behind this. I'll ask around and see what I can dig up. I'd sure like to know who we're dealing with. I'd heard about this bill, but I was so busy I didn't pay any attention. Besides, in essence, it's the kind of measure I've been advocating."

"I guess our own cause has boomeranged on us."

"It appears that way."

Maureen felt as if she'd had the wind knocked out of her. She'd been hoping to hear something different from Brandon. Why wasn't he giving her answers? "Oh, no."

He pulled her into him. "I said 'appears.' I didn't say there wasn't a way out."

"What do we do first?"

"First, we go through every paper in your house."

She gasped. "Have you ever seen Mac's study? You don't know what you're asking. But I'll do it—if it takes forever."

"It'd better take less than ninety days."

Maureen put her arms around him, feeling secure and strong again. She always felt as if she could take on the world when she knew Brandon was at her side. "It won't. I know it."

"Yeah? And on what facts do you base that assumption?"

"Only on myself—knowing what I can do when I'm pressed to the wall."

Brandon kissed her gently, allowing his lips to savor hers. They were making great strides together. He no longer doubted the outcome of this relationship, or their life together. If they'd been honed of one kind of stone, they couldn't be more alike. They believed in the same goals, the same virtues. They wanted the same things out of life and were willing to fight for what they believed in. But more than Texas, more than justice, Brandon believed in the love he had for this woman. When all was said and done, it was Maureen he was fighting for. He wished he were an ancient Greek oracle who could change the world for her with a simple proclamation. He would create a paradise for her . . . she deserved nothing less.

Lynn Bean made use of every second while Burt was away. Armed with false identification that Eagle Eyes provided for her, she was able to open all of the safety-deposit boxes. Lynn carefully eyed the identification cards she had to sign at each bank as she went into the deposit box area. All of the boxes had been assigned to Burt *after* the crash had been felt by their friends.

What she found boggled her mind. Besides cash, which she had expected to find, there were gold and silver coins and gold bars. By the time she visited the fourth bank, which was located in Dallas, Lynn had already found over half a million dollars. She didn't need any more evidence to tell her it was all drug money.

She found that the passbook accounts were easier to wipe out than she'd thought. She'd spent days forging the different names Burt had used. She almost felt like thanking him for using only initials for his first name on each of the accounts. She knew he'd thought he was covering his tracks. Instead, he'd only paved the road to her freedom . . . and he'd paved it with gold.

Lynn put a three-thousand-dollar deposit on a town house in Turtle Creek in Dallas. The real estate agent went into a lengthy and exuberant explanation of the amenities of the property: the Jacuzzi tub, the mirrored dining area, the security system, the plush carpet, the built-in vacuum system, the microwave, the self-cleaning ovens and the Sub Zero refrigerator. She could have saved her energy, Lynn thought. She was only after a temporary haven until the divorce was final. Then, eventually, she would have the house, too. She would move herself and the children back to Kerrville, and Burt could find some other place to live. When she finished with him, she knew his ego would never allow him to remain in Kerrville. She intended to humiliate him the way he had humiliated her all these years.

Lynn placed the copies of the drug logbook in a safety-deposit box in Dallas. Then she called on John Kimberley, her attorney, signed her petition for divorce, and left the key to the safety-deposit box in his safe hands.

Lynn arrived in Kerrville at four o'clock in the afternoon. She'd made enough purchases at Lina Lee to quash any suspicion on Burt's part about her trip. Before leaving for Dallas, Lynn had arranged for Brian and Stephanie to stay with Charleen. They were home from Boston for a mid-semester break, but she knew they would jump at the invitation because Charleen would spoil them with junk food and rented VCR movies until Lynn called for them.

Burt was due back the following night. That gave Lynn just enough time to make her final arrangements. Her insides told her what she was doing was right and that she was going about it in the right way. But Lynn believed in double protection. For that she needed Brandon.

She telephoned Brandon's house and found him at home. They agreed to meet in an hour. She would pick up the children at Charleen's on the way home.

When she pulled up to Brandon's house, she was a bit surprised to see Maureen's pickup in the drive.

Shirley opened the door for Lynn and showed her into the living room, where Maureen and Brandon were having drinks by the fire. Lynn hugged Maureen and accepted Brandon's kiss on her cheek.

"You two look happy," Lynn said as she sat on the sofa.

Maureen glanced at Brandon. "We are . . . despite the state government."

Lynn's face was etched with confusion. "What are you talking about?"

"Yesterday I received a delinquent land tax bill for eight hundred thousand dollars."

"Jesus! Are they serious? Maybe it was a computer error."

"No such luck," Brandon said as he handed Lynn a glass of chilled zinfandel. "I checked and it's accurate all right. Seems Mac hadn't sent in his taxes since 1955."

"It still doesn't ring true to me. There's something more to it than that."

"Damn right," Brandon said. "Only we can't prove it.

Right now, Maureen's trying to find a way out of paying those taxes. Otherwise, she'll lose the ranch."

Lynn's heart went out to her friend. "God, Maureen. Is there anything I can do?"

"I don't think so. We need a miracle."

Brandon ran a soothing hand over Maureen's shoulder. "We've got three months. We'll find our miracle. I'm sure of it." He looked at Lynn. "So, what brings you over here?"

Lynn was so caught up in Maureen's dilemma she'd nearly forgotten. "This is your week to play Sir Galahad, Brandon. I need your support, too. I'm going to ask Burt for a divorce as soon as he gets back from Houston.

"I've been very busy this past month getting my ducks lined up, as they say. I found everything I need to keep him from ever taking the kids from me. But it could be dangerous, too."

Maureen felt the hairs on the back of her neck bristle. "How?"

"I followed up on your suspicions, Maureen. Burt *is* very involved in drugs. I found everything—money, bonds, coins, and all registered under false names. More important, I found a logbook."

Brandon's eyes widened. "Are there names in the book?"

"No. But there're dates and times of drug drops. The amounts of each drop are given and how much Burt made off each deal. It's incredible. Where does all this stuff go?"

"It's frightening . . ." Maureen said, thinking of the millions of drug users in the country.

Lynn looked at Maureen. "You have no idea how little he thinks of me, of his children. He brought this terror into our own backyard. He was landing planeloads of drugs on our airstrip!"

"The airstrips!" Brandon was suddenly bombarded by a thousand thoughts, and they all made sense. The mob wanted Maureen's land for the airstrip. Hers was the longest and had the best clearance of any around. There was also plenty of acreage surrounding the strip on all sides so that planes coming and going would not create a disturbance for any other ranchers. The McDonald Ranch was needed for drug smuggling. As Brandon thought more about it, he knew a ranch that size could even be used to launder the drug money through a legitimate cattle business, oil possibly and . . . the gold mine. The possibilities were endless. He was certain that the mob had investigated her land to the nth degree. It was his guess that there were even more reasons for the mob's wanting the ranch. But for him, just the ones he'd thought of were enough to kill someone over . . . someone like Wes Reynolds. Someone like Maureen.

Brandon's mind was racing. Lynn might have just come to them with the key that he and Maureen had been so desperately seeking. "Do you mind if I ask a few questions?"

"Of course not."

"When did all this start?"

"In March sometime. I can't pinpoint when he made his first contact with the dealer or shippers or whatever you call someone like that. But I don't think it was long after Burt was informed by our attorney that he would have to file for bankruptcy. It explains how he pulled himself out of the mess when all his buddies were going down for the count."

"Interesting. Is there anything in this book that I could use to help me fight the mob?"

Lynn hesitated. She'd been so embroiled in her own world she'd not realized the full ramifications of the evidence she'd found. Of course Brandon would want to use the logbook and anything else to shut down Burt and his higher-ups, who were calling the shots. But Lynn had different ideas that weren't quite so noble. Lynn was concerned with survival.

"I can't do that, Brandon."

"Lynn," he said pleadingly, "do you know what you've got? Through Burt we might be able to track down some very heavy hitters. We could stop the mob dead cold."

"I know that." She gulped. It wasn't like her to be selfish, but this time she felt as if she had no choice. "But don't you understand, Brandon? I've been trying to get out of this marriage for years . . . a lifetime. I want my children to be safe. If I let you have this book and you go to the authorities, then not only is my husband in jail, which I don't want, but my children could be threatened, kidnapped . . . even killed. I don't owe anybody that much, do I?"

"No, you don't," he said slowly.

"I want to be rid of Burt, but I also don't want his children knowing their father is a criminal. If I handle all this my way, I'll have the power to keep Burt away from us for the rest of our lives. He could never hurt us again. He could still go away and make a life for himself, just not here in Kerrville.

I want to help you. You know I do. But, please, try to see it from my side. . . ."

Maureen did see it from Lynn's angle. Not only had she taken a great risk in finding the evidence against Burt but, in the weeks to come, his retaliation could be vicious. He was the one with mob connections. He was also an egomaniac. How much more did he love himself than his wife and children? Lynn was right to protect herself and her children.

Maureen put her hand over Lynn's. "If it were me, I'd do the same thing. I wouldn't let anyone jeopardize my children."

Lynn was somewhat surprised. She knew how important this campaign was to Maureen and Brandon. And yet, Maureen had the kind of compassion Lynn needed right now. Lynn knew she was letting them down. But Maureen didn't care.

"Maureen's right," Brandon said. "I guess I was too zealous there for a minute. After all, what is Texas if not her people?"

Lynn smiled radiantly up at him. "Thanks for understanding. It's important to me that you're behind me. I also wanted you to know all this in case something *does* happen to me, or Brian or Stephanie."

"Good God! Don't even think such a thing!" Maureen exclaimed.

"I have to, Mo. I know a lot . . . too much . . . about all the wrong things. There are plenty of people who might want to see me out of the picture."

Maureen nodded. Lynn was being realistic and courageous. She was taking a greater chance that they were. *They* were fighting an unknown monster, which sometimes is easier to do. Lynn was fighting from knowledge, past history and emotions that were more volatile than a gangster's vendetta. Passion pulled more triggers than hit men. The odds were greatly against Lynn.

"We'll do whatever we can to help," Maureen said.

"I'm going to have it out with Burt soon. It won't take him long to find that his money is gone. I took all of it. At least all that I could find. I'm sure he's got more hidden away . . ." Lynn said snidely. Then she looked down at her hands, at the thick wedding band she wore. "I wish it wasn't like this." Tears stung her eyes, but she caught herself and choked back her sob. She couldn't cave in. Not yet.

"You're going to be fine," Maureen said. "You've got more courage than I could ever hope to have."

"I don't know about that. I just know I have to save my children . . . and myself."

"And you will," Maureen said. "I know you will."

37

◆

HURRICANES HAVE CREATED less havoc than Maureen did during her quest for the document that would save her ranch. In
the three days after she received the tax bill from Austin,
Maureen began a search that made her quest for gold look
like page skimming.

She combed the record books at the Kerr County Courthouse. She placed requests for deed descriptions of all five
parcels of land and all legal documents on the ranches that
Mac absorbed in his purchases of 1976, 1978, 1980, and 1981.
She went over all the information she had on the gold mines,
looking for legal descriptions and tax forms dating back to
before Texas applied for statehood.

She requested all the tax papers from Austin through the
state comptroller's office and the tax assessor's office. She had
to submit not only Mac's name but the names of the previous
owners of the other four ranches. She was informed by telephone that it would take over a month to garner the requested
information.

She started in the study and again went through the files,
books, records and logs page by page. She read every line of
every tax bill until she was bleary-eyed.

She found nothing. In 1955, Mac had paid his tax on the
original McDonald Ranch. Then, in 1956, he did not pay it.
There was no attached addendum to explain why. She telephoned the accountant who had assisted Mac on his taxes
that year. The number was no longer in service.

She found that on the purchases of the other four ranches,

Mac had paid those land taxes. There was no record of who had advised him to do this.

None of it made sense. Mac hadn't been the kind of man to shirk his responsibilities, and she had a difficult time drafting him in the role of a tax dodger.

"The answer is here somewhere," she mumbled to herself. Mac had been an incredible pack rat. He'd saved what she needed. She just had to find it. She was beginning to feel desperate. She'd try just about anything at this point. "Hell, I'd even go to Charleen's psychic!" She laughed a bit despondently to herself. She sighed. "Mac, if you're listening to me, I need your help. Now show me where to look!"

Just then Juanita came into the study. She had her head tied up with a red bandana and she wore an enormous bib apron that was covered with dirt smudges. Her sleeves were rolled up and her hands and arms were filthy.

Maureen looked at her quizzically. "What on earth happened to you?"

"I told you yesterday . . . I clean the attic."

"Oh, yes. I forgot."

"It a mess! Rusty, he take out all the garbage for me. But what you want to do with these old wood boxes?"

"What wooden boxes?"

"The ones Mac put all those funny papers in."

"Comics?"

"Not Sunday papers. Papers. You know. The ones he no need. Like that." Juanita pointed to the stacks of papers around Maureen.

Maureen's eyes flew open. She felt chills sprout, regenerate and sprout again all over her body. She grabbed a legal paper and held it up. "This kind of paper?"

"Si."

Maureen bolted to her feet. "Hallelujah! Oh, thank you, Mac!" She grabbed Juanita's arm and pulled her toward the staircase. "Show me those papers!"

Burt had been at the office all day. Things were going well. He needed to pull some cash out of his "reserves," as he called his special accounts, to make his payroll, but these days that was no big deal.

Tonight was another drug drop and he'd be a hundred thousand richer. It was such easy money he wondered why he hadn't thought of it a long time ago. It made life easy; it made life sweet.

After he spent an hour or so at home with Lynn, Burt was planning to see Shane. He had a couple of bottles of Dom Perignon in the trunk just for tonight. He hadn't seen her since the week before his trip to Houston. He couldn't believe how much he'd actually missed her.

Nothing was out of order when Burt arrived home. He could smell the roast in the oven as soon as he came through the door. As he went to the bar, as was his routine, he noticed there was no sound coming from the family room. There was no television, no video games bleeping and no children's voices.

"Lynn! I'm home!" he said, walking to the doorway to the family room. It was empty and unusually organized. He had expected to see bookbags and crayons and notebook paper everywhere. It was as if the children were gone.

Lynn stood at the top of the enormous staircase and watched him go from room to room. She had her things packed in her Mercedes.

"I hear you, Burt," she said, starting down the stairs. She wore a smashing black dinner suit she'd bought at Tootsie's in Houston a month ago. It had cost twelve hundred dollars. It was the kind of suit that emphasized her curvaceous body. She wore her best copies of her Bulgari jewels. She looked dressed to kill.

He watched as she came down the stairs. She looked every inch the lady she was. Breeding *did* show, he thought.

"Are we going out? Isn't that a roast I smell?" He sipped his drink with an easy smile.

"*Your* dinner is in the kitchen. *I'm* the one who is going out . . . for good."

"What are you talking about?"

Slowly, she opened her purse and pulled out the keys to the safety-deposit boxes. She held them out to him, then with her steady, unemotional eyes on his, she dropped the keys onto the marble floor. They clattered and clanged like church bells.

It took a moment for Burt's mind to register what was happening. Because he'd never prepared himself for this moment, he didn't want to recognize the keys. He stared at them as they glistened in the light from the chandelier. Dumbly he raised his head and saw Lynn pull out from her bag the passbooks to all his secret accounts. She dropped them, too, onto the floor. She hadn't missed a one. She'd found his wall safes, his floor safe, and his hiding places in the furniture.

As he looked at her, he realized he didn't know this woman at all. Her eyes glinted like hard steel. Her lips were drawn in a fine, firm line on her face. She held her head proudly on her squared shoulders. She reminded him of Barbara Cottrell at that moment. She looked like the kind of woman he'd always feared . . . a woman with power.

"How did you find all this?"

"Wouldn't 'why' be a better question?" She glared at him. For the first time in her life, Lynn knew how a trapped animal felt when it tore at its own flesh to gain freedom. She would do anything tonight to make this break with Burt.

"Why?"

"I've filed for divorce, Burt."

He laughed at her. He felt fear and panic grab at his gut and come rolling out into his mouth, expelled as nervous laughter. She'd threatened to divorce him before, but she never had. She'd always known she could never have custody of the kids. "Where's Brian? And Stephanie?"

"Safe . . . from you. Don't bother looking. You won't find them. And if you did, you won't see them."

"What makes you so sure?"

Her lips curled up sardonically and her eyes narrowed as she reached into her purse again and pulled out the logbook. It was the piece of evidence that would sever their marriage like the edge of a guillotine.

"This is my insurance."

"Christ . . ." Burt felt as if he'd received a blow to the kidneys. He was speechless.

"Everything is in here, Burt. I'll have my divorce on my terms . . . not yours. I want the kids. No custody battles, no arguments, and you'll see them only when I say you can. I want the house and you'll keep up the mortgage notes on it. I figure with your new business it shouldn't be a problem financially. Don't bother looking for your gold or money. I took it all. I deserve it. When the divorce is final, I'll move back here. Where you live is up to you. If you're smart, you'll go away. There's nothing left for you here."

Burt knew he had no options. There was nothing to decipher in his mind, no points needed debating. It was not a time for thought. It was a time for action.

Anger boiled through Burt's blood as he flung his drink on the floor. The crystal shattered into a thousand pieces. Particles skitted across the floor and hit Lynn's ankles. Her jet-black hose became dotted with tiny holes, and blood seeped through the nylon.

"You bitch!" Burt hurled himself at Lynn.

Lynn had anticipated his action. She jumped aside and out of his path. She snatched a revolver out of her purse and let the purse drop to the floor. As he regained his stance, she leveled the gun at his face.

"You'll always be a gutter rat, Burt."

"Shit! Where'd you get that?"

"I found it in your desk. In the locked drawer, which I learned how to pick. Don't *ever* try to screw with me again, Burt. I'd just love the opportunity to blow your head off."

Beads of perspiration broke out on Burt's forehead. "You would, wouldn't you?"

"Yes," she said, knowing that what frightened her most was that, at that precise moment, she *could* shoot her own husband. "You don't know what it's been like for me. Knowing you were with Jennie Sloan or Shane Cottrell or a dozen other women. Knowing you thought so little of your family that you would put our lives in danger with this drug business."

"You don't understand. I did it for you . . . for the kids. . . ."

"Bullshit. You did it for yourself. At least be honest, Burt. It's your ego you're feeding. *We* don't have to have this mansion, or the cars or the clothes. But *you* do."

"You'd leave me if all those things weren't there."

"I'm leaving you and they *are* there."

"Lynn, think about this."

"Forget it." She carefully scooped up her purse, still holding the gun on him. "Look at the bright side, Burt," she said, moving around in a circle toward the door. "You won't have to divide your time or your life between me and Shane. She can have all of you now."

She went out the door, and just as she started to close it, she tossed the gun to him.

"Catch! It wasn't loaded. I found the bullets and threw them out. I told you a long time ago it was dangerous to have guns in the house. You didn't listen then, either."

She slammed the door, raced to her Mercedes and sped

down the drive. Lynn was over a mile down the country road before she took a full breath.

She thought she'd be shaking, or nervous or sad. But she wasn't. She'd never known such relief in her life. She felt as if she were eighteen again and her whole life was ahead of her. She could do *anything* with her life now. The possibilities were endless. She'd always wanted to believe that somehow her existence in this world would make a difference. When she was married to Burt, she believed that the world moved in a collective mass. One person could never be strong enough or wise enough to change things. Tonight, she found her philosophy evolving. Maybe there was a chance for her, a chance for them all.

38

◆

MAUREEN SAT in the Texas State tax assessor's office holding the papers she'd found in the attic. Brandon sat next to her. They were both smiling.

Maureen remembered that time almost a year ago when she'd first come to Austin with Brandon. She'd been so angry about her cattle, angry at the government official and angry at Brandon for just being who he was. How different her life was now.

That afternoon, when she and Juanita had brought the wooden boxes down from the attic, she had been more excited than the day Ryan Lassiter, the geologist, told her there was gold on her land. She had asked God for a miracle; she had asked Mac to help her. This time she was sure they both had had a hand in it.

The papers she needed were called condemnation papers. The set of yellowed documents was dated July 1956. The United States Army Corps of Engineers had condemned the entire McDonald Ranch. She had the secretary of defense's signature and Mac's signature to prove it.

At that time, when patriotism was running high after the end of World War II and Korea, Mac had been called upon to dedicate his lands for defense and flood control. The papers cited the Omnibus Flood Control Act of 1938 as the original federal law under which such practices were taken. In the papers it was stated that should the Army Corps of Engineers ever need Mac's land, especially the southernmost areas that bordered the Guadalupe River, they could, for the

357

fee paid him, utilize the land for the good of the country and the state of Texas.

Being the proud and patriotic Texan that he was, Mac had signed the papers. Though he was paid a meagre sum, Mac retained all mineral rights to the land. At any and all times, Mac was free to drill a rig wherever he wanted and free to mine minerals, including gold, at his discretion and expense. Interestingly, he was not allowed to sublease the land to anyone for the purpose of grazing cattle. And Mac was *not* allowed to ever sell his land to any individual, though it could be passed on as an inheritance.

Maureen realized that the offers *she* had had on the land, both from Alexander and from the mob, meant nothing; the land actually belonged to the federal government, and it had never been up to her to accept or reject an offer.

The only real concession out of the deal was that Mac never had to pay state or federal land taxes on any of the condemned property.

As soon as Maureen told Brandon about the papers, he enlisted the aid of Blane Arlington of the state senate and Bill Archer in Washington. Both men wrote letters to the state tax assessor in Maureen's behalf, stating that if anything, Maureen was due an apology by the state for the inconvenience it had caused her.

At stake now was only the matter of the taxes due on the four parcels bought since 1978.

"Miss McDonald, you can go in now," the receptionist said.

"Good luck, darling," Brandon said as she rose.

"You're not coming with me?"

He winked at her. "You don't need me."

"I love you," she said, feeling confident and very, very loved.

William Stevens greeted Maureen as she walked in. Courteously, he ushered her to a chair, poured her a cup of coffee from the automatic coffee maker on the console behind him. He smiled as he spoke.

"I received your copies of the condemnation papers, Miss McDonald. And I spoke directly with Blane about this matter. I agree with him, this state does owe you an apology."

Maureen smiled back, thinking how different he was from the agriculture official. "Thank you. I brought the originals . . . in case there was a question. . . ."

He held up his hand. "It isn't necessary. I'm satisfied. The only thing we have to discuss is the tax due on the parcels that were purchased in the last few years. My investigations have not turned up anything on this end as to why your uncle didn't pay the tax. I can only guess that it was ignorance on his part—and a great deal of ignorance on the part of the state for not finding him delinquent long before this. In other words, both parties are at fault."

"There's just about twenty thousand due on that land, am I correct?"

"Yes. And under the circumstances, I think it only fair that this office make provisions for your repayment. If it's all right with you, we could extend those payments over a three-year period without interest or penalty."

Maureen's eyes flew open. "It would make all the difference in the world to me. I don't have twenty thousand dollars right now."

"I know."

"You do?" Then she chuckled. "Of course you do."

"Miss McDonald, we're not here to punish our citizens. We're here to see our state become strong again. If I were to knowingly put you out of business, what kind of Texan would I be?"

"Indeed."

"We will do all we can to get this matter straightened out. I think now that we understand one another, perhaps we can work amicably together."

"Mr. Stevens . . . I'm sure of it."

Wearing a happy smile, Maureen rose and shook William Stevens's hand. He showed her out of his office and chatted for a moment with Brandon before being called back by his receptionist for a telephone call.

"I think we should celebrate," Brandon said.

"Me, too. Lunch? Champagne?"

"Hmmm," he said, while he thought for a moment. "I have a better idea."

"What could be better than champagne?"

"Come with me, Miss McDonald."

He grabbed her hand and they raced down the hall to the elevator. They scurried on just in time behind two businessmen. Brandon punched a button and then pulled Maureen close to him and kissed her. Maureen felt as if she were floating. She didn't know if they were going up or down, and she didn't hear the snickers and coughs from their two uncomfortable elevator companions.

The doors opened, and Brandon looked at the lighted indicator panel above his head. "This is it."

"This is what?" Maureen asked as he hurried her down the hall.

"It's almost noon and sometimes they close up if they're shorthanded."

"Who closes?"

"They do," he said with a grin as he pointed to the sign on the wall.

Maureen looked. It was the License Bureau. "Brandon?"

"Will you marry me?"

She nearly started laughing she was so happy. "What a dumb question. Of course I will!" She flew into his arms and kissed him.

"We'll get the ring after the license."

"I don't need a ring."

"You *need* a ring," he said firmly.

"Okay. I *need* a ring."

They went through the door. They stood behind a star-struck young couple who couldn't keep their hands off each other. Maureen looked at Brandon and he smiled at her.

She tilted her head toward the boy and girl. "Can you believe that?"

"Looks like a good idea to me," he said, putting his arms around her.

"Teenagers. What do they know?"

Brandon kissed her deeply, thanking God for bringing Maureen to him. She made him believe in miracles.

39

◆

DRESSED IN A BLUE SATIN NEGLIGEE, Charleen lay on top of her bed mindless of the chill in the room. Next to her was a stack of reports from her attorney, her accountant and the statistician she employed at her oil company. On the very top was Maureen's prospectus.

The conclusion of all the reports was that the mining investment would be a sound one, but that there was a thirty-five-percent risk involved. It was the same as when she'd drilled for oil.

She'd promised Maureen she wouldn't consult her tarot cards or call her psychic. However, she had *not* promised to refrain from talking to Charles.

As always, she smiled when she spoke his name. "Charles?"

"Yes, my love. I'm here," he said to her.

After years of communication with her dead husband, Charleen had realized that recently she'd had a new perspective on many things. She was being more critical and analytical about everything in her life. She'd gone two weeks without talking to her psychic. She hadn't played with her own deck of tarot cards, or with the Ouija board. And she'd also not spoken to Charles. She'd felt terribly lonely.

"I'm so glad you're here," she said with relief. "I was afraid you wouldn't come."

"You haven't called me. But that was good."

"It was?"

"You have needed this time for introspection. You, of all

361

people, should know that the answers to all your quests come from within."

"I know," she said a bit sadly. "You know what Maureen has said to me."

"Of course," he said. "You also know, in your heart, that she is right."

Charleen was frightened. "I don't know anything of the sort!"

He seemed to look upon her with compassion. "You have been living too much in fantasy."

Charleen's eyes filled with tears, and there was a tremendous lurch in her stomach. "No I don't! If you say that, Charles, it means everything you and I have is a joke . . . a sham."

"That's not what I'm saying at all. I am here for you. I always will be. But what you perceive to be reality and what *is* reality are not the same."

"Oh, Charles," she cried.

"Look at me, my love. Really look at me. When I speak, my lips do not move. I speak to you through mental telepathy. You hear me in your mind. You cannot touch me and I cannot touch you. I am energy. You are human."

Suddenly, she felt icy cold. She yanked the down comforter over her trembling body. "This isn't happening!" She was crying and couldn't stop. "Why didn't you say something? Why didn't you put an end to it all?"

"Because it was not the time. You had lessons to learn. This woman was brought to you so that she could show you reality. At the same time, it was meant to be that you would interact with her, so that she would learn to listen to her inner self."

Charleen thought about this and knew intuitively that he was right. "But I'll be alone."

"No. There is another man in your future. I want you to find him and love him, for that love is meant to be just as ours was. You were meant to be happy, my love. I have always seen to that. But now you are growing and it is time for you to have a fuller life . . . a life I cannot give you."

She looked at him and absorbed the glowing energy around him. She became warm again. Charleen did not need to question the rightness of what Charles said. Her heart told her this was the path she must follow. It might have some detours, but it was right for her.

"I'll miss you," she said softly.

"I'm not going away . . . not really. I'll speak to you through my heart. But I won't come to you like this again."

"It still makes me sad. . . ."

"Not for long. I want you to know, Charleen, that I will always love you."

"And I'll love you."

He smiled at her and the room filled with brilliant salmon-pink color. It radiated from him in huge waves of energy. Charleen had never seen anything like it. Then, slowly, he disappeared, but for a few minutes after his leaving, the color remained, and as it did, she felt all her fears melt away. He *would* take care of her future for her, in that she could trust.

Gently, she lay back on the pillow and closed her eyes. She placed her hand atop the prospectus. It felt warm and good. She knew what she would do tomorrow. And it would be the right thing, for she had listened with her heart.

Maureen had been up since dawn tending to chores. She'd brushed and groomed Esprit after a short ride to check on the herd. She was pleased that there were four new calves on the way.

She was standing in the kitchen and had just poured herself a cup of coffee when the doorbell rang. Juanita looked at her quizzically.

"Who can that be? It's only seven-thirty," Maureen said.

Juanita shrugged her shoulders, and went to answer the door.

Charleen walked into the kitchen and hugged Maureen. "I couldn't sleep all last night. I couldn't wait to bring you this."

"What is it?" Maureen asked, taking the envelope from her friend. She opened it. It was a check for five hundred thousand dollars. "What?"

"I want to invest in the gold mine. I took it to my advisors . . . I have their reports in the limo to prove to you that I did as you asked. . . ."

"I believe you," Maureen answered her.

"I want to put up two and a half million. This will get you started today if you want. I'll have my bank in Dallas wire the rest to you when you need it. Now, may I use your phone?"

"Sure." She pointed toward the wall phone. "Charleen, I just don't know what to say. . . ."

"Say that you're going to make me *very* rich." Charleen smiled and then punched out the long-distance numbers that would connect her with Lynn Bean at her new condo in Dallas. "Hi. Yeah, I'm here. I'll let you tell her." Charleen handed the receiver to Maureen.

Maureen was confused. "Who's this?"

"Lynn." Charleen nudged her and then chuckled with a conspiratorial laugh.

"Hi, Lynn. I got your note. . . ." Maureen kept staring dumbfounded at the check in her hand. It didn't seem possible that her dreams just might come true.

Lynn's voice was bright on the opposite end of the line. "I just wanted to tell you that besides the check that Charleen gave you, you'll be seeing one from me this week for another half a million."

"What?" Maureen nearly lost her voice. "You can't do that, Lynn. You need your money . . . the kids . . ."

"There's plenty. Besides, you think I'm going to let Charleen be the only one who makes a killing on this deal? I just *know* you're going to strike it big. Actually, it's kind of selfish on my part, bullying my way in like this, but when Charleen called me last night—"

"Last night?" Maureen looked over at Charleen. There was something different about her that Maureen couldn't quite pinpoint.

"She told me about the deal and she graciously is allowing me to have part of her share. She could put all the money up, Maureen, but, well, she and I go back a long way. I need something to get involved in once I move back to Kerrville."

"Oh, Lynn. When do you think that will be?"

"I hope for Christmas. But it depends on Burt. I don't see any problems there, though. He's not stupid. If he doesn't give me the divorce the way I want it, he'll go to jail."

"I don't know what I would do without friends like you," Maureen said.

"Well, one thing's for sure," Lynn said. "Life sure would be boring!"

Maureen said her good-byes and then, her eyes welling with tears of gratitude, she turned to Charleen. "I don't believe this."

"Well, believe it." Charleen hugged Maureen. "Boy, I'm glad this is settled. Now I can go home and get some sleep."

"You don't want to stay for breakfast?"

Charleen turned around with a shocked look on her face. "Breakfast? Please! I don't even get up until noon."

Maureen watched until Charleen's limousine disappeared down the road. Then she looked down at the check. "Half a million dollars . . ." she whispered to herself.

Juanita glanced up from the morning newspaper. "Señorita?"

"Juanita, we're officially in the gold-mining business!" Maureen said.

"Si," Juanita said, and casually lowered her eyes back to the newspaper. Gold mining or cattle ranching didn't make any difference to her. She still had the same number of meals to prepare.

40

◆

SHANE WALKED into the dining room and found Alexander reading the *Wall Street Journal*. She stuck the copy of the Kerrville newspaper under her arm as she poured herself a cup of coffee from the silver coffeepot.

"You're reading the wrong paper, brother dear."

She tossed the Kerrville paper at him. "Page nine. The society page. I think you'll find it very interesting," she said.

He ignored her and went back to the *Journal*.

"You better read it," she said in a childish, singsong voice that had always grated on his nerves.

"Oh, for Christ's sake, all right." He opened the paper and scanned it quickly. He was just about to put it back down when he saw it. "Oh, my God," he gasped incredulously.

There in the center of the society page was a huge photograph of Maureen McDonald and underneath was the announcement of her engagement to Brandon Williams.

The wedding was set for the Saturday after the November elections.

"I don't believe it."

"Why not? They've been lovers for almost a year," Shane said maliciously.

"Shut up!" He reread the article. He still didn't believe it. He wouldn't believe it. He couldn't handle this . . . not now . . . not on top of his other defeat.

He'd been so sure about her, about his plans to tax her out of her land. God! What a mess he'd made of things! Who the hell had ever heard of condemnation papers anyway?

367

Alexander had heard through his source in Austin, an administrator in the tax assessor's office, every detail of Maureen's case. He knew now that there was no chance of ever divesting her of that land. Alexander was out of ideas, out of hope.

And now, this announcement showed him just how futile his battle had been—obviously, for a very long time. It made him look like a fool. Alexander had never looked like a fool . . . to anybody. Not even to his addict sister.

The heat from Alexander's anger roared through his body. Suddenly, it was almost as if he couldn't even see. He blinked his eyes and tried to focus on Shane, but all he saw was Maureen's face. He wanted to throw himself at her, feel his hands around her throat and squeeze the life out of her. He wanted to hurt her, the way she'd hurt him. She should know this kind of humiliation, too.

He could feel his hands ball into fists, and he had to consciously force them to remain relaxed and steady.

Think. He must think. There had to be a way to avenge all that she'd done to him, all that she'd put him through.

It came to him in a flash and he knew it was the answer. Her gold mine. He must destroy the mine. Without that sense of accomplishment, Maureen would be crushed. In that, she was like him.

Alexander felt he knew her better than she knew herself. He knew how she needed to prove herself to Texas, to all those who had told her that Mac had been a kook. She was doing it for Mac as much as for herself. Yes, he thought, he knew exactly how to get to Maureen.

He looked down at the engagement picture. He still didn't think Maureen knew her own mind when it came to love. Most women were that way. They had to have someone tell them what was what. Alexander had made a mistake by allowing that someone to be Brandon and not himself.

He would take care of Brandon later. Right now, he had to strip Maureen of her self-esteem. Then they would be equals.

Alexander said not another word to his sister. He got up and walked calmly out of the room.

"Alex? Where are you going?" Shane asked indignantly. This wasn't fair. Why was he leaving just when she was about to have some fun with him?

The phone rang and she picked it up.

"Hello?"

"Shane, baby, I—"

"Burt? Is that you? You sound awful. And where the fuck have you been?"

"I need you. . . ."

"No kiddin'? Then how come you disappeared for almost three weeks?"

"I was in Mexico. . . . She left me, Shane."

Shane couldn't believe her ears. "Lynn? She's gone?" This was too good to be true. It was the answer to all her problems . . . it was her dream come true. Shane had known that if she waited long enough, if she believed strongly enough, one day she and Burt would be together. And she'd been right.

"I don't know where she is."

"Who gives a shit? Where are you? I want to see you."

"I'm at the house. Please, can you come over now?"

"Of course, baby," she said sympathetically. "I'll be right there."

For Shane it was the longest drive of her life. During that time she planned her wedding, her first two children, the house she and Burt would build, the trips they would take. They were going to have a perfect life. She'd waited too long for happiness. At last it was *her* turn.

She knocked on the door, but there was no answer. No butler, no maid greeted her. She rang the bell, and finally frustration pushed her to try the door. It opened. "Burt?" she called, walking into the foyer.

He was sitting in the raw silk Georgian wing chair in the living room. Shane almost didn't recognize him. He'd lost at least ten pounds. Maybe fifteen. His cheeks were sunken and hollow, and there were bags under his eyes. His hair needed a trim, and it looked as if he hadn't combed it in days. He wore a knit shirt and a pair of crumpled-looking, baggy pants.

"Shane?" He raised his head mechanically.

She put her purse on the coffee table and sat on the floor next to him, placing her hand on his knee. "You look like shit."

His eyes were vacant, which frightened Shane tremendously. It reminded her of when Barbara was in a coma and the doctor would lift her eyelids to examine her. Burt looked just as dead.

"She left me. She took everything. The kids. . . ."

Shane smiled. This was what they'd wanted. She didn't

understand why he was so upset. He didn't love Lynn. Or did he? "Come on, honey. Snap out of it. It's not the end of the world. I'm here, aren't I?"

He placed his hand on her head. "Yes, you are. But . . ." Tears filled his eyes and rolled slowly down his cheeks.

Shane was getting angry. "What is this? Why are you so upset? You told me you didn't love her. You love *me!* Remember?"

"She was my wife. . . ." he said faintly.

"And so now she's not. You're acting like it's a big deal. Come on"—she tugged gently on his arm—"let's go upstairs. . . . I'll show you how to forget Lynn."

Suddenly, Burt understood what Shane was saying. He jerked his hand away. "Have you no heart at all? My goddamn wife *left me!*" he yelled at her.

"So what?" she yelled back. "You don't love her! You never did. If you had, I never would have existed in your life. Quit giving me this shit, Burt. It's only your goddamned ego that's bruised. Big fucking deal."

She stood up. "That's the trouble with you men. You can dish it out but you can't take it. Look at you! You keep this up and no one will even so much as look at you. No guts— you got no guts, Burt. Jesus! I can't believe this. All this time I thought you were the strong one. Brother! Was I wrong."

"Shut up!"

She picked up her purse and started for the door.

"You can't go," he said snidely, trying to find some courage. "After all, you need me. You need your fix and you need me."

"I don't think so. I've learned a lot in the past few weeks, Burt. And today you showed me that you're no better than I am. At least I know what I am. I'm an addict. But you . . . all you are is *lost!*"

She walked straight to the door. She didn't listen to him screaming at her. She didn't let the sting of his barbs hurt her, or his insults touch her. She closed the door quietly behind her, still hearing his voice, but not his words. She got into her car and drove away.

Burt raced to the doorway, stunned that Shane would leave him. She had been like putty in his hands. Why was everything falling apart like this?

He tried to remember the things Lynn had said to him over the years, but it was all a muddled ball of confusion in his head. Nothing made any sense to him. It was as if someone had changed all the rules to the poker game and hadn't told him. But that was preposterous. He was Burt Bean. He was rich. Someday his oil company would be back on top, and it wouldn't be long for him, because he'd been smarter than his cronies. He was smarter than Lynn and Shane—and half of Texas, for that matter. He was a winner, wasn't he?

He listened as the late October trees dropped their leaves. Everything was so still he could hear them as they rustled on the ground. It was still warm—a good sign to him. When he'd been poor it meant what little money they had needn't be spent on heating fuel.

He closed the door and returned to the empty house. Funny, it felt much cooler inside, nearly cold, he thought. Just like the coldness he felt in his soul.

41

✦

THE CHAIRMAN OF THE BOARD PLACED the spreadsheets in front of him on the long conference table. The results of the latest polls were in. With only a week until the election, the polls were mixed. The *Dallas Morning News* believed that Brandon Williams and his supporters had a good chance of defeating the gambling bill. However, the word out of San Antonio, Amarillo, Houston, Lubbock, and Waco was leaning to the pro side. The battle was intense.

The chairman had bought more air time than five Brandon Williamses could afford. He'd even gotten a Baptist minister to go on "A.M. Houston" and state that the proceeds from a state lottery would save the homeless, hungry and jobless of Texas, just as the lotteries had done in New Jersey, Illinois and other states. The following day, they gained four share points in the polls.

Satisfied that they would win in Austin, the chairman found only one matter disturbing: the problems in Kerrville.

"Gentlemen," he addressed his colleagues. "I have given a great deal of thought to the entire matter of our 'Texas plan.' I'm afraid the time has come for revision."

There was a hush around the table. Revision meant that many of them could lose their jobs.

373

"Let me ease your minds by saying that you have all done well. I am pleased. It is apparent that we will win this election. Everyone has worked diligently, and your efforts will see fruition in a few days. What I'm referring to is not the entire plan itself but merely its location."

"Sir?" It was the second vice-president. He was the one responsible for bringing the McDonald land into the fold—an assignment he'd failed. "Our research shows that Kerrville is the only place—"

The chairman held up his hand, but smiled graciously. He was in too complacent a mood to let it be disrupted by anyone. "That's not entirely true. What we found was that Kerrville would be the most profitable in twenty years for us, should we begin the casinos this year. However, we've encountered too many difficulties there. That was unfortunate, as was our partnership with Alexander Cottrell. I've decided to sever our ties there and move."

"Move?" The young vice-president asked with a startled hush. The others at the table were equally surprised.

"Yes. To Galveston. It's perfect for our operations. Condos are dirt cheap and what Hurricane Alicia did not destroy last year, the crash took care of this year. We'll rebuild it. Hotels, casinos, boutiques. It's more quaint and historic than Atlantic City. There's already a proposed rail system going in that will connect Houston and Galveston. If we can't advertise gambling to bring tourists, we'll advertise history—Americana. If there's one thing I've learned in our venture this year it's that patriotism *sells*. And that's what we're going to give them."

The faces surrounding the chairman were beaming. To a man, his staff was in total agreement. They even applauded him. He nodded his head graciously.

"Consider it done, gentlemen. As of this moment, Kerrville is past business to us. I conclude that we have no loose ends there?" He looked at the vice-president.

"None at this time, sir."

"Good. All in favor then?"

"Aye." The response was unanimous.

42

◆

A GENTLE BUT THICK FOG RESTED in the valleys of the hill country. The grass was incredibly green, and there would be no sign of frost until December. Alexander drove his chocolate brown Jaguar down the country roads thinking that it had been years since he'd been up this early in the morning. He'd forgotten how beautiful it was in the fall. He'd forgotten what it was like to see the dew glistening on the scruffy bush plants and the gold leaves of the oak trees.

When he was young, he'd never liked the fall. It was the time that followed summer; it was the lonely time after Maureen had gone away.

He drove the car off the road and down the two ruts in the ground that the large mining machinery had made. He glanced at his watch as he pulled up to the entrance to the mine. It was a quarter to six. The sun wouldn't be completely up for half an hour. He had just enough time.

He pulled the car to the left of the mine behind a huge pile of excavated earth, sand and rock. That way, his car was hidden from any oncoming cars.

He jumped out of his car and opened the trunk. He took a deep breath as he looked down at the bundles of dynamite that would blow Maureen's dream to kingdom come.

His hesitation lasted only a split second. He believed in what he was doing. It was his only chance to bring her back to him.

Quickly, he picked up the four bundles, the spool of coiled fuse and the mountain-climbing pickax he'd brought from home. It was an instrument he'd used on hiking trips, and it was light enough for him to wield easily.

He entered the front of the mine. The opening was huge and gaping, and once inside the mine it was dark. But already the mining company had rigged up electric lights run by a generator that sat just outside the mine. He turned the generator on. Now he was able to see the three shafts that radiated off the main area. He intended to destroy them all.

He went down the first shaft and found it went only fifteen yards before stopping. He placed his gear on the ground and went right to work. He chopped a hole in the softest part of the wall and inserted the dynamite bundle. He attached his fuse. Then, out of his down vest pocket, he pulled a small black box and inserted the fuse wire into it. He placed an AA battery inside the black box and then flipped a tiny silver switch. A red light went on.

"Bingo!" he exclaimed to himself when he saw the remote control device really was going to work.

The second shaft went four times deeper into the mountain. Here, he placed two bundles and attached similar remote control devices to each. The third shaft was almost as long as the second, but its walls were much harder and it took him longer to set the dynamite bundle.

When he finished, he raced out the entrance, making certain to turn off the generator. It was lighter outside than he'd expected it to be.

He heard a car in the distance. He looked around and saw that it was Maureen in her pickup truck with another truck behind her.

"The mining crew!" He looked at his watch. It was almost seven. Alexander had greatly miscalculated.

He ran to his car and backed it up, keeping it behind the mound of earth that obstructed any view of him from the road. He circled around, over a small hill, weaved through the oak and scrubs, and drove away from the mining area and back to the main road. He headed away from the mine in the opposite direction from which he had come.

Maureen pulled up to the mine, parked the pickup truck and got out. She went directly to the generator and turned it on. But as she did so, she had an eerie feeling that someone was watching her. She glanced around the area, but saw no one. She started toward the mine entrance as the mine workers piled out of their truck and went inside.

Maureen stopped dead in her tracks. Something was not right. She couldn't explain it; it was just a feeling. As she moved forward, she swore she smelled Alexander's cologne.

"Impossible," she said to herself as she went inside.

The men were checking their gear, when suddenly, like a flash of lightning, Mac's face shot across her mind. She felt chills course her body. Dread flooded her heart. She didn't know what was happening.

"Something's not right!" she said aloud.

The foreman turned around and looked at her. "What did you say, Miss McDonald?"

Maureen was shaking as her instincts screamed a warning. *"Get out!"* she screamed. She raced from one man to another. "Everyone get out!"

It took only one look at the panic on Maureen's face to convince the foreman. *"Run!"* he yelled.

The men went charging for the entrance, their minds not registering their actions, but their bodies carrying out an ancient instinct for survival.

When he knew he was completely out of sight, Alexander pulled the car to a halt and got out. He took the remote controls out of his pocket. He could see the trucks, but he couldn't see where Maureen had gone because the mound of earth was cutting off his vision. She was probably over by the generator, he thought.

He held the remote control gently. It was much like the toys he'd played with when he was a child. Remote-controlled airplanes and cars had been favorite Christmas gifts.

Without thinking any further, he pushed the black button.

Like an awakening demon, the mine rumbled as the dynamite exploded within its walls. Enormous clouds of dust, sand and debris bellowed through the shafts, following the mining crew and Maureen as they raced for safety.

Maureen's legs felt as heavy as the rock the crew had been chiseling from the walls of the mine. She was running, but she felt as if she were standing still. She screamed, but no one could hear her over the tremendous roar of the explosion. Beams split and crashed from the shaft ceilings to the floor. Rocks tumbled on top of each other, damming up the entrances to the three shafts. It was as if the world were coming to an end.

As she raced for the light, she felt the earth tremble beneath her. She screamed again. She could see the men as they sprinted into the daylight.

Now she was the only one left. There was a second explosion.

The noise was deafening, and she felt as if her head were being crushed by its powerful vibrations. Cold air rushed over her and engulfed her in a bubble. Then she realized it was only her fear.

She saw the men as they gasped for breath, coughing up the dust and sand that had filled their lungs and throats. She saw her foreman as he turned and, startled, realized that she was not safe yet.

She could feel the rocks falling around her. She felt the waterfall of sand and dirt as it brushed her back. When she finally reached the entrance, she was hurled forward by the next and most forceful explosion.

She bit her lip as she landed face first outside the mine.

The foreman grabbed her hand as they raced away from the entrance. They all knew there could be more explosions. The danger was not over yet.

Alexander heard the explosions as they ticked off one by one precisely as he'd synchronized them. As the roar from the third explosion filled the air, he put his remote control in his pocket and returned to his car.

"That ought to teach her a lesson," he said as he started the car. As he pulled away to the main road, he heard the fourth and last explosion. He wore a smile of self-satisfaction as he dropped his Ray Bans over his eyes and headed home.

Maureen and her men were well away from the mine when the last explosion occurred. They were all shaking and speechless, looking to one another for explanations. No one had any answers . . . except Maureen.

She'd never seen him. She had no evidence. Without proof there was nothing she could do to convict him—but Maureen knew in her heart that Alexander was responsible.

"God will make you pay for this, Alex," she whispered to herself. "This time, you won't get away."

Charleen Sims drove herself down the country road that ran behind her ranch and connected her land to Maureen's.

Since the day she'd told Maureen she would financially back the mining of the gold, Charleen had felt like a new woman.

No more did she sleep till noon. The days of taking two hours to dress were over. She tied her blonde hair in a knot, used little makeup and wore only Levi's and cotton blouses. Her only concessions to fashion were the eelskin boots she wore. She was a working woman now, and she loved it.

She was like a kid with a new toy. Only this toy was going to make her, Maureen and Lynn very wealthy. It was a challenge she'd needed for a long time. And she had Maureen to thank.

The road she took was little used by anyone and especially not early in the morning. Had this been another time in Charleen's life, she would have chalked up what she saw to the fact that it was seven-thirty in the morning and she wasn't awake yet. But she was as wide awake and keen-eyed as if it had been noon.

She saw the car approaching. Then suddenly it slowed a bit and turned off the road and down a wooded drive to the left.

"Was that . . . ? No, what would he be doing here?" she said aloud.

This road was used only by ranch trucks or the oil riggers in delivering equipment. Charleen had only used it of late because it cut fifteen minutes' time from her normal drive to Maureen's ranch. And, most important, it led directly to the mining area.

"Oh, God." Charleen knew instantly that something was dreadfully wrong. She hadn't been seeing things. That *had* been Alexander.

She depressed the gas pedal. The car jumped from forty to fifty to seventy.

She wheeled around the bend and came up to the familiar mine entrance. She saw Maureen and the men huddled together outside the mine. They were safe, but Charleen could still feel the vibrations of danger all around her.

She picked up her cellular telephone and dialed Brandon's house.

"Brandon! It's Charleen. There's been some kind of accident at the mine. I can see Maureen from here and she looks okay, but come quickly. And Brandon . . . I saw Alexander Cottrell driving away from here. I don't know . . . I don't like it, either."

43

◆

THE CHAIRMAN OF THE BOARD PROPPED his feet on a blue leather ottoman in the den of his River Oaks mansion. His wife was at a dinner meeting for the March of Dimes charity. She was to be the ball cochairman in the spring. Because she was gone, he'd had no one to share his supper with. It was a thrice-monthly occurrence, and he'd come to enjoy the time alone.

He picked up the remote control for the television and turned on the evening news.

Brandon Williams and Maureen McDonald were surrounded by nearly two dozen reporters and a group of men wearing mining helmets.

"Who do you think is responsible for this explosion, Mr. Williams?"

"We can't say for certain, but we have our suspicions. I'm just thankful that my fiancée is safe and that these men were not injured."

The chairman leaned forward eagerly, as if the television would have better focus that way. He pushed the volume button twice. "What the hell?" he muttered.

Maureen stood by Brandon's side, not saying anything. The reporters badgered her with questions that she either declined to comment on or indicated that Brandon would answer.

381

The chairman realized that Maureen knew who had studded her mine with dynamite. The investigator that the newsmen interviewed next verified that this had not been an accident.

The chairman ground his teeth. He didn't like being upset. He'd had everything tied into a tidy ball yesterday and now somebody was screwing it up. If Maureen McDonald knew who was responsible, it wouldn't take long before someone else did.

The chairman picked up the telephone and pushed the second button. It was a direct line to his president.

"Did you see the news this evening? I want your people to take care of those loose ends in Kerrville. Immediately."

Alexander took his black leather hanging bag and stuffed two pairs of shoes into it. He packed only one suit, but four sweaters, two pairs of casual pants and a half dozen sports shirts. He placed the cash he'd taken from his savings account and from his safety-deposit box in the pockets of his clothes. He grabbed his passport—he would definitely need that. He placed the coach airline ticket in the breast pocket of his seven-year-old tweed jacket. He grabbed underwear, socks, cologne and a toothbrush.

Shane stood outside his door watching him through the crack. She was incredibly high. And she intended to stay that way for as long as possible. She didn't understand what was going on, but she intended to find out. She pushed the door open.

"Going somewhere?"

"Yes," he said flatly.

"Mind telling me?"

"Yes, I do."

Shane was buzzing. She swooped into the bedroom and plopped herself on the bed. He yanked his robe out from under her and laid it on top of his clothes.

Shane grinned up at him. She took out her Vicks Inhaler, which was filled with cocaine, and took a snort.

"You're disgusting," he said.

"Look who's talking," she said. She could hardly focus on him. For a moment, he looked alarmingly like her father. It was an appropriate thought; she'd felt childlike, lost and alone since she walked out on Burt. She reached out to touch Alexander's hand, but her arm was too heavy. It fell with a thud on the bed. "Don't go," she said pleadingly. It was probably the first emotional thing she'd ever said to him. She wondered why she'd said it.

He shook his head and continued packing. "Forget it."

"Tell me why you're leaving!" Shane demanded.

Neither of them had noticed her as she edged her way down the hall on wobbly legs, but Barbara had been standing just around the corner of the doorway during their entire conversation. She chose this moment to show herself to them.

"He can't tell you why he's leaving," Barbara said in her imperious voice. "Can you, Alexander?"

He looked at her. "No, I can't." Jesus! he thought. She knows. Mother knows exactly why I'm going, but how did she find out? It didn't really matter. He'd made a terrible mistake by blowing up that mine. Ten hours later, he still couldn't believe he'd done it. Thank God no one had been hurt. Especially Maureen. He loved her. He knew that much, and he didn't want to hurt her. He only wanted her to himself. He had been wrong and now he was going to pay for it.

Barbara looked into her son's eyes, the eyes he'd inherited from her. He was her child, her baby, and now he was going away. She knew as sure as the sun came up in the morning that she would never see him again. Not alive, anyway.

"It was on the news, Alex."

"I know, Mother."

Barbara flung mind to the edges of her life, past, present and future, to find a way to save her son. But it was not meant to be. They had both come to the precipice where he would have to live his life alone, without her. It was the last thing she'd ever wanted. She'd wanted him to stay on the ranch, inherit the land, and hand it down to his children one day. She'd mishandled everything.

She'd had many days and nights to think about her relationship with her children. She knew now how she'd failed them. She had not given them the love they'd needed at a time when they had needed it. But she also knew that, given the same set of circumstances and a chance to live her life over, she probably would do it all the same. Barbara *had* done her best. But being both father and mother and breadwinner had been tough. She had failed them, but they had failed her, too.

"I'm glad you're leaving, Alex," Barbara said.

"What?" Shane was incredulous at what she was hearing. She instantly started to sober.

Alex went to his mother and put his hands on her shoulders. "So am I. Maybe now I'll have to grow up."

Barbara nodded.

"They'll come after me. You know that."

"Yes." She felt tears in her eyes. But this time being in control didn't matter so much. She let them fall. "I love you, Alex. I always have. I want to help you."

"You can't. I have to help myself."

"I know that now. Maybe I tried to help you too much."

"Maybe." He wiped her tears with his fingertips. "Don't worry so much. I'm a Cottrell. I'm smart . . . maybe even smarter than they are. I'll outrun them. You just watch me."

"See that you do." Barbara damned the day she had found her heart again. Now it was breaking. She knew no one could ever mend it.

Shane rolled off the bed and stood. "Would someone tell me what the fuck is going on here?"

"Shut up!" Barbara yelled at her. "If you want to stay in this house you can clean up your mouth. Clean up your whole life. I won't have a druggie living here, Shane. I won't let you go down the tubes anymore."

Shane raised her head and jammed her hands on her hips indignantly. "And I suppose you're gonna stop me?"

Barbara looked at her. "No, I'm not. *You* are. *You're* going to stop yourself."

Alexander looked at his sister. He knew he would always keep one step ahead of the mob. He could dodge bullets as well as the next man. He'd make a new life for himself . . . get a new name . . . a new identity. He wouldn't be Alexander Cottrell anymore. And maybe it was just as well. He didn't like Alexander much. But Shane, her future looked even more bleak than his. He was a survivor. Shane was weak. All her life she had blamed Barbara for her weakness. She had used Barbara's very existence to feed her weakness. It was a sin he, too, was guilty of.

Shane was shaking as she looked at her mother. This time Barbara meant what she said.

"There're going to be new rules here, Shane. Very strict rules. You can either abide by them or leave. And if you leave, it will be the same for you as for Alexander. You won't be welcomed back unless you change your life."

As Shane looked into her mother's hard green eyes, she realized that Barbara meant business. She was giving no slack this time. And as she looked further, she saw something she'd never seen before. Shane realized that what she was seeing was love. Her mother loved her enough to give her the guidelines that would make her grow up. She was surprised that she wasn't trembling. She was frightened of the future, of the days ahead when she would have to learn to live without cocaine. But now that she was seeing—and believing—what they *might* build between them . . . she wondered if it wasn't worth the risk.

Alexander picked up his bag. He started to say something to Barbara, but couldn't. The lump in his throat was too big.

He went down the stairs. Barbara and Shane followed. Shane remained at the bannister railing. Slowly, Barbara started down the stairs.

Alexander stopped at the bottom of the stairs and looked up at her. "No, Mother. Don't follow me. It's too much of a strain."

"No it isn't," she said, watching her son leave.

"No, Mother. Stay . . . for me." He rushed out the door and flung his bag into the trunk. He had to get away before it was too late. He knew now that his mother had always loved him, always respected him. It was *he* who had been too blind to see it. He'd wasted his whole life searching for something that had always been his. He'd been a fool. He rammed his foot against the pedal and sped away. He had to hurry. He had to get away before his mother saw his tears.

Epilogue

♦

BRANDON AND MAUREEN WERE STILL WATCHING the local election returns as they came across the screen when the gold-and-glass clock on the mantel chimed twelve.

"It looks like we've made it," he said, kissing her cheek.

"Brandon, they declared the gambling issue dead over two hours ago. We've known since nine that Bradley is our new governor. What did you think would happen?"

"I just had to be sure." He looked at her. She was beautiful, and he liked the way the firelight danced in her dark hair. He touched it and then pulled her closer to him. "It won't be long till you're Mrs. Williams."

"Only four days. I can't wait." She kissed him. She let his lips linger on hers. She felt she could stay here in his arms forever. Whenever they were together like this it was as if there was nothing in the world except the two of them. No gold mines, no political campaigns. She wondered if heaven could offer this much happiness.

She smiled at him.

"What are you thinking?" he asked.

"I was just thinking about my friend Bitzy. She always told

387

me I had to have a plan. That if I didn't, things would never work out for me. Ever since the day I met you, *nothing* has gone according to my plan. I didn't sell the ranch; I didn't even do very well with the herd. I found a gold mine. I helped stop a group of criminals. I guess you could say I've been flying by the seat of my pants for a long time."

"I think, if you had a plan, you probably would have botched everything up."

"What?"

"I had a plan since the night we met. And my plan worked out just the way I wanted it."

"Is that right?"

"Yes—we're getting married on Saturday."

"True," she said, leaning back on the sofa. He slid his arm around her.

"Have you thought about where we're going to live?"

"Of course . . . at my—" Her eyes widened. "I just got my house repaired. I can't let it go vacant. And there's Juanita."

He tapped his temple with his forefinger. "Ah, you see? What would you do without me and my plan?"

"What are you talking about?"

"I've already made the preliminary move—I called Bitzy . . . the number was on your desk. When she and John come out for the wedding, they're going to look the place over and see if they might not want to lease from us."

"Lease?"

"They're following *her* plan. Getting married, babies, his novel . . . you know . . ." he teased her.

"Oh, Brandon! That's a wonderful idea!"

"I'm sure you would have come up with it in time."

"I'm sure . . ." She leaned over and kissed him again. "What do you say we celebrate our victory at the polls tonight?"

He caressed her cheek, her neck and started to unbutton her blouse. "Shall we go upstairs?"

"No," she said breathlessly. "Let's stay here. It's unplanned."

Barbara Cottrell turned off the television, assured that the gambling issue was dead . . . at least for this year. The battle had been worth the pain she suffered in the helicopter crash, and it was worth losing her son over. Barbara had hope these days because she knew in her heart that Alexander would find what he was looking for.

She'd spent many years in the dark, espousing the wrong virtues, venerating lineage and a person's background instead of the person. The "good old boy system" was not dead, but it had been dealt a mighty blow. There was a new Texas rising. It was a place where people with courage and strength would lead into the next decade. Texas was people like Maureen McDonald and Brandon Williams and, yes, people like her, who believed in themselves. They had been the ones who had put themselves and their reputations on the line. And they had come up the winners. Barbara felt good about the future. More than ever, she was proud to be a Texan.

BESTSELLERS FROM

BOUND BY DESIRE   75451-7/$4.95 US/$5.95 CAN
The beloved saga of Steve and Ginny Morgan continues as their legacy of passion shapes the destiny of a new generation.

SWEET SAVAGE LOVE, STEVE AND GINNY BOOK I
                          00815-7/$4.95 US/$5.95 Can
DARK FIRES, STEVE AND GINNY BOOK I
                          00425-9/$4.95 US/$6.50 Can
LOST LOVE, LAST LOVE, STEVE AND GINNY BOOK III
                          75515-7/$4.95 US/$5.95 Can

THE WANTON	81615-8/$3.95 US/$4.75 Can
SURRENDER TO LOVE	80630-4/$4.95 US/$5.95 Can
THE CROWD PLEASERS	75622-6/$4.95 US/$5.95 Can
THE INSIDERS	40576-8/$4.50 US/$5.95 Can
LOVE PLAY	81190-1/$4.95 US/$5.95 Can
WICKED LOVING LIES	00776-2/$4.95 US/$5.95 Can
WILDEST HEART	00137-3/$4.50 US/$5.95 Can

If you enjoyed this book, take advantage of this special offer. Subscribe now and . . .

GET A *FREE* HISTORICAL ROMANCE
— NO OBLIGATION (a $3.95 value) —

Each month the editors of True Value will select the four best historical romance novels from America's leading publishers. Preview them in your home Free for 10 days. And we'll send you a FREE book as our introductory gift. No obligation. If for any reason you decide not to keep them, just return them and owe nothing. But if you like them you'll pay *just* $3.50 each and save at least $.45 each off the cover price. (Your savings are a minimum of $1.80 a month.) There is no shipping and handling or other hidden charges. There are no minimum number of books to buy and you may cancel at any time.

send in the coupon below